About the Author

INGRID FRY was born and raised in Berkhamstead in the UK, but spent much of her childhood commuting with her family between England and Austria. Emigrating with her parents to Melbourne, Australia many years ago, she has called Australia home ever since.

A business development consultant, writer and minder of a husband and a beagle with superpowers, she lives in a leafy suburb on the outskirts of Melbourne. Lakes Entrance is her second home, and it was from there, much of the Crystal Sphere series was developed.

In her spare time, Ingrid enjoys pistol shooting at the local gun club, dancing her socks off at The Caravan Music Club, and is a passionate karate nerd, well on her way to a black belt in karate. Ingrid models the belief that it is never too late to achieve your dreams, and age is definitely just a number.

You can find out more information about Ingrid via her website www.ingridfry.com.au
Email: Ingrid@ingridfry.com.au

Other Books
by
Ingrid Fry

Crystal Sphere Series

Descent into Darkness
Journey to Hell
Quest for Light
Search for Truth
Battle for Blood (forthcoming)

Copyright © 2020 Ingrid Fry

Content Warning: The Crystal Sphere Series is intended for mature readers and contains sexual situations, violence, and other representations that may cause some readers distress. Please prepare accordingly.

National Library of Australia Cataloguing-in-Publication entry:
Creator: Fry, Ingrid, author.
Title: Quest for Light: Crystal Sphere Book 3
/ Fry, Ingrid.

ISBN: 978-0-6486816-3-2

Tale Publishing
Melbourne, Australia

Tale

For this book, I would like to acknowledge the Gunaikurnai, Traditional Custodians of the Gippsland area which includes the Den of Nargun and the Buchan Caves, and the Traditional Custodians of Hanging Rock in the Macedon Ranges Shire — the Wurundjeri, Taungurong and Djadja Wurrung people, and the Wajarri Yamatji people in Western Australia, whose ancestors and their descendants are the traditional owners of this Country.

For my friend and fellow writer, Carl Lakeland

Follow Maggie's music playlist on Spotify!

Type *all* of the following ridiculously long code into the Spotify search bar:

spotify:user:zs8xyxpxzbt1mjcir59qz1jzw

Click the Follow Button for Crystal Sphere

I was in the kitchen, standing ankle deep in blood — the floor a shimmering lake of red, which flowed slowly into the hall.

Lifting a foot from the warm, bloody soup, I made my way carefully towards the sink, trying not to make waves. The musty, metallic smell of iron filled my nostrils.

I found a sponge and turned the tap on. Nothing happened. No water. The pipes clanked. There was a rattle and a splutter before a gob of congealed blood spat from the nozzle. It sat like a lump of liver, dark against the stainless-steel sink. The pipes protested — rattle, gurgle, thump, groan.

I screamed as a torrent of blood gushed from the tap. It hit the bottom of the sink and blasted up into my face. Hands slippery with blood, I tried in vain to turn off the tap.

A waterfall of blood overflowed the sink and ran down the cupboards to join the lake at my feet.

I shoved my finger into the tap nozzle and tried to stem the flow. Bad idea. Jets of blood spurted out around my finger. Mental note: next time keep mouth closed. I spat a mouthful of blood into the sink and dry retched.

Jason walked into the kitchen and laughed. 'Maggie! What the hell are you doing? 'Some sort of mime act?'

'Oh, thank God, you're here! Turn off the mains! Get the mop! The blood, I can't stop it! Don't just stand there … help me!'

Jason flopped his head back and stared at the ceiling. 'Shit. Here we go again.' His face was a mask of despair as he strode through the blood towards me.

'Don't make waves!' I yelled.

He grabbed me by the arm and slapped my face. I would never get used to the sting and shock of it. I gasped, my body jolted, and the blood disappeared.

'I'm so sorry.' He held me tight, and I could feel his heart pounding.

My heart pounded too as adrenaline pumped through my body. 'It was hideous. The whole house was filled with blood. It poured from the tap, and I couldn't stop it.'

'You haven't had a vision in a while. Did you see anything else?'

'No. Only blood. Horrible.'

'I hate having to hit you.'

'Yeah, but it's the one thing that snaps me out. Please promise me you'll never hesitate.'

'I promise.'

The terror of my vision was mildly offset by my relief that I didn't have to clean up all the blood.

'What do you think it means?' Jason asked.

I sighed. 'I don't know, but it can't be good.'

* * * * *

Aside from trying to decipher the meaning of the blood vision, the other issue bothering me was how anyone could mature from a child into a young adult in a matter of days?

It was the question that continued to haunt me after the dark force and Tapakah had returned as a deadly duo to take me and kill the others.

If it weren't for my dad, the Prof, using every last bit of his strength — no, make that sheer will — to get out of his sick bed and bowl a crystal into the dark force, everyone would be dead. And me, I'd be ... I'm not sure what I'd be. A Bride of Frankenstein. Except in this case, Frankenstein would be called Tapakah.

Tapakah means cockroach in Russian. We think that's what he could be: a human cockroach hybrid. The Prof reckons the cockroach he accidently brought to Australia from the Hadron Collider could be Tapakah.

The Prof's cockroach had the ability to generate black holes, which it used to destroy its enemies. His roach destroyed a lab assistant at CERN because the lab assistant was always trying to kill it. The roach never hurt the Prof as he doesn't like to kill anything. As a child, I was the one who had to catch and release spiders and bugs from the house. The Prof wouldn't kill a fly. He was similar to a Buddhist, in that way.

What the roach did do — whether by design or accident — was become a minion of the dark force. Now they were in cahoots. The Prof thinks it's a symbiotic relationship of convenience. The dark force feeds on the negative energy of humans, so it instigates killing and mayhem to satisfy its hunger. Its MO is to keep humans whipped up into a state of frenzy. The roach wants to survive and reproduce. It wants to eliminate humans, because humans always want to eliminate roaches. Humans *hate* roaches, so we think Tapakah is delighted to have a working relationship with an entity that's culling them.

A roach can get inside you, take you over so you do its bidding, or, actually, Tapakah's bidding. He controls them. We know this because of the number of humans who've tried to kill us. When a roach infested human dies — or really, when we kill them — the roach exits their body and disposes of it by causing it to disappear into a black hole, along with anything else in the vicinity not tied down.

I won't share the Prof's theory as to how a hybrid human roach evolved. It's too disgusting. I mean, we don't know for sure that's what Tapakah is, but all evidence seems to point that way.

The dark force is gaining strength. The only thing that will restore balance is if everyone stops getting angry. That's not going to happen though, hence, we have to find the crystal meteors. We need at least eleven of them to kick the dark force back to kingdom come.

As for the roaches, we're not sure. Maybe eliminating Tapakah would eliminate them too, similar to cutting the head off the colony. Tapakah wants to breed with me because I've been infected by the dark force. That makes me special. He's saving himself because I'm that special to him. Lucky me.

There are eleven of us fighting the good fight. Me, Maggie 'cursed with psychic powers' McLaine, a computer programmer, gamer, music lover, corporate couch potato and the love interest of a roach. My abilities have been enhanced by contact with the crystals. I'm stronger and more intuitive. I also have an atom of dark force lodged inside my brain. If I get angry, I'm awfully dangerous. I nearly killed Jason, Ashley, Luca and my dog, and they're my best friends.

Jason is my SO (significant other), plumber by trade, love of my life and probably, at this point in time, we suspect, compromised by a roach. Jason's contact with the crystals has significantly boosted his physical strength.

The Prof. My Dad. He's just come back after being stuck in another dimension for twelve months. We'd thought him dead. He's a brilliant astrophysicist. He discovered the radiation-affected roach and accidently brought it back to Australia. Big mistake. But then again, maybe not. We may be the only people on Earth who can fight this thing.

Boo is our beagle cocker spaniel cross. She can levitate and communicate with us telepathically. We have no idea why her telepathic voice sounds identical to Prince Charles. As a girl dog, it peeves her no end. Boo had first contact with the crystal. She's now super intelligent, courageous and fantastic to have around in a crisis.

Ashley Beringer is rugged and tough, with a build comparable to a tank. He's Jason's best friend. And mine. More than a friend really. We used to be an item way back when. He's a boozehound, stoner, motor mechanic, war veteran, landscape gardener, prospector, sheep shearer, cook, miner, postman and paramedic. He's saved our lives and we've saved his.

Bella is my sister. We were estranged when Dad disappeared, but she's come back into our lives. She left her partner in New Zealand — for a while anyway — and is helping us in the fight. Her nursing skills come in handy. She used to be a cop, which is excellent. She can handle a gun.

Then there's the Maestro, alias Chiara. She's a brilliant conductor, musician and she's an alien from the planet Sonus. She's an MTJ — a multi universe time jumper, stuck here 'cause her Maestro gadget ran out of power. I'm not sure how old she is, but she alleges she's sixty years old in Earth time. She looks sexy and sensational and makes me feel shabby in comparison.

Christos is the Maestro's SO, and like the Prof. has just been freed from another dimension. The Maestro has been on Earth for a while so has adapted to our "puritanical" ways. Christos' arrival is causing havoc. The Maestro and Christos feed on sexual energy and sound. I'll leave the integration problems to your imagination.

Detective Inspector Fox Johnston was investigating all the crimes in which we always seemed to be near. Of course, we couldn't tell him the truth. He wouldn't believe us. Nobody would. But one day, he became caught up in a dark force situation and saw for himself the alien forces we were dealing with. He's now one of our "musketeers", and it's great to have a member of the police on our side. It's not easy for him though because now he can't tell anyone either.

Dromeus, or Drom, is a freelance dark force fighter. Tall, lanky, looks a bit like Richard Gere. He makes a living playing the stock market and prospecting. He's a graphic designer, barista, masseur, personal trainer and producer and seller of organite. He reads two books a day, is telepathic and is an amazing traceuer — you know, one of those people who does parkour, basically jumping over everyday obstacles that most people go around. He's accomplished so much in his life because he practices polyphasic sleep techniques. That means he doesn't sleep much.

Luca is a priest in the Catholic Church. Well, probably not for long. He's decided to quit. He's the only person I know who beat a cockroach, expelled it from his body by a force of will and faith, I guess. He trained as a doctor before deciding to become a priest. He saved my life. Luca's gay, which is one of the reasons he wants to leave the church. He's tired of having to deny who he is.

That's our motley crew of musketeers, and now we're back at square one with three dead crystals. We need to find at least eleven crystal meteors to defeat the dark force and restore balance. And we need to find them fast. We drained the three we had to get the Prof and Christos back, save Fox and Ashley, and send the dark force and Tapakah packing.

Now we have nothing to protect ourselves with. If the dark force strikes again we're history. The odds are stacked against us, but I'd rather die than give up the fight. I'm not afraid to shed some blood along the way. Especially yours, Tapakah. Especially yours.

---

[1] *Maggie's Playlist: White Flag — Bishop Briggs*

"I love you like a sister. I love you like a friend. I cherish and respect you, but there the journey ends. You don't ignite my soul with passion; you're not music to my ears; you don't know how to comfort me when my mind is full of fears. I'm afraid I have to leave you; there's no longer any spark. I'm gonna walk the twisted highway that leads me to the dark.' — Maggie McLaine, Quest for Light

Ashley's severed arm hung off his shoulder, secured by a thin strip of muscle. Blood drenched his white T-shirt. Fox had a hole the size of a tennis ball in the palm of his right hand. As he held it up to examine the damage, I saw his horrified expression through the gaping wound. These images, and the vision of the blood flood, lingered in my mind's eye. How the hell would I get them out of my brain?

I rubbed my eyes and shook my head to try and dislodge the grizzly visions. I was sitting at the dining room table nursing a cup of coffee and reflecting on what had happened yesterday. It was ten in the morning and everyone, except Jason, was still in bed recovering from the ordeal.

I couldn't get my head around Tapakah. He'd been around seven years old when I'd last seen him a few weeks ago. Yesterday he'd appeared to be in his late twenties. I speculated on what he might look like in another few days. Maybe he'd grow old fast and die. He could have a short life span. *That* would be excellent. The thought gave me a shot of hope.

Ashley staggered into the room rubbing the sleep from his eyes. 'Are you okay?' he asked.

'Yes. Just trying to get nasty images out of my head.'

'That's the story of my life, luv. It's not good, is it?'

He pulled up a chair and sat next to me before raking his hands through his hair, putting his elbows on the table and dropping his head into the crook of an arm.

I ran my hand across his shoulder, checking out the musculature. 'Want coffee?'

He looked up and smiled. 'Checking to see if it's still attached?'

'Actually, yes.'

'It's fine.' He stretched out his arm and rotated it. 'See?'

'I can't get rid of the image of your arm hanging off. Thank God for Dad. He saved us.'

'He sure did. I need to thank him again.'

'Did you go anywhere special when the crystal hit?'

'I can't remember. A blast of light and then nothing. When I woke it was hours later and I was completely healed. Same as Fox. I've never been so grateful. I thought my time was up. I remember wondering how I'd protect you with only one arm if I survived.'

'I'm sure you would've found a way. I'll bet the Maestro could've whipped up a robot, terminator arm. Thanks to Dad we're all okay. Physically anyway. Thanks for always looking out for me.' I moved across to the kitchen to make him a coffee.

'That's my job, luv. How's Jason?'

'Still weird. He was up early working in the shed. Ever since he was attacked, he's been so distant towards me. It's like he's just going through the motions. His heart's not in anything. Luca mentioned personality changes could be part of the concussion, but if it continues he could have more serious brain damage. He needs to have a scan, or something.'

'Drom still thinks he's been roached,' Ashley said quietly.

'If that's the case maybe a brain scan would show something.' I put a cup of coffee in front of Ashley. 'Long black, very strong, very hot. Exactly how you like it.'

'Thanks, Mags. You're a legend.'

'Are those drugs helping your combat nightmares?' I asked, sitting next to him.

'It's early days, but yes, I've been sleeping better. Who knows, one day you might be able to sleep with me.' He flashed a grin.

'Yeah, right.' My mind went back to the last time we'd tried to wake Ashley from a nightmare. Jason had poked him with a broom, and Ashley had put a twelve-inch dagger right through the middle of it. I had to be careful what I said. This was delicate territory. Ashley had put his girlfriend in hospital with serious injuries and killed his dog during a bout of combat nightmares. Since then he'd made a vow to always sleep alone. 'I hope the drugs do the trick for you. Maybe the Maestro could wipe out more of your memories, like she did with—' Damn. Damn it. He'd had that memory wiped, and I was about to bring it up. Jesus, I was an idiot.

'What memory? What are you talking about?'

'It slipped out. I shouldn't have said anything.'

He squeezed my arm. 'What memory?'

'You asked the Maestro to wipe out a specific memory. I'm hardly going to tell you what it was.'

'Jesus, why would I say that?'

'Because you couldn't handle the memory. You said it ruined you.'

Ashley was silent, looking into his coffee. His biceps flexed as he gripped the mug. The ceramic creaked. A muscle on the side of his jaw twitched.

'The cup is ready to break, Ashley.'

'You need to tell me.'

'You wanted it gone.'

'Tell me.'

'No.'

'Tell me.'

'All righty then. You know how Christos can transmogrify himself into the image of whatever a particular human may find sexually attractive so he can feed off their sexual energy?'

'Yeah, like how he appeared to Luca as Carey Grant, and to Bella as Liam?'

'Well, he did that to you one night—'

'Oh, fuck. You're kidding me. And I thought he was you?'

'Yep.'

'Oh, Jesus. How far did he go?'

'I'm not sure.'

I had to lie. I couldn't say he went all the way.

Boo saw what was happening and attacked Christos. Christos couldn't maintain the illusion and changed back right in the middle of things. You freaked out. One minute it was me the next it was a big, burly bloke. You said it ruined something precious. You were devastated. The Maestro mentioned her device had a memory erase function and you begged her to use it. So she did.'

'Crikey. I'm glad she did. No wonder I wanted rid of that bloody memory. Jesus. What a slime bag.' His brown eyes locked onto mine. 'I realise I don't have a snowball's chance in hell of ever being with you again, so there's no way I'd want that nightmare ruining my fantasies.'

'So, you can't remember any of it? Not even the "good" bits?'

'Not a thing. And that's fine with me. I've enough good memories to keep me going,' he said, raising his eyebrows.

'So perhaps the Maestro could delete a few more of your awful memories?'

'Maybe. But where do you stop? Those things make you who you are. What happens when your mind is full of holes? Delete all the bad memories and my brain would look like a block of Swiss cheese. With all the crap I've been through, there'd be nothing left.'

'How do you deal with the horrific images in your mind?'

'When a shit image comes to mind I try and paint over it. In my imagination, I take a paintbrush and change the picture to something else. Something I like.'

'Does it work?'

'Sort of. You have to keep doing it. Keep painting over those pictures. If you persevere they lose their intensity.'

I closed my eyes and attempted to paint a leather jacket over Ashley's detached arm. I painted the blood-stained T-shirt black, but red bits kept coming through. This would take time.

'We've got no crystals left to regenerate us,' I said. 'If we're fatally injured now we'll die.'

'Yep. We're absolutely vulnerable. I wonder if the dark force knows it?'

Fox joined us at the table. He looked quite chipper given the circumstances. 'Who's vulnerable?' he asked me.

'We are, with no crystals left.'

He held his hand up to the sunlight streaming through the window and examined it carefully. 'I was thinking that myself.'

'As good as new?' Ashley asked.

'Better than new. Looks younger, feels stronger.' Fox flexed his fingers and made a fist. 'I love the way those crystals work.'

I nodded. 'That's what happens when the crystal regenerates you. The bits you've lost come back improved. Something else happens too. You get better at certain things. It happens slowly, over time.'

'It seems you've won another heart, Maggie,' Fox said.

'What do you mean?'

Who was he talking about? Ashley? Had he overheard us?

'Tapakah, of course.'

A wave of nausea surged through my body. 'Thanks for reminding me.'

'Sorry, but we're going to have to keep an even closer eye on you now. I still need to take you to the shooting range.'

'I managed to shoot a grenade launcher with just theory, no practice.'

'Yes, you're a natural. But each pistol is different. You need to be familiar with using a few different types and calibres. The larger calibres are more powerful, have more recoil, and are harder to shoot accurately.'

'The .22 calibre is the assassins' choice,' Ashley said. 'That's a smaller calibre. Better for you. If you shot someone in the head with a .38 it would blow their skull apart. Very messy. Shoot someone with a .22 and it's much cleaner. Goes in, rattles around and comes out nice and neat.'

I screwed up my face. 'Charming. Beaut breakfast conversation.'

Jason came in and pulled up a chair on the opposite side of the table. 'Is Ashley being inappropriate as always?'

'I was saying Maggie needs to get up to speed with handling a pistol, given she's number one on Tapakah's A-list.'

Jason shook his head. 'We can look after her. There's no hurry. I worry about Maggie having a gun.'

There he went again. It was fine for the guys to have guns but not the girls.

'For Christ's sake, Jason, I thought you'd moved on from this attitude already. What about Bella? She needs protection too and should reacquaint herself with handling a gun. All our lives might depend on it. You're saying we're incompetent to handle a gun because we're female.'

'I'm not saying that at all. I don't want to put you at risk.'

'Sounds like the same thing to me,' I snapped. My blood pressure was starting to rise. I was tired of his attitude. Breathe, Maggie. Breathe. Don't get angry. Let it go.

I took a deep breath in, slowly let it out and walked across to the kitchen.

Remove myself from the situation. Breathe. Relax. I would not get angry.

Once I'd focused myself I asked Jason and Fox if they wanted a coffee, and when they said yes, I set my mind to making it.

In the meantime, Drom, Luca and Bella had resurfaced, followed closely by Christos. They joined Jason, Ashley and Fox at the dining table.

'Morning all,' I said. 'We have a full house … no, where's the Prof?'

'Here.' The Prof dashed across to the kitchen and gave me a kiss on the cheek.

'How are you feeling, Dad?'

'I feel fantastic. That crystal energy sure does amazing things. I feel ten years younger.'

Bella came into the kitchen and hugged him. 'That's wonderful. We missed you so much. It's hard to believe we have you back.'

'I'm glad to be back. We need all hands on deck.'

'It's even more dangerous now we have no live crystals to protect us,' I said. 'We need to get cracking and find some.'

The Maestro flounced into the kitchen and held her arms out to the Prof. They embraced and kissed passionately and deeply. We looked away, embarrassed, but Christos watched the action with amusement and obvious enjoyment. I didn't think I'd ever be able to get my head around the Maestro and Christos. Imagine having a relationship where you were totally free to be with whoever you wanted, yet have no feelings of jealousy. Still, they were aliens and that's how they were wired. It'd be fun to be them for a day. Mmmm. I knew who'd be on my list.

Bella looked at me. 'I bet I know what you're thinking.'

I grinned. 'Probably the same thing you are.'

'Um, you guys gonna come up for air sometime soon?' Ashley asked.

She pulled herself away from Dad and directed her violet-eyed gaze at Ashley.

'What's wrong, my love? Jealous? There's plenty for you if you want it, darling.' She slunk over to him and massaged his shoulders. 'Look at you. You're as good as new, Ashley Beringer. Shoulders still as broad, maybe broader. And check out those biceps.' She ran her hands over his arms. 'You need TLC. Don't tell me you don't.' Her laughter tinkled out across the room, sounding like a melody. Her voice was so seductive. God, anyone would fall for her. I couldn't blame Dad for being head over heels.

A twinge of envy tugged at me when the Maestro touched Ashley's body. Bella flapped the top of her T-shirt in and out. I wasn't sure if she was getting overheated about the Maestro or Ashley. Maybe both.

I certainly knew who made me hot under the collar.

Ashley grabbed the Maestro's wrists and pushed her away. 'Cut it out. You're not my type, sweetheart.'

'Yes, I guess that's true. We know who you really like.' She looked directly at Christos.

Oh no. What the hell was she doing?

Her expression changed when she realised her mistake. Ashley's eyes narrowed and his jaw clenched. He looked ready to pounce. The Maestro tried to remedy the situation. 'Of course, Bella would have to be on your list, darling, wouldn't she?' She wrapped Bella in her arms and Bella dissolved into them. 'How gorgeous is this girl, Ashley?'

'Yeah, she's gorgeous. But she's married. That actually *means* something to some people.'

Jason observed quietly. He'd done that a lot since he was attacked. His face had healed and he was physically better, but mentally, not so good. Distant. Quiet. Totally unlike him. I didn't know who he was anymore and couldn't read him. How could the love of my life suddenly turn into a stranger?

Bella had told us it had happened with her husband, Liam, and there'd been no accident involved. That was why she'd decided to stay in Australia. She'd run away from the stranger in her home. Where could I run to? I couldn't leave Jason. I needed to stick by him, help him through this. Events had been tough on everyone; we were all worse for wear.

As though he'd read my mind Luca looked at Jason and said, 'How are you feeling today?'

'Just fine.' He looked across at Luca. Jason's laser beam eyes had lost their lustre. The lights were on but no one was home.

'You don't seem yourself,' I said softly. 'You're distant. I feel like I can't reach you anymore. I'm worried.'

'Don't be.'

Drom seemed concerned. 'Luca, do you think Jason should have a brain scan so we can be sure everything's okay?'

'It wouldn't do any harm. I think he should.'

Excellent. This has turned into a spontaneous intervention.

Jason sat upright. 'I don't need a frigging brain scan. Get off my back.' There was a coldness in his voice I'd never heard before. I shivered involuntarily.

'But Jason, you need to rule out brain damage. I'm concerned for you.' I moved over to him and placed my arm around his shoulder. He aggressively shrugged it off.

I felt my eyes prick with tears. 'Why do you keep pushing me away?'

'Did you ever consider the reason I keep pushing you away is because I don't feel the same anymore?'

His statement hit my stomach like blunt force trauma.

'The same way about *me*?' I whispered, dreading his answer.

'Yes, about you.' He pushed back his chair and walked up the hall and out the front door.

I felt tears spill down my cheeks.

It couldn't be. What had happened? After everything we'd been through. What had I done wrong?

Voices sounded from far away. Bella's arms were around me. 'Ashley, go after him,' she said.

'What the hell's got into him?' Fox asked.

'Poor, Maggie. She didn't deserve that,' the Maestro whispered.

'He's *roached*. Doesn't anyone get it?' Drom snapped.

'You're right. People don't change overnight,' Luca said.

'We shouldn't let him out of our sight,' Fox said.

'Maggie? *Maggie?*' Dad squeezed my shoulder.

'I'll make her hot chocolate like Ash does,' Luca said.

Drom shook his head. 'I had a feeling this was coming.'

'Here, let me, Bella.' Strong arms embraced me. A voice whispered in my ear, deep and resonant, 'He didn't mean it. It's not him talking. I can feel it. I understand a great deal about love. Believe me. It's not him saying those things.'

The voice belonged to Christos. He purred soothingly in my ear. Enveloped by comfort, I slipped back into my body and looked up into his icy blue alien eyes. 'Are you sure?'

'Yes, little one, I'm sure.'

Gosh, no wonder Bella had fallen for this Yul Brynner look alike.

'Sit on my knee, Maggie.'

He took me into his huge arms, and I tucked up against his chest as he rocked me ever so slightly. My pain and shock evaporated, replaced with a sense of calmness and acceptance. Everything would be okay. Such peace. Christos had taken me to a different plane of consciousness. 'Thank you. You're amazing. You made me transcend my emotions. Incredible.'

'My pleasure. But you transcended. I simply created the conditions.'

'That's why you don't get jealous, isn't it? You transcend.'

'I'm not sure what you mean. We don't feel the same as you. I haven't been here long enough to understand.'

'Well, Earthlings would pay a fortune to get a dose of what you gave me.'

Christos looked at the Maestro. 'I'll keep that in mind.'

16

Maybe that's why she had so much money. It wasn't just from the conducting.

The Maestro blew me a kiss. Her smile was so warm and caring that its energy penetrated my heart, a dart of pure love. Crikey. We hadn't even begun to scratch the surface in understanding, or appreciating, what these two aliens could do. The Prof caught my eye and winked. Well, maybe someone had.

---

[2] *Maggie's Playlist: Wild Hearts Can't Be Broken — Pink*

 **Chapter 3: Infected**

I left Maggie crying at the kitchen table and chased Jason up the driveway. Her shocked face was still in my mind's eye. Jason had certainly dropped a friggin' bombshell.

Drom shouted from the front door. 'Be careful!'

It was another cold, grey day, made brighter by the vibrant yellow clouds of wattle trees that bloomed along the fence line. They were a blazing symbol of hope in this shit time. I soaked up their beautiful colour.

I had to fix this for Maggie. But to be honest, part of me had been stoked when those words had come out of Jason's mouth. My spark for Maggie had come back with a vengeance. I was never over her. I'd never get over her. But Jason and Maggie were my best mates. I loved Maggie, but I couldn't allow it for the sake of her, or him.

'Jason! Wait up! I want to talk to you.'

'I want to walk on my own.'

'You know that's too dangerous. Our rules are we always have someone with us.'

Jason continued to walk away. 'Whatever.'

'Listen, you're my best mate; I need to talk to you. What's the story with Maggie? You love her; how could you say that?'

Jason stopped walking and turned to face me, his mouth a thin line. His eyes clouded over. 'I said it because it's true. I don't feel anything for her anymore. I don't love her. It's gone. I don't know why; it's nothing she's done. What we had is over.'

'Something's happened to you. You don't stop loving someone overnight. She's the love of your life, you told me so yourself not long before you were attacked.'

'What's happened is that things change. I don't have feelings for her anymore.'

'Mate, we need to get away for some R & R. Remember the time we went to Bali? How relaxing was that? Those two gorgeous chicks we met, and you tried windsurfing for the first time, remember?'

Jason furrowed his brow, and his eyes turned up and moved from side to side as though searching for something in the sky. 'Yeah … yeah, it was great. No chance of that happening anytime soon though.'

'It's still great to have the memories to get by on. I'm your mate and here for you whatever happens. Remember that. I think you need to get yourself checked out. After the pummeling your cranium went through, you should get a scan. Do it for your own sake, mate, please? Will you at least think about it?'

'I'll think about it. Thanks, Ash. I appreciate it. You're a good friend.' The tone in his voice was robotic and flat.

It was like Maggie said. He was going through the motions. He'd totally disconnected from himself and us. Shit, I hated to see him like this. I understood how Maggie must feel. 'Come inside, Jason, you look tired.'

'I've a terrible headache. I have them all the time now. My head never stops aching.'

'Jesus, all the more reason to get yourself checked out. Come on, go to bed, mate. I'll make you a cup of my sleepy time tea and get you some painkillers.'

I put my arm around him and guided him through the front

door and into his bedroom. He pulled off his boots and flopped down on the bed. I covered him with blankets. 'Here you go. Close your eyes and rest. I'll be back with a brew and painkillers.'

When I returned to the kitchen, a group of anxious faces greeted me.

Maggie's eyes were red from crying. 'What did he say?' she asked.

Christ, I wanted to take her in my arms and kiss those tears away. 'He's gone to bed with a shocker of a headache. Said he has them all the time now. Maggie, can you get me the rum. I'm going to make a brew of my sleepy time tea.'

She pulled a bottle from the drink's cabinet. 'What's that you're crumbling into the cup?'

'Valium. I'm going to knock him out for a while.'

'Without telling him?'

'Yep. I can confirm beyond any doubt that Jason's been compromised. Who knows if he's been roached, but the person I was talking to out there was not Jason.'

'How do you know for sure?'

'I said we needed a holiday and reminded him of the time we went to Bali together.'

Maggie looked confused. 'But you've never been to Bali. Neither has Jason.'

'Exactly. I reminisced about the girls we met and the first time he tried windsurfing, and he agreed how great it was and how he'd love to go back. Jason may be in there somewhere, but right now, he's someone or something else.'

Fox ran his hands through his hair. 'Holy shit, you were right, Drom. We have the enemy in our midst.'

Drom sat quietly and nodded. He was smart. He'd known all along. I needed to listen to him more. He could say "I told you so", but that wasn't his style. It was like Maggie said. Just because he carried a man bag, sorry, satchel, it didn't mean anything. He reminded me of my little brother when he was alive, minus the bag.

Maggie's face lit with hope. 'You think it's not true what he said about not loving me anymore?'

Jesus. I wanted to say sorry, Maggie, but it's true, he doesn't love you anymore. He doesn't deserve you. I do. I want you.

'I'm sure he still loves you. No doubt about it. That man in your bedroom is someone else. It's not Jason. Take what he says to you with a grain of salt.'

'Poor Jason,' the Prof said. 'So, now what?'

'I'll take him this brew and then we'll work out a plan.'

* * * * *

In the bedroom Jason lay motionless and deathly pale on the bed. Those roach bastards were going to pay for this, arseholes. 'Jace, here, drink this and take these.'

He groaned and opened his eyes. I jumped back, nearly spilling the tea. His eyes were black. No iris. Totally black. Holy shit.

He blinked, and then Jason's blue grey eyes were staring at me. I rubbed my eyes on the back of my sleeve. Christ, I was losing it.

'Drink,' I said. 'You know this tea fixes anything.'

He nodded and gave me a weak smile.

'All of it. And take these. You'll feel better soon, mate. Don't worry about anything. We're here for you.'

'Thanks, Ash.' He collapsed back on the bed.

I tucked him in and left the room wondering how I'd cope if we lost him. What if we couldn't get him back?

Everyone was having an animated, whispered discussion around the kitchen table. Maggie had made coffee for everyone, including me, and she made it just the way I liked it.

'We were talking about what to do,' Fox said. 'A brain scan would at least show us what we're dealing with.'

'I guarantee you he won't go willingly,' I said.

'We could knock him out and take him to hospital. That way they'd *have* to do a scan,' Christos suggested.

'I think his cranium has been beaten around enough,' Fox replied. 'Even if we drugged him, covered his head with blood and took him into hospital saying he … I don't know, fell off a roof, and they scanned him and there, on the image, was a cockroach. Then what? They couldn't operate and remove it; the thing would generate a black hole and take out Jason and the whole hospital.'

Maggie bit her lip and stared at Luca. 'It doesn't appear Jason has the ability to de-roach himself like you did. God knows how you did that.'

Luca crossed himself. 'That's exactly right. God knows. I wish I could tell you more. It was faith and love, but it was also disgust. My body and soul rejected the thing. I thank God every day for that blessing.'

The Professor put his arm around Maggie. 'We only have one option.'

I could see the poor bloke was worried sick about her and Jason. He loved Jace like a son.

'What's that, Dad?'

'The crystals. You said fake Jason couldn't stand to be near them, so they may be the only safe cure. Jason is a Crystal Keeper, so it's in the crystals best interests to keep him safe. He's of no use to them if he's working for the dark force, so my bet is a crystal will de-roach him.'

'But, Dad, I still have a dark force atom lodged in my brain, and the crystals haven't eliminated that. I can sense it's still there. Why would Jason be different?'

'You don't have a roach in your brain. We're assuming Jason has. From my experience with the original roach, it hated to be anywhere near a crystal.'

'I saw it myself. It went berserk,' the Maestro agreed.

Maggie slumped down in a chair, put her elbows on the table

and clutched her head. 'Oh, Jesus. Poor Jason.'

Bella rushed over and put an arm around her. She stroked Maggie's hair. 'He'll come through this. He will.'

Maggie sat upright. 'We've got to find crystals. We don't have the crystal map because all the crystals we have are dead, but we do have the general locations.' Maggie stood and took a pink piece of paper from a drawer. 'The list says there are two crystals located at the Den of Nargun, which is in Gippsland, about three hours away. There's another one a bit further on at the Buchan Caves, another at Hanging Rock, one at the Grampians, one at Beechworth, one at Murchinson WA, and one at Uluru, which is fixed apparently, can't be moved. We have to bring the rest of the crystals to it. I reckon we go for the ones in Gippsland. If all goes well, one trip should bring home three crystals.

'Because we don't have a crystal map we can't pinpoint exact locations, but I can track them by a buzzing in my mind. I'm a walking crystal detector. I'll go get them.'

'There's no way you're going alone,' the Professor and Bella said simultaneously.

'Yeah, that's fine. But we have to keep fake Jason at bay. As soon as he's dead to the world, we must leave. When he wakes and asks where I am, you can say I went to … to the Hanging Rock location. If he's in contact with dark force minions, he'll give them a red herring that'll keep them off my tail.'

'Our tail, Maggie. I'm coming with you. We can take my truck,' I said.

She looked at me through her long, dark lashes. 'Thanks, Ashley. I appreciate it.'

How the hell was I going to stop myself kissing those lips?

'Wouldn't have it any other way, luv.'

'If the two of you go bush looking for a crystal, there should be someone staying with the truck for backup,' Fox said.

Stuff Fox. Always wanting in on my turf. I'd seen the way he looked at Maggie. Shit. He was right though. I looked at Drom.

'Are you free?'

'Yep. I'd be happy to get out of the city for a while.'

'Someone should keep an eye on Jason at all times,' I said. 'Fox, you'd be ideal, but you have to work.'

'We will stay,' Christos offered. 'I will guard.'

'Christos, I have a rehearsal to go to,' the Maestro said, 'but I'll be back later today. Will you promise to stay here and not feed on any of these people?'

'Yes. I understand this now. I promise.'

'I've made Christos a lasagna,' the Maestro said. 'It's the only food he can tolerate at the moment. Bella, if he gets hungry, can you heat it up for him? He doesn't comprehend how things work, or how to cook yet.'

Bella smiled. 'I'd be delighted to.'

Maggie smiled too. I knew she was thinking the same thing as me — that this was a job Bella would enjoy, given her huge Christos crush.

'So that's it,' Maggie said. 'We have a plan and we'll head off ASAP. We'll keep you in the loop and let you know when we're due back. Once we're nearly home, you guys need to restrain Jason and keep him locked in the bedroom so we can use the crystals on him as soon as we walk in the door.'

Maggie seemed calm and confident. That was my girl, always happy with an action plan.

Fox's phone rang and made us all jump. He answered and walked outside onto the deck. His whole persona changed when he was in police mode. He strode back and forth, expression fixed. He was rugged, tough and an exceptional detective.

I'd hated his guts when he was on our case — when he didn't have a clue as to what was really going on. He'd been relentless, but now he knew the truth, he couldn't tell anyone. He knew police resources were being wasted investigating and searching for people who weren't there anymore, but his hands were tied. It was a bastard. He was a good cop.

His eyes locked onto mine as he came back in. His expression was grim.

'Bad news?'

'Very. They've slapped a D-Notice on this. They want to keep it under wraps for as long as possible until they work out what's going on.'

'What's happened?' the Professor asked.

'There's been a sharp increase in missing persons, rising steadily over the last few weeks. All based in this state.'

'There were six missing persons reported on the news, along with all the other muggings, stabbings, house invasions and car jackings,' Drom said. 'I thought it was strange there were so many at once.'

'There's a lot more than that now,' Fox said.

'How many?' Maggie asked.

'One hundred and two. All women.'

'Holy shit,' Drom said.

Bella looked visibly distraught. I put my arm around her and felt her shaking.

'They've been taken, haven't they? By … it,' she whispered, her voice cracking.

'Probably,' Fox said. 'The police have no clue. These women have vanished. Because of the volume they're thinking human trafficking, some sort of slave trade. The women range in age from seventeen to twenty-five. This kind of thing is unheard of.'

'Even more reason to get moving.' Maggie looked at me with a determined expression, then she bent and gave Boo a back rub. 'She's coming with us. We need her.'

Boo looked intensely at Maggie, and I knew they were communicating telepathically. I wished I could hear what they were saying.

Testing. Testing. Hello, Ash. Can you hear me?

Jesus. Who the hell was in my head? Prince Charles? What the?

Oh, not you too, Ashley. It's Boo. I don't understand why I sound like Prince Charles. I'm a girl dog. Surely the Queen's voice would be more appropriate if it has to be royalty. It's such a puzzle, and frankly I find it annoying and embarrassing.

Jesus, Boo, if that is you can I get a word in? How come I can hear you?

Not sure. Seems Jason is out and you're in. Maybe our wavelength can only take so many. I'm unsure. Still, it's a good thing Jason's out. He's definitely not himself. He stinks of roach.

You can smell it?

Yes.

Have you told Maggie?

I don't want to upset her more than she already is.

She seems to be handling herself all right.

You haven't seen her crying every day. She goes into the bathroom. I follow her in and try to comfort her. It's the only place she can go where she's alone. She's cried every day since Jason was beaten up. She knew straight away but wouldn't admit it to herself. When she's not crying, she listens to music. You've seen her. Those AirPods are never out of her ears. It's how she copes.

Fucking hell, I wish I'd known. We could've done something sooner.

Please refrain from using course language, Ashley. Previously, we never used profanities in this household, except in enormously trying situations. We need to keep up standards of polite behaviour.

Yeah, yeah. Jesus. Sorry. You know me, it's too hard. I'll try. Christ, I can't believe I'm talking to a dog.

Not any ordinary dog.

I realise that, Boo. Do you ever shut up?

I do indeed. Particularly when the occasion warrants silence.

See this look on my face, Boo?

Now would be such an occasion.

---

[3] *Maggie's Playlist: Never Get Over You — Paul McDonald*

'Life happens - chocolate helps.' — *Unknown*

It felt strange to be sitting in Ashley's truck, cosied up between Ashley and Drom. Normally it would've been Jason and me.

Ashley looked at me intently. 'Are you all right?'

'I'm fine. Just thinking is all.'

Jason had been looking forward to searching for the crystals. He loved the bush and exploring. Now he was stuck at home dosed up on Valium and red herrings. I couldn't have described how much I missed him — it was as though he was dead, and I was grieving. An enormous aching hole of emptiness gnawed in my gut. But things were what they were. I'd have to build a wall around the pain and get on with things. I'd have to be strong for him. He would be for me.

Thank God I had Ashley and Drom. It felt fantastic to be out on the road with them watching the suburbs and McMansions giving way to the greener sweeping spaces of paddocks and farms.

We drove through open expanses of pastureland, green hills, and valleys dotted with fat cows and woolly sheep soon to be shorn. The land felt spacious, the farms and homes neat and cared for indicating the owners took pride in their lives and surrounds. The vibe was pleasing, clean and peaceful.

'I could live out here,' I said to Ashley.

'Me too,' he agreed.

'Me three,' Drom said.

You can count me in too.

Boo was in the back of the truck, ears flapping. The wind rushed up her nose, and the sides of her mouth fluttered. Exactly how she liked it. Fox had given us Schmoo's dog goggles to use and Boo liked them. She said they made her look cool.

We didn't talk much along the way. I reckon we were all enjoying the drive, watching the world go by. It seemed … normal. Normal was good. It'd been ages since we last managed normal.

'There's a hitchhiker,' I said as we whizzed by someone. 'It's just a kid.'

Drom craned his neck to look back. 'A young woman. She's tiny. She looks desperate. She's waving at us.'

Ashley looked at me. 'Reckon we should go back?'

'We should. It's not safe to be hitchhiking alone.'

'Oh, jeez. Here we go then.' Ashley pulled over, dropped a u-ey and went back, but the girl was nowhere to be seen.

'Maybe she was picked up?' I said.

'She couldn't have been; we were here two seconds ago,' Drom said.

I caught sight of a flash of colour in the bushes at the side of the road. 'She's there, behind the bushes.'

Ashley pulled the truck to a stop and took his pistol out from the console. He saw my look. 'We need to be careful. This could be a trap.' He ejected the magazine and checked to see how many rounds were in it. He pushed the magazine back in and engaged the safety. 'Stay here. I'll check things out.'

'I should come too,' I said. 'You'll scare the bejesus out of her if she's alone.'

'I don't look *that* scary, do I?'

'You're over six-foot-tall, built like a brick shithouse, with wild hair, a beard, leather jacket and biker boots. I'd say that looks slightly intimidating,' Drom said dryly.

Ashley flashed his new choppers. 'But my beard's nicely trimmed and I've a great smile now my teeth are fixed.'

I rolled my eyes. 'Yeah, that makes all the difference.'

'Come on then. Drom, get your gun out and be ready to cover us if anything turns to shit.'

We jumped out of the truck and headed towards the bushes. Ashley grabbed my arm and pulled me behind him. 'Stay back, just in case.'

I pointed to a small form huddled behind a tree stump. 'There.' Stepping out from behind Ashley I spoke softly. 'Hello. My name's Maggie. We saw you on the side of the road waving and came back to give you a lift. Are you okay?'

'We won't hurt you. Do you still want a lift?' Ashley asked.

'Yes please.' The young woman unfolded herself from her crouched position and stood.

She was tiny, probably under five feet, slim, with long black hair, brown skin and dark eyes. Her jeans were covered in dirt, and her jumper had burrs and grass seeds stuck in the fibres. She picked up a small backpack and walked tentatively towards us.

'You've been sleeping rough?' I asked.

She nodded.

'Where are you headed, luv?' Ashley asked softly.

'Anywhere. Away.'

'What's your name?' I asked.

'Jasmine.'

'Well, we're heading up Bairnsdale way, Jasmine. You tell us when and where you want to get out,' Ashley said.

Jasmine was unsteady on her feet, and I noticed she was trembling. She had a flag on her backpack, two horizontal red stripes on a white background and a green tree in the middle. It was half hanging off, waving in the breeze.

'What flag is that?' I asked.

She looked at it blankly before speaking. 'Lebanese. I hate it.' She tugged at it fiercely until it pulled away. Dropping the flag as if it were red hot, she ground it into the dirt with her boot and spat on it. 'I will never go back.'

Ashley looked shocked. 'Crikey.'

We walked back to the road where Drom was waiting beside the truck.

'Drom, meet Jasmine,' Ashley said.

Drom scanned her with his blue eyes. 'Hi, Jasmine.'

I knew he was taking in every tiny detail, and he probably already knew more about her than we did.

'Do you want to sit in the front or back?' I asked.

She glanced nervously up and down the highway. 'I'll sit in the back. Can we go now?' She clutched anxiously at her jumper.

'Sure thing,' Ashley said. 'Let's hit the road.'

Drom sat in the back with Jasmine, she as far away from him as she could. There was silence for a while before Drom said, 'You haven't had anything to eat or drink in days, and you've been sleeping rough. You've ditched your rings — and your watch — probably cashed them in for money. People are after you. They want to hurt you. They've hurt you already. You're on the run aren't you, Jasmine?'

Tears streamed down Jasmine's face leaving streaks on her dusky skin as they washed away the grime. I handed her Ashley's crushed box of tissues. She took it gratefully, grabbed a handful and wiped her eyes. She pulled at a thread on her jumper and without looking at Drom said, 'Are you psychic?'

He smiled. 'No, well sometimes. That's more Maggie's domain. I'm observant.'

She blew her nose and looked at him shyly. 'But how ... how do you know so much?'

'You look dehydrated. You're shaking, I assume from low blood sugar caused by not having eaten. You have dirt on your clothes, grass seeds in your jumper, and the paler skin on your hands and wrist shows where your jewelry used to be. You have bruises on your wrist and neck. You're scared and anxious, and you keep looking around to see if anyone's following us.' He brushed some remaining tissue off her nose with his thumb. 'Am I right?'

Her voice broke. 'Y ... yes!'

I looked at Ashley. 'Can you stop the truck so I can get the Esky from the back? I've made sandwiches. We need to eat.'

When he pulled over I slid out. 'How are you, Boo? All okay back here?'

Yes. Indeed, Maggie. Thank you. Anything to eat for me in there?

'Yep.' I handed Boo one of her favourite treats, a dried rib bone.

Thank you, Maggie. I'm a lucky dog.

I left Boo hoovering down her treat and climbed back in the truck. Ashley took off at speed. I knew he was concerned we were losing time, and maybe about who was after Jasmine.

I passed her a sandwich. 'I hope you like curried egg.'

Her eyes lit up at the sight of food. 'Thank you so much.'

Drom watched her tear off the cling film. 'Eat and chew slowly, even though you're starving.'

She took a breath before biting into the sandwich. From the expression on her face it appeared I'd made the best sandwich in the entire universe.

I passed sandwiches to everyone, and when we'd finished I found the Thermos and made us all a cup of tea. Jasmine drank from the mug with her eyes closed, as if it were nectar of the Gods.

'Feeling better now?' Drom asked her.

She smiled. 'That was the best sandwich and tea I've had in my whole life.' Her smile was broad and lit up her face.

'Are you up to telling us what's going on with you?' Drom asked.

Jasmine nodded. 'You were right; I am running away. I'm

running away to avoid a forced marriage. Because of this, my family is trying to kill me. My brothers, my parents, all want me dead. I'm a curse on their family. They won't stop until they find me and kill me.'

'Jesus,' Ashley said.

'I have two older sisters. Serena is already married, forced to be with an old man, a business associate of my father. My other sister, Bassima, is dead. She was forced into marriage too. She ran away. She was desperate. Nearly every day, her husband beat and raped her. Bass contacted my family in Australia and told them what happened. My dad said he would save her and sent my brothers to bring her home. But my brothers went to Lebanon to kill her. For the family honour. My brother Kadar slashed her lip, her nostrils, cut off her ears, slit her throat and stabbed her forty-seven times.'

Ashley's face reflected the horror we all felt. 'The sick bastard! What happened to Kadar?'

'Eight months in a Lebanese jail.'

'Eight months for torture and murder?' Drom said.

'It was classed as an honour killing. The laws have changed a bit since then, but men get away with it all the time.'

'Oh my God, Jasmine. That's terrible. And you have nowhere to go?' I asked.

'No. I had to leave all my friends, family. I can't trust anyone. I need to change my identity, how I look. Disappear. Maybe try and go overseas. I've no money. I had to leave everything behind. I'll have to try to find work.'

'I'll give you cash, luv,' Ashley offered.

'So will I,' Drom said.

'Maybe Jasmine could stay with us for a while?' I suggested.

'I'm not sure we could offer her the right sort of environment, with everything that's going on an' all,' Ashley said quietly.

'You have troubles too?' Jasmine asked.

32

Drom nodded. 'Unfortunately, we have troubles too. 'Different to yours, but just as nasty.'

Jasmine looked worried. 'Oh dear.'

Drom touched her arm. 'Don't worry. You're safe. We won't let anything happen to you.'

Ashley slowed the truck and looked at Jasmine in the rearview mirror. 'We have to turn off here; we're driving to a national park, The Den of Nargun. We can let you out here if you want, or you can stay with us.'

Jasmine looked to Drom for confirmation. 'I will stay with you? If that's all right?'

We all muttered acknowledgement.

It worried me having Jasmine with us. I didn't want to involve her in a situation more horrible than what she was already dealing with, but we couldn't abandon her. I figured we didn't have a choice. I knew Drom and Ashley were thinking the same thing. Ashley met my gaze and gave me a *"what can you do?"* shrug before we drove on.

The highway wound its way into flat lands, flood plains close to the river, rich expanses of fields; a tapestry of vegetables — corn, cabbages and lettuce — sat in contrast against newly ploughed fields the colour of dark chocolate. A large upturned plough sat on the edge of the road, its eight circular yellow blades rotating gently in the breeze. Metal sunflowers. It was a serendipitous art installation worthy of any gallery.

During the course of our trip, Drom had moved closer to Jasmine. She was exhausted and her head jerked as she tried to stay awake.

With a match-making motive in mind, I said, 'Why don't you lean up against Drom and get some shuteye? I'm sure he won't mind.'

Drom flushed. 'No, I don't mind.'

She scooted up next to him and leant against his shoulder. 'I hope I don't smell,' she said. 'I haven't had a shower for days.'

'Oh, I wondered what that was.' Drom grinned at Jasmine's shocked expression. 'Just kidding. You smell fine... kind of like hay. I love the smell of hay.'

She gave him a gentle punch on the arm, leaned back against his shoulder and was instantly asleep.

I grinned at him. 'I've never ever seen you blush before. What would your powers of observation say about that?'

He flushed again. 'It's hot in here. That's what they'd say.'

Ashley checked out Drom's face in the rearview mirror and chuckled. 'Yep, someone's got the hots, no doubt about that.'

Drom opened the window to let air in.

'You don't have a girlfriend do you, mate?'

'My itinerant lifestyle makes it too hard to get serious. All the girls I've been with get sick of me being away. They can't give up their lives to traipse around with me. That's just how it is.'

'I can relate to that,' Ashley said.

'Anyway, I haven't met a woman who feels like "*the one*", if there is such a thing.'

'Oh, believe me, there is,' Ashley said. 'The trouble is, "*the one*" may not be available. Timing is everything, mate. Everything.'

I turned around. 'I thought you did believe in soul mates?'

Drom looked at me intently. 'I do, and I believe you can have more than one. Imagine if you met two at the same time. That would be a dilemma.'

'It sure would.'

Oh, this was hitting close to the bone. Not wanting to continue the conversation, I turned away and looked out at the scenery. Lone farmhouses with the ubiquitous wrap-around veranda sat high and alone on their individual hills. Kings of their own domain with a view to forever.

'Wish I was up on that veranda, in a rocking chair, with a glass of champagne, gazing out at the view,' I muttered to myself.

'Ditto that,' Ashley said. 'And a log fire, a big bed and a fridge full of beer. And a barbeque to cook steak and sausages on.'

'To burn them on you mean,' Drom said.

'Ha ha. No sausages for you, Drom.'

We took a sidetrack to a small town called Glenalandale, which made my mouth feel funny every time I said it. The Glenalandale footy field was an oval of soft green grass framed by rough-hewn benches for the fans to sit on. Surrounding the oval were paddocks adorned with cows grazing peacefully.

Ashley pulled into the parking area, and Boo jumped out of the car and hightailed it to the centre of the oval. She was a dog on a mission.

'What's Boo on to?' Drom asked.

Jasmine was now sound asleep tucked underneath Drom's arm, her arm draped across his waist, her mouth slightly open, a soft snore escaping it.

I grinned. 'Hmm. Cozy. You stay put. Come on, Ashley. Let's see what Boo's so interested in.'

We were hot on Boo's heels as she finally skidded to a stop, nose down, exploring a small dome protruding from the grass. Boo gave her classic faux sneeze — a loud '*Pffpht!*' accompanied by a sideways flick of her head — followed by intense eye contact with us.

Ashley laughed. 'Ha! Boo, it's a mushroom! She thought she'd found a new ball!'

I grinned. 'Bad luck, Boo!'

Boo looked embarrassed.

We walked slowly back to the car, enjoying the feel of the sun on our faces as it broke through the clouds.

Ashley checked his watch. 'Let's have a cuppa here.'

'I have cake the Maestro made, coffee and walnut torte.'

'Bring it on. Looks like Drom and Jasmine have made a connection.'

'I've never seen him blush before, and he's gone kind of shy. Never seen that before either. He's normally mister cool and confident.'

'Good ole Dromski, ay? I reckon it's fate.'

'But why does fate bring us complicated things? Look at Drom's life, look at Jasmine's, and at ours. It's too crazy.'

Ashley draped an arm across my shoulder. 'You don't have to tell me that, luv.'

I fitted nicely underneath Ashley's arm, but it was heavy on my shoulders. 'Your arm weighs a ton.'

'Nah, that's your weak knees not holding you up properly.'

'Oh, don't go *there*. My knees are fine, thank you.'

'Want me to test 'em out for you?'

Before I could answer, he picked me up underneath the arms and swung me around.

He chuckled. 'I bet I've still got it.'

I felt the pressure of Ashley's hands near the sides of my breasts and the heat of his breath in my ear.

'Stop, I'm dizzy. Put me down.'

He stopped, held me suspended and then slowly lowered me to the ground, my body brushing against his all the way down. My toes barely touched the grass and still he held me up. His arms didn't have a single shake or tremble.

He whispered throatily, 'So, how are the knees holding out now?'

His breath was hot, and the back of my neck tingled. An involuntary surge of desire coursed through my body. 'You're incorrigible, Ashley Beringer.'

'So you keep telling me.'

'Put me down. I'm absolutely fine thank you.'

I took a deep breath as he let me go, willing the strength back to my knees. Friggin' Ashley Beringer. I'd be damned if I was going to give him the satisfaction. He thought he was God's gift to women. Well, he wasn't going to be able to turn me on at his whim.

I made my way back to the car as steadily as I could. Drom laughed when I lost concentration and a knee gave way oh so slightly. Ashley was right behind me and grabbed my arm. I pulled it away and felt my face go hot. 'I tripped on a rock is all.'

Oh shit. Shit. Shit. Shit. Damn you, Ashley.

Drom opened his window and said, 'What's up, Maggie? You look hot and bothered. I don't get it — it's *freezing* out there. How's the knees?'

Friggin' Ashley! He'd been blabbing to Drom. But surely, surely, he wouldn't do that. It was too personal. I'd kill him.

'What do you mean?'

'I don't know. You looked a bit wobbly.'

I flashed Ashley the most furious look I could muster.

'Hey, luv. Come here a minute.' He took me by the hand to the back of the truck.

I pulled my hand away and pushed him against the tailgate. 'What the hell?'

'Hey! Take it easy. What's wrong?'

'How the hell does Drom know about my knees? You've been blabbing to him. How could you?' I tried to whack him.

'You need to calm. Please. Take a breath. Now.'

'Yes. Okeydokey. You're right.'

Adrenaline had started to course through my body. It could easily trigger the dark force atom. I breathed in and out slowly until I felt in control.

Ashley earnestly searched my face for any sign of the demon. 'You right now?'

'Yes. Explain yourself.'

'I didn't say anything to anyone. I would never do that.' He linked his pinky finger with mine. 'I have no idea why Drom said that. But he comes out with things, personal things, about people all the time. He's done it to me. He's like a bloody radar. He picks things up and then spits 'em back out. I don't think he understands what the things mean though.'

'I don't know about that.'

'Whatever the case; please believe me. I would never give away our confidences. *Never.*'

'Even under torture?'

He smiled. 'Even under torture.'

'Extreme torture?'

'Yes, even then.'

'Okay. I believe you.'

'Thank you.' He enveloped me in his leather jacket and we held each other silently for a while before letting go.

He grinned at me. 'I've still got it though, haven't I?'

'You don't know when to quit do you?' I shook my head and walked away, glad to note my knees had fully recovered.

* * * * *

I set everything up on a nearby picnic table and we sat around enjoying our hot coffee and the Maestro's cake. Jasmine was eyeing off the cake. 'You must be starving,' I said. 'Please, have more.'

She quietly took another piece. Drom watched her a moment and then said, 'So, who exactly is hunting for you?'

'My brothers, Kadar, Amal and Ghassan, and probably cousins too. It's their duty to kill me for the dishonor I've brought on the family.'

Ashley shook his head. 'I can't get my head around how anyone could do that to their sister. If men treat women badly we say, "*You wouldn't do that to your sister.*" But your brothers have done that and don't give a damn. It's sick.'

'My brothers and cousins have no respect for women. They gang raped my girlfriend because they said she was "an Aussie slut". She was too scared to go to the cops. They said they'd kill her.'

38

'They got away with it?' Drom asked.

Jasmine closed her eyes. Her face quivered. 'Yes.'

An image blasted into my mind. I gasped and lurched forward. The vision and its associated agony king hit me in the guts. There are some things you can't unsee.

White bath. Utter despair. Burning pain. Red water. A young girl floating. Naked. Dead. Breasts protruding above the water, islands in a sea of blood. The word "free" written in blood on the white tiles.

Ashley grabbed my arm. 'Maggie! What's wrong?'

Tears streamed down my face. 'Elissar. She killed herself. She wrote the word "free" in her own blood on the white tiles.'

Jasmine stared at me wide-eyed with shock.

I shuddered as an icy chill enveloped me. 'I see things. And feel them too, unfortunately.'

Ashley took off his jacket, draped it over my shoulders and put an arm around me. 'You look like you've seen a ghost.'

'I have.'

'Your girlfriend, Elissar, took her own life?' Drom asked.

Tears ran down Jasmine's face. 'Yes. I found her.'

Drom put his arm around her. 'I'm so sorry.'

She held his hand. 'Elissar is free now. I'm glad for her. She was in so much pain, depressed and sad.' Jasmine stared coldly into space. 'Drom, if I could, I would kill all my brothers and cousins. I want them to pay for what they did to my sisters, my friend, me … and other girls. I want them all dead.' She grabbed the cake knife and stabbed it down hard into the tabletop. She stared at the knife as it wobbled back and forth. 'I would kill my father too.'

Ashley and Drom shook their heads, lost for words. My head shook too as I tried to comprehend how your family could treat you so badly that you wanted to kill them. Fox had told me about such cases, and how prevalent forced marriages were in Australia, but the horror of it hadn't hit home until I'd heard

Jasmine's story.

'I can't believe this is happening in Australia,' Ashley said.

Drom looked at him. 'It's happening all over the world.'

Jasmine wiped her eyes. 'I'm sorry to burden you with my troubles. You are all so lovely. I'm sorry.'

'Don't be sorry,' Drom said. 'Come on, there's four pieces of cake left. Chocolate makes you happy. Let's finish it off.' He gave each of us a piece.

'Hey, I've got something.' Ashley pulled out a hip flask from his jacket pocket and put a shot of golden fluid in everyone's coffee. 'Grand Marnier liqueur. Goes great with chocolate cake and peps you up. This'll put colour back in your faces, girls.'

'Here's to chocolate and happiness,' I said. We clinked our mugs and downed the contents. The pungent scent of oranges filled my nostrils, and a sense of warmth ran down my gullet and soothed my churning stomach.

Ashley smiled at me. 'See, your cheeks are pink already.'

I handed him his jacket. 'You always have a remedy at hand. Thank you. I feel better now.'

Jasmine smiled. 'Me too.'

'Come on, let's hit the road, kids,' he said, packing up the Esky.

* * * * *

We made excellent time, and finally, when the asphalt gave way to a rough, potholed gravel road, we knew we didn't have much further to go. Boo was inside and rode shotgun, front paws balanced on the window ledge. She studied the scenery with as much interest as we did.

The Den of Nargun is a sacred aboriginal site located at the bottom of a deep valley. I'd been there years ago and remembered the legend of the Nargun, a fearsome creature, half stone, half flesh that lived in the cave. The Nargun would steal any child that came near its den, and spears thrown at it would be repelled. Men were asked not to go near the den, as it was a woman's spiritual place, used for female ceremonies and initiations.

We drove into the car park. It was deserted. Good news. My heart started to beat faster and my gut tightened as I got out of the car. I had a sense of what was about to befall us.

[4] *Maggie's Playlist: Hitchhiker — Demi Lovato*

 **Chapter 5: Skull Crusher**

'The trouble with the world is that the stupid are cocksure and the intelligent are full of doubt.' — Bertrand Russell

Maggie and Ashley were kitted up and ready to roll, their faces tight and determined. The Den of Nargun awaited them.

Ashley tucked his pistol down the back of his pants. 'We'll probably be a couple of hours, Drom. Give us three hours max, and if we're not back by then come looking for us. There's no reception here, so phones are useless.'

'No worries. Be careful.'

Maggie gave me a grin. 'Look after Jasmine.'

I gave her the thumbs up. 'Will do.'

I returned to the truck and peered in the window. Jasmine was lying on the back seat fast asleep. I had a few hours to kill. I could probably get through a couple of books. If Jasmine woke she could go on watch and I could get my twenty-minute shuteye.

I checked my phone. Yep, the two books I'd downloaded were ready and waiting. The truck rocked as Jasmine sat up and rubbed her eyes. She looked confused as she got out.

'You okay?' I asked.

'Yes. I didn't know where I was for a minute.' She stretched her arms over her head. 'It's wonderful to have a bit of sunshine.' Leaning back against the truck, she closed her eyes and turned her face to the sun.

She was so petite and pretty. How could anyone want to hurt her? I couldn't believe what she and her sisters had been through. And her best friend. I would kill her brother myself if he ever crossed my path.

Jasmine opened her eyes and caught me looking at her. She pulled a grass seed from her hair. 'I can't wait to have a shower. I must look terrible.'

'If you want to freshen up, there's a toilet block over there.'

'Good idea. I'll make us a cup of tea when I get back.' She flashed me a beautiful smile.

'I'll make it for us. See you soon.'

I hunted around in the back of the truck for the Thermos and Esky. Boo was sitting in a sunny spot dozing. She opened her eyes and stared at me, ears pricked, on high alert.

There's a car coming, Drom.

I couldn't hear anything for a moment, but then the sound of crunching gravel and a car coming at speed was unmistakable.

'*Shit!* Boo, go hide in the bushes. Keep an eye out. I'll get Jasmine.'

Boo hovered out of the truck and floated away into the bush mimicking a gigantic bumblebee. She looked back at me, pink tongue hanging out, mouth open in a crazy cartoon like smile. Boo always loved the possibility of a bit of action.

A four-wheel drive blasted into the car park. It did a three sixty hand brake slide, spinning around and spraying Ashley's truck and me with gravel, before coming to a stop facing the opposite direction. Loud music blasted from the car.

The music stopped and the car doors opened. Six men leapt out of the car. A tall, dark skinned man approached me as I brushed dust and gravel off my clothes.

'How *you* doin'?' he said as he sauntered over.

'Doin' fine. Except for the dust.'

He rubbed his beard and scanned the area. 'You here by

yourself, buddy?'

I wasn't his buddy. Dickhead.

'No, my mates went for a walk. They'll be back soon.'

'How come you didn't go?'

'Sprained ankle. Can't walk. Just came along for the ride. You here to walk too?' I said, knowing full well they weren't.

'Nah. We're lookin' for someone. You haven't seen a Lebanese girl, long black hair, tiny? Perhaps you picked up a hitchhiker like that?' He narrowed his eyes and stared at me.

'Can't say I have. Who is she?'

'My slut sister.' He spat on the ground. 'Hey Ghass, put some music on. Too fuckin' quiet here.'

'What sort, Kadar?'

'Blood Ink, man. Skull Crusher.'

I willed Jasmine to stay put.

Ghass opened the door and turned on the ignition. After a couple of seconds, the air was filled with screaming heavy metal music. A flock of rosellas took off from a nearby gum tree in terror.

I willed Jasmine to lock the toilet door and put her feet up so she couldn't be seen.

Kadar pumped his head up and down. 'Good music, 'ay?'

Two of the men sauntered towards the toilets. 'Going to take a piss, man.'

Kadar stomped his foot to the frenetic noise and shouted, 'Take a look around while you're there. Make sure no one's hiding, ay?' He grinned at me, then fished around in his pocket, pulled out a toothpick and stuck it in the side of his mouth.

He was staying close to me. There were six of them, all built, heavy boots. They didn't seem to be packing heat, but they probably had blades. Maybe they had guns in the car. Jasmine must've realised who it was by now. She'd lay low. The music was seriously doing my brain in. I could barely think for the racket.

Above the noise of the music I heard a toilet door crash open, then wood smashing against wood. *Bang! Bang! Bang!* Smash. The sound of another door giving way.

Kadar chewed his toothpick and looked at me. 'The boys are making a bit of fire wood, ay?'

'Hey, Kadar, look what we've found.' Ghass appeared, grinning proudly. He held Jasmine in a headlock, pulling her behind him.

A surge of blood rushed to my head and my heart started to pound.

'Huh. Look what the fuckin' cat dragged in, would yah. My slut sister.' He grabbed Jasmine by the hair and dragged her over to me. He wound her hair around his wrist until her head was tight up against his arm. He jerked his forearm back so Jasmine's face was tilted skywards.

'This is the skanky bitch we've been looking for,' he growled, yanking her hair viciously. 'Makes me wonder how she got here, ay?'

The other men slowly gathered around. My mind was busy calculating strategy, distance, odds, and factoring in the sun, wind and spin of the Earth. Well, not the spin of the earth, but everything else I could think of.

I finished my calculations. 'I'll give you three seconds to let her go, get in your car, and leave.'

Kadar put a finger in his ear and poked it around. 'What's that, Skip? I thought I heard you say you'll give us three seconds to let her go, get in our car and leave.' He threw back his head and laughed, revealing a set of tobacco stained teeth.

'You heard right.'

Kadar and his henchman looked at each other and grinned. 'And who's gonna make me? You? Little Skip, with the sprained ankle?'

I could use the Dirty Harry line! I'd wanted to use that line all my life. Ash would be rapt. Here goes. 'Well, we're not just gonna let you walk out of here.' An involuntary smile twitched on my lips.

Jasmine whimpered as Kadar yanked her hair again. 'Jasmine's coming with us, fucker. So, what *"we"* are you talking about?'

'Smith & Wesson and me.' I whipped out my pistol and pointed it at his head. It made a satisfying click as I cocked the hammer.

A look of shock flashed across Kadar's face. He took a step backward. His cronies made a move for the car.

'Nobody move or Kadar gets it,' I yelled. Jasmine's eyes were wide open and staring at the gun. 'Make like a statue, Kadar. The rest of you, down on the ground, now!' I didn't take my eyes off Kadar. 'Let. Jasmine. Go.'

In a split-second Kadar flicked his arm forward. A knife shot out in his hand and was up against Jasmine's throat. He grinned. 'I'll slit her throat like a pig. Mister Smith & fuckin' Wesson won't be fast enough to save her.' He pressed the knife into her neck. A trickle of blood flowed across the blade.

'So, Skip, whatcha gonna do now? Listen, you put that gun down and we'll be gone. This has nothing to do with you, man. This is Lebo business. I promise you. Put the gun down and we'll be outta your hair. Gone.' He cocked his head at Jasmine and jiggled the toothpick in the side of his mouth. 'We've got what we came for.'

I slowly leant forward as if to put the gun on the ground. 'You're right. This thing isn't even loaded. I'm no hero.'

'Wise move, Skip.' Kadar nodded and grinned, pumping his head to the music again. 'Kick it over to the guys. We'll take it along as a souvenier.'

Over your dead body, arsehole.

'Stop stalling. Put the gun on the ground. Now!'

As I bent forward I quickly pulled out three throwing knives from my pocket.

Flick one — straight into Kadar's arm. He screamed and dropped his knife.

Flick two — another knife into his thigh. He let go of Jasmine.

I pulled the knife out of his thigh, grabbed Jasmine and pulled her behind me. 'Get in the car. Lock the doors.'

Kadar staggered forward. I delivered a kick straight between his legs. Blunt force trauma. *Bang!* Nerve endings in overload. Kadar hit the ground like a sack of spuds. He wouldn't be going anywhere for a while.

Flick three — knife deep into the shoulder of arsehole number two. He reeled back screaming. I pulled another three knives from the other side of my jacket. One guy was at the car.

Flick four — a knife into the shoulder blade of arsehole number three. Another blood curdling scream. He collapsed to the ground and called for his mother. I stepped forward to meet approaching arseholes numbers four, five and six. All three of them had knives, which flashed in the sun. My blades were matt black. They didn't flash as I dispatched them right on target. Maim not kill. Right through the arm, top of the thigh, and you — you got the side of the stomach, scumbag.

They toppled like dominos and fell in a crying heap. I collected all their shiny little knives that had never had the chance to leave their filthy hands.

Kadar was on all fours, crawling to his car. I dispatched another flick kick to his guts and he went to sleep.

Jasmine opened the truck door. 'What can I do?'

'There are black cable ties in the glove box. And duct tape.'

She scrabbled around and came over with a bundle.

I took a cable tie and tied it around Kadar's feet. I pulled it tight and it made a satisfying *zip* noise. I did the same with his hands, then ripped off a piece of duct tape and slapped it across his mouth.

Gotta love cable ties and duct tape. Or duck tape, as Maggie would say.

I picked up my gun, which was loaded and ready to fire. Arsehole number two quivered like a bowl of jelly. I strode across to him. My brain hurt, as though it was filled with razor blades. 'Before I take care of you, there's something I have to do.'

I opened their car door and let the sound system have it. Blessed silence. 'Thank Christ for that,' I muttered, blowing the smoke away from the end of my gun.

Arsehole number two had thrown up over his jeans. 'Try anything and I'll blow your brains out. Just like your sound system. You have shit taste in music, by the way. Keep your eyes down and do what you're told. Jasmine, you saw what I did with Kadar over there. Do the same to him.'

Between us we bound them all. Jasmine was calm and efficient, and seemed to take pleasure in making sure the ties were extremely tight.

'Great work. Let's drag 'em up against this rock wall.'

One by one we dragged the motley crew over until they were all lined up in a nice neat row, sitting on their arses.

'Oh, mustn't forget them.' I squatted down and extracted my throwing knives, using their pants to wipe the blood off my knives.

Ghass wailed pitifully. 'I'm gonna die.' The duct tape hadn't stuck to his beard that well.

'I wish you would. But unfortunately, you're not. If I wanted you dead you would be already. It's up to Jasmine whether you live.'

Ghass stopped wailing in an instant. Jasmine looked at me. They all looked at Jasmine. I pulled a bullet out of my pocket, flicked open the revolver and poked the bullet in. 'There's six shots in there now.' I held out the gun. 'Don't point it at anything you don't want to shoot. Don't put your finger on the trigger until you're ready to shoot. There's a bullet for each of them, if you want. It's cocked and ready to fire.'

Jasmine's beautiful brown eyes were set and determined as she carefully took hold of the gun. Her hands were as steady as a rock as she pointed it at Kadar.

---

[5] *Maggie's Playlist: Knife Thrower — Charming Disaster*

"Our spirituality is a oneness and an interconnectedness with all that lives and breathes, even with all that does not live or breathe." — *Mudrooroo Narogin*

Ashley and I rock hopped our way along a narrow track. The climb was steep. A slip and fall would probably result in severe injury or death, so I kept my eyes fixed on the path. Every now and then, I would stop and gaze up at the sandstone cliffs blazing with yellows, reds and oranges, and then down into the green, moist depths of the valley below. The large lichen covered rocks that flagged our path changed their apparel to soft green moss as we climbed down to the bottom of the valley.

The path to the Den of Nargun appeared before us, an immense jumble and tumble of boulders — an ancient God's forgotten game of marbles. You had to earn your way to the Den of Nargun. The air was fresh and cool, redolent with the scent of rainforest. The presence of spirits surrounded me, those who had walked this way for hundreds and thousands of years.

'We need to be quiet now,' I whispered to Ashley. 'We're getting close.'

The energy here was sacred and complex. My mind hummed as it tuned into the crystals. My brain felt an uncomfortable fullness as it picked up and amplified the psychic vibrations to the power of way, way too much.

Whenever you're in a sacred space the best thing you can do

is be quiet and listen. Even with a bog-standard brain, when you stop talking, you can perceive truth. Silence is truth. And silence is alive with sound.

I was surprised at how tuned in Ashley was. I always thought he never got the whole spiritual thing. I stopped to let him pass, and he appeared larger than life, a gentle giant picking his way through the boulder strewn path. He fitted in here, resonating with the energy. Who would've thought?

Shortly, the Den appeared before us — a long, horizontal cave in the cliff face, surrounded by a body of water about twenty feet wide. Ashley took my hand and helped me over the final few boulders. We sat quietly on a rock next to the water and gazed into the cave.

Our presence was still, bringing with it the silence and respect that is the finest gift we could offer the spirits who lived here. The stillness was intense, as though the whole valley and all life within it held its breath.

Ashley's expression reflected the stillness we felt, which rolled over us like a wave of peace so deep it dissolved all thought. We could've been sitting here for a minute or an eternity.

A thought drifted into my mind breaking my reverie. *Sitting still with my eyes closed, like this, would make me easy pickings for a predator.*

As the thought concluded, something cold and hard clutched my ankle. I screamed and pulled my foot back, but I couldn't shake the grip loose. Whatever it was yanked me off the rock and into the lagoon. I spluttered and thrashed my arms as I was dragged through the water at speed. Above me, the brackish water distorted the sunlight and trees into a murky collage. I tried to grab something but found only soft mud. Gasping for air, I was finally dumped on the sand.

It was dark and cold. The dankness of the Den filled my nostrils — rotted leaves, mud and bat poo, I reckoned. I was wedged up hard against the back wall of the cave by … a rock.

From the darkness of the cave, the outside world appeared as a splice of light framed in blackness. Ashley was a statue sitting on a rock.

'Ashley! Help me! Wake up!' I screamed. He couldn't hear me. I was in a cone of silence. I heard something. A voice. The voice had the timbre of gravel and rock.

'I am Naaarguunnn.' The voice thundered, reverberating around the walls of the cave.

The Nargun's voice was like a cross between Darth Vader and the Predator with a bad sore throat. A noise followed, similar to the sound of stones churning in a cement mixer. It was clearing its throat. I had the feeling the Nargun hadn't spoken in quite some time.

'You are Crystal Keeper. Where is our friend Boooo-ooh?'

'Yes, Nargun, I am a Crystal Keeper. Boo couldn't come. Unfortunately, they don't let dogs into National Parks, so we had to leave her behind in the car, with the doors locked and windows open, in the shade of course, with our friend Drom, but…'

'Enough!' the Nargun growled.

The sound of the rocky, raspy voice had an added rumble of thunder, and with my nervous babbling, I may have annoyed the Nargun. An annoyed Nargun was not the outcome I intended, or wanted.

A wave of terror rushed over me as a large section of rock shifted, rising up out of the sand with the sound of suction. As my eyes grew accustomed to the darkness, I could make better sense of what confronted me. The rock pinning me to the back wall of the cave was a large rocky hand, connected to a massive rocky arm, attached to — you guessed it — a humungous rocky body.

The Nargun's hand covered my whole torso, and my ribs ached as it increased the pressure, pushing me against the back wall of the cave. Sharp rocks dug into my back. One pierced my skin.

I gasped. 'You're hurting me.' Terror and claustrophobia grew rapidly. 'I. Can't. Breathe,' I whispered, barely able to get the words out.

A large stony object moved close to my face and blocked my view out of the cave. It was blackness within blackness until two small upturned crescents of light appeared where I thought eyes should be.

The crescents expanded into round pools of exquisite amber and gold light, a light from the beginning of time. The amber pools moved closer until they were no more than an inch from my face. A breath of rock, forest and ancient lands swept over me.

The pressure on my body released as the Nargun backed off a little. I gasped for air.

'Balance must be restored,' the Nargun rumbled. 'I entrust these to you to fulfill the task. You must not fail. To help you succeed, every rock will be your friend. Fail, and every rock will be your enemy.'

'That's a bit harsh,' I said. 'If we fail, we won't mean to. We'll die trying. I don't want to have rocks as my enemy. I love rocks. So does Boo. She collects them. She has a whole basket of them on our coffee table. I don't work well under threat. Take that back.'

Crikey, I had enough to worry about without adding rock worry to the list. I wasn't in a strong bargaining position and probably should have kept my mouth shut.

The Nargun responded to my ultimatum with a long, sulphurous belch of air that blasted back the wet hair plastered across my face. A Nargun blow dry — that was a first. I was going to smell like a hard-boiled egg.

'I am sorry, Maggie. I will always protect you. But it is a bad time now,' the Nargun roared. 'See…'

My psychic senses cranked into overdrive, flooded with images from the Nargun. A display of the beauty and holiness of the land, air, waters and all its creatures raced through my mind, from the beginning of time to the present day. Harmony and balance followed by cruelty, savagery and destruction.

The Nargun was ancient and immeasurably forlorn, but I sensed a flicker of hope as it presented me with two glowing crystal spheres.

The light from the spheres illuminated its stony hand, a structure woven of rock and flesh, the palm iridescent with opal fluorescence. I took the crystals and placed them on the sand next to me.

'So beautiful!' I stroked its hand feeling a texture of warm rock and course skin. The Nargun emitted a long, low ominous growl, which continued in a familiar rhythm.

Grumble, growl, rumble, growl, grumble, growl.

My heart settled. It wasn't going to eat me, it ... was ... *purring!*

As I sat there stroking the hand of the Nargun, I pondered what moment would be the most opportune to disengage. Hmmm. This could be tricky. Maybe it liked this so much it would never let me go, and would keep me here as its personal masseuse for eternity.

'I must go now, to restore balance,' I said in my deepest voice, attempting to mimic the words the Nargun had used.

A rocky hand patted my head, and I was glad it finally seemed able to measure its own strength. Not an easy task to pat a cranium with a hand the size of a boulder.

I picked up the two crystal spheres. 'Thank you, Nargun. I'll see myself out then, shall I?'

The Nargun nodded, slowly and rhythmically nestling its stony body down into the watery sand. Its head remained halfway out of the sand and it resembled, for all intents and purposes, an ordinary boulder.

I stepped out from the dark chill of the cave, clutching two crystal meteors. Welcome sunlight and warm air hit my body. I turned and the boulder opened its beautiful eyes. I held its gaze, which seemed softer somehow. The Nargun blinked slowly and closed its eyes. A rumble shook the earth, leaves showered down from trees and the water jumped and rippled around me.

As the Nargun's eyes closed, Ashley's opened. I walked through the water towards him holding out the crystals in upturned palms. I don't ever recall seeing Ashley's jaw drop before, but drop it did, and if I'd had a ping-pong ball I would've liked to try my luck at lobbing it in that open mouth.

Ashley sat dazed and speechless. Later, as he explained what he'd seen, I understood why. When he opened his eyes from the Nargun induced slumber, he saw before him a woman rising up from the rippling waters. Tight wet cloth clung to her body, wet hair glistened in the sun, and a tornado of autumn leaves whirled in the air around her. Held in her outstretched hands were two orbs of dazzling radiance that refracted the sunshine and mist into a thousand shimmering rainbows.

'Jesus. I thought the Goddess of the lake was coming out of the water for me. I couldn't believe my eyes. It was beautiful.' He grinned. 'I'm going to revisit that in my mind on a regular basis.'

Unfortunately, the reality that stood before him was somewhat different. A sulphur scented, wet, muddy woman with chattering teeth. The only thing going for her was she had two crystal spheres in her hot little hands.

Well, actually, my hands were freezing, but I had the crystals. My teeth chattered from the cold, and the excitement and adrenaline rush of my encounter with the Nargun.

Ashley held out his jacket. 'Here, take this.'

'Thanks, but I'll warm up on the climb out of here. Could you put the crystals in your pockets?'

'Sure.'

I handed over my precious possessions. 'The Nargun was

beautiful. I wish you could have seen it.'

'Well, I saw what it could *do* … with that impromptu earthquake an' all. You wouldn't want to get on the wrong side of it.'

I buckled as a strong feeling hit me in the gut. 'Agh!'

Ashley grabbed my arm. 'What's wrong?'

'It's Drom. He's in trouble. We need to go!'

I looked up in dismay at the steep cliffs towering above us. 'Crikey! It took us thirty minutes to get down, it'll be even longer going back. Drom's going to have to deal with whatever it is by himself.'

'I'll run ahead. Will you be okay?'

'Yes, I'll be fine. You go.'

Ashley looked down his nose at me as though wearing imaginary spectacles. 'Be. Careful.'

'Yes, Ashley.'

He turned and raced up the track, leaping sure footedly from one rock to the next.

I followed. After ten minutes of rock hopping as fast as I could, my legs shook and my lungs burned. Ashley was nowhere to be seen. His long legs had made easy work of it.

Oh my God, I was unfit. This was killing me. I'd be dead before I got to the top. I'd be of no use to Drom. I was a liability. I'd seriously have to do something about my fitness. I was a corporate couch potato. I usually sat in front of a computer all day. My body couldn't cope.

'God, hear me now. I promise you, if I don't die on the way up I'll go on a fitness campaign.'

Three quarters of the way up I stopped to catch my breath and hoped whatever trouble Drom was in that Ashley was there helping him.

The path ahead was tricky. It was a steep climb, and it was narrow and stony. I clambered over the rocky terrain on all fours, trying to go as fast as I could and keep safe, like Ashley

56

said. But my legs decided otherwise. They went on strike and developed a severe case of the wobbles. I could barely make them do what I wanted them to do.

Come on. Come on. Behave. One more step. You can do it.

I placed my foot carefully on the next rock and everything gave way. My ankle collapsed, and I slid down the incline at speed. I scrabbled for a handhold as rocks and branches ripped through my grasp. Sliding over a ledge, I linked my hands and latched onto a rock sticking over the edge. Dangling in space, I held on to the small boulder as though my life depended on it.

Well, hello. My life did depend on it. Okay. Don't panic, Maggie. This was not so bad. I had a strong handhold. I just had to find a foothold. I could do this.

I glanced down to see what lay below me, hoping to see a tree close by, maybe a ledge, perhaps the path below. Instead, there was a sheer drop to the valley below. My body responded to this with a weird tingling in my base chakra.

I focused upwards, swung my legs, tried to find somewhere to put my feet. There was nothing. I was hanging in midair. I tested my arms, tried to pull myself up. Hopeless. There was no way I had the strength to lift my body weight. I stretched a leg to the side. The only foothold was shoulder height. If I could swing my leg up and get traction I may be able to heave myself up. I'd have to get a swing up to do it.

I stretched out my leg as far as it would go. Shit. Not very far. I couldn't hold on and swing high enough. My arms burned. My hands were numb. 'Help! Help! Somebody *help*!'

The rock and bush absorbed my screams into their embrace. Crikey. There's not a chance in hell anyone's gonna hear that.

Who'd have thought I'd go this way? Maybe I could survive the drop? I was kidding myself. I'd be a broken heap of bones when I kissed the ground. But people had survived. You had to try and hit the ground feet first. I remembered reading that somewhere. Keep your knees relaxed. Bending them reduced impact. Wrap your arms around your head to protect from secondary impact. Try and fall to the side. Not backwards. What else? Use your mobile phone to call for help. Yeah, right.

I wondered how long my arms would hold out. How much life had I left? As much as my arms would allow.

I didn't want to, but I had no choice. I opened my mind and sent out a telepathic distress call. I knew Drom would get it, if he was still alive, and Ashley and Boo, but they were probably in the middle of something. I'd be making things worse. Distracting them.

If they came, it'd take twenty minutes to reach me. Maybe Boo could get here faster? There was no way I could hold on for another *five* minutes. I was screwed.

Focus. Look up. Look at the sky, the trees. Hold on.

I directed all my energy into my hands. I was not going to die smashed to smithereens on the rocks below. I simply was not. The pain in my arms was excruciating. I distracted myself. Dolphins, beautiful dolphins, spinning, swimming. Jason — the last time we made love, oh my God, how phenomenal? Bacon and eggs. My favourite playlist. Oh, Ashley, how I'd love to f...

For a split second, I didn't realise I'd let go.

I screamed as air rushed past my body.

Maggie, it's Boo! Hold on. One minute. I'm nearly there. Hold on.

Too late.

---

[6] *Maggie's Playlist: In The Outback — Dreamtime*

"The crash of your thunder was in the whirlwind; your lightnings lighted up the world; the earth trembled and shook." — Psalm 77:18

Kadar was still unconscious, unaware of the gun pointed at his head. Jasmine kicked him. 'Wake up.' She kicked him again. No response. Either he was playing possum or I'd hit him harder than I thought.

'I want to look into his eyes as I kill him. I will wait.'

'He'll come around soon. Are you sure you want to do this?'

'Yes. I'm sure.' She took her finger off the trigger and nodded in the direction of a group of shrubby wattles. 'Something's moving in the bushes.'

'Be careful with the gun. I'll go check it out.' I raced back to the truck and grabbed another pistol. Someone was working their way towards the back of the stone wall. I checked my watch. I'd double back and go around the other side. Take 'em by surprise.

I moved low and quiet, keeping to the bushes. Making my way to where I thought they were headed, I squatted down behind a tree to wait.

Cold steel pushed into the back of my neck, then the familiar click of a hammer being cocked. 'Hello, Ash.' His body towered above me and blocked out the sun.

'How'd you know it was me?'

'The sound of your gun. It has a certain kind of click when you cock the hammer.'

'Dead set? And what if somebody had taken my gun, mate?'

'I knew it was you anyway. There were other indicators. Lucky for you I didn't kill you.'

'Yeah right. In your dreams. Anyway, what's going on? I busted a pooper valve trying to get here. Maggie's still coming. What's happened?'

I stood and brushed a bull ant off my jeans. 'Come and see. It's all under control. Did you get the crystals?'

Ashley's face split into his trademark smile. 'Mission accomplished.' He patted his jacket. 'Right here.'

'Thank God.'

'Thank Maggie.'

'You move quietly for a big bloke.'

'Yep. All that sneaking around in Iraq.'

Ashley followed me to the car park. Jasmine was still holding the gun. She smiled when she saw Ashley. He stared at the collection of bound and gagged hoods.

'Holy hell, Jasmine, you did all *this?*' He laughed. 'Drom was lucky to have you around.'

Jasmine giggled. 'It was Drom, silly.'

'Hoo-whee! Spectacular work, Drom.'

'Hey, I used the line. The one from Dirty Harry.'

'*Really?* Shit, I wish I'd been here to see it. I'm proud of you.' He gave me a huge, crushing, man hug, then slapped me hard on the back, nearly knocking me over.

'Good ole Dromski. You sure have proved yourself today. So who are these dudes?'

Jasmine pointed the gun at the still sleeping body. 'That's Kadar, my brother. My two other brothers, and three cousins. Drom saved me. They were going to kill me. Now I'm going to kill Kadar. When he wakes up.'

Ashley looked shocked. 'Jesus, are you sure you want to do

that? Killing someone, even your enemy, does something to you. It leaves a mark, something bad on you.'

'I want him dead.'

'Then I'll do it for you,' Ashley said quietly. 'I'm stuffed as it is. One more won't make much difference. I'd be happy to take out that piece of trash. I don't want you with blood on your hands.'

'It's my choice.'

'Yes, it is. Take a minute to think about it, okay? I'll be back in a sec.'

Ashley grabbed my arm and pulled me over to the truck. 'What are you thinking, Drom?' he hissed. 'Why the *hell* did you give her a gun? Have you lost your mind? We're all going to end up in a world of hurt. Aside from what it will do to her.' He glared at me.

'He's a murderer. They're *all* murderers and rapists. I wanted her to have justice. For herself, her sisters and her girlfriend. She won't get it any other way. She won't get any peace. They'll hunt her down. For the rest of her life, she'll be looking over her shoulder. I wanted to give her a gift. A gift of justice. Freedom.'

'She'll feel a real lot of freedom and justice in jail, mate. Everything has strings attached. I see where you're coming from. Believe me, I want that too. But you can't let her do it. You ... you really like her, don't you, mate?'

'Yes. There's something. You know me. I'm calm, rational, controlled. With her ... I feel so protective ... it's as if I've known her all my life. My heart pounds; I feel nervous. When I was fighting those guys, it took all my strength not to kill them. I can't get her out of my head. There's something wrong with me.'

Ash whacked me on the shoulder. 'Oh, jeez. The boy has finally got it.'

'Got what?'

His belly shook with laughter. 'You're in love, or lust, you idiot. That's all.'

'I don't like feeling out of control. I don't want to get emotionally attached.'

'You'll get used to it. But you understand better than anyone that we must make rational, careful decisions. As best we can anyway. It's not just our lives that depend on it.'

'I get that. That's why I'm worried. I have to end it, now.'

'You'll do nothing of the sort. Don't even think about it. We need love. Especially now. Even if it makes us crazy. *Don't.* Okay?'

I looked at him and said nothing.

Ashley's body suddenly jerked and he clutched his head. 'Did you get that? Maggie. Bloody hell, she's in trouble!'

Ashley raced full pelt back from whence he'd come, his long legs pounding the ground like a machine. He yelled, 'Stay here and don't do anything stupid!'

The bones of my skull began to vibrate as a rumble similar to the sound of ten freight trains assaulted my ears. Ashley's mouth was moving, but I couldn't hear what he was yelling. The ground began to heave and shake. Leaves fell from the trees. Birds flew away in clouds of panic.

Ashley was knocked clean off his feet mid stride. He hit the dirt. Jasmine tried to keep her balance and not point the gun at anything she didn't want to shoot. Bless her. The truck bounced up and down next to me. Everything was in motion, and then everything stopped.

Silence. More than silence. No wind. No birds. No insects. Everything was holding its breath — waiting. I held mine, wondering what the hell was going to happen next.

---

[7] *Maggie's Playlist: Gunpowder & Lead — Miranda Lambert*

"Rocks and minerals: the oldest storytellers." — *A.D. Posey*

The earth roared as my hands let go and I fell into the abyss. Ashley's yell echoed in my mind: 'I'm coming!'

Too late.

I felt the earth shaking even in midair. A flurry of leaves hit my face, and I opened my eyes, wondering at what point I should get ready to land.

Shit! Maybe now! A wedge of rock popped out of the cliff face below me and I screamed. It was coming up fast — I knew that — but everything was in slow motion. Sound muffled, and the world condensed until there was only me and the approaching rock. My mind was still water into which crystalline thoughts dropped like depth charges.

Plop. Bang! If you're drunk, you can better survive a fall. See, that was another reason I should've had champagne for breakfast.

Plop. Bang! If you fall out of a plane, your body will be 7,500 times its normal weight when you hit the ground. At that exact moment, your brain will weigh ten tons.

Plop. Bang! Impact may disconnect your aorta from your heart.

Plop. Bang! Your skull could shatter and your cells may burst.

Plop. Bang! Massive internal bleeding is a distinct possibility.

Plop. Bang! Death is the likely outcome.

Why the hell did my brain retain that stuff? It was so not helpful.

I covered my head with my arms.

I didn't want to die. Not now. Not like this. Relax your knees.

I was going to hit hard.

The back of my jumper snagged and I jolted, my head snapping backwards. The rock ledge approached.

Relax. Relax. This was it!

An inch away from ground zero, I was hoisted up slightly. As lightly as a butterfly, I landed feet first on the rock ledge.

You beauty!

Then my bloody knees gave way. My feet slipped, and I found myself balanced on the edge of a precipice, arms waving like windmills.

Shit, here we go again.

I fell forward but didn't fall. Whatever had snagged me was holding.

Maggie, it's me. Boo. I've got you. Lean backwards.

I did as I was told and Boo dragged me to safety. She floated down and sat in front of me.

That was a close call, Maggie.

I hugged her. 'That's the understatement of the year, Boo.'

My body shook from head to foot. 'You saved me, Boo. Thank you.' I could hardly speak for exhaustion.

I'm sorry I wasn't there sooner. And to be honest, it wasn't me. I helped. But it was Nargun who saved you.

'Nargun made the rock pop out?'

Yes. Nargun said he would protect you, and he did.

'Jeepers. I didn't think his guarantee extended to things caused by my own stupidity.'

Obviously, it does. Boo grinned.

Whoever said dogs didn't have a sense of humour didn't understand dogs.

'Boo, we have to get back. Drom's in trouble. That's why Ashley had to leave me.'

Relax, Maggie. Everything's under control. Drom handled it. He normally wouldn't call for help, but it was Jasmine. She's got him rattled.

'It's called love, Boo … like you and Schmoo.'

'*Pffphht!*' Boo gave me her faux sneeze.

A familiar voice echoed through the bush. It was Ashley, calling frantically. 'Maggie! Maggie! Where are you?'

'Down here! I'm okay. Down *here*.'

Ashley's head poked over the edge. I'd never been so glad to see his rugged face.

He grumbled. 'Bugger me dead, *really?* I swear you've taken twenty years off my life. I'm getting too old for this shit.'

I grinned. 'I love you too, Ashley, and I'm glad you're still alive.'

He shook his head and sighed. 'Ditto. Sit tight. I'm going to have to get a rope to haul you out of there.'

I'll get it, Ashley. I'll whizz back faster than you. I know where the rope is.

'There's an abseiling harness in there somewhere. Get Drom to help you find it. It's in a blue plastic crate. Thanks, Boo. Looking out for Mags has me plumb tuckered out.' He groaned and lay flat on the ground like a lizard, his face peering over the edge.

I yelled upwards, 'Nargun saved me. And Boo.'

'So that's what the quake was all about. I thought you were dead. Honestly, from now on, no matter what trouble anyone gets in, I'm not leaving you. You can't be trusted on your own.'

I didn't say anything. I was too tired to argue. I sat and looked out at the trees. The birds had started chirping again. The sun broke through the clouds, and the bush burst into colour. The aroma of eucalyptus and wattle permeated the gentle breeze.

I took a deep breath and pulled the fragrant air into my lungs.

I patted the rock under me and whispered, 'Thank you, Nargun. I'm alive.'

The earth trembled and rumbled gently in response.

'Whatever you're doing down there stop it!' Ashley yelled.

The rock felt warm and comforting beneath me. It's heat seeped into my bones. I gazed out at the beauty surrounding me. 'I'm being grateful, Ashley. Immensely grateful.'

* * * * *

Ten minutes later Boo returned, flying through the trees carrying the harness in her mouth. Drom must've wound the rope around her body as she looked twice the size with all the gear. It didn't seem to slow her down one bit.

Ashley lowered the harness and told me what to do.

'Ready?' he yelled.

'Yep. Get me outta here!'

My feet lifted off the rock as he hauled me upwards. I reached the top and grabbed for rocks to pull myself back onto the path. It didn't happen. My muscles were fried. Ashley grabbed the back of the harness and pulled me onto the path. I sank in a heap on the ground.

'Jesus, Maggie, you're a dead weight.'

'I feel like one. Every muscle in my body is absolute toast. I must've been hanging there for twenty minutes before my hands and arms finally gave out.'

Ashley's face was awash with concern. 'Christ, I feel bad for you having to go through that. It's my fault. I should've never left you.'

'Please, don't do that to yourself. It's not your fault. Decisions have to be made. You can't babysit me all the time. Everything turned out fine. So please, move on. I get upset when I see you upset.'

He pulled me to my feet. 'Come on, luv.' He held my face and kissed my forehead. Then he hugged me so hard I could barely breathe. He smelt of sweat and leather, and the hair on his chest tickled my face.

Tie a rope around Maggie's waist. I can pull her along and stop her going over the edge again.

'Good plan, Boo.' Ashley found a shorter length of rope and secured it around my waist.

'Oh, Boo, I have a present for you.' I pulled a feather from my back pocket. 'It floated down from the trees while I was sitting on the rock, landed right in my lap. I'm not sure if it's a power feather though.'

Boo took one look at it and spun around in circles. *It's a white-bellied sea eagle feather, Maggie! It's extraordinarily powerful. It means I'll be able to fly across oceans. Quick! Put it on the ground.*

I'd never seen Boo so excited. Previously — before Boo and I could communicate telepathically — I'd always wondered why she rolled on feathers. She was obsessed with them, and would pick particular feathers up and bring them home. Now I knew they gave her the power of flight. Eagle feathers were her favourite. Ideally all of them would have fallen straight from the bird and not been touched by a human. But I was a Crystal Keeper, so it didn't seem to matter that I'd touched them.

I placed the beautiful black and white feather on the ground, and Boo carefully lay beside it and slowly and methodically wriggled and rolled onto it, her legs in the air, body gyrating from side to side.

Once the rolling was complete, Boo leapt up and shook herself from head to feet. Showers of sparks flew from her coat: exquisite, unearthly shades of red, gold, yellow, blue, and violet droplets sprayed out in an arc. The smell of ozone filled my nostrils as they hissed and sparked through the air. Tiny red-hot pinpricks of energy zapped me as the droplets hit my bare skin.

All done! I feel amazing. Thank you, Maggie.

Boo shot up into the air and made like a bullet, ricocheting from tree trunk to tree trunk before finally coming to land at our feet.

Ashley laughed. He'd never seen Boo recharge before. 'That was the most beautiful thing.' He grinned and fanned himself. 'Well, except when you came out of the Nargun's den that is. Phew!'

I'm so charged I could probably fly you back, Maggie.

'Thanks, Boo, but save your power.'

I'll tow you then. That's easy.

Boo took the end of the rope attached to my waist, and off we went. I blessed her all the way back. Having her pull me up the hill made it a breeze. As we walked, Ashley filled me in with what happened. He was so proud of Drom.

I reflected back to when we'd first met Drom. Ashley had thought him all talk and no action and hadn't trusted him, particularly as he carried a "man bag". Now, he seemed to respect him and talked about him as though he were a kid brother.

'We can't let Jasmine kill them, Ashley. No matter what they've done. You can't kill them either. We're not executioners.'

'I know. I'll put a stop to it. It's a bastard though. Now we'll have them on our tail, and I don't think they'll scare off easily. They've got too much of that honor shit going on in their heads. Brainwashed zombies. Can't think for themselves.'

Just great. The thought of having another bunch of thugs hunting us down filled me with dread.

---

[8] *Maggie's Playlist: Always Looking Out For You — The Beez*

"If I sharpen my flashing sword and my hand takes hold on judgement, I will take vengeance on my adversaries and will repay those who hate me. I will make my arrows drunk with blood, and my sword shall devour flesh, with the blood of the slain and the captives..." — Deuteronomy 32:41-42

I froze, unable to believe the vision of horror stretched out before me. We had reached the end of the track leading to the picnic area, and the car park opened up before us.

Ashley noticed my horrified expression. 'What is it? What's wrong?'

The area was crammed with hundreds, no, thousands of injured, beaten, bleeding, decomposing women. Women were everywhere, en masse, stretching out to the horizon.

'Ghosts,' I whispered. '*Thousands* of them.'

'Holy shit.'

Two of the ghosts separated from the crowd and flew towards me at speed. I stepped back as they screeched to a stop in front of my face.

I knew who they were. Bassima and Elissar, Jasmine's dead sister and girlfriend. Bassima was frightening to look at. She chose to appear just as she'd looked after Kadar's frenzied attack. Elissar had bloody wounds along her wrists.

'Hello, Maggie,' they said. 'We were waiting for you. You can give us justice.'

'I can't give you justice. Go to the light. It's the only thing that gives true justice. You don't have to stay here and hold onto your pain and anger. Think about it. That's what the bastards would want. They want you to suffer. And you're still letting them hurt you.'

'We want to hurt *them*. We want them to feel our pain. All of us.'

'Who are all these women?' I asked, hoping the answer wasn't going to be what I thought it was.

'Woman like us. Abused by men, by their families, their brothers, their fathers, their husbands. For seven thousand years and more there has been no justice. They crave this justice. They will not rest until they get it.'

'But those men, Jasmine's family, they're not responsible for all these women's pain.'

'They are the offspring. They carry the evil. From father to son, down the centuries. They *are* responsible.'

'What do you except me to do?'

'Give them our pain. Make them feel what we feel.'

'For all those women?' I scanned the sea of ghostly heads around me. 'I can't do that. It would kill me. I can do it for you two, that's it. I'll do it for Jasmine, so she won't have blood on her hands.'

I pushed through the sea of ghosts. I hated walking through them. It didn't feel right, or polite, but I had no choice. I tried not to look at them. Imagine being stuck in the middle of a sea of zombies. That was me. Ew.

I hurried to Drom and Jasmine. Jasmine was in front of Kadar, holding a gun.

'Can you feel it?' I asked Drom.

'Yep. It's awful. What's going on?'

I explained the situation to them. Jasmine's face turned white.

'Bassima and Elissar are *here?* You can see them?'

'Yes, along with thousands of other women.

'If I do this for Bassima and Elissar, give your brothers their pain, will you let them live?'

'They will experience the same suffering?'

'Yes.'

Whimpers arose from the brothers. Fear was etched across their faces as they began to comprehend their fate.

Jasmine nodded. 'That is a greater punishment than dying. I will let them live so they can suffer until they die. And Bassima and Elissar, they will be at peace?'

'If they choose to go to the light.'

Ashley looked at me uncertainly. 'This sounds dangerous. Have you done this before?'

I screwed up my nose. 'It's more distasteful than dangerous. I have to go into their heads.'

'I don't like the sound of that,' he said.

'Let's do this. Give me a minute to get my head ready.' I breathed rhythmically, pulling energy into my mind. Similar to a mind meld, the ballroom appeared, but this time it had thousands of doors around the outside of the room. I knew what they were, and I certainly wasn't going anywhere near them.

Bassima and Elissar were already standing in front of their open doors. I crossed to them and they each handed me a ball of energy. It was dark, muddy and revolting.

I made myself energetic gloves of crystal light and hoped they would protect me. Taking the energy balls of pain and despair, I placed them on the floor and opened the doors to the minds of Kadar and his henchmen. They were now of one mind, and into that opening I cast Bassima's and Elissar's pain.

The screams from the outside world reached my physical ears as Kadar and his henchmen experienced Bassima's and Elissar's suffering physically, mentally, emotionally, spiritually and more. I left them with the pain and closed their doors.

Bassima and Elissar's faces looked serene.

'Thank you, Maggie. We will never forget you.' They turned and walked through their doors into a blaze of light.

My brain hurt. A noise reverberated through my skull. The ballroom had expanded to the horizon and thousands of doors appeared. It was the women. They wanted in. Thousands of women, going back thousands of years wanted in. They pounded on their doors, pushing with all their psychic energy, pain and rage.

I had to get out of there. There was no way I could hold them off. I tried to close the link but I couldn't. There was too much psychic energy pushing in on me. My head felt ready to burst. If all those women got in, my brain would end up like Kentucky coleslaw. Recipe: take one cabbage, shoot the hell out of it with a .38 calibre handgun, and that was all you had left. Coleslaw, Kentucky style.

A voice rang out, clear as a bell. It came from Kadar's door, which opened. And out stepped — *Tapakah!*

'Hello.' He smiled his soulless smile. 'All that pain, all that despair. It's what the dark force feeds on. You've arranged a real banquet here.'

The dark atom in me vibrated and quivered in anticipation.

'We'll have their pain, combined with the brothers, blended with yours, to create a never-ending feast of spiraling rage. All thanks to you.'

I could barely formulate words as I struggled to keep the doors closed. 'How. Did. You. Get in. To … my head?'

'Kadar. He's been 'roached' as you call it. Funny how things work out. Quite a coincidence, don't you think?'

I gasped. 'But this will kill me and then you won't have me. You said you want me.'

'I do. But—' He shrugged his shoulders. 'The dark force is my ally and it wants to feed. All this energy, here in one place. Too good to be true. Its power will expand tenfold. More humans will die and that, Maggie, is a marvellous thing.'

The sound of screaming assaulted my physical ears. A new scream added to the mix. Mine.

'Yes, be frightened, Maggie. We *love* frightened.'

Tapakah flew across the room. He took me in his arms and stroked my face with his lacquerware hands. He ran his tongue down the side of my cheek. 'Ah, disgust. We like disgust, Maggie.'

Oh my God he was repulsive. I couldn't hold out for much longer. I must though. Concentrate. Focus.

'We can enjoy ourselves while I wait for you to release the doors. You can't fight me and hold them out. What a dilemma to find yourself in, sweet Maggie.' He ran his hands over my body, then pulled out a knife and cut open my jumper.

Concentrate. Focus. Push against the doors.

He cut my bra and pulled down my jeans.

The doors, think of the doors. Kentucky coleslaw. I didn't want that. Focus. Do it for Jason. He needed me. Everybody needed me.

Tapakah pulled down my underwear and shoved me to the floor. I was powerless to resist, all my energy directed at holding off the psychic assault.

'If I can't have you in real life, I can have your etheric body. It will feel the same.' He forced my legs apart and pressed himself on top of me. He spat, or rather regurgitated, a thick yellow mucus into his hand.

'It seems I'm not turning you on,' he hissed. 'Perhaps lubrication will help.' He rubbed his slimy hand between my legs.

My stomach somersaulted, and I projectile vomited into his face. 'Eat my etheric vomit, arsehole!'

He ran his tongue around his mouth and licked his lips. 'It's time to open the doors, Maggie. I'm going to fuck you.'

My strength was gone. A door opened.

That was it. I was fucked, all right.

A figure stepped through the door.

It was Ashley, holding a Desert Eagle pistol. He pointed it and pulled the trigger.

My head exploded. The world disappeared.

 ## Chapter 10: Ghost City

"Monsters are real, and ghosts are real too. They live inside us, and sometimes, they win." — Stephen King

Maggie stood braced, her left leg forward, her right leg back, foot slightly angled out. Her face was pale, her eyes closed. Her gaze darted about under her closed eyelids.

'How long has she been under?'

Drom looked at his watch. 'Two minutes, fifteen seconds.'

'How'd I know you'd be keeping track?'

'It's what I do.'

Kadar and his henchmen sat quietly scowling at us. Drom's knife wounds would be giving them grief.

'Why is nothing happening yet?' I asked.

Drom pointed upwards. 'Something *is* happening. Check out the sky.'

A massive black cloud was forming. It hung so low I could just about reach up and touch it. Its pitch black centre sat right above us and spun slowly, drawing in other clouds. The cloud boiled and churned. It appeared alive.

'Jesus, where'd that come from? It's getting bigger by the minute. We're in for one helluva storm.'

'It's already here,' he said softly. 'Can't you feel the psychic energy? It's so intense my head hurts.

Jasmine watched Kadar. She looked pale, despite her dark

skin. After her decision to let Maggie intervene, she'd given the gun back to Drom. Fantastic decision for Jasmine. I hoped it was a good one for Maggie.

Jasmine ripped the duct tape off Kadar's mouth.

'What are you doing?' I asked her.

'I want to hear them scream.' She systematically ripped the tape off each of their mouths.

'Fair enough.'

As soon as she'd removed the last of the tape, the men started to groan. They rocked their bodies backwards and forwards. They writhed and flinched, as though at the hands of an invisible attacker. Then the screaming began as they relived the pain they'd caused Bassima and Elissar. They sobbed, they begged, they pleaded, they whimpered, they howled. They grovelled and called for their mothers, for God. They pissed and shat themselves.

Jasmine clutched at her clothes and watched with tears streaming down her face. Her knees shook.

Drom remained impassive.

I motioned towards Jasmine. 'Drom, take care of her. She's doing it tough.'

He shook his head in the negative, his expression tense and unhappy.

What the hell was he playing at? Oh, Jesus. He wanted to keep his distance. Not get involved.

I put my arm around Jasmine, and she responded immediately, wrapping her arms around me and burying her face in my stomach. Crikey, she was tiny, and trembled like a puppy in a thunderstorm.

I guided her to Drom, detached her arms from around me and tucked her under his arm. 'She needs you, mate. Do whatever you need to do later, but not now. Now is not the time.'

He enfolded her in his arms and her face relaxed, as did his.

76

She stopped shaking, and Drom became himself again. Calm. Confident.

You can't fight it, mate. When it's right, it's right and nothing feels better.

The wind had sprung up, creating eddies of dust around us. The temperature dropped. The air became icy. The cloud hovered above us impersonating a gigantic flying saucer, pitch black and ominous. A rumble of thunder sounded deep in its belly. The air smelled of rain.

Maggie twitched and flinched. Drom looked at her, worried.

'Can you get into her head?' I asked him.

'I've been trying. I can't get in. What about you?'

I thought back to the last mind meld. 'Oh, I'm so not going there, not after my last cock up.'

There was a massive crack of thunder and we jumped, as did Kadar and his henchman. They had finally settled down, albeit into a whimpering, quivering mess. I pointed at them. 'I think it's over.'

'Then she should be out by now.'

A bolt of lightning smashed into the ground nearby illuminating us in an eerie light. A smell of ozone and charcoal filled the air. Kadar leapt to his feet as though he had a rocket up his arse. He stood frozen, fists clenched, eyes closed, face tilted skywards. He shuddered, shifted his head to the front and opened his eyes. They were pitch black.

I pulled out my gun. Maggie was writhing and twisting. She clutched her temples and screamed.

Drom and Jasmine clapped their hands over their ears. My spine tingled, and the hairs on the back of my neck stood up. The sound was unbearable. The wind began to shriek and howl along with Maggie, as though a thousand voices were wailing in despair.

'It's got her!' Drom yelled through the maelstrom. 'She can't break the link.'

I closed my eyes. My mind's eye revealed a door. I had to get in. Mustering every shred of my strength of mind and will, I kicked that fucker down.

I stepped through the shattered door into the ballroom. Maggie was on the floor with a creature on top of her. They were on the far side of the ballroom. The space resembled a stadium, surrounded by thousands of doors. I'd never reach her in time. *Shit.*

I made a split-second decision. I exited the ballroom and returned to the real world. Kadar's eyes were still black, and his body shook with diabolical, hysterical laughter. It wasn't that funny, mate.

I blew his head off.

You can shoot a hole in an engine block with a Desert Eagle pistol. There was nothing left of his skull. He pitched forward and fell at Jasmine's feet, his blood spilling out around her boots. A cockroach crawled out of his neck. I knew from its posture it was hissing.

Drom pulled Jasmine back. 'We need to go. *Now!*'

Maggie collapsed to the ground. I quickly felt for a pulse. She was still alive. I shook her shoulders. 'Wake up! Maggie! Wake up! We've got to go. A roach is gonna blow.'

Her eyes opened, but she looked through me, her face filled with horror. She was speaking, but I couldn't hear over the noise. I put my ear to her mouth.

'The women — thousands of them — dark force is using them — got to stop it. Get me a crystal—.'

I reached into my pocket and pulled one out. 'Here you go.'

'Give … it … to me.'

I dragged her upright and slapped the crystal into her hand. The darkness was rising from Kadar's body. 'We have to go!'

Drom had put Boo and Jasmine in the truck and driven it a safe distance away. He ran back, bent low against the force of the wind, and pointed to the huddle of men.

'What do we do with them?'

'Cut 'em loose.'

Maggie swayed on her feet, so I supported her while she held up the crystal. My view of the world flipped on its head. 'Christ almighty, what the *hell?*'

I was in Maggie's mind and could see what she saw. All around us, right to the horizon, were thousands of women, all ghosts, shrieking and wailing. The cloud above us was comprised of whirling, howling women. Some were beautiful, but mostly they looked like friggin' zombies on a bad day. The things clawed and pawed at us, at Maggie especially, shrieking for vengeance.

The crystal in Maggie's hand fired up, glowing gold, then yellow. A blast of white light exploded from it, mushrooming out like an atom bomb. I closed my eyes. Keeping them open was impossible. Everything was radiant, shimmering light. All sound disappeared.

When I opened my eyes again I saw lightning streaming upwards from the crystal. The sky split open, maybe it was the universe, and into the blazing fissure streamed rivers of ghosts, until the last one, a young girl all alone, floated through into the light. The aperture snapped shut as the crystal light retracted.

Kadar and his henchmen had vanished. There was no black hole. The black cloud had disappeared, along with the ghosts. The atmosphere felt light, cleansed. Beautiful.

'The crystal did it,' Maggie whispered. 'All those ghosts, they're *free,* gone to the light. The dark force didn't get to use them. It's a victory.'

I stared at the lifeless crystal in her hands. 'I hope so.'

She rubbed her eyes. 'It is. I wouldn't have done it otherwise.' Maggie staggered and I grabbed her arm.

Jasmine and Boo joined us, Boo wagging her tail and Jasmine looking shell-shocked.

Drom put his arm around Jasmine. He nodded towards where the men had been. 'What do you think happened to them?'

'Black hole took them,' Maggie said. 'Their car's gone too, and all the litter they left lying around.'

'Why not us?' Drom asked.

'The crystal protected us and let them go.' Maggie took Jasmine's hand. 'I'm sorry, there was nothing I could do to save them. We'll explain everything.'

Jasmine nodded, her eyes wide. She was speechless with shock and confusion.

'We're safe now,' Maggie assured her. 'At least for a while. I need a cup of tea.' Her hands shook uncontrollably. 'And food. I'm starving.'

'That's my girl,' I said. 'If you ever lose your appetite, that's when I'll know something's seriously wrong.'

Drom grinned. 'Yeah, Maggie's good on the tooth, isn't she?'

'She's on the seafood diet. See's food and eats it,' I said, knowing I was going to cop it any minute.

Drom winked at me. 'Wasn't it Maggie who said, "If we shouldn't eat at night, why is there a light in the fridge?"'

'Do you have the truck keys, Drom?' Maggie asked quietly.

Oh, she wasn't seeing the funny side.

He held them out. 'Right here.'

'*Run*, Jasmine!' Maggie grabbed the keys and took off like a bat out of hell. She flung open the truck door, pushed Jasmine in, climbed in herself, and slammed the door shut just as we got there. The locks clicked shut.

Maggie and Jasmine's grinning faces looked out at us. Maggie opened the Esky and handed Jasmine a sandwich. 'That'll teach you, you pair of smart arses,' she yelled through the glass. She took a bite from a sandwich. 'Mmmm.'

I fished around in my jacket, found a spare key and held it up. 'You are so in trouble,' I mouthed.

When I opened the door, Maggie and Jasmine slipped out the other side and ran away as fast as they could, carrying the Esky between them.

Drom and I soon had 'em cornered. Drom seized Jasmine. Maggie took off with the Esky again.

She tried but couldn't outrun me. I grabbed her by the back of her jumper, and when she spun around she tripped and I fell on top of her. We lay in a panting heap.

She wheezed. 'Get off me. I can't breathe.'

'Promise you won't run off with the food.'

'Promise.'

'Where the hell did you get all that energy from?'

'No idea. But I've used every last skerrick of it.' She closed her eyes and her arms flopped to the ground.

I leaned back on my elbows. Maggie's black hair shone almost purple in the sunlight. Her normally pale face sported pink cheeks.

She had beautiful lips, full and sensuous. Her bottom lip was slightly fuller.

I wiped some dirt off her face and her thick lashes fluttered. She opened her eyes, and I was lost in their green depths.

You're a witch — a goddamn, frigging beautiful witch.

I leant forward and kissed her.

She kissed me back.

I reckon she would've kept on kissing me, if it hadn't been for Drom. His timing sucked.

---

[10] *Maggie's Playlist: Ghost City — Thomas Azier*

Maggie **Chapter 11: Bairnsdale**

"The lovely town of Bairnsdale will hide us from the swarm, a haven on our deadly quest, a refuge from the storm." — Maggie McLaine, Quest for Light

Footsteps crunched on the gravel behind us and Ashley quickly pulled back from our kiss.

'What's going on?' Drom asked.

'What the hell's it look like?' Ashley snapped. 'The chase must've tipped Maggie over the edge. Lucky for her I'm good at CPR. You okay now, Maggie?' He helped me up.

'What happened? I feel so dizzy.'

'Um, looks like you fainted,' Ashley mumbled.

'No wonder with you lying on top of her like that,' Drom said dryly.

I squeezed Ashley's hand. 'Can you help me back to the truck? I'm cactus.'

He scooped me up and strode towards it.

'You don't have to carry me. I can walk.'

'Thanks for covering for me. I'm sorry. I didn't mean to kiss you. Well, I did, but I shouldn't have.'

'I kissed you back. I'm so grateful for what you did today. You saved my life. After what we've been through, I want to kiss everyone.'

'Yeah. Of course.'

All I could think of was Ashley. And Jason. Ashley had me in his arms, and I wanted to stay there forever. He was always there for me. But Jason. He needed me, now more than ever. I loved him. But I wanted Ashley. And Jason. I wanted both of them. I wished I was a Sonusian like the Maestro and Christos. That would've solved everything. They could have as many partners as they liked, no problems.

Suddenly overwhelmed by the day's events, I sobbed into Ashley's chest. Huge, shuddering, heaving sobs.

'It's okay, luv.' He stroked my hair. 'It'll all be okay.'

* * * * *

The truck was packed and ready to go. Drom and Jasmine sat quietly in the back, and Ashley, Boo and I were in the front. We sat and stared at the spotless car park, too tired to talk, too tired to move.

Eventually Ashley started the engine. 'I guess we'd better go. We're running out of daylight. I reckon we should go into Bairnsdale and find a hotel for the night. Get ourselves cleaned up, fed and rested. We'll head off to Buchan in the morning.'

Drom leaned over to the front. 'We leave at dawn?'

Ashley laughed. 'No, we don't, but we probably should.'

'Why dawn?' Jasmine asked.

'It's a movie thing,' I said. 'You may have noticed Drom and Ashley quoting movie lines. This is a Musketeer thing. They always say, "We leave at dawn!"'

'They do it in Westerns too,' Drom said. 'They always have to leave at dawn.'

'Probably 'cause there wasn't street lighting back in the day. Too dark to go anywhere before dawn,' Ashley said.

Drom checked his phone. 'As soon as we get reception I'll ring some hotels. We need to tell the others what happened. They'll be worried. Then we need to explain to Jasmine what's going on.'

She sighed. 'Maybe I don't even want to know. All I have is fifty dollars. I don't have enough money for accommodation.'

'Don't worry about money. Drom and I will take care of it,' Ashley said.

'Thank you. I'll pay you back as soon as I can.'

'Nah, don't worry about it.'

The drive to Bairnsdale was uneventful. We were all lost in our own thoughts. Drom found us a serviced apartment with a double bedroom. When we arrived he said, 'You guys wait in the truck while I check in. We look like outlaws on the run.' He combed his hair and tried to tidy himself up. 'Don't want to scare the receptionist.'

He was back in a flash. 'Room eighteen. Park out the front.'

Boo spoke in my head. *Maggie, I'm going to stay in the truck. I can get some sleep and keep an eye on things.*

Okay, thanks, Boo. I'll bring you out water and get you a serve of healthy take away.

'Ashley, did you hear her?'

'Yeah, got that. Seems I'm still in the loop.'

The apartment was spacious and inviting. Ashley went straight to the fridge and got beers for him and Drom and poured a sparkling wine for me. 'Anything for you, Jasmine?'

'Sparkling wine too, please.'

We sat around the table and downed our drinks in two seconds flat. Ashley and Drom offered to get supplies from the bottle shop next door.

Ashley tapped my arm. 'Don't let anyone in. Stick a chair under the door handle.'

'Roger that.'

When they'd gone Jasmine looked around. 'Where will we sleep, Maggie?'

'I guess us girls will have one room and the guys have the other. But Ashley has to sleep by himself, so he'll probably use the fold out bed. Did you want to be with Drom?'

Jasmine flushed and looked down into her hands. 'He's kind. He makes me feel safe.'

'He's the loveliest guy. You couldn't go wrong with him.'

'I get mixed messages. One minute I think he likes me, the next it's as if he doesn't care. But I've only known him for five minutes.'

'I can tell he cares. But he's frightened of his feelings and of getting involved, of putting you in danger.'

'I don't care about danger. I've felt in danger for most of my life. With him I feel safe.'

'You don't understand what we're facing. You may not want to stay when you know.'

'This is fate. I'm meant to be here.'

'I think you are too.'

'I hope Drom thinks so too,' she said softly.

Jasmine headed off to the bathroom for a shower, and I sat on the couch drinking the last of my bubbles. I couldn't remember ever feeling so tired. I closed my eyes. Just for a second.

The touch of cold steel on my forehead jerked me awake. I found myself staring down the barrel of a shotgun.

I froze in shock, not only because of the shotgun, but because of who was holding it.

---

[11] *Maggie's Playlist: Can't Fight This Love — Austin Mahone*

"The young boy was no longer. Stolen innocence, given evil. Black eyes devoured my soul. A slithering demonic weevil." — *Maggie McLaine, Quest for Light*

The shotgun was nearly as large as him. He must've been about eight years old, with a round face and short black hair. Wide set, amber coloured eyes gazed serenely out of his pale face. Spindly white arms covered with tattoos poked out of a black T-shirt. His hands were black with grease.

He spoke in a little boy's voice that sounded as if it came from beyond the grave. 'Get the crystals. You're coming with me.' He poked me in the head with the shotgun. 'Now.'

'Ow! *That hurt!*' I spoke loudly, hoping Jasmine would hear. 'Haven't you been kept up to date? Your boss doesn't want the crystals. He told me so himself. Which is just as well because I don't have them.'

He hissed at me. 'Keep your voice down. I may look young but I can shoot.'

'I'm sure you can. Well, since you know my name, what's yours?'

'Leon.'

Behind him, the bathroom door opened ever so slightly and a big brown eye peered out. The door closed again.

'Okay, Leon, if you back up so I can get off the couch, I'll retrieve the crystals and come with you.'

Jasmine crept out of the bathroom with her arm up to the elbow in a ceramic toilet brush holder. Leon caught sight of her reflection in a glass cabinet. He wheeled around, and she smashed the container over his head. He caught the full force of the solid base on the back of his skull, and his legs crumpled beneath him. I ripped the gun from his hands before he hit the deck.

Jasmine stood wide-eyed looking at the small boy at her feet. Blood trickled from a gash on her arm and dripped onto his face. When she caught sight of the injury she swayed unsteadily. I sat her down and threw her a tea towel. 'Apply pressure to the wound. I'll be with you in a sec.'

I rummaged through Ashley's bag. 'Ah, here it is.' I pulled out a fat roll of duct tape. Ashley never travelled anywhere without it. "Duck tape", as I called it, was handy for so many things. I bound Leon's hands and feet.

I checked his pulse. It was strong, but I figured he'd be out for a while. I put a tape across his mouth, grabbed another tea towel and tied it around his eyes. If he came to, I didn't want him to see us. Maybe I should block his ears as well. I reckoned everything he saw and heard would be transmitted straight back to the boss at roach central.

I dragged Leon to the wall and propped him against it. That's when I heard a noise from the front door. The handle clicked. Jasmine sat bolt upright.

'*Shit.* I forgot to secure the door!' I slid a pistol to Jasmine and grabbed the gun off the couch. Standing with legs spread, I pointed the shotgun at the door as it slowly opened.

It was Ashley and Drom. I felt relieved. *Thank God.*

Ashley raised his hands in surrender. 'Welcome home, boys,' he said, in response to being greeted by (a) me with a shotgun and (b) Jasmine pointing a pistol at his head, held by tremulous bloodied hands.

'Jasmine!' Drom leapt forward and took the gun from her.

Ashley shut and locked the door and jammed a chair under the handle. He relieved me of the shotgun. 'Jesus, Maggie, are you okay? Who the *hell* is this?'

'Leon.'

Ashley looked at him. 'He's just a kid.'

'About eight, I reckon.'

Jasmine sobbed. 'I think I've killed him.'

I shook my head. 'I checked his pulse. It's strong. He's breathing.'

'Jasmine took him out?' Ashley asked.

I grinned. 'Yep, with a toilet brush holder. Her arm has a nasty gash, on the inside, under the bicep.'

'Shit.' Ashley bent next to her. 'She could've done an artery.'

He examined the wound and replaced the towel. 'It's a nasty gash, but it's not an artery.' He fished around in his bag and threw a first aid kit to Drom. 'Here, catch!'

I dashed to the kitchen sink. 'I'll get a bowl of water to wash it out.'

Ashley checked Leon's pockets. 'How did the kid get in?'

'Um, I think he…'

Ashley scowled and held up a key. 'With this? What the hell did I tell you? What's rule number two?'

'Always barricade the door. I fell asleep. It was just one second. Before I knew it, there he was. I woke with a shotgun pointed in my face.'

Ashley snarled at me. 'You're an idiot, Maggie. Irresponsible. Your negligence could've got you both killed.' He pushed his hair back off his face, crossed his arms and glared at me, his eyes blazing with fury.

Drom gave him a look. 'Hey, take it easy. That's not helping.'

'I'll tell you what's not helping. What's not helping is Maggie putting everyone's lives at risk. Fuck me!' He slammed his fist against the wall.

Jasmine jumped and looked up at Ashley in terror.

'Stop it!' Drom shouted. 'What's got into you? You're scaring Jasmine and you've upset Maggie, you idiot.' He shoved Ashley away from me.

'Don't bloody touch me!' Ashley grabbed Drom by his T-shirt, twisted it, and shoved him against the wall, rattling the picture frames.

I knew Drom could take care of himself, but he chose not to react. He held up his hands in surrender. 'I'm sorry, Ash.'

Drom put his boot on the throat of his own ego and subjugated it to his will. It was a psychic move, and it worked instantaneously. Ashley let go of Drom's T-shirt and pulled him into his arms.

'Shit. Jesus. I'm sorry. I don't know what got into me.' He gave Drom a man hug and let him go.

Drom straightened out his T-shirt. 'It's okay, man, we're all on edge.'

The force of Ashley's rage had hit me like a slap in the face. He was right. I'd put our lives in danger. I was careless and irresponsible. I took one look at poor Jasmine and burst into tears. 'I'm sorry, Jasmine. It *was* my fault. I'm sorry I put you in that position. I'm so sorry — and your arm — and everything.'

Drom hugged me. 'You're exhausted. If we're into the blame game, I'll take the blame. After what you've been through today I shouldn't have left you on your own.'

Why was it when people were nice to me, it made me cry even more? I started to sob again.

Drom rubbed my back and led me to a seat. 'It's okay,' he said softly. 'Let me get you a drink.'

Ashley sat at the end of the couch and stared at me as if he'd never seen me before. He looked dog-tired.

I met his eyes. 'What?'

How dare he speak to me that way. And after everything I'd been through. It was humiliating.

He looked away. 'Nothing.'

Drom handed me a champagne and put a beer on the coffee table next to Ashley. 'We all need to settle down.' He moved to dress Jasmine's arm, then he took her by the hand and led her to an armchair and covered her with a throw rug. He put a glass of bubbly in her hand. She sipped it gratefully.

He stood, hands on hips, and looked at us. 'I'm making an executive decision. We're eating in tonight. Takeaway. There's a great café across the road. I'll go get it now.'

We nodded, too tired and upset to speak.

He pulled a pistol from the back of his jeans, checked it and slipped it back in his pants. 'I've got my phone. I'll be thirty minutes max.'

Once he'd gone, Ashley jammed a chair under the handle and sat back down. 'See. Not that hard is it, Maggie?'

My face felt instantly hot. 'Well, stuff you, Ashley Beringer! You're an arsehole. How dare you speak to me like that and humiliate me. It was a simple mistake, for Christ's sake. You couldn't think to cut me some slack after what happened today?'

Rage swelled. I began to shake. My vision narrowed to focus on the cause of my anger. My heart thumped so fast I felt sick. I glanced at the Fitbit on my wrist — 250 bpm. *Impossible.* It spiked as my heart pumped the wrath, madness and violence to my brain. The room was a haze of red. I picked up the shotgun and aimed it at Ashley. The word *exterminate* echoed through my mind as the dark force atom ignited in my brain.

Surprisingly, through it all, I remembered the gun safety laws Ashley had taught me.

First law: *Assume the gun is always loaded.* Yep. Check.

And the second: *Never point a gun at anything you don't want to shoot.* Check.

And the third: *Always be sure of your target and what's behind it.*

'And that's a check.' I pulled the trigger.

A woman screamed somewhere. A man shouted. It seemed close. Bloody red pervaded my vision. I squinted, trying to distinguish if the slow motion firework of red was Ashley's head exploding. Everything went black.

"Every tree that does not bear good fruit is cut down and thrown into the fire." — Matthew 7:19

I awoke to the sticky, tight feeling of duck tape across my mouth. My arms and legs were bound tight. I was encased in the stuff. Cocooned in it. Someone had put me on a bed and tied me to it. Looked like I wasn't going anywhere, anytime soon. Where the hell was I?

Bang! Bang! Bang!

A wine barrel size Japanese Taiko drum was thumping away in my head. What the hell had happened?

A sense of dread washed over me as I struggled to recall something — anything. I stared at a picture on the wall, a field of blood red tulips. Then I remembered. The haze of red. The shotgun. *Ashley!*

I screamed into the tape, thrashed my body backwards and forwards. The bed creaked and knocked against the wall. Voices. The door burst open, and three anxious faces stared down at me. Drom. Jasmine. Ashley.

Oh, thank God.

Memories of the night I'd nearly killed Jason flooded back. In my memory, all I could see was blood. Blood on Jason, on me, all over the walls, all over everything. I remembered the feel of my bare foot in a shoe full of sticky, congealed blood. Claustrophobia struck. I screamed as loud and as best I could through the damn duck tape.

Ashley stroked my hair. 'Maggie! Stop, settle. I'll take off the tape. Stop making noise, will you?'

I nodded and Ashley slowly pulled the tape away from my mouth.

Tears streamed down my face. 'I thought I'd killed you, like with Jason.'

He smiled and wiped my eyes with his sleeve. 'No chance I'd let that happen, luv.'

'It got me again, Ashley.'

'Yep. And it was my fault. Not yours.'

'How long have I been tied up?'

Drom checked his watch. 'Three hours.'

Jasmine looked at me with wide eyes. 'They have told me everything. I know. My mind is spinning. It's insane.'

'I'll find scissors and cut you loose.' Drom left the room.

I looked back to Ashley. 'How'd you not die?'

'I kicked the gun out of your hand. It had jammed anyway. I'm sorry, it took a lot of strength to subdue you. I had to knock you out.'

'Jason had to do the same. I'm so sorry.'

'No, I'm sorry. It broke my heart to hit you, but I had no choice.'

'Hence my pounding head and all the duck tape.'

'Yep. And its *duct* tape.' Drom returned and handed him a pair of scissors. He began cutting through the tape. 'Unfortunately, I didn't have any red silk ribbons. I didn't expect to be binding you up like this,' he said ruefully.

'Did I cause much damage?'

Ashley rubbed his ribs and the back of his neck. 'Well, I'm black and blue. It's as if I've done ten rounds with a heavyweight boxer. Luckily not too much is smashed. Jasmine ran around pulling stuff out of the way.'

'Crikey. I can't believe I can do that. Turn into such a

monster.'

'We need to film you in action next time. Get a GoPro or something. It's nuts.'

The thought horrified me. 'God, I hope there isn't a next time.'

When Ashley finished, the duck tape was piled up at the foot of the bed. He helped me sit up and rubbed my wrists to get the circulation back. Leaning across to the bedside table, he picked up a glass of water and some tablets. 'Here, take these.'

'Paracetamol?'

He nodded and I gratefully took them and downed the water.

He turned to Drom and Jasmine. 'Would you mind leaving us for a minute?'

They left, closing the door behind them.

Crikey, what was coming now? Was he going to tell me he was leaving? I wouldn't blame him.

Ashley took my hands and looked at me. 'I owe you an apology. My behaviour was unforgiveable. I should never have spoken to you that way, or said the things I said. I feel sick about it. No wonder it triggered you. Part of me knew that's what would happen, that it would tip you over. Can you forgive me?' His voice choked and he looked away. 'And, I had to *hit* you, for fuck's sake. I can't live with myself.'

'I forgive you. It's okay.'

'I'm the one who can't be trusted. It's me. I was so worried about what could've happened to you. I should've stayed. I broke the promise I made to you only hours earlier. All I could think about was having a drink … and then, we came back to see you both in that state. I was angry at myself and I took it out on you.'

'It's not your fault. It didn't all come from you.'

'It didn't?'

'No. Leon reeked of dark force. The energy in the room was thick with it. It triggered both of us. That's what it does, creates violence and mayhem, and if you're not aware, it takes you over. It ambushed the both of us tonight. We let our guard down. We all have violence in us, if we didn't, it'd have nothing to work with.'

'I still feel like shit.'

'We have to be tougher than this. Smarter. Thank God we're still both alive. All of us are alive. This is war. Things happen and we have to move on, wiser and stronger for the experience.'

My head began to spin and my hands trembled. 'I need to eat.'

He smiled. 'Blood sugar levels critical?'

I nodded.

'That's my girl. If you ever lose your appetite, I'll know you're really sick. I love you. You realise that, don't you?'

I squeezed his hands. 'Yes. I love you too.'

Ashley pulled me off the bed. When I faltered on my feet he steadied me. 'Here, luv, let me.' I didn't protest as he picked me up and carried me to the next room. He put me on the couch and tucked me in a throw rug. Jasmine handed me a bowl of food and a fork. The spicy aroma of Thai green curry filled my nostrils. It reminded me of home and Jason.

I ate until I could eat no more and soon the strength returned to my body. Leon was still where I'd left him. 'He's still unconscious?'

'We're worried about him,' Drom said. 'He hasn't moved, but he's still breathing, and his pulse is strong.'

'What do we do with him? He's been roached.'

'Maybe we dump him somewhere he's likely to be found,' Ashley suggested.

Drom shook his head. 'So he gets to come after us again? Wreak havoc on us and everyone else?'

Ashley frowned. 'What are you saying? We kill him? We're not murderers, especially not of children.'

I put my empty bowl down and moved to look more closely

at Leon. 'Something's different. Did you notice he's changed colour?' I touched his arm. 'He's gone from white to brown ... and his skin's ... dry ... hard. Yuk.'

'Maybe he's dying,' Jasmine said.

I removed his blindfold and hooked a fingernail under the corner of the tape over his mouth. When I pulled it back, it made a sound similar to ripping cardboard.

Jasmine screamed. The guys rushed over.

'Holy shit!' Ashley said. 'The skin's peeled off his face.'

A large slash of brown skin had stuck to the tape, leaving behind a raw, glistening patch of white. The flesh looked crinkled and silvery.

Drom studied the skin. 'That's like no skin I've seen before. On a human, anyway.'

Jasmine clamped a hand over her mouth. I wondered if she was going to be sick. The Thai green curry certainly rose up in my stomach.

'*Look!*' Ashley said.

Leon's face began to crack. It appeared crazed, resembling an ancient oil painting or the old lacquerware fruit bowl my mum had. The skin on his arms cracked and split revealing a slimy white surface underneath. Soft crackling sounds accompanied the process, reminding me of the snap, crackle and pop of a bowl of Coco Pops.

A loud crack made us jump as Leon's skull split, and the expanding flesh underneath pushed apart the cranium.

Mesmerised, we watched the hideous slow-motion display. The skull casing fell away with the hair attached and clattered to the floor. A glistening, wrinkled head — if you could call it that — remained.

'It's like an albino prune,' Ashley said. 'That. Is. *So*. Wrong.'

Leon's body twitched violently and we yelled in fright. Two white indentations that should have been eyes snapped open. A pair of large, pitch black, luminous orbs stared back at us.

Ashley threw the tea towel over its head and shuddered in disgust. 'Holy hell!'

Leon's body twitched and pulsed underneath his clothes. He was trying to shed his skin, but his clothes and bindings were in the way. I grabbed the scissors and started to cut off his T-shirt.

'What the hell are you doing?' Ashley asked.

'Cutting these off. They're stopping him transforming.'

'Ah, do we really want to do that?'

'We can bind him up again once he's finished.' I pulled Leon's T-shirt free and cut the tape from his wrists and ankles. I took off his shoes and socks, then his jeans and jocks.

There lay Leon, completely in the altogether. The shell across the front of his torso cracked open and the body beneath it expanded. The silvery skin was almost translucent. Bodily fluids surged beneath it. Organs and muscles pulsated and throbbed in violent rhythmical contractions. Leon convulsed along the floor extracting himself painfully and slowly from his brown shell.

We watched in horrified fascination until finally, the pure white, glistening body of Leon lay before us.

He pulled his silvery arms and legs up beneath him and swayed on all fours, quivering with the exertion.

Behind me a hammer clicked as Ashley cocked his revolver. Then a metallic clunk as Drom snapped forward the slide on his semi-automatic handgun.

Jasmine stood next to me, and I swear I could hear her heart beating. Or maybe it was mine.

With his eyes closed, Leon pushed himself slowly upwards. Taking his body weight on his feet he unfurled his spine until he was standing upright. He faced us and stood frozen.

'It looks … *beautiful*. Amazing,' Jasmine whispered.

Leon's eyelids snapped open. Two large, pitch-black pools of luminosity gazed out at us.

There was an all-around sharp intake of breath. Leon stared at us. We stared at Leon.

Now what?

Leon twitched. The guys stepped in front of us and raised their guns. Leon shuddered, convulsed. His mouth opened in an agonised, soundless scream. His chest split open in diagonal rents. A blast of air hit our faces as a terrifying hissing noise assaulted our eardrums.

Jasmine covered her ears as the hissing increased. Leon sank to his knees and his torso tipped backwards. *Crack!* His spine snapped and his head thunked to the floor. The rest of his body followed, and the hissing sound changed tone as Leon's body deflated like a balloon.

The sound of hissing faded away, and finally — silence.

Leon lay at our feet, a gelatinous pile of crumpled flesh.

---

[13] *Maggie's Playlist: Transformation — Nona Hendryx*

"Evolutionary plasticity can be purchased only at the ruthlessly dear price of continuously sacrificing some individuals to death from unfavourable mutations. Bemoaning this imperfection of nature has, however, no place in a scientific treatment of this subject." — *Theodosius Dobzhansky*

The glutinous mass that was Leon bubbled and shimmered on the kitchen tiles. Sprinkled with crunchy bits of brown shell, it reminded me of tapioca. I loved tapioca with a sprinkle of palm sugar on the top. Not anymore.

We stood in silence trying to process what had happened.

'Where's the roach?' Ashley asked.

'He was the roach,' Drom said.

'So, no black hole to worry about?' I asked.

Drom looked around. 'Doesn't look like it. Seems Tapakah has started without you, Maggie.'

'What do you mean?'

He pointed at Leon's remains. 'He's already begun creating his new master race.'

'If they're all like that we'll be sweet,' Ashley said.

'Do you think Leon came out of a test tube?' I asked.

'The doctored-up egg would've, but someone had to give birth to it.'

'Oh my God, that's *awful.*'

'Sure is.' Drom fished around in his bag and brought out a small glass tube. He stuck the end of it into Leon's remains.

'What are you doing?'

He screwed the top back on. 'Collecting a sample. I want to get the DNA analysed.'

'What do we do with the remains?' Jasmine asked.

Ashley grabbed some garbage bags from the kitchen. 'I'll scrape him up and chuck him in the trash.'

I shook my head. 'That's not right. He was a person, sort of. We should do something better than that.'

'I recommend we burn him,' Drom said. 'We don't want to leave any of that stuff around. It could contain bacteria, viruses, who knows.'

We all took a step backwards.

'Good point,' Ashley said. 'I'll bag him up and put him in the freezer. We can burn him when we get to Buchan. There's nowhere to do it here.'

Drom examined the sludge in his glass tube. 'Tapakah must have access to labs and research facilities to do this. He's either brilliant in the field, or has a team working for him. Probably both.'

'He's probably roached all the scientists he needs and has them working twenty-four seven doing his evil bidding,' Ashley said.

'I wonder if Leon was experiment number one or fifty?' I said.

'This is too horrible,' Jasmine said.

'Still glad you met us?' I asked.

'If it's like this every day I don't know how you cope.'

'I like a drink,' I said.

'You get used to it,' Ashley said. 'I love a drink too. It helps.'

'I keep fit and read two books a day. I meditate and don't get too attached to anyone or anything,' Drom said.

Ashley grinned. 'And you drink too.'

'Yeah, and that.'

'Not getting attached to anyone or anything sounds miserable,' Jasmine said.

I patted Drom's shoulder. 'He's like the Buddha.'

'You've no one in your life?' Jasmine asked.

'These guys are my family at the moment. But nothing stays the same. The only thing you can bank on in life is change. Everything changes.'

Jasmine looked sad. 'You're making me depressed.'

'It's liberating,' he said.

I plonked down on the couch. 'Time to have a liberating drink. A nice big glass of red.'

'I'll join you as soon as I've finished bagging up,' Ashley said.

'I'll help you,' I said, not really wanting to.

Ashley donned rubber gloves and waved at me. 'No, it's all good. I've got this.'

Ashley bagged up Leon and cleaned and disinfected the floor. He opened a bottle of red and poured everyone a glass. He handed me a glass and sat next to me.

'How's your aches and pains?' I asked him.

He raised his glass to me. 'Nothing a few of these won't fix. It's slightly less painful than when I was jumped on by five guys in Iraq.'

'Oh, I'm so sorry.'

'No, luv, I'm fine.' He rubbed his ribs and grimaced.

'Oh, stop it! You're making me feel terrible.' I tried to punch him in the arm.

He pulled away in mock fear. 'No, don't!' His face darkened and he looked at me with a serious expression.

'What?'

'I wanted to ask you about what happened today, in your head, with Tapakah. When I broke down the door you were on the other side of the room, and he was on top of you. I didn't think I'd get to you fast enough, so I took a chance, went back to the real world, and blew Kadar's brain's out.'

'You made the right decision. You saved me.'

'From what?'

'He was going to rape me. He knew I couldn't hold him off *and* keep out the psychic energy of thousands of women. I was powerless to stop him. You did though.'

The colour drained from Ashley's face. 'That piece of ... so, he ... he didn't?'

'No, he didn't.'

I told Ashley everything that had happened. Ashley listened, growing paler as I spoke. Jasmine buried her face in her hands.

When I'd finished, Ashley slammed his fist down on the couch. His face was dark with anger. The muscles in his jaw twitched. 'What a sick fuck. I will kill him. I promise you here and now, he's going to die at my hand and it won't be pretty. You couldn't be impregnated when you're in your etheric body could you?'

'Yes, you could.'

Ashley looked horrified. 'But how would you give birth?'

'The etheric baby would stay in the etheric womb until a body is created by a physical union. Then it would populate that body.'

'So, if you and Jason created a baby, and Tapakah's devil child was there waiting…'

'It could displace our child and download itself.'

'Holy hell.'

Jasmine's expression was distraught. 'This just gets better and better.'

I squeezed Ashley's hand. 'I owe you big time, Mr Beringer.'

He took both my hands. 'Crikey, I knew we could be attacked physically and psychically, but not to that extent. How can I protect you on that level?'

'You did.'

Drom moved and sat next to Ashley. 'You have brute force. You're a warrior in the physical world. That'll play out in the psychic realms too.'

Ashley chuckled. 'Jesus. That's good to know. Who would've

thought? Down to earth old Ash, a psychic warrior. I'll have to get a T-shirt made. You'll have to teach me more about this psychic stuff so I can be better prepared.'

'I can't promise I'll have all the answers.'

Ashley sat back, ran his hands through his hair and looked at Jasmine. 'So, this has been a day in the life of the Musketeers. Can you hack it?'

'I ... I'm not sure.' She looked at Drom. 'Maybe I don't have a choice.'

Drom met her gaze. 'You always have a choice. It's just that sometimes the choices suck.'

---

14 *Maggie's Playlist: Prototype — Viktoria Modesta*

"Monsters are made to warn, to threaten, and to instruct, but they are by no means always monstrous in the negative sense of the term; they have always had a seductive side."
— Marina Warner

Ashley and I remained on the couch when Drom and Jasmine went to check on Boo and take her some food. Judging from Ashley's expression, he had something on his mind.

'So, hypothetically, in the interests of learning more about the psychic world, could we get together in your mind, so to speak. I mean, we could be sitting here, but in our heads, we could be chatting together in the ballroom?'

'Yes.'

'So, it's a secret meeting place. No one would know what was going on.'

'Yep.'

'And we could do whatever whenever?'

'Technically, yes.'

'That's awesome. Can we try it now? And how come it looks like a ballroom?'

'That's my thing. I can make it appear however I want. I find the ballroom is easier for me, clean and simple. The images of the doors help me to separate minds.'

'So, you'd have to invite me in?'

'Generally, yes, but you managed to force your way in by yourself today.'

'We could have an affair, in your head. No one would be the wiser.'

'*Ashley!*'

He gave me his evil grin. 'Just saying, hypothetically.'

'Cheating is still cheating. Doesn't matter on what level.'

'It's hypothetical. Can we try now? Before they get back? I want to see what it's like with no danger present.'

'Okay. Close your eyes. Take a few deep, slow breaths in and out.'

While Ashley was doing his breathing, I did the same and opened my mind. I changed the appearance of the ballroom so it didn't remind me of what had happened. There was only one door this time, and I knew it was Ashley. I opened it, and there he was. I smiled at the expression on his face. He looked as excited as a kid with a new toy. 'Come on in.'

He walked around the ballroom. 'I love what you've done with the place. Can you have furniture?'

I materialised two wing back chairs, a rug, an open fire, a small table and two glasses of red.

Ashley sat in a chair and ran his hands over the fabric. 'This is fantastic! I can feel the material, as if it's real.'

'Try the wine.'

He picked up the glass and took a sip. 'It's my favourite red. How did you know?'

'Lucky guess.'

'Can I create things in your space?'

'If I let you.'

'Can I?'

'Try away.'

'I'll give you two guesses as to what I'm trying to create.'

'I don't even need one guess. A bed.'

'You've got a one-track mind. I was going to create a gun. But now you've brought it up, let's give that a go.' A California king materialised. He looked happy with himself. 'That wasn't so hard!'

'Well done. That's amazing for a novice. The detail is perfect.'

'Seems a shame to let it go to waste then.' He sat on the edge of the bed and lay back. 'This is the best bed I've ever laid on. Try it.'

'I believe you.'

'So, hypothetically, could we go to sleep here, all night?'

'That'd be too hard.'

'You need awareness?'

'Yes.'

'Come on, try it, be a sport.'

I lay on the bed. 'You've done a fantastic job for a beginner.'

'I may be a beginner in that area, but I'm certainly not in this one.' He rolled towards me and put his arm around me.

'*Ashley.*'

'Just a cuddle. I need to gauge what it feels like.'

'You know how it feels to cuddle someone.'

'Please?'

'Oh, all right then.' He put his arms around me and held me close.

'I could stay here forever. If you materialise food, does it nourish your physical body?'

'It can, but I'm not advanced enough for that. If we don't come out, our bodies would eventually die.'

'Can I kiss you? Just for research purposes.'

'You don't give up do you?'

'I like to be thorough with my research. It's important I comprehend everything.'

I turned my cheek towards him. 'On the cheek.'

'No, a proper kiss. It won't matter because it isn't real.'

'You know that's not true.'

'Well, how will I understand if you won't let me find out?'

'It will be exactly the same as when you stole that kiss in the car park today.'

'Show me.' He leant over and looked into my eyes. His hand caressed the side of my face. '*Show me*,' he whispered into my ear.

'Ashley, please, I really—'

Something caught my attention. I stopped and listened. 'What's that noise?'

I heard a rhythmic thumping noise and sat up in alarm.

'I can't hear anything. Lie back.'

'Can't you hear it? Listen.'

'It's the pounding of my heart. Come on, let's have fun.' He pushed me back and straddled me. He grabbed my wrists and pulled my arms over my head. 'Now you're all mine.' He bent forward to kiss me.

I turned away and tried to buck him off. 'Ashley, enough!'

'Oh, you've got strength in you. I like that. Sorry, babe, I'm not going anywhere. Neither are you.' He conjured up lengths of black silk.

The silk ribbons undulated and slithered, winding themselves around my wrists. Snaking along the bed head, they secured themselves and yanked my arms taut. They slipped around my ankles and pulled my legs wide apart. The muscles in my groin ached from the pressure.

'Ow! Stop it! This isn't funny; you're hurting me.'

'Come on, Maggie. It's your fantasy. Play along.'

A large pair of shears materialised. They looked sinister and vaguely familiar.

'Let me help you slip into something more comfortable.' Ashley inserted the shears under my top. The steel was cold against my flesh as he cut through my clothing and my bra. He ripped the material out from under me.

'Ashley, you're freaking me out. Stop it!'

'You stop it, babe. It's your head, your fantasy.'

'It's not my fantasy! You've gone too far. I'm stopping this right now.'

How could he do this? Ashley was a scoundrel, but he'd never cross the line like this. Stealing a kiss was one thing. This was something else.

I began the process of closing my mind and redirecting the energy back to the physical plane. Shutting everything down. Leaving the ballroom. Cleaning it out.

Nothing happened. Everything stayed the way it was. My brain was entwined with barbwire. The harder I tried, the worse it hurt. I couldn't escape. I was trapped in my own mind.

How could this be? I had to try again. I cried with the pain of my effort, but no matter how much I tried I couldn't get out. I was a prisoner in my own mind.

Panic rushed through my body as I struggled to escape.

'I knew you wouldn't leave. You want me. It's obvious.' Ashley moved to the end of the bed and inserted the shears into my jeans. The cold steel burned as the shears made their way up my leg.

'Actually, I can probably do this no hands.' He let go of the shears. They kept going. They cut through my underwear, nicking my skin. Once at the top of my first leg, they spun around in midair and made their way back down my other leg. Slowly and methodically, the shears finished their work, and flew back into Ashley's hand. He ripped the material of my clothes from under me and threw it on the floor. He stepped back, legs spread, rubbing his chin as he ran his eyes over my naked body.

The pounding noise continued to echo in the background. It was louder, frantic. What was it?

I could trust Ashley with my life. He was going to stop. Still, I said, 'You've gone too far. Please, let me go. I'm not sure how you're doing this, but *please* stop.'

He grinned. 'You can stop anytime you want.'

'But I can't, I've tried!'

'That tells me you don't want to.' He moved to the side of the bed and ran his hand up the inside of my thigh, pausing between my legs before moving upwards to my breasts.

'This is wrong. What about Jason? I'll never forgive you for this. He'll never forgive you. You've gone too far.' I started to sob.

'Babe, you're the real little actress, with tears on tap. You don't give a shit about Jason. He doesn't give a shit about you anymore either.'

Ashley's clothes vanished and he stood naked before me. He climbed on top, grabbed my face and kissed me, forcing his tongue into my mouth. He pulled back just as I tried to bite it off. His hands were all over me, his mouth on my breasts. All I could do was scream and twist and writhe. In the background, the frenzied pounding continued.

'Shut up, Maggie, or *I'll* shut you up.'

I kept screaming.

Ashley forced something in my mouth. He lifted my head by the hair and pulled a strap tight. My mouth was held wide open. I couldn't talk, only moan and gurgle.

'That's better. No noise. Easy access. I'm not going to blindfold you. I want you to see what I'm going to do to you.' A long steel cane appeared in his hand. 'Over you go.'

The bed disappeared and I flipped onto my stomach, suspended in midair. He brought the cane down hard across my buttocks. I felt it cut me. The pain was excruciating. I gurgled and moaned trying desperately to find a way out of my mind. It was as if I was banging my head against a brick wall imbedded with nails. I tried to materialise weapons. I tried to dematerialise my bonds. Nothing I did made any difference. How could he do this to me? How could he think I wanted this?

The cane came down again. And again. And again. And — again.

'Say you love me.'

'I hate you!' I gurgled. It came out as meaningless babble.

My bonds rotated in space and I hung upright, arms

suspended above me. Black silk snakes encircled my knees and pulled them outwards. I hung there, my arms aching, completely vulnerable, embarrassed and humiliated. Tears ran down my face. Horrible, futile sounds came from my mouth. The pounding hammered in my ears.

Ashley stepped forward and stood between my thighs. 'I've been waiting for this. So have you.' He grabbed my hips and pulled me towards him. Blood dripped onto the floor from the cuts of his whip.

I felt rather than saw a door appear in the ballroom. It warped and buckled as though someone was trying to get in.

Drom? Is it you? Help!

I noticed an armoire next to the door I hadn't seen before. It rocked slightly. It was a Japanese antique wardrobe similar to my dad's. A soft yellow lacquer highlighted the panels, which were heavily decorated with horsemen, dragons, mountains and flowers. It had black, engraved, heavy metal hinges and locks. The pounding came from inside it.

A bloodied finger thrust into my mouth. 'Focus. Now, babe, I can do whatever I want to you.'

I gagged and retched as the taste of copper filled my mouth.

Don't call me babe, you mother fucker. I hated being called babe. Ashley knew that. I hated Ashley. I'd never forgive him. Never.

'You're going take more than a finger in your mouth, babe.'

More black snakes materialised and entwined themselves around my body, arms, legs, breasts, throat; they pulled tight. I couldn't breathe. I choked, started to black out. They released. I gasped for air. I screamed in my mind. I was screaming for help. I hadn't stopped screaming.

Ashley grabbed my buttocks and squeezed hard. His cupped hands were full of blood. He dragged them over my face and breasts. He squeezed out more blood and wiped it over my torso, arms, and legs. His expression was ecstatic, insane, as he smeared it over his body, face and head. Blood was everywhere. Holding his cupped hands underneath me to catch the flow, he poured the rest of it over my thighs and between my legs.

His hands slippery with blood, he grabbed my hips again and pulled me towards him. His hair was drenched in my blood, which ran in rivulets down his neck and chest.

Spinning into madness, my mind was frantic. It raced. It latched onto words and ran them over and over and over.

Babe. Shears. Blood and black ribbons. Babe. Shears. Blood and black ribbons. Babe. Shears. Blood and black ribbons. Shears. Shears. Rib cutting shears.

The truth slapped me hard.

I screamed in agony as the barbwire tightened its grip on my mind and he tightened his grip on me.

---

[15] *Maggie's Playlist: When You're Evil — Aurelio Voltaire*

"Man's enemies are not demons, but human beings like himself." — Lao Tzu

'Show yourself, Demon! You. Are. Not. Ashley Beringer. Reveal yourself!'

'It's not him. It's an imposter,' a voice shouted through the door. It was Luca. *'Burn this evil in hell, that they may never again touch you or any other creature in the entire world. God the Father commands you. God the Son commands you. God the Holy Ghost commands you. Christ, God's Word made flesh, commands you.'*

"Ashley" released his grip on me as the skin on his body cracked and blistered. He bellowed as it exploded into a cloud of black dust around him.

Was the demon gone? I couldn't see through the haze.

As the dust settled a figure revealed itself.

Tapakah.

My bonds disappeared and I fell to the floor at his feet. He stared down at me with black eyes. He opened his mouth to speak just as the doors on the armoire burst open with an ear-splitting crack.

A shadowy figure emerged, blasting out from the explosion of shattered wood, dust and splinters. It was Ashley, his face twisted with rage and determination as he ran towards Tapakah, a samurai sword raised high, ready to strike. The skin on his knuckles was stripped to the bone. The white of them glistened in the light. He charged forward emitting a battle cry that shook my atoms.

'Fahaaaaaaaaaarrrkkk!'

Tapakah looked over his shoulder in time to witness Ashley plunge the sword into his back. The blade emerged through Tapakah's stomach and withdrew leaving a waterfall of black blood gushing down his legs.

Leaping side on to Tapakah's body, Ashley raised the sword, and with a merciless, double-handed slash, ran the blade down along the front of Tapakah's torso. Pieces of flesh fell to the ground. Tapakah looked down at them in horror. Ashley scooped up the bits of bloody meat, pulled open Tapakah's jaw and jammed the bloody mass into his mouth.

'Eat that, you cocksucker!' Ashley stepped backward, paused for a second, then raised the sword. In one clean stroke, he swept the blade through Tapakah's neck. Black blood sprayed in an arc and hit my body, burning against my skin.

Tapakah stood motionless, his face devoid of expression. Silence was palpable as we froze, staring at him.

We started as Tapakah's legs moved. Oh, my God, he was going to come back to life. Please die. Please die.

He leant slightly to the side dislodging his head, which slowly slid from his shoulders, to land with a thud at my feet. His black eyes stared up at me from the puddle of blood pooling around his head. My gut somersaulted violently, and I threw up over his face.

Ashley sank to the ground, his knees hitting the floorboards with a *thunk*. Gripping the sword in his bloodied hands, he jammed the tip into the floor and rested on the hilt, his breath ragged. Blood ran in rivulets down his body. His muscles twitched from exertion. He personified a ferocious and slightly insane Ninja warrior as his eyes blazed out from the black blood covering his face. The muscles in his neck stood out like rope as he tilted his head back and roared. The savagery of his howl rang in my ears as I materialised a jerry can of petrol and doused Tapakah. I hadn't had a chance to use C4 yet, so I manifested two pieces. After inserting the timer sticks, I joined Ashley.

He looked up at me as I held out my hand. No spoken words were necessary. Twelve words flew between us on silent wings.

Thank you. I love you.

Maggie, I love you more than life.

Ashley took my hand and rose to his feet. Together, we walked through the door and closed it. I pressed the remote control. Through the glass insert in the door, we saw the room explode into flames. Tapakah's body writhed in the inferno and disappeared.

I opened my eyes.

I was back on the couch, naked and covered in red and black blood.

Ashley sat next to me, a bloodied, crazy eyed, wild haired warrior with a fully formed samurai sword clutched in his hand.

The front door opened. We'd forgotten to chair it. Drom and Jasmine walked in and their jaws dropped. We stared at them. They stared at us. I guess we must've looked pretty ghastly judging by the horrified expressions on their faces.

'Please, tell me that's it for today,' Ashley croaked.

Drom chaired the door, while Jasmine ran to the bathroom for a towel and covered me with it.

'Jesus Christ,' Drom said. 'Are you badly hurt? Do we need to get you to hospital?'

We shook our heads.

'You need to wash?' Drom asked. He spoke to us slowly, as though we were children.

We nodded our heads.

Ashley handed Drom the sword. 'Stand guard.'

'Against what, specifically?'

'Everything.' Ashley picked me up, carried me to the

bathroom and closed the door. He turned on the water then put me down and guided me into the double shower.

'Do you want to be alone?'

'No.'

'Then I'll shower with you.'

We stood and leant our foreheads against the tiles and watched the blood run off our bodies. It flowed down the drain in a swirling river of red and black.

I washed my hair, scrubbed my body and checked out the reflection of my buttocks in the glass screen. Six angry red welts ran across them, but luckily, I didn't bring the cuts back with me.

Ashley's hands were in terrible shape, but I noticed at least he had skin over his knuckles. He washed my back and I washed his. We must've been in the shower for at least an hour, maybe more. Finally, we left the shower and dried ourselves with fluffy white towels.

Drom had made us mugs of hot chocolate with marshmallows on top. Jasmine had cleaned Ashley's sword. It lay gleaming on the table.

She dried my hair with a hairdryer as I sipped my hot chocolate. Later she brushed my hair, with gentle, methodical strokes. As an adult, I'd never had anyone brush my hair before. It felt wonderful.

We were all silent. Too exhausted to speak.

Finally, Drom said, 'I'll take watch. You three go sleep. We can debrief in the morning.'

'Set your alarm for two hours,' Jasmine offered. 'I'll take second shift.'

Ashley took my hand, gave Drom and Jasmine a tired wave and led me into the bedroom. He closed the door, pulled back the bed covers and motioned for me to get in. Then he flopped face first onto the rollaway bed and was asleep as he hit the sheets.

I slipped out of bed, pulled the covers over him and kissed

the side of his face. The sheets of my own bed felt cold when I got back in. I felt lost. The loneliness of an empty bed was more than I could stand. I wanted to sleep in the arms of someone who loved me. Anyone who loved me would do. I ached for Jason. My heart, mind and soul were wracked with a deep sense of desolation. I'd shed more tears in the last few days than I had in my lifetime. I buried my face in the pillow and sobbed some more.

A hand touched my hair and I jumped.

'It's me. The real Ashley. What's wrong?'

I blubbered. 'I can't stand to be alone after everything that's happened. I'm frightened. I miss Jason. My body aches. I feel so awful, it hurts.'

'I can hold you, if you want, but I can't guarantee I'll stay awake. I'm beat.'

'Could you? I'll take the risk. I don't care if you stick a knife in me. At least I'll die happy.'

'Well, I wouldn't be too happy.'

Moving quickly around the room he collected various items and threw them into a bag. He opened the door to the lounge. 'Hey, Drom. Here are all my weapons. Maggie needs to be close to someone tonight, and I'm it. It's a risk, but she wants to take it. I'll leave the door ajar. Can you keep an ear out for anything untoward? I'm so tired, I'm sure it'll be okay.'

'No worries.'

Ashley climbed in bed next to me and stretched out an arm. I snuggled up against him, feeling warm and safe. Sleep took me in an instant.

We slept soundly in each other's arms all night. It was a healing balm for our two shattered souls.

* * * * *

I opened my eyes and looked straight into Ashley's.

116

'Mornin', Magster,' he whispered. 'I think I've died and gone to heaven, waking up and seeing you next to me.'

I smiled. 'Is that a gun in your pocket, or are you just pleased to see me?'

'Got no guns here, so I must be pleased to see you.' He grinned. 'We made it through the night.'

'Thank you, Ashley. I had the best night's sleep I've had in ages.'

'Thank you. It's a milestone for me, I can tell you. I haven't slept through the night with anyone for years. I can't tell you how happy I feel. It's like I've been in solitary confinement and, finally, I've been released. It's funny how things work out.' He stroked my hair. 'If it hadn't been for ... anyway, it's all good.'

'I guess we better get up.'

'Five minutes more. We deserve it. Let's just lie here, I want to make the most of this.' He pulled me in close.

'Me too.' I snuggled into the warmth of his arms.

We must have dozed off again because, when we awoke, it was to the glorious smell of bacon and eggs.

Drom's face appeared around the door. 'Congratulations, mate! How good is it you slept right through? It's fantastic.'

'Sure is, Dromski. A huge thanks for getting me onto those drugs. And thanks for keeping watch. You must be buggered. Tapakah draining me of every ounce of my energy probably had something to do with it too.'

'Tapakah?'

'Yep. That evil piece of slime. We've got to debrief.'

'Only after bacon and eggs and copious amounts of coffee. Jasmine and I have cooked up a storm.'

I smiled up at Drom from the crook of Ashley's arm. 'Smells divine. You're a legend.'

'See you out there.'

Ashley slipped out of bed to search through his duffel bag. The morning light filtered through the curtains and highlighted his muscular physique. His back muscles rippled as he rifled through his things.

He looked back over his shoulder and caught me staring. 'Enjoying the view?'

My face went hot and he laughed. Ashley pulled on jocks and a T-shirt.

'Here.' He handed me my robe and politely turned away as I stood and put it on.

'I guess we've seen everything there is to see of each other,' I said.

'Yep. I've lost count of the times I've seen you naked. Well, I haven't lost count, but it's a shame, you always seem to be covered in blood. Either yours or somebody else's.'

He pulled on a pair of jeans. 'I'll leave you to get dressed.'

Breakfast was bacon, eggs, grilled tomatoes, hash browns and toast. I was in heaven. Ashley and I hoovered up our food and he went back for seconds. Over coffee we told Drom and Jasmine about Tapakah.

'But how could that happen?' Drom asked.

Ashley leaned back in his chair and took a sip of coffee. 'When I stepped into Maggie's mind, someone king hit me from behind. I came to and found myself trapped inside an antique wardrobe. Go figure. I could see everything he was doing to Maggie through the keyhole. He wanted me to see it. He was torturing her and me at the same time.' Ashley rubbed his battered hands. 'It was just a bloody wooden wardrobe, but I couldn't get out. I kicked, punched and clawed with everything I had, but it seemed to be made of steel.'

'Oh, Ashley, Tapakah must have been waiting and gained access to my mind the precise moment you did. With you out of the way, he was free to play his sick games and impersonate you.'

'Christ, how long did it take you to twig it wasn't me?'

'I thought it was you. I believed you'd gone insane.'

Ashley looked distraught. 'You're fucking kidding. How the

118

hell could you think I'd ever do anything like that?'

'I was in a trance. Part of me knew things weren't right, knew it couldn't be you. The black ribbons, they were from my nightmares. The shears, they were the rib cutting shears Adam used in the morgue. Black blood, again, from my nightmares. Tapakah constructed a virtual world using thought forms from my nightmares. It was so real until I latched onto those elements. They were the keys that unlocked the illusion. And Luca. He helped break the spell. Have you rung him, Drom?'

'Yes, he knows you're safe. I said you'll ring him later.'

'So that was the point I could break free of the wardrobe?'

'Yes.'

'Do you think he's still alive after what Ashley did to him?' Jasmine asked.

'Probably,' I said. 'But his etheric body was destroyed, so I don't think he'll be very well. He's not human though. Who knows how long it'll take for him to recover. I wouldn't be able to recover from that sort of attack.'

'Where did the samurai sword come from?' Drom asked.

'It was in the wardrobe. I found it just before I broke free.'

'Dad has a wardrobe similar to the one you were in. He collects samurai swords. The one you have is made of Damascus steel. I know, 'cause Dad told me all about it. Tapakah must've stolen that from my head too.'

'But how did Ashley bring it back here?' Drom asked.

'Dunno. I brought it out with me,' Ashley said.

'But how?'

'Fucked if I know.'

Language please. I'm under the table, Ashley. Can we have some decorum?

'Sorry, Boo. Apologies. I forgot.' Ashley grinned. 'Jesus, a man can't get away with anything around here.'

A loud '*Pfhpppt!*' sounded from under the table as Boo snorted in disgust.

'For you to materialise a thought form is incredible. The energy to do something of that magnitude, that skill … it's …'

'Mind boggling,' I said, finishing Drom's sentence.

Ashley puffed out his chest and displayed his biceps. 'I guess it's all part of being a psychic warrior.'

Drom rolled his eyes. 'Oh, please.'

Jasmine squeezed one of Ashley's biceps. 'Heavens!'

Ashley laughed. 'That's what all the women say. Squeeze harder. I can't feel a thing.'

'I'm squeezing as hard as I can.' She let go, giving up. 'Amazing.'

Drom shook his head. 'It is bloody amazing. We'll have to find you a scabbard for the blade.'

'We'll have to be extra vigilant with mind melds in future,' Ashley said. 'I wouldn't want anyone experiencing that head fuck.'

A low growl issued from under the table. Ashley rolled his eyes.

'Maybe we need code words to verify identities,' I suggested.'

'Wouldn't he be able to glean those from our minds?' Ashley said.

'Maybe we need an incantation. Something that makes an entity reveal its true form. I'll talk to Luca about it.'

'I'll do some research,' Drom said.

'What was it you yelled out when you ran Tapakah through with the sword?'

'Fu — sorry, I don't know.'

'It seemed to be a specific war cry. I've never heard anything so scary.'

'It's probably from karate,' Drom said. 'I've been doing it for years. It's a battle cry, Kiai. Ki means energy and Ai means join, so it's a cry to facilitate the convergence of your energy and scare the bejesus out of your enemy.'

Ashley looked surprised. 'Huh. I've never done karate, only

dirty tactics fighting. Where the hell did I get that from?'

'Maybe you were channelling the energy in the sword,' I said.

'I sure felt like a Samurai, and I reckon I was dressed as one. Did you see the clothes?'

'No. I just saw the spirit of a Samurai. The most ferocious warrior I've ever laid eyes on.'

Drom gazed at Ashley in awe. 'Wow. I wish I could've seen that. Sounds amazing.'

I shook my head. 'No, you don't. Trust me. You'd have nightmares forever. I will.'

Ashley's expression turned desperately sad as he took my hand.

'What?'

'Now I'll be in your nightmares. I don't want that.'

'No, no I didn't mean that. But if it does happen, and you are in my nightmares, I'll get the Maestro to erase my memory. All but the part where you chopped Tapakah to bits.'

'Things are tough enough as it is without a Musketeer featuring in your nightmares. Promise me. If you have nightmares, you'll do it?'

I squeezed his hand. 'I promise.'

He flashed me an evil grin. 'I want to give you dreams of the wet variety not nightmares.'

'*Ashley!*' everyone said. He ducked, as a hail of plastic cutlery came his way.

---

[16] *Maggie's Playlist: My Demons — Starset*

After breakfast we brought out the live crystal and placed it on the table. Instead of using sunlight, we decided to try using a torch to activate the crystal maps. Ashley shone the torchlight on the crystal, and pale reflections appeared on the tabletop.

I expanded the map of Australia with my fingers. 'It's not as powerful as sunlight, but it works.'

Drom compared his caving map to the crystal map. 'It appears the Buchan crystal is somewhere right in the middle of the Fairy Cave. That's a major tourist attraction.'

'The caves close after three, so we'll have to wait 'til everyone's gone,' Ashley said.

'We should get going now so we have plenty of time to check out the area. My "spidey" sense will guide us once we're there,' I said.

Drom continued to study the crystal map. 'I wouldn't imagine the crystal will be sitting in public view, right in the tourist trail.'

'I wish it was. I don't fancy the idea of having to crawl around in underground caves. In fact, I hate that idea.'

'Yeah, not my cup of tea either,' Ashley agreed.

Drom folded up his maps. 'Okay, let's get this thing done.'

We arrived at the Buchan Caves Park about an hour and a half later. The road to the caves ran along the river, which had been planted with English deciduous trees. The trees were in full autumn colour and provided a magnificent spectacle.

We stopped the truck and climbed out. The place was deserted. The sun had come out and the sky was vivid blue. We stood and looked up at it through the blaze of autumn leaves. When the wind blew a flurry of autumn leaves floated down in a storm of radiance. The air was filled with the rustle of their flight.

Jasmine stretched out her arms and spun around in the floating leaves. 'This is divine.' The leaves crackled and crunched under her feet.

Boo ran around like a lunatic chasing the leaves. She checked the area and, seeing no one around, launched herself into the air. She spun and circled through the trees, trying to catch leaves on the fly.

'This is amazing,' Ashley said. 'I feel like I'm in England.'

'It's so beautiful,' Drom agreed. 'Let's have morning tea right here.'

We spread our rug on the green grass by the river and had mugs of tea and cake. The sun filtered down through the trees and warmed our backs. Our rug was soon covered in a sea of coloured leaves.

Ashley stretched out his arms. 'This makes you remember why it's great to be alive.'

'After yesterday, I had my doubts,' I said.

'Ditto,' Ashley said.

After morning tea, we drove into the main tourist area, which contained the park information centre, rest rooms and picnic areas. A few cars were there, with people ready to go on the first tour.

'Drive up to the Fairy Cave car park,' I said to Ashley. 'We can walk around, and I can get a sense of things. I'm not getting anything yet.'

Once out of the truck we walked up the path to the Fairy Cave entrance. A small building surrounded the entry point. The doorway was protected by a strong metal gate, which was chained and padlocked.

Drom rattled the gate. 'It's fantastic these caves are protected now. It's stopped irresponsible cavers and stupid people trashing them. You can't get access to any main entry points now, unless you get special permission.'

Ashley shook his head. 'Yeah, it's always a few dickheads that spoil it for the rest of us.'

I walked up to the metal gate and my pulse quickened. A gentle hum buzzed through my body and brain. 'It's down there. I feel it. Why does it have to be in a friggin' cave? Why can't it be lying in a paddock somewhere?'

Drom's mouth tightened. 'It doesn't seem to work that way, does it? We'll have to work out a plan.'

'Hey, maybe Boo could go in and find it?' I suggested. 'She doesn't mind tight spaces. She helps the council by digging sand out of storm water drains at the beach, and she goes down wombat holes.'

'That's a great idea,' Drom said. 'She could easily sneak in, do a recky and report back. With her size and skills at levitation she may even be able to retrieve the crystal without damaging any of the formations.'

'That's if it's not buried somewhere,' I said.

Ashley looked at me. 'It's a good plan. I wasn't keen on the idea of you going down there.'

'Me neither. And more than that, I don't like the idea of breaking into the place.'

Drom shrugged. 'We don't have a choice. They're not going to believe our story, are they? Maybe this way won't have to break in.'

'I've two LED headlamps in the truck. I use them for prospecting,' Ashley said. 'We can kit out Boo so she can see where she's going. It's pitch black in those caves. We'll have to wait until after hours. Dogs are banned here.'

We walked back to the truck and told Boo about our idea. She was as excited as a puppy about her new mission.

I'm perfect for this mission, aren't I? How exciting. I'm sure I'll be able to sniff out that crystal. I've done it before.

Drom checked his watch. 'Let's find a place to chill out.'

We drove out of the park and around the corner to the other side of the river, following a track down to the river's edge.

Ashley looked up at the huge granite cliffs that towered above us. 'This is Shangri-La Dee Dah.'

Soft green grass ran right down to the water's edge, and sand and small pebbles allowed easy access to the river. Boo was into the water in a flash. She could've been mistaken for an otter as she serpentined along the river. The water flowed super-fast around the bend, large river rocks creating a waterfall.

Shaking out the rugs, we all lay on our backs staring up at the cliffs and listening to the sound of the water.

Jasmine was tucked in the crook of Drom's arm. 'Just beautiful.'

'What? The scenery or Drom?' Ashley asked.

She blushed. 'Both.'

Boo flew out of the river and hovered above, shaking water all over us.

'Agh, Boo!' Drom yelled. 'Shake somewhere else. Why do dogs always do that?'

It's what we do. I can smell crystal up the river, Maggie.

'Where abouts?'

See that large river rock sticking out into the water, half way up? There's a small cave opening, but it's underwater. It stinks of crystal.

'I reckon that's about level with the Fairy Cave,' Drom said.

You think it's connected to the Fairy Cave?

'Most likely.'

Shall I try and get in?

'No way, Boo. It's too dangerous. It could be submerged. You might get in and not be able to get out. You could drown.'

Okay. I'll wait then.

Boo floated down to the ground and rolled on her back in the grass. She lay, her legs akimbo, staring up at the cliffs.

Drom fiddled with his phone. 'It's doing my head in.'

'What is?'

'Not having phone coverage here. I wanted to check in with Bella.'

'I spoke to her this morning. Everything's fine,' I said. 'Jason's up. They're keeping an eye on him. He said his headache feels better and the rest is helping. Luca said he's going to spike Jason's coffee so he sleeps more.'

Ashley made a face. 'We'll go straight back after we get the crystal.'

A strong tide of emotion swelled in my body, and my eyes filled with tears. 'The sooner we try the crystals out on Jason, the better. I can't handle the way he is and what we're doing to him.'

Drom handed me a tissue, and I blew my nose with my signature trumpet sound.

Ashley put his arm around me. 'It'll be okay. The crystals will fix Jason. I know it.'

'It's breaking my heart, having to drug him. What he must be going through and ... and maybe it's true ... he doesn't love me anymore.'

'There's no way,' Ashley said softly.

'I hope you're right.'

I'll go now. The tour should be nearly over. If you can kit me up with the light I'll zoom over from here. No need for you to come.

'Okay, Boo.' Ashley went to the truck and returned with a headlamp. We secured it so it sat on the front of Boo's chest and set the LED light to low.

See you later!

Boo took off and flew along the side of the cliff face and then up and over the top towards the Fairy Cave.

Ashley looked concerned. 'I hope she stays low. Farmers have guns out here.'

A knot of fear twisted my stomach. 'Oh crikey, I didn't even think about that.'

---

[17] *Maggie's Playlist: Autumn Leaves — Ed Sheeran*

I flew up and over the cliffs. It was great to have a mission.

Oh, there's a rabbit down there! Oh, and ducks! No, focus, Boo. Crystal hunting. That's what we're after. Crystal. Not ducks. Crystal.

My nose buzzed with a trillion different scents; the air smelt fresh in this place. I loved how my ears flapped in the breeze when I flew.

There was the entrance. Just a couple of kids there.

I took the corner at speed, sucked in my gut and whizzed over the top of the gate. The kids screamed. They'd seen me. Bother.

'Mummy, Daddy!' they shrieked. 'We saw a ginormous flying one-eyed bat. It flew into the cave! It was as big as a pig, Mum. It was *scary*. It's going to eat the people in there! Tell them! Get the people out!'

'Don't be silly. There's no bats as big as pigs.'

'But it's in there, Dad. We saw it! We saw it!'

'Well, we'll look for it when we go in on the next tour.'

'No! We're not going. There's a one-eyed flying pig bat in there. It will eat us! You can't make us go! Noooooo—'

The children's screams faded as I slowly descended into the

cave. Pig bat indeed. I thought I looked quite svelte. Children were so rude these days. No manners. No respect.

Floating through the narrow pathways was easy. The LED light worked a treat.

I'd imagined the caves would be freezing cold, but the temperature was pleasant and slightly humid. Everything was moist, and I could smell iron in my nostrils from the walkways and ladders.

I'd never been in an underground cave before. It was exciting! I turned a corner and before me shimmered a pool of still water, which reflected the formations hanging above. It was as though the rock had melted, dripped and fused into crystalline icicles. My light illuminated the heavy curtain-like folds, transforming them into drapes of soft pink and orange.

Glassy spears hung from every point above me. Strange towers rose up resembling stacks of dinosaur bones shimmering eerily in the light. A ginormous striated cocoon hung in honeycombed pleats, cradled in the arms of a fossilised alien octopus. I couldn't help myself. I *had* to bark at it.

'Woof! Woof! Woof! Woof! Grrrrr.'

The thing deserved to be barked at. I started and leapt sideways as the sound echoed and bounced back at me.

I moved on and barked again as the head of a gigantic Chinese dragon with teeth the size of baseball bats appeared out of the gloom. The space I found myself in was reminiscent of a Gothic cathedral. Immense rippled columns towered above me, a row of ancient rust coloured angels stretched out across the wall, a huge eagle with feathers made of glass clutched a petrified lectern that dripped with candle wax. Its eyes were fixed heavenwards towards a group of archangels soaring above. The angels' powerful wings glittered, and their flowing robes shifted in the light as I passed by.

The hair on the back of my neck stood up. *Bats!* I could smell bats.

Groups of them hung from the ceiling resembling bunches of black grapes. Focus, Boo. Move on. Crystal. That's what we were after. I gave them a quick yap, just to let them know who was boss.

I smelt crystal. I could feel it in my bones. It was right here, so close the smell punched me in the face. I stuck my nose in a small hole the size of a tennis ball. It was there, and judging by the scent, about thirty feet in.

I scratched at the hole, but it was surrounded by concrete. Even with my superpowers there was no way I could get through, and if I came at it from a different angle, well, I'd have to dig through two stalagmites. Maggie wouldn't be happy about that. I gave the tiny tunnel one last, good long sniff and headed back out as fast as I could fly.

The place was deserted as I rocketed out into the sunshine. It felt wonderful to be out of there. I shook myself thoroughly to get rid of the stale energy. A sulphur-crested cockatoo flicked its crest and screeched at me as I sailed by. My eardrums vibrated with the ear-splitting cacophony of cicadas, as the sound rose and fell in the wind.

Warm air rose up off the cliff face as I flew over the top and I paused to enjoy a bird's eye view of everyone down below.

Maggie was paddling in the river, Drom and Jasmine were cuddled up on the rug, and Ashley was sitting on a river rock watching Maggie.

I flew in at speed and hit the water creating a perfect wave to douse Maggie.

'Boo, you mongrel!'

Ashley laughed his head off.

Debrief back on the rug, Maggie.

I couldn't wait to tell them about my adventure.

---

[18] *Maggie's Playlist: Pigs Can Fly — James Bourne*

After Boo filled us in with all the details, I gave her one of her favourite chicken wrapped hide chews. She snatched it with glee and settled down in the grass holding it between her paws. Boo always zoned out into Zen mode when she chewed those things, her big brown eyes gazing off into the distance.

'Well, that's not the news we wanted to hear,' Ashley said.

'It *must* be accessible,' Drom insisted. 'The crystal wouldn't be anywhere unreachable. They have to be accessible to crystal keepers, otherwise what's the point?'

'Looks like I'm going in for a swim then,' I said.

'Not the river cave. I won't let you,' Ashley said.

'Well who died and made you boss? I have to go. For Jason. For everyone. I have no choice.'

'You do have a choice,' Drom said. 'We could leave this one where it is and head straight to Hanging Rock to get that one.'

'But then we'd be a crystal short, and we're running out of time.'

'Better short one crystal than short one life,' Ashley said.

'Boo, how wide is the river cave entrance?' I asked.

Just wide enough for you or Jasmine.

I stood and took off my jeans.

'No, hang on,' Ashley said. 'Why *can't* Boo go?'

'Because I can hold my breath longer and I have hands. I don't have to carry the crystal in my mouth. It's more dangerous for Boo. At school, when I was bored, I used to hold my breath for three minutes. I can do this. You could tie a rope around my waist. If I'm not out in three minutes you can pull me back out.'

'This is dangerous,' Drom said. 'If you're moving and stressed, you probably won't be able to hold your breath for more than thirty seconds. Forget three minutes. And, you could get cerebral hypoxia from holding your breath.'

'What's that?' Jasmine asked.

'Oxygen starvation to the brain. It's called shallow water black out. It can happen when you've been holding your breath underwater. You lose consciousness before you even feel the need to breathe. Then you drown.'

'I'll go in for thirty seconds then. Maybe it's only the entrance that's underwater. At least let me go down and check.'

Ashley looked upset. I knew he was thinking of all the hundreds of things that could go wrong and how to prepare for them. So was Drom.

'Are those headlamps waterproof?' I asked him.

'Yeah, I've used them in rivers when prospecting.'

I took off my top. 'Okay, kit me up with one. And don't look so gloomy. I'll be fine.'

Ashley fitted the lamp securely around my head. He pulled a bundle of 6mm nylon rope from the truck and tied one end around my waist, then smiled at me. 'You look a real picture.'

Feeling self-conscious, I covered myself with a jacket. 'Yes, I'll bet. If I'd known I was going swimming I would have brought my bathers.'

'Love the G-string,' Drom said.

My face went red hot. 'Oh, shut up. I hate it. They're the most stupidest things ever. I grabbed it by mistake when we left in such a rush.'

132

'You can borrow my jocks,' Ashley offered. 'Turn them inside out and they'll be good to go.'

I screwed up my nose. 'Ew! This is hard enough as it is without you all making fun of me. Come on. Let's get going. I'm getting cold.'

Drom handed me a small packet. 'Use these ear plugs. They're supposed to help you feel warmer by keeping the cold water out of your ears.'

Ashley grinned. 'Shouldn't we be rubbing you all over with lanolin or Vaseline? I'm sure I've got Vaseline somewhere.' He rummaged around in his toolbox.

Drom laughed. 'That's for long distance swimmers, and the jury's out as to whether it keeps them warmer. I think it's more for chaffing.'

'Well, it probably wouldn't hurt. Here it is. I knew I had some.' He held up a jumbo jar of Vaseline. 'Come here, Maggie, and let me grease you up.'

'Oh, you're *so* funny. You are not coming anywhere near me with that stuff. Goodness knows what it's been used for.'

'Vaseline is as handy as duct tape. I've used it to unzip a stuck zipper, lubricate various mechanical parts, fix squeaky door hinges. And if you get an oil stain on your clothes, just dab it with Vaseline and throw it in the wash. The oil comes right out. I used it on a squeaky hotel bed once,' he said, raising his eyebrows up and down. 'Last year when I was camping, the mosquitos were so bad, in desperation, I smeared myself in Vaseline and the bugs left me alone.' He dipped his fingers into the goo. 'Here, try it.'

Ashley chased me around the grass waving his Vaseline laden hands at me. Drom and Jasmine giggled their heads off. I laughed so hard I could barely breathe. Ashley stepped on the rope, bringing me to an abrupt halt. Collapsing on the grass, I giggled hysterically as he smeared me with goo. Boo had stopped her Zen chewing to watch us with amusement. She raced over and began licking my ear, which made me laugh even more.

'Agh! Stop. Stop you two! I can't take it anymore.' I pushed Boo away. My sides were sore from laughing.

'Here let me help you up.' Ashley attempted to get a grip on my hand, but I was as slippery as a seal and we both fell back on the ground.

'I'm probably going to pollute the river with all this stuff on me.' I wiped my hands on the grass.

Drom took off his jeans and T-shirt. 'Okay, enough hijinks. Let's get in the river.' I noticed Jasmine appreciating his fine physique. He was tall and lanky, but well-muscled.

'Are you okay to stay with the truck?' he asked her.

She lowered her eyes. 'Yes, Drom.'

Ashley handed me some swim goggles. 'They're a bit old, but they'll do.' He stripped down to his jocks, picked up the rope, and pulled me a couple of steps forward. 'Mmmm, I like having you on the end of a ro — *oh shit*. Sorry, I didn't mean—'

'Ashley, it's okay. I'm fine. I want you to be yourself around me.'

'I don't want to remind you of, you know, *stuff*.'

'Say what you want. I'm happier when you're being yourself. You can't censor everything you say, particularly as most of the things you say are inappropriate anyway.' I winked at him.

'You've got a cheek.' He grinned and tugged on the rope again. 'Let's go, slave girl.'

I gasped as I entered the water. It was icy. The bottom of the river felt sandy under my feet as we waded towards the river rock. Thank God it wasn't muddy and squelchy. I hated squelchy. When we reached the rock, the water was up to my armpits.

'At least we can stand. That makes it easier,' Drom said. 'I'm going to check out the cave.' He took a breath and ducked under the water, resurfacing a minute later. 'Looks extremely narrow. There's no way Ashley or I would fit.'

Ashley disappeared under the water. He bobbed back up and pushed the wet hair out of his eyes. 'You're right. With shoulders as broad as mine, there's no way.' He puffed out his chest and grinned at Drom.

Drom rolled his eyes.

'Okay, my turn,' I said. 'I'm going down to have a look around first. Not go in.'

Earplugs. Check. Goggles. Check. I switched on my headlamp and ducked down under the water.

The surface rippled in a green roof above me. Long strands of bright green grassy weed grew up from the bottom of the river and waved in the current. Towards the bank the weeds were flowing inwards. The cave entrance.

I swam towards it and stuck my head in the hole. The rock was worn smooth. There was a bit of green slimy stuff at the front, but inside the cave tunnel the rock looked clean. The headlamp illuminated about six feet of tunnel in front of me, and then the light was sucked away into blackness.

I pushed forward testing the cave for size. I fitted, but it was too narrow to swim. I would have to kick with my legs and drag myself along the cave walls. I pushed back and up towards the surface.

'How long?' I gasped.

Drom checked his watch. 'Forty-two point zero four seconds.'

'Crikey. Is that all? It felt like ages.'

'What did I say?'

'All right, I'm going in as far as I can. I'll have to drag myself along. It's too tight to swim.'

Ashley seized my arms, his face stern. 'Now listen. I'll try and hold the line taught, but not impede your movement. If you get to breathing space, and want to stay in, tug the rope hard, three times, so we know you've got air. If you're in there for more than forty seconds and I don't feel anything, we're hauling you out. When you want to come out, tug the rope twice. Got it?'

'Um … I got everything except for the bit after *now listen.*'

Ashley looked taken aback before he realised I was kidding. 'Oh, ha ha. Always the joker.'

Drom laughed. 'She's trying to beat you at your own game. Good luck, Maggie.'

Ashley checked the rope was properly secured and the headlamp was working. He held my face and kissed me on the forehead. 'Be careful.' His voice was hoarse. 'I'll duck down and watch you swim in. It's a great view.'

I whacked him hard on the arm. 'Don't. You'll put me off my game.'

'Just kidding.'

I took a breath and entered the cave by kicking off from a rock. With arms stretched out in front of me, I hoped the momentum would carry me up the tunnel without expending too much energy.

One cat and dog … two cat and dog … three cat and dog. I counted off the seconds in my head.

Rock surrounded and confined me, the ambience oppressive and sinister. The water was hazy. I began to feel claustrophobic. Eight cat and dog … nine cat and dog.

I hit a bend in the cave and my momentum stopped. The cave narrowed, forcing me to use my hands to pull myself along. My head hit a rock sticking down from above. The strap on my head lamp snagged. Twelve cat and dog … thirteen cat and dog. There wasn't enough room to use my hands to unsnag myself, so I pushed back, wiggled my head and the strap came free. Seventeen cat and dog, eighteen cat and dog. My heart pounded.

I was past the point of no return. I had to risk it, keep going. I yanked hard on the rope three times so they wouldn't pull me out, and dragged myself forward. Twenty-one cat and dog, twenty-two cat and dog. The tunnel grew even smaller. The rock scraped along my back, stomach and sides. My arms were restricted. I could only make small pulling scrabbling movements with my hands.

I fluttered my legs and feet. Twenty-seven, twenty-eight. My lungs felt ready to burst. My limbs ached from the cold. The tunnel continued into blackness, another six feet. Thirty-two, thirty-three, thirty-four. Terror flowed through me. I wanted to scream.

Have trust, Maggie. Trust. Shit. I'd lost count. Thirty-nine? — cat and dog … forty cat and dog. The tunnel dipped upwards, the light changed, my back arched with the tunnel and my arms left the water. Grabbing the edge of a rock, I hauled myself upwards. I couldn't feel my fingers. Forty-four cat and dog. I burst out of the water.

My gasp was so loud it sounded like a scream as I sucked precious air into my lungs. Dragging myself out of the water, I shivered and shook uncontrollably, and my teeth chattered so hard I thought they may shatter. Dark lines crisscrossed my skin — my body was covered with cuts and scrapes.

Crouching on all fours, I clung to the rock ledge. My pale skin was almost blue in the LED light. Oh my God, I looked like Gollum from Lord of The Rings. Precious? Where was my precious?

The cave I found myself in was small and not high enough to stand upright. My brain buzzed with the sense of crystal. Weird noises came out of my mouth. My head was spinning. Then the thoughts stopped dead, as one particular thought entered my cranium.

How the hell was I going to get out? I'd have no momentum! Momentum gave me at least an extra ten seconds. If I found the crystal, I'd only have one hand free. I'd be going twice as slow. How many seconds was it? Forty? My brain was so cold it could barely function. If it was forty, that meant it'd take double to get out. Eighty seconds. One minute and twenty seconds! I used to hold my breath for three minutes. But I'd been nearly dead at forty seconds. Shit. The others wouldn't realise what I'd done. No, wait. They could pull me out. Duh. They'd be able to tell how far I was in by the length of rope. Thank God. It was okay.

I felt for the rope around my waist. It wasn't there.

Shit. It had gone!

I leant over the pool and looked in. No blue rope to be seen. It must've come loose as I'd dragged through that last section. It should still be there. It wouldn't be too far away. Jesus, but Ashley would be pulling it taut. He may have pulled it all the way out.

Don't pull out the rope! Don't pull out the rope! I sent out a telepathic scream and hoped Drom, Ashley or Boo would pick it up. I didn't want to use a full-blown mind meld. I was gun shy after what had happened last time.

I decided to focus on what needed to be done first. Find the crystal. It had to be there. The buzzing in my mind was intense. I crawled on hands and knees and felt along rocky ledges and crevices. I hoped nothing nasty lived in those cracks. I felt along a protruding rock above me, and then everything went black as the headlamp died. And when I said black, I meant black. The blackest black ever. My irises expanded. It made no difference. Shit. *Shit. Shit!*

Keep going, keep going. You can do this. You still can.

Something warm ran down my cheeks. Tears. My breath was shallow and raspy. My heart was banging in my ears. I fiddled around with the headlamp switch. Nothing. I couldn't see to play with the batteries. I needed to find the crystal. It would give me light.

Slow down. Breathe. Quiet yourself.

I took deep breaths and thought about dolphins. More deep breaths. A sense of calm descended. It was so still. Silent. Black. Just an occasional drip of water. My teeth had stopped chattering. That was a relief. What was that noise? Rain? There was a rustling sound, the crackle of static.

Please not roaches. Don't let it be roaches. Crystal. Find the crystal.

I fumbled around the ledge and found something round. It was stuck. I ran my hand around it. It was the size of a crystal. My hand tingled. It *was* the crystal. I grabbed it with both hands and pulled. The rock cracked and gave way. I fell and landed on my backside. I must be near the edge of the water. I tapped the rock on the floor of the cave and the outer covering cracked open. A beautiful luminescence bloomed in my hands and grew brighter until every part of the cave was lit up.

The noise makers were revealed. Spiny shadows danced creepily across the walls. Holy Shit! *Spiders.* Thousands of them, each the size of crabs! They scuttled towards me.

One neared my foot. I kicked at it, and the bug launched itself at me. It was aggressive. I screamed and brushed it away. One crawled up my leg. It *wasn't* a spider. What in God's name were these things?

More of them jumped at me. They were on my head, in my hair. My body was covered in them. Their legs pricked my skin as they hooked onto me. The cave walls were moving, melting, flowing towards me, a molten lava flow of insects.

I threw the headlamp at the advancing army and brushed the insects off my hair. Putting on the goggles, I took a deep breath and leaned head first into the water. I let myself slip down into the tunnel, arms stretched out before me, the crystal illuminating the dark. The prick of insects left my legs and body as I fully submerged. Holding the crystal in one hand, I dragged myself along with the other. I could still use the side of my crystal holding hand to help pull me forward.

Eight cat and dog, nine cat and dog … I began counting the seconds again. It was harder going back. Slower. No sign of the rope. It was so narrow. Jesus. I didn't understand how I'd done it. I felt the skin on my hipbones grinding into the rock. Tiny currents of blood flowed up from the underside of my arms making patterns in the water. It felt narrower. Was it getting narrower?

A piece of weed floated across my face and stuck over my goggles. I shook my head to try and dislodge it. Twenty cat and dog, twenty-one cat and dog. It was so narrow. I was hardly making any progress. I could barely see through my goggles. Still no rope. Something dug into my side. My bra was snagged on a rock. I was stuck. I wiggled and shook from side to side, I moved backwards.

Thirty-one cat and dog. It was no good; I couldn't shake free. Dragging myself forward, the material strained under the pressure. I wished I hadn't bought a quality product.

I clawed at the rock and dragged myself forward. I pulled against the material. It strained against my body. I kept going. The straps cut into my shoulders. It was too narrow to get my arms around and release the bra.

Thirty-nine cat and dog. I was screwed. Icy cold penetrated my bones. My muscles were losing strength. My hands ... I couldn't feel them. Suddenly, the material gave way and I shot forward and dragged myself around a bend.

Forty-one cat and dog. A piece of blue floated in front of my face. The rope! I grabbed it, wound it around my hand and yanked hard, twice.

I surged forward at speed, feeling like superwoman. The cave wall pummeled me as I flew by. I closed my eyes and prayed I wouldn't black out. Prayed I wouldn't lose my grip on the rope. It was fifty-one cat and dog when I finally sucked air back into my lungs.

I was never so glad to breathe. Never so glad to see and feel the sun on my face. And never so glad to see the faces of Ashley, Drom and Jasmine.

'Thank Christ.' Ashley supported me in the water while I gasped for air.

'I got it!' I spluttered and held up the crystal.

'I knew you would,' Ashley said.

'Good work,' Drom said. 'We were beside ourselves. Jasmine was ready to go in after you.'

Jasmine swam over to me. 'You're bleeding everywhere.'

'Only a few cuts and scrapes. I'll live.' The words were garbled, sounding nothing like I wanted to say.

Jasmine gave a little scream. 'There's something in her hair, under the goggle strap. Yuk! Get it out!'

'Looks like a prawn,' Ashley said.

Drom pulled the critter out from under the strap. Its legs wriggled. It *was* as big as a prawn.

'It's a cave cricket,' he said. 'They're harmless.'

'There were thousands of them in the cave. They were jumping at me and crawling on me. It was a nightmare.' My teeth chattered uncontrollably.

Jasmine's face was a picture of horror at the thought.

'Come on, luv, let's get you out of here. You're blue with cold.'

My body was shivering and I could barely move. Drom and Ashley carried me to shore. Jasmine had gone ahead and was pulling towels out of the truck.

I tried to speak and mumbled something unintelligible.

'She has hypothermia,' Drom said. 'We need to move fast and get her warm.'

'Christ, Maggie.' Ashley looked me over as I shivered in his arms. 'Oh, luv, my God, your poor body. Draw on the crystal power. Heal yourself!'

Even though every part of me was cut, grazed and bruised, there was no way I'd even think about using the crystal. We needed every atom of power to complete our mission. Also, I had the feeling the crystal would only part with energy if our injuries were life threatening.

'Na ... n n n no, wu ... won't use it ...' I stuttered. My body shook so much I thought I was having convulsions.

Drom tried to pry the crystal from my hands. 'Maggie, let go. Come on, work with me here. Let it go.' He finally managed to prize it free. I couldn't feel my fingers; they looked snow white and waxy. Lifeless.

That was what I'd look like when I was dead.

I tried to tell Ashley what happened, but my words wouldn't coincide with my mouth.

Ashley looked at Drom in confusion. 'I can't understand what she's saying.'

'It's the hypothermia.' He grabbed the towels from Jasmine and covered me. 'She's shivering, so that's a good sign. Ash, get your sleeping bag. We'll use that. Turn the heater on in the truck and get her inside.'

'I'll make her a hot drink,' Jasmine said. 'What about her injuries?'

Drom shook his head. 'We need to warm her up first.'

Ashley pulled off my G-string which was the only bit of clothing I had on, and Drom supported me while Ashley dried me with the towels. He dashed to the truck and pulled something out of his bag.

'Here you go, luv. I've got just the thing that'll help.' He held out a set of yellowing, full body, thermal underwear. 'These little beauties will keep you warm as toast. Arms up.' I dutifully obeyed as he pulled the top down over my head. I stepped into the long johns and he pulled them up. I wondered how long it'd been since they'd seen the inside of a washing machine. I decided to not think about it.

When they'd finished, I was a mummy sitting in the front of the truck. Thermal underwear, sleeping bag, blankets, a towel around my hair and the heater in the truck going full bore.

Ashley climbed in and sat next to me. 'Come here and cuddle up. You need the extra body warmth. It'll help.'

'You're having me on. Your warmth won't get through the wrapping.'

He grinned. 'That's better; I can understand what you're saying now. We should've put me in there with you in the first place.'

'You're slipping,' I said.

Jasmine handed Ashley a mug of hot tea, and he held it to my mouth for me. I took a sip. It was the best cup of tea I'd ever had. The warmth trickled down inside me. 'Oh, that's divine.'

Drom, Jasmine and Boo climbed into the back of the truck.

It's beautiful and warm in here, Maggie. Just perfect for a snooze. Boo snuggled down between Drom and Jasmine, her head in Jasmine's lap. Boo's front legs were curled up tight. She licked her lips, making noises with her mouth similar to sucking a lolly.

'Boo always makes those noises prior to settling in for a serious sleep,' I said.

Drom stroked her soft ears. 'Schmoo does the same.'

Boo looked up at Drom with adoration. *I miss Schmoo.*

A wave of homesickness washed over me. 'I miss Schmoo too, Boo … and Jason, and Fox, and everyone.'

'The day's getting on,' Drom said. 'Should we book into a hotel for the night?'

'I need to get the crystals to Jason,' I said. 'We should go home.'

'If we leave now, we'd be back by about nine-thirty,' Ashley said. 'I'm happy to drive.'

'What shall I do?' Jasmine asked. 'I don't know what to do.'

'You're coming with us,' I said. 'You can stay until you work out what you want to do. Put that worry out of your mind for the time being, okay?'

'Thanks, Maggie.'

Ashley untangled himself from me and secured the seat belt around my body. 'All right, let's hit the frog and toad.'

Drom looked at his phone. 'I can't wait to get mobile reception back. It sucks out here. I can't believe they don't have coverage. The Prof and everyone need to know what's going on.

They'll be worried.'

'We should have reception in about thirty-five minutes,' Ashley said. 'Oh, and Drom, when you speak to them, you have to say we had a Buchan good time.'

'Of course. It's Buchan beautiful here.'

A long, sleepy growl issued from the depths of Boo's throat.

Ashley rolled his eyes. 'That Buchan dog has no sense of humour.'

We all laughed, including Boo.

---

[19] *Maggie's Playlist: Under the Water — Dirty Heads*

Everyone's phones sounded as we hit reception.

Drom read a text. 'Shit. Ashley, ring Fox. Now. Put it on car speaker.'

'What's wrong?' we all asked.

'Jason's gone. He's been missing for two hours.'

My stomach contracted in fear.

Fox's deep voice sounded out through the speakers. He was in police mode. 'We've got problems, guys. At two-thirty p.m. this afternoon, Bella went to check on Jason and he was gone. Luca, Christos and Bella searched the whole property; he's not on site. From what we can ascertain, he hasn't taken anything with him. Just the clothes on his back. Car, motorbike, money, credit cards — everything's still here. Oh, except his gun. He's taken that.'

I tried to speak through my fears. 'Do you think he … would he—'

'Self-harm?'

'Yes, do you think?'

'My gut instinct is telling me no. But I have no evidence. I've sent in a photo and organised a priority KLO4 for him.'

'What's that?'

'Sorry, it's notifying the police to a *Keep a Look Out For* a person of interest. In Jason's case, it's a missing person request. I mentioned his head injury. They're on to it, Maggie. We'll find him.'

'I reckon he's coming after Maggie,' Drom said.

'If he is, he'd be heading towards Hanging Rock,' Ashley said.

'I've got the local crew keeping an eye out already,' Fox assured us.

'Damn it, Fox. We have the crystals. You must find him.'

'I'm doing my best, Maggie,' he said softly.

'This is the worst news. We should have chained him to the bed.'

'I did. But he was restless, tossing and turning, talking gibberish. I handcuffed him to the bed before I left. I didn't tell you because I thought you wouldn't like the idea. But I did it anyway. He broke free. I'm sorry.'

Ashley thumped his fist on the steering wheel. 'That's my fault.'

'How can it be your fault?' I said.

'I taught him how to get out of cuffs. Ages ago. It's a cinch. He can get out of cable ties and duct tape as well.'

'Oh, great. Thanks for teaching *me* that!'

'Yeah, well, we kinda need you to stay taped up on occasion, or we'd be screwed.'

Of course. How could I forget I had evil psycho-bitch tendencies?'

'Did you have any hair pins in the bedside drawer?'

'Probably. There's all sorts of stuff in there.'

'All he needed was a hair pin or similar to be out of those cuffs in seconds.'

A sigh came through the car speakers.

'Great, thanks for telling me, Ash,' Fox said.

'Well, it never came up in conversation. Plus, I wasn't going to tell a cop I could get out of cuffs.'

'So, what now?' Drom asked.

'Well, there's no point in rushing back if Jason's not there,' I said. 'We should sleep somewhere and set off early in the morning to Hanging Rock, as planned. No matter what, we have to get crystals.'

'Tell me the timings and I'll meet up with you,' Fox said.

Drom seemed thoughtful. 'Given that Tapakah was in Kadar's head our red herring may not have worked. Jason could be here.'

'He could be bloody anywhere,' Ashley agreed.

'I'm handing over to Luca, he wants to speak with you,' Fox said.

'Hi, Maggie. I wanted you to know I convinced Jason to get a brain scan, because of his shocking headaches. I took him yesterday. Everything was normal. He's fine.'

I wasn't sure whether to feel happy or sad. If he wasn't roached then he was normal. If he was normal then he didn't love me. Sadness won. I burst into tears. 'So, he doesn't love me,' I said to no one in particular.

'Just because nothing showed up on the scan doesn't mean he hasn't been compromised,' Luca said. 'I think he has. All of us think so. Boo said he stunk of roach. At least he doesn't have a brain injury, and that's the good news. Stay strong.'

'Okay,' I mumbled.

I listened in a daze as Ashley and Drom filled in the folks at home with what had happened. Dad was in the background, worried if I was okay. I couldn't speak; I was numb. I should've been happy Jason was roach free, but instead tears continued to run down my face, and I couldn't wipe them away because my hands were bound in all the wrappings.

I jerked around in the front seat like a frustrated caterpillar. I had expended my last ounce of energy to get those friggin' crystals for Jason. To save him. To save us. And now he was gone. It wasn't fair.

'Gotta go, guys,' Ashley said. 'Call you back later.' He swerved to a stop, jumped out and opened the passenger side door. He undid my seat belt and hauled me out of the car. Propping me up against the side of the truck, he pulled away the blankets, rugs and towels and unzipped the sleeping bag, letting it fall to my feet. I stood next to the truck, my body lost in the folds of his yellowing thermals. He held me tight for a moment, before pushing me gently back onto the passenger seat. 'Back into the car before you get cold.'

He piled all the wrappings around me and handed over his crumpled tissue box. 'Blow your nose. Everyone cover your ears.' I laughed through my tears.

When we set off again, Ashley turned the heater up to high.

'Thanks, Ashley. I'm okay now, not cold anymore.' I felt calmer now I could move my limbs.

He squeezed my hand. 'It'll be okay.'

'We all know Jason loves you,' Drom said. 'From what we've seen, it's a given.'

'I hope so.'

Ashley let go of my hand and didn't say another word. He just kept staring at the road ahead.

* * * * *

We drove in silence, Ashley gripping the steering wheel and looking drawn and tired. Drom, Jasmine and Boo were asleep in the back. I had no idea how I looked, but I figured it wouldn't be particularly pleasing.

'We should stop sooner rather than later,' I suggested.

'We're coming into Lakes Entrance. We'll find somewhere here.'

'The Prof's holiday house is here. I know where the key is.'

Ashley gave me a tired smile. 'I was hoping we could. That's why I came this way.'

My spirits lifted. I loved Lakes Entrance; it was a beautiful coastal township. I hadn't been for ages. Mum and Dad built the house in their spare time, and it sat right on the lake's edge, overlooking the waters of the North Arm.

Ashley turned off the highway to head towards the house, and a feeling of impending doom hit me.

'Stop. Don't go there. Go into town. We'll stay somewhere else. I have a terrible feeling.'

'Anything specific?'

'No, just don't go to the house.'

'Okay.' Ashley headed into town.

As soon as he drove away my feeling lifted. All our phones beeped with a message from the Prof.

'Danger. Don't go to Lake House. I'll call soon.'

Drom mumbled from the back, 'Your spidey sense is working well.'

Ashley slowed the truck. 'What about this hotel? It's got a vacancy sign.'

'That'll do. It's close to the Central Hotel; we can go there for tea. The food's great, and they have an open fire.'

While Ashley and Drom checked in, I took a call from the Prof. I'd just finished speaking when they returned to the truck.

'Dad checked the security footage at the Lake House. A group of bikers rented the house next door. They've been poking around, staking our house out. Prof rang one of the neighbours, old Dicko. He's been keeping an eye on things. He confirmed their suspicious behaviour. Said they look like a nasty bunch of thugs. The Prof thinks the dark force minions are on our tail. They must think it's logical we would stay here.'

'Maybe we shouldn't eat out tonight,' Drom said. 'Maybe best to lay low in the hotel room and head off early.'

My stomach rumbled. 'That's probably the sensible thing to do, but I'd love to have a counter meal.'

'Me too,' Ashley said.

Drom shrugged. 'Yeah, let's go out. Stuff it.'

I snuck into the hotel room without anyone seeing my beautiful thermals, and I went straight to the bathroom for a shower. Peeling them off was a painful task, as the material had stuck to my open wounds. I stood naked in front of the mirror. It wasn't a pretty sight. My hipbones were red raw, and my body was crusted with blood. Anything on my body that stuck out had copped abrasions. My breasts had taken a beating after I'd lost my bra, and my elbows and knees were a mess. The front of my body had so many abrasions I didn't know what to do. How the hell was I going to treat this? The thought of putting on clothes made me shudder.

'Ashley, I need the first aid kit,' I yelled through the bathroom door. My voice sounded small and squeaky. I tried again. 'Ashley, I need the first aid kit!'

Emotion choked in my chest. The reflection in the mirror was overwhelming. I wanted Jason. I needed him. Anger and frustration surged. Just as I was going to scream again, the door opened and a hand poked in proffering a first aid kit.

'Thanks,' I sobbed.

'Can I come in?'

I draped a towel around me. 'Please.'

Ashley came in and closed the door.

I held out my bloodied arms. 'I don't know where to start.' My bottom lip trembled. Don't cry. Don't cry. Be strong. Don't look at him. I stared at the bathroom ceiling and blinked away tears.

'Jesus, Maggie, you can't do this alone. Don't worry, I'll get you cleaned up or they'll get infected. I'm not sure if we have enough dressings. Drom, can you come here?' he yelled.

Drom opened the door and stuck his head in. 'Holy shit.'

'You haven't seen the rest of me.'

'We're going to have to wash and dress a million abrasions

and there's no way I've got enough stuff,' Ashley said. Can you find a chemist and get me lots of gauze and dressings, a bottle of something to wash out the wounds with, like sodium chloride and antiseptic cream. We'll need to change the dressings every couple of days and make sure the wounds stay moist so they heal properly. See if you can get antiseptic cream with pain relief in it. Oh, and Dermabond and Steri-strips.'

Drom rattled off the list back to Ashley. 'I saw a chemist on our way in.'

'I'll get started with what I have. Thanks, mate.'

'I'll take Jasmine with me. Boo's guarding the truck. Chair the door.'

'Thanks,' I said, as he and Ashley disappeared.

Jasmine and I waited until we heard Ashley chair the door.

'Is it safe to leave?' she asked.

'They'll be fine. Let's check on Boo.'

Jasmine walked quietly beside me. I liked the fact she didn't feel the need to talk all the time. I liked quiet. Quiet was good. For me, there was nothing worse than someone who didn't know when to shut up. I couldn't get the image of Maggie out of my mind, her poor, busted up body. She looked worse than when we first carried her out of the water.

The truck looked undisturbed. 'Hey, Boo, everything okay?'

Yes, thank you, Drom. Just catching up on a bit of shuteye. Be assured, however, that I am always on high alert, even though it may seem I'm fast asleep.

'I get that, Boo. You're like me.'

Indeed.

'We're going to the chemist to get first aid supplies. Won't be long. What do you want to eat, Boo?'

Nothing yet thanks. Maggie will bring me back steak from the pub. She always does.

'No worries. Back soon.'

'You can hear Boo talking in your head?' Jasmine asked.

'Yes, she sounds exactly like Prince Charles. It's so weird.'

'Why Prince Charles?'

'We have no idea. Boo doesn't know either. It annoys her.'

'I hope Maggie isn't left with scars. Those abrasions are deep.'

'If we give her proper wound care, she'll be fine. At some stage, she'll probably cop another dose of crystal and that'll fix it.'

'You're all so knowledgeable, with so many skills. I feel out of my league. I want to contribute, but I have nothing like you do.'

'You have a good heart and you care. You're brave and passionate. You stand up for justice. That's all you need. You can learn skills, but it takes too long to teach someone love, compassion and kindness. Those qualities are innate in you. You don't have a bad bone in your body. That alone makes you a worthy musketeer.'

Jasmine blushed. 'That's the nicest thing anyone's ever said to me.'

'Well, it's true, and you deserve a whole lot more. This is a turning point for you. You're free to create a new life, to be what you want to be, do what you want to do.'

Jasmine pulled at my sleeve. 'Look, there's a bakery next to the chemist. I'll get fresh bread. I'm going to make curried egg sandwiches for tomorrow. Maggie loves them.'

'We all love them. Wait right out front when you've finished.' I left Jasmine and headed into the chemist.

When I exited the chemist ten minutes later Jasmine was nowhere to be seen. A loaf of bread lay on the ground. I picked it up and yelled into the bakery doorway. 'Hey! Where's the girl who just bought this? She's tiny, long black hair, dark skin, big eyes—'

'Went off with a bloke, mate. He said he was family and she was a runaway. Had a picture of her in his pocket an' all. Said he was taking her home to her mum and dad. Called her a slut and a whore. Dragged her off. We didn't want to get involved, mate. You know, all that wog family business.'

'How long ago?'

He leant over the counter. 'Ten seconds ago. See that red car pulling out. She's in there.'

I hurled the loaf of bread at the gutless baker and ran down the mall towards the car. Jasmine was in the back seat between two men. She was struggling. Another two men sat in the front.

I ran at full pelt. I had to get them before they left the car park. Leaping up onto a car park railing, I launched myself at the car and landed square on top of its roof, slamming my feet and fists onto the metal.

As anticipated, the noise made them jam on the brakes. I used the forward momentum to roll over the top of the car. I landed on my feet at the front bumper. I pulled out a throwing knife and slashed the sidewall of the left front tire and then the right. When the driver opened the front door to get out, I kicked it shut against his arm.

While the driver nursed his arm, the other three men leapt out. I stood my ground as they circled towards me.

The driver screamed, 'You're going to fuckin' die for this, Skip.'

'Let the girl go and I won't hurt you.'

'Get the prick!' the driver screamed.

The men sprang into action. I waited until they were almost on me before I leapt onto the car, rolled across the top, and landed beside the rear car door. I opened it and dragged Jasmine out. Her eye was red and swollen. One of the arseholes had punched her.

'Get behind me.'

The men approached, their faces ugly with rage. Well, they were ugly anyway. The rage didn't help.

'Which one of you courageous arseholes punched her?'

154

A brutish looking bloke with a beard and a gut stepped forward. 'That'd be me, Skip. She's a slut and a whore. Just your type.' His belly shook as he laughed at me.

'That's my Uncle Lail,' Jasmine whispered.

'This is family business, Skip. Stay out of it. She's got it coming. You haven't seen her brother or cousins, have you? They're looking for her. We're looking for them. Allah's on our side, Skip. It's justice we found her. So just fuck off.'

'Do you believe in an eye for an eye?' I asked.

'Yes, Skip. It's in the Qur'an — 5:45. I like that passage. "We ordained for them therein a life for a life, an eye for an eye, a nose for a nose, an ear for an ear, a tooth for a tooth, and for wounds is legal retribution."'

'It actually says more than that. You left out the bit about charity. It goes on to say, "But whoever gives charity, it is an expiation for him. And whoever does not judge by what Allah has revealed — then it is those who are the wrongdoers."'

Uncle Lail's jaw dropped and he screamed, 'There ain't no fuckin' charity here, mate. And you? You quote the Qur'an to *me*? That's a fuckin' insult coming from your mouth.' He moved a couple of steps closer and pulled a gun from the back of his pants. He pointed it at my face. 'Give me the girl!'

I could tell he was a novice by the Vulcan death grip he had on his gun.

I raised my hands to gun level, in surrender. 'Please don't shoot me. Here, take her.'

He relaxed. In that split second, I whipped the gun from his hand and had my gun pointing in his face. 'The difference between my gun and yours, arsehole, is that my gun has bullets in it.' I pistol-whipped him across the head with his gun. He crumpled to the ground clutching at his head. The other hoods stepped forward.

I cocked the trigger. 'Don't even think about it. Here's what's going to happen. You take Uncle Lail here and drive away. You go home and you don't come back. You leave Jasmine alone. If any one of you, your family or friends comes after Jasmine, I *will* kill you. You make it your business to tell everyone she's off limits. Promise this, and you get to live. Do you promise, arseholes?'

The men looked at each other. Uncle Lail whimpered on the ground before suddenly lunging at me. My foot connected with his chin before his hand even touched me. His teeth crunched as they bit through his tongue. Hopefully that would shut him up for a while.

'Well?'

The men mumbled.

I stepped forward. 'I can't hear you.'

'We promise,' they muttered.

'Louder.'

'We promise!' they yelled.

'Now, I want you to sincerely apologise to Jasmine.'

'No way.'

I raised my revolver and took aim.

The men spoke. 'We're sorry, Jasmine. Truly sorry. We'll never bother you again. Yeah, sorry Jasmine.'

'Why are you sorry? Tell her.'

'Um … we're sorry for hurting you … um, for frightening you … we're really, really sorry, Jasmine.'

Uncle Lail was out cold, with a large lump growing on his face. His tongue was swollen and sticking out of his mouth, impaled by his yellow teeth.

I waved my gun at them. 'Take Uncle Lail and go. If I see any of you again, I will kill you.'

Two of them scurried over and dragged Uncle Lail into the car. They hurried in after him and slammed the car doors. The engine started and the car limped out onto the road, its two flat front tires flapping on the asphalt. I stood and watched as they disappeared around the bend.

156

Tucking the guns down the back of my pants, I started as a round of applause echoed around the car park. A crowd had gathered outside the bottle shop, and they stood and clapped.

'Bloody ace, mate.'

'Best thing I've seen all year,' an old lady in a yellow cardigan, shouted.

'He's a warrior, Mum,' a little kid yelled. 'I seen him on TV before.'

'You showed 'em. Don't need scum like that around here, 'ay big fella?'

'Bloody marvellous, Maude. The way he catapulted off that railing reminds me of me back in the day.'

The baker stepped hesitantly towards me, leaning back as he handed me a couple of bags. He obviously thought I might hit him. 'Here's your stuff from the chemist and a new loaf of bread for you.'

'Thank you. I appreciate it.' He jumped back as I took the bags from him.

A lady with tattoos and missing teeth came forward and held out a bag of frozen peas to Jasmine. 'For your eye, darls.'

'Thank you so much.' Jasmine took them and pressed the bag to her eye.

I took Jasmine's hand and we walked across the car park towards the hotel. The sound of applause followed us. So much for keeping things low key.

We walked through an alleyway. The sun was shining, and I could feel warmth radiating out from the red brick walls. Jasmine pulled me to stop and leaned back against the wall, looking up at me.

'Thank you, Drom. You risked your life for me.'

Her long dark hair gleamed in the sunshine and floated up around her face in the breeze. She looked so beautiful, even holding a bag of peas against her eye. Her one brown eye glistened with tears, and her dark lashes fluttered. Her lips were soft and pink, and I wanted to press her up against that warm brick wall and kiss her like she'd never been kissed before. I wanted to run my hands over her beautiful body and tell her I loved her.

'No worries, Jasmine. Let's get back.' I brushed the dust off my jacket and walked away.

---

21 *Maggie's Playlist: Because I Love You — The Master's Apprentices*

I counted bathroom tiles to distract myself from the pain. At one hundred and ninety-three, Ashley came back with a bowl of water. 'Drom and Jas shouldn't be long. The door's chaired, so we can get started.' He placed the bowl on the bench.

'Shouldn't I shower first? I won't be able to shower with all the dressings.'

'I guess you should. It'll sting though.'

'I have to wash my hair. Makes me itchy all over thinking about those spider crickets.'

'Cave crickets, luv. Drom was telling me about them. They're cannibals. If they run out of food, they'll eat a couple of their own legs. If there's still no food, then they'll eat each other. They're harmless to humans, but.'

'I'm not so sure about that. I'm psychologically scarred.'

'Yeah, well there's always that.'

'Still, if they hadn't been there, I don't think I would've been able to make myself swim back through the tunnel.'

'So, I have the cave crickets to thank for getting you back.'

'I guess I owe them. Funny that.'

'I'll have a beer while you shower. Give me a hoy when you're ready.' He grinned. 'Or I could have a beer in here and keep you company?'

I laughed. 'You don't quit, do you? Have a beer and see if you can catch the news. Find out what the dark force is up to.'

The soap on my skin stung like a bastard, so I showered just long enough to wash my hair. It was excruciating. With hindsight, we should've taken a wet suit, but who knew I'd have to go underwater. I certainly didn't have an inkling. We'd need a semi-trailer if we had to prepare for everything.

I called Ashley back in and he began washing and dressing my arms and shoulders. He'd brought me in a glass of wine, which I sipped gratefully.

'I feel like such a sook. But it's so painful.' My bottom lip started to quiver again.

'Abrasions are painful. Heaps of nerve endings exposed. I had road rash when I came a cropper on my bike, and its agony. You're not a sook. You're the bravest girl I know. I'll leave the gash on your shoulder for the Dermabond. Now for your legs.'

Ashley worked gently and methodically, cleaning and dressing the wounds on my legs. Between wounds, he sipped his beer and I guzzled wine. By the time he finished, I resembled a patchwork quilt.

'Wonder what's keeping them?' Ashley said. 'Thought they'd be back by now. Still, I have more stuff than I thought, so we can keep going. What do you want to do about your torso? I'm happy to take care of that too, but you might feel more comfortable doing it yourself.'

'I can't. You've seen me naked heaps of times. My hipbones are trashed, and I wouldn't even know what to do with my breasts. Maybe I should put a dressing in my bra?'

'Are you sure? Looking is one thing, touching is another.'

'I'll pretend you're a doctor. Well, you were a paramedic anyway. For heaven's sake, we used to be together. It doesn't matter.'

'Doctors and Nurses. My favourite game.'

'Oh, stop it!'

'We'll wait for Jasmine. She can help you.'

'No, it's fine, keep going. Let's get this done, already.'

'Okay, drop the towel, luv.'

The towel had stuck to my nipples, and I winced as I pulled it free. I hoped the hotel's laundry service could get out bloodstains.

'Holy hell.' Ashley stood and took in the extent of the damage. Turning away from me, he looked up at the ceiling and raked his hands through his hair. His voice was hoarse. 'Just going to get more grog.' He left the room.

When he returned, he plonked a stubby and bottle of wine on the bench. 'Right.' He topped up my glass, then twisted the top off his beer and took a swig. He handed me a couple of tablets. 'Painkillers. Take them.'

Ashley hadn't shaved in days, and a beard was well on the way. I had a cave man for a paramedic. He washed his hands, dried them, took a robe off the door and draped it around my shoulders.

'Okay, what do you want me to do first?'

'Hipbones. They're killing me. No nipples … oh, whatever.'

He grinned. 'Okay, as I'm a breast man, I'm going for the boobs first.'

'Oh, for Christ's sake.'

'Hold the bowl of water for me.'

I held the bowl and fixed my gaze firmly on the ceiling as Ashley gently bathed my raw nipples. I bit my lip and screwed up my face. Tears came. It was agonising.

'This is doing my head in,' Ashley mumbled. 'I'm sorry. I'm so sorry it hurts. Nearly done. This is wrong. Everything's so wrong. I should've had a wet suit. God is an arsehole, a twisted, sicko arsehole, Maggie. I've dreamt of touching you again, you know that. And this is how it is.'

'Stop it, this isn't helping. It will heal. I'll heal. You can't

161

prepare for every eventuality. We do our best. And it's not God's fault, it's just the way it is.'

'Well, the way it is sucks. I've dealt with torn off limbs, people with their guts hanging out and half their faces blown off, but this, I'm sorry, it's hard for me to handle.' He jammed his fist into the side of his skull. 'I get why Drom does what he does. Why he keeps his distance. When you get too close to someone, you can't function. Can't do what needs to be done.'

'You always do what needs to be done, and you care. Caring makes you vulnerable yes, but it keeps you human, open, kind, loving. That's what we're fighting for.'

Ashley took a deep breath and finished dressing my wounds. 'That's the best I can do until Drom gets back.' He stood up stiffly and rubbed his knees. 'I'll dress your hipbones better once I have more supplies.'

'Thank you, Ashley. I owe you big time.'

'Have a look at you. You're an advert for Steri-strips.'

I checked myself out in the mirror and laughed. 'I'm a piece of abstract art. You might as well have bound me up in one enormous bandage.'

'Come on, luv. Dry your hair and put some clothes on. We'll go to the pub as soon as Drom and Jasmine get back. I'm starving.'

'Me too.'

'Glad to hear it. If you ever lose your appetite, that's when I'll know something's really wrong with you.' He flashed me a cheeky grin and ducked out of the bathroom, narrowly escaping the bar of hotel soap directed at his head.

'We'll have to work on your throwing skills,' he yelled, as the soap hit the back of the door with a clunk.

* * * * *

A specific series of knocks came from the front door.

162

Ashley laughed. 'Drom's secret knock code. He cracks me up, that guy.'

Despite the secret knock code, I noticed Ashley still had his gun at the ready. He removed the chair from under the door and checked the peephole before he let them in.

'Jesus, Jasmine, what happened?' Ashley asked.

Drom looked grim. 'We had a visit from Uncle Lail.'

Jasmine held a bag of frozen peas against her face. 'It doesn't hurt as much now.'

'She's going to have a nasty black eye,' Drom said. 'Friggin' arseholes.'

'Come on, sweetheart, let me take a look,' Ashley said.

Jasmine reluctantly let him take away the bag of peas. I tried to put her at ease. 'He was a paramedic. He knows what he's doing.'

'What happened?' Ashley asked.

'He punched me in the face.'

Drom filled us in with all the details while Ashley checked and bathed Jasmine's eye.

Ashley put his hand on her shoulder. 'Well, like Drom said, you're gonna have one cracker of a black eye, little Miss. You'll get a shock when you look in the mirror, but don't worry, it's not serious. The white of your eye is bright red. It's called a subconjunctival hemorrhage. It's when the blood vessels in the white of the eye rupture. It can take about ten days to clear. You'll be fine, luv, but you'll look somewhat worse for wear for a while. We need to keep up the ice compresses for the first couple of days, and then warm compresses. Tell me if you get any headaches, blurry vision or nausea.'

Jasmine stood and headed for the bathroom. 'Okay, thank you. I'd better have a look at myself.'

'The incident drew a crowd,' Drom said. 'I'm sure there'll be video footage. The police are bound to be involved, particularly with guns being drawn. We need to leave.'

There was a knock at the door. Drom leapt up and looked through the peephole.

'It's a lady. I think she's from reception.'

'Open it. I've got you covered if anything goes down,' Ashley said.

Drom opened the door to an attractive middle-aged woman. She stood there, nervously clutching her cardigan.

'Hello, how can I help?' Drom asked.

She looked anxiously from side to side and whispered, 'Hello, darls. I'm Judy from reception. I was at the supermarket today, in the car park. I saw what you did. I recognised you and the girl. The police have been around. They're looking for you. Showed me a blurry picture. I told them I hadn't seen anyone in the hotel that resembled you.'

'You lied to cover me?' Drom asked incredulously.

'Well, the photo was blurry, I couldn't be sure. Just wanted to give you the heads up, darls. How's the poor girl?'

'Nasty black eye, but she'll be okay.'

'If there's anything you need, let me know, luv. You're a hero. We need more people like you to get rid of scumbags like those. To tell you the truth, I think the cops are just going through the motions searching for you. They want the hoods that bashed the girl.'

'The hood that did it is her uncle.'

Judy looked shocked. 'Holy Mother of God. Well, you take care of yourself, luv, and that girl. And as I said, anything you need.'

Drom closed the door and came back into the lounge area.

Ashley grinned. 'Dromski the hero warrior 'ay? You're the talk of the town.'

Drom's face was stern. 'Yeah, great. Just what we need. I've cocked up.' He pulled out his phone. 'I'm calling Fox. Better tell him what's happened. He could help to take the heat off us.'

Ashley looked disappointed. 'Looks like we'll be eating in,

Maggie.'

'Bummer. It sucks having to lie low all the time. We should become masters of disguise so we can go wherever we want. I've always wanted to own a wig. I'm going to get one. It'll be fun!'

'That's not such a crazy idea. It would be extra protection for you too, given you're number one on Tapakah's hit list.'

Drom came back looking happier. 'I spoke to Fox. He's going to make a few calls and try to stop any vids getting aired on the news. How come you two are looking so chipper?'

'That's good news,' Ashley said. 'And we're looking happy because we have a new project. We're going to kit up with stuff to disguise ourselves. Maggie was bummed about not being able to go out for tea tonight, so we thought we should get disguises. That way, we can do what the hell we want, rather than feel like escapees all the time.'

'Good plan. I was thinking about it myself. The easiest way to change your appearance is to change hair length and colour, eye colour, add glasses, hats, make yourself older. Changing your posture and gait is important too.'

'We should each have a couple of disguises we can use as required. Keep a kit with us when we travel,' Ashley said. 'Stuff it. I noticed a Salvos store in town. I'm going to duck down and get us a selection of different clobber.' He grinned. 'We're going out tonight, guys! I'm looking forward to having one off the tap.'

I giggled. 'We can turn Drom into an old man. We should get Jasmine a beret. She could pull it down over her eye and tuck her hair up underneath.'

Drom screwed up his nose. 'I don't want to be an old man. I'd prefer hippy surfer dude.'

Ashley went to the door. 'Once we get back to Melbourne, we can go shopping and invest in decent wigs. In the meantime, we'll have to make do. If I can't find anything, we'll have to eat in. Secure the door. I have my phone if you need me.'

I waited until he'd gone then screwed up my nose. 'I hate

wearing second hand clothing. The previous owner's vibes are ingrained in them.'

Drom screwed his nose up too. 'Yes, it's not my cup of tea either. Anyway, it'll be fun to see what Ashley comes up with.'

Jasmine came out of the bathroom looking miserable. 'I'm hideous.'

She'd been crying, as her other eye looked red too. I hugged her. 'It'll get better. We can use makeup to cover the bruising. You're lucky he didn't cut you with a knife.'

'Yes, they did that to my sister. I am lucky. Thanks to Drom.'

Drom shook his head. 'I can't fathom how they can do that to their own flesh and blood. They treat you like you're not human. I mean, calling a member of his own family a slut and whore and punching you in the face. It's sick.'

'And the thing is ... I'm not a slut. I haven't been with anyone.'

Drom and I exchanged surprised looks.

'You're kidding. A beautiful girl like you. Guys would be lining up,' I said.

'With arranged marriages, the family want us to be virgins. And yes, I've had opportunities, but there's been no one I wanted to be with, no one I really liked. No one who I felt respected me as a person.'

'I hate the whole slut-shaming business,' I said. 'Just because a woman enjoys sex, has sex a lot, or maybe, God forbid, has a number of sexual partners, they're degraded by being called a slut. They don't do that to men. Poor Jasmine hasn't even had sex and she's still called a slut.'

'Women slut-shame other women too,' Drom pointed out.

'True. But look at all the derogatory terms for a woman who sleeps with her choice of men. You have slut, whore, tramp, wench, floozy, harlot, prostitute, strumpet, trollop, loose, slag, skank, jezebel, hooker, vamp, tart, minx, hussy, hustler, slapper — the list goes on.'

166

'What do you call a male slut then?' Jasmine asked.

'Um, man-whore … philanderer, womaniser, playboy. But they don't have the same moral contempt attached to them. I mean, *hello*, sex *is* a two-way endeavour.'

'You're right. The words are vicious in their condemnation of women. It appears women shouldn't be having sex at all,' Jasmine said.

'Yeah, but it's okay for the blokes to have as much sex as they want, with whoever they want. It's almost admired. So, who are the women having sex with all those blokes?' I said. 'Obviously all the *sluts*. Jeez, don't get me started.'

Drom grinned. 'I think it's too late for that.'

'It wouldn't be an issue on Sonus, would it? They wouldn't have any such labels for men or women.'

'Too right,' Drom said. 'Now, I reckon it's time for a cleansing one while we wait for Ash to get back.'

Ashley came back laden with bags. 'I have awesome stuff here, guys. I picked up a few things from the op shop, but I thought I'd also go with Drom's surfer dude theme, so I went to the surf shop. They're having a sale.'

I laughed, reflecting back to our time at the Hyatt. 'You're like Jon, the clothes dude. We don't need him anymore when we've got you.'

Ashley emptied all the shopping onto the couch and started sorting things into piles.

'Okay, Dromski, here's what I have for you. So cool.'

Ashley was having the time of his life. It still surprised me that he liked to shop.

'We have one acid wash jacket, one T-shirt with printed fruit labels on the front, a pair of drainpipe striped jeans and a pair of skate shoes.' He pulled out a cap with a ponytail attached to it. 'Oh, and this is fantastic.'

Ashley slapped the hat on Drom's head, and Drom was instantly transformed.

'That's amazing. With the long hair coming out the back you look like a surfer already,' Jasmine said.

Drom checked himself in the mirror and laughed. 'Yeah, the

hat and the hair tell a story. You can picture my panel van outside.'

Ashley took out a small paper bag. 'I have these. Fake nose rings and piercings.' He tipped out the assorted jewellery. He clipped a silver ring into the side of Drom's nose. 'This is a fancy gold, tribal style one I thought would suit you, Jasmine. It goes in the middle of your nose.' He handed it to her and she popped it into her nose and smiled. 'How does it look?'

'Gorgeous. Exotic,' I said.

'It suits you,' Drom said. 'You look hot.'

Ashley passed some clothes to Jasmine. 'Here's a pink top with a cartoon girl on the front, a black hoody, pink beach pants, and to cover your eyes, a pair of pink framed, rose coloured glasses. Oh, and a pair of surf shoes, in blue. One more thing, an oversized beanie hat in blue. You can tuck all your hair inside it.'

'I love everything, Ashley. I'm going to try it all on now.' She ran into the bedroom.

Ashley opened a large paper bag. 'You're gonna love these.' He pulled out sheets of paper and laid them on the table. 'Fake tattoos. None of us have tattoos, do we?'

Drom shook his head. 'No, we're all clean skins.'

'You wouldn't believe the shit I went through in the army because I didn't have tattoos,' Ashley said. 'The guys got me stone drunk one night and had me tattooed. I had the damn thing lasered off.' He passed one of the sheets of paper to Drom. 'Here's a skull dream catcher tattoo and feathers for your arms, and abstract shapes for your face. I bought these coloured butterflies for Jasmine. Maggie, for you, a set of vintage guns, a sun, a moon and a heart that says Ashley.'

He saw the expression on my face and laughed. 'Just kidding about the last one.'

I picked up the sheet of tattoos. 'I love the vintage guns. The designs are so intricate.'

Jasmine returned from the bedroom grinning like she'd won

Tattslotto. She spun around to show off her new gear.

'You're unrecognisable and awesome,' Ashley said.

Drom grinned. 'Right on. Seriously rad, salty sister.'

Ashley rolled his eyes. 'You've been boning up on surfer vernacular, haven't you?'

'Yes, indeed.'

Jasmine pointed to her head. 'Check out my ear!'

'Oh, that's hilarious.' I counted ten piercings going all the way around her ear. 'No one would ever know it was you. Amazing.'

Ashley rubbed his hands together. 'Your turn, Maggie. I've kept it simple. They're all new. I know you don't like second hand stuff. Drainpipe jeans, a cool black T-shirt, a hoodie jacket to cover your arms, and a pair of black sketchers. I have these black leather necklaces with pearls and silver and bracelets to match.'

'This stuff is rad, man. I love the leather.'

'I knew you would. I love buying you stuff. Oh, I have this too. I walked past a hairdresser and saw it in the window. They style wigs for woman going through chemo. Anyways, this is a new wig, excellent quality, and she let me have it for a great price.'

He pulled out a short, honey blonde wig, and I jumped up and down in girly leaps. 'Oh, wow, wow, wow, Ashley! That's super rad.'

He handed me the clothes. 'Go on, here's everything. Get your gear on. I'll have champagne waiting for you when you come out.'

I hadn't seen Ashley so upbeat in ages.

When I came out of the bathroom, Drom and Ashley were kitted out in their new clothes. Ashley looked amazing in a pair of black beach pants, a white T-shirt, a military green hurricane jacket and a pair of cool looking surf shoes. He'd done something to his hair that made it look like he'd been in salt water all day. He had amazing beach hair.

Drom looked unrecognisable and five years younger. He'd gone to town with the tattoos. They covered his arms and neck.

Drom eyed me up and down. 'Holy Cooha, you're one hot babe. The blonde hair suits you. I'd never realise it was you.'

'You look beautiful,' Jasmine said. 'So different. I wouldn't have recognised you either.'

Ashley stood hands on hips checking me out. 'I'm in total fambo.'

'Fambo?'

'It means to really like someone apparently. Drom's been teaching me surfer words. The wig looks ace, very natural.'

'I feel like a new person. How did you get your hair all beachy?'

'Jasmine dipped it in salt-water solution, scrunched it up and dried it. Looks awesome, doesn't it?'

'You look the part.'

Drom referred to the surfer's dictionary on this phone. 'In the lingo, Ash's called a senior.' He grinned. 'An old surfer who can still paddle out and catch a ride.'

'Senior? I'll show you senior!' Ashley grabbed Drom around the waist and flipped him upside down. I knew from past experience that friendly tussles between blokes could result in bad things as they tried to outdo one another. I intervened. 'We need to go soon. Can you help me put on a couple of tattoos, please?'

'Sure, luv.' He chucked Drom on the couch and Jasmine started tickling Drom as he lay prone, making him laugh out loud. The sound of laughter in the room made me happy.

'How about a couple of tats on the side of my neck? That's about the only skin that isn't covered in dressings.'

When he finished, I had a beautiful black and white feather on one side, and a small, ornate pistol on the other. He stood back and admired his handy work. 'Christ, you look hot.'

'What about some for you?'

'Okay, give me the old dagger through the heart with two bluebirds, and I dig that wolf head.'

We drank copious amounts of wine and beer as I applied the tattoo transfers. With the encouragement of Jasmine and Drom, I did get a bit carried away. After fifteen minutes, Ashley's arms were covered from top to bottom.

'You look like one tough mother fucker,' Drom said. He pulled a face, realising he'd dropped the 'F' bomb.

'It's okay, Boo's outside,' I said.

Yes, but I can still hear what's going on. You shouldn't encourage them, Maggie. Wash your mouth out Drom, and put two dollars in the swear jar. With Ashley's contribution, we already have fifty dollars for the Lost Dogs Home.

'Crikey, what's Boo's listening range?' Drom asked.

I'm not telling. You always need to be on your best behaviour.

We laughed. It felt great to be always close to Boo, except when it came to swearing that was.

We took selfies and sent a group photo to the folks at home saying we'd made friends with a group of surfer dudes and dudettes. We couldn't wait to hear back.

'Okay tribe, let's go to the pub,' Ashley said.

It was a short walk to the Central Hotel. On the way, we saw Judy, the lady from reception. She eyed us up and down. 'Are you looking for a room? Can I help you with anything?'

Drom changed the tone of his voice and slouched slightly. 'Which way's the Central Hotel?'

Judy looked straight at him. 'Around the corner to the left. You can't miss it.'

'Thanks, Judy.' He spoke in his normal voice and gave her a wink as he walked off. Judy spun around and stared at him, her face breaking into a huge smile. She hurried off shaking her head and chuckling.

'Shouldn't you have kept quiet?' Ashley said.

'Nah. Judy can be trusted. I like her. She's an all right dudette.'

Feeling rather self-conscious, we walked the short distance to the hotel. Having an appearance so different from our normal look made us think we stood out. But no one gave us a second glance. Going up the steps of the hotel, we met a couple of surfer dudes coming out.

'Got a slammin' fat wave down at Eastern Beach, man,' one of them said to Drom.

Drom gave them the surfer's hand signal: he stuck out his thumb and pinky, folded the other three fingers in and rocked his hand back and forth.

'What's that mean?' Jasmine asked.

'Surfer's hand signal. Means hello, hang loose or cool, apparently.'

She grinned. 'You're loving this, aren't you?'

'Yep. I always wanted to surf. It's the one thing I never made time to try. At least now I can pretend.'

Ashley ordered drinks and Jasmine and I secured a table for four by the open fire.

Jasmine looked relaxed. 'It's lovely here. Such a great atmosphere.'

I flicked through the menu. 'It's our favourite pub at Lakes.'

After ordering up big, we waited for the meals, enjoyed our drinks and boned up on surfing vernacular. We were all high on laughter and alcohol. It was as if I had brand new friends, and I couldn't stop looking at them. 'This is such fun. I feel like a different person because I look so different, and it's like I have new mates too.'

Drom slapped Ashley's shoulder. 'It was the best idea. Thanks for all the clobber. Let us know how much we owe you.'

'Forget it. I don't want any money. You pay for the meals and we're good.'

'Hey, we should have new names,' I said. 'That's important.'

Everyone chose a new name. I chose Zara, Jasmine chose Kali, Drom wanted to be Joe, and Ashley was Dave.

Ashley leant over and whispered, 'I can't take my eyes off you, Zara. You look so *hot*,' he said throatily. 'You are totally another girl, so to make this charade even more realistic we should pretend we're an item.' The throaty whisper in the ear did it to me every time, and he knew that.

Drom watched us from across the table. 'Dave thinks that to make things more realistic, he and I should pretend we're an item,' I said to him.

'I reckon that's a top notch idea, Zara.'

'That's not the answer you were supposed to come back with!'

He grinned. 'Kali and I should do the same.' He put his arm around Jasmine, and she looked like she'd arrived in seventh heaven.

Ashley had a fit of the giggles and was still laughing when the waitress brought our meals over. He pulled a crumpled packet of cigarettes from his pocket and put them on the table. He responded to my glare by wrapping an arm around me. 'It's all part of the disguise, Zara.'

Silence reigned as we tucked into the delicious food. I was now in seventh heaven. It felt good to be alive.

Jasmine dropped her knife. It hit her plate with a clatter and bounced onto the floor. She bent down to get it, and on the way up, tugged at Drom's sleeve. She looked pale.

'What's wrong?' he asked.

She kept her eyes down and fiddled with the packet of cigarettes. 'Uncle Lail's here.' Her hands shook. 'I knew he'd come back.'

'Sit up straight, Kali. Act confident. Where is he?'

'Behind you, ordering a meal at the counter.'

'What shall we do, Joe?' I asked.

Joe and Dave answered simultaneously. 'Nothing.'

'Just act like merry surfer dudes and dudettes,' Joe said.

Uncle Lail was at the counter. I pretended to read the menu board above him. He walked towards a table about four feet away from us and looked around the room checking out everyone nearby. His eyes ran over our table and quickly moved on. He didn't register us, or Jasmine, even though he looked right at her.

'He didn't recognise you,' I whispered.

She clutched her glass to steady her trembling hands. 'That was the scariest thing ever.'

Drom was busy texting on his phone.

'What's up, Joe?' Ashley asked

'Fixing up scumbag Lail.'

Three other men entered the pub and joined Uncle Lail at a table. They scanned the area. One settled his eyes on our table and stared at Jasmine.

I held up a beer glass and spoke loudly. 'Want another drink, Kali?'

She gave me the thumbs up, revealing the tattoos on her hand and arm.

The man looked away in disgust.

Ashley stood. 'I'll get the drinks.'

He returned with four glasses of beer and plonked them on the table.

Jasmine gasped as the side doors to the bar burst open. Six armed police made a beeline for Uncle Lail's table.

Lail and his pals leapt to their feet, hurling glasses and chairs at the police. They made a run for the front door, but three officers were waiting for them. Uncle Lail and his cronies were handcuffed and marched to the awaiting divvy van.

Drom smiled at Jasmine. 'That should keep him out of our hair for a while. Kidnapping and assault is a serious crime.'

Jasmine let out a sigh of relief and leant forward and kissed Drom on the cheek. We raised our glasses, clinked and took a sip.

I screwed up my nose. 'It's not our favourite tipple.'

'Leave the beer for us, girls, it was a clever ruse. I'll get you some wine.' When he returned with our wine he looked at Drom. 'You sent a text to Fox, I assume?'

'Yep. The old Swamp Fox is a great ally to have around. He rallied the troops to get here ASAP.'

Ashley raised his glass. 'To the Swamp Fox.'

'To the Swamp Fox.'

Jasmine and I downed our drinks in one go and banged the glasses back down on the table. The guys looked at us in surprise.

Kali grinned. 'Well, we are totally stellar surfer chicks.'

'You two are da bomb, man,' Drom said.

Ashley raised his glass. 'I'll drink to that.'

And we all did, well into the night.

---

[22] *Maggie's Playlist: Disguise — Dirty Heads*

It was late when we arrived back at the hotel. We were in high spirits because of having the chance to do something normal, albeit in disguise. The masquerade affected everyone's personalities, and like actors, we embraced our characters.

Ashley decided we'd made ourselves too rowdy and hyped up to go to sleep, so he made us mugs of hot chocolate. 'We have a big day tomorrow, so need to get some shuteye.'

'Yes, Dad,' Drom said.

I connected my iPhone to the small Bose speaker Jason had given me. 'I need music.' I pressed play.

'That sounds like belly dance music,' Jasmine said.

I nodded. 'Middle Eastern sounding. The song's called Marco Polo, by Loreena McKennitt. She's Canadian.

'I can belly dance,' Jasmine said.

'I love belly dancing. Come on, Jasmine, show us. This music is perfect.'

'I have a hip scarf in my back pack.' Jasmine rummaged through her bag and pulled out a gorgeous long blue scarf. It had scalloped edges and was covered in gold beads. Gold coloured coins dangled and glittered in the light, and tassels hung down from the ends.

'That is so beautiful,' I said. 'Please give us a demonstration. *Please.*'

Jasmine went all bashful on me. 'I feel too embarrassed.'

'You would've danced in front of people before.'

'I used to teach classes, but I feel shy in front of you.'

'I took belly dancing classes years ago,' I said. 'I loved it. I can still remember a few of the moves.' I stood up and made a few figure-eight rotations with my hips.

'That's it!' she said.

'Come on, Jas, do a dance ... please?' I dashed over to the dimmer switch and turned down the lights. We had lit candles earlier, so the ambience in the room was lovely. I dragged the coffee table out of the way so she had plenty of room.

'You win, Maggie.' She tied the scarf around her hips. 'I'll put my sports top on. I didn't bring the full outfit.' She raced to the bathroom.

The guys had been rather quiet, and out of the corner of my eye I saw Ashley give Drom the thumbs up. They were being unobtrusive so as not to put her off, and obviously looking forward to the show. Drom pulled his legs up on the chair and settled back.

Ashley patted the couch next to him. 'Hey, Zara, you're my old lady. Come and sit here.' I sat and he put his arm around me.

Jasmine came out of the bathroom wearing a black sports top, which was short enough to give her a bare midriff. She knelt on the floor in the middle of the room. With her forehead touching the carpet, she swept her long hair over her head so it lay on the floor in front of her. Her arms lay outstretched beside her hair.

I turned up the music. Bongo drums beat a slow hypnotic rhythm, and a sitar sent its mournful spiritual sounds into the room.

Jasmine's arms moved backwards and out to the sides like a bird stretching its wings. Her dusky shoulders began to rotate in turn, and her arms flexed, reminding me of an Indian goddess, as she raised her torso upwards. Her long black tresses hid her face. As Jasmine rose to her knees, she swept her hair backwards in a flourish to reveal her face.

She tentatively moved her hips to the beat of the music, swaying from side to side. Her hair flowed over her shoulders and her eyes were closed. Her hands moved slowly through the air as though drawing intricate designs. Her hips moved independently from the rest of her body, gyrating in smooth and intricate orbits in harmony with her upper torso.

Jasmine's eyes flicked open. Her gaze was confident and direct. A shapely bare leg revealed itself through the shimmering blue material as she slowly rose to her feet.

The music quickened. She took a step forward, and a bare leg skimmed through the glittering material. Her hips gave powerful flicks up and down. She walked towards Drom, each step creating a cascade of movement though her body. Her arms moved up and down through the air, and her torso twisted in sensuous circles.

The buzzing, exotic sound of a hurdy-gurdy added its voice to the song. An accordion, more drums and the insistent chiming of finger cymbals filled the room. The pulsing, hypnotic rhythms transported us to another place and time, a harem of old.

Jasmine spun around and faced away from us. Her hips flicked forcefully from side to side in time with the music, creating a mesmerising display. The beads on her hip scarf caught the light and shimmied and bounced as her torso followed the rhythm. Stretching out a leg, she twirled around, her arms moving over her head. Hands joined at the wrists, like the wings of a bird, they spun around each other as her whole body gave itself to the increasing tempo of the music. Every part of Jasmine matched the intensity of the drums, beat for beat, sound for sound.

She flipped her hair forwards and back, and with each clash

of the cymbals, she collected the edges of her scarf and pulled the material to the sides, revealing her legs. On her toes now, she rotated, her feet moving up and down in tiny steps that translated to impossibly fast movements of her hips.

Her arms moved fluidly mimicking a bird in flight, her breasts shimmied from side to side, and her entire body pulsated to the music. She *was* the music.

The music climbed to a crescendo. Jasmine twirled around faster and faster, creating a shimmering whirlpool of gossamer around her. As the music hit its final note, Jasmine dipped her head forward and then with a flick, tossed back her mane of hair and froze.

The only sound in the room was Jasmine's breathing, as her chest heaved from exertion. We sat spellbound and speechless.

Ashley's voice was hoarse. 'Your jaw's hanging open, Drom. It's not a good look.'

Jasmine laughed. The spell was broken, and we gave her an enthusiastic round of applause. Ashley fanned himself with a magazine. 'I've never seen anything so beautiful, so damn erotic, in my whole life.'

'Truly stunning, Jasmine,' I said, 'I was transported.'

Drom sat there shaking his head. When he finally could put words together he said, 'You were divine. It was transcendent. You were totally in the "now", and you took us all with you.'

'I just thought it was damn hot,' Ashley said. 'You'll have to teach Maggie.' He looked at me and grinned, and I rolled my eyes. Jasmine giggled. Her eyes, despite the injury, sparkled with joy, and her whole persona was vibrant with energy.

She knelt in front of Drom and looked him straight in the eye. 'I really like you, and I want you to be my first. Tonight.'

I felt Ashley start and he looked at me with raised eyebrows.

Jasmine paused, took a breath and continued. 'If you say no, I will understand. If you don't feel the same about me, I will understand. I realise this is being forward, but I don't want to play games. I'm asking for what I want. You can do this tonight with no strings attached. I understand you don't want to be in a relationship with anyone, so there's a bus to Canberra tomorrow, and I will be on it. Ashley has given me money for the ticket. But before I leave, I would like you to be my first.' Jasmine gave a tiny nod for emphasis.

It was one of the few times I'd seen Drom lost for words. I could hear his brain spinning. It was stuck in a groove called fear.

Ashley grinned. 'What the hell is there to think about?'

Seeing Drom's gob smacked face, I said, 'Um, I think Ashley and I should go in the other room. Give you two privacy.'

Drom woke from his trance. 'You knew Jasmine wanted to leave?'

I shrugged my shoulders.

'We had a bit of a chat about things,' Ashley admitted.

I yelled to Drom in my mind: *Drom, talk to Jasmine, you idiot. Say something to her. At least acknowledge what she said. She's put herself out there.*

'Um, Jasmine, I don't know what to say. I mean it's sad you're leaving, but I guess you've made up your mind. I'm not sure if…'

'Oh, jeez,' Ashley muttered.

'Um … perhaps you'd be better to…'

I could see Jasmine was becoming upset.

'What are you trying to say?' she asked him. 'It's either yes or no. It's not that hard.'

He looked up at her. 'It is that hard. Some things I don't take lightly.'

'You're frightened,' she said softly. 'You feel fear for yourself, not me. Scared for your heart. You lock it away. I'm sad for you, but I understand.' She stood and turned away. Drom leapt to his feet and took her by the shoulders. He looked into her eyes.

181

Jasmine flushed. 'I'm sorry, my face…'

'Your face is beautiful. You're beautiful, and I am honoured.' He took Jasmine by the hand, led her into the bedroom and closed the door.

Ashley let out a sigh. 'Halle-bloody-lujah.'

---

[23] *Maggie's Playlist: Marco Polo — Loreena McKennitt*

'When love beckons to you, follow him, though his ways are hard and steep. And when his wings enfold you yield to him, though the sword hidden among his pinions may wound you.' — Kahlil Gibran

Ashley could easily kill me with his bare hands, but it was a risk we seemed willing to take for some human warmth and comfort. He lay next to me, fast asleep on his stomach with one arm cuddling a pillow.

The morning sunlight filtered through the curtains highlighting him in a golden hue. Shadows played in the contours of his muscled arms. His hair was swept back off his face. I wished I had my sketchbook.

He said he'd wake us for an early start, but when I checked my phone it was after nine.

Thankfully, we'd made it through another night together without incident. Ashley religiously took his drugs, plus he added a Valium whenever I shared the bed with him. He also made sure his weapons were in the other room. The risk of him having a combat nightmare would always be there.

Despite our strong bond and attraction, Ashley never crossed the line. He was the perfect gentleman, which surprised me. He treasured his friendship with Jason and would never do the dirty on a mate, even though he had certainly pushed the envelope in the past.

I missed Jason so much that I physically ached for him.

Having Ashley next to me at night made it easier. Sort of.

My mind turned to Drom and Jasmine. I smiled as I wondered how their night had turned out and thought of how Jasmine had won his heart.

Ashley woke and saw me. 'What are you smiling about?'

'Mornin'. I didn't realise you were awake. I was thinking about Drom and Jasmine. She did well to change his mind, go against his philosophy.'

'It was the dance that did it. Hooley dooley. Who could resist after that?'

'Drom's stronger than that. He's not easily swayed. He must have feelings for her.'

'He has. He told me. And it's doing his head in. He wants to be a free agent, fighting the good fight.'

I leant up on one arm. 'We've slept in. It's nine already.'

'I know. Change of plans. I wanted to give Drom and Jasmine more time together. We didn't get to bed until late. I mean, it's her first time, it should be special, not rushed.'

I ruffled his hair. 'You're sweet for a big tough guy.'

'We need to change your dressings. How are you feeling?'

'I'll be glad when I can get all this stuff off me. It's irritating. What time are we going to leave?'

'Just after ten I reckon. If we can get to Hanging Rock around four, most people should be gone by then. That gives us about three hours of daylight. Do you think that's enough?'

'Who knows? I'll text Fox and tell him our plans.'

He rolled over onto his back and stretched out an arm. 'Do I get a morning hug?'

'Never say no to a hug.' I snuggled into the crook of his arm. 'Hugs are scientifically proven to be beneficial for your health.'

'How so?'

'Hugs decrease stress, boost your immune system, increase oxytocin levels, which help to increase the feel-good hormones such as serotonin and dopamine. They keep you feeling calm.

Hugs reduce inflammation due to the release of oxytocin, plus they lower your blood pressure, improve pain tolerance and reduce depression and anxiety. We need as many as we can get.'

'Yep, I knew about the oxytocin levels.'

'A piss weak hug won't do it though. They need to be firm and meaningful to stimulate oxytocin release.'

'I can do firm and meaningful.' Ashley swung me on top of him and made like a koala. He laughed. 'How's the oxytocin levels now, luv?'

I giggled. 'Getting right up there.'

There was a specific series of gentle knocks on the door.

'Come in, Drom,' Ashley said. 'We're working on our oxytocin levels.'

Drom stuck his head around door. 'So that's what you call it.'

'I'd say your levels would be pretty high right now, Dromski,' Ashley said. 'You've got a glow about you.'

Drom came in and sat on the edge of the bed. I rolled myself off Ashley.

'I thought we were leaving early. You slipping, Ash?' he asked.

'Nah, last minute change of plans. Thought I'd let you two love birds have extra time. Still, it was probably all over in a couple of seconds. It would've been awhile for you, hey Drom?' Ashley said, baiting him.

Drom wasn't taking the bait.

'Jasmine's ready to go, if you want to say goodbye. The bus is leaving at ten thirty,' he said softly.

Ashley sat up in bed and looked shocked. 'What the hell? What do you mean she's leaving? You can't have been that bad!'

'That was the plan. She told us last night she was going to leave. Don't act so surprised. You gave her the money for the ticket.'

'You didn't ask her to stay?' I said.

'No, why would I? She'd already said she was going.'

'You two did … you know?' I said.

'Yes. Like I said I would.'

Ashley shook his head. 'You are fair dinkum unbelievable. You told me you had feelings for her. Why the hell didn't you ask her to stay?'

'You know why. I don't want to get attached. It gets too complicated. Too dangerous.'

'So you never want to be in a permanent relationship?' I said. 'Have someone to love and who loves you?'

'I have people I love. You're my family, I love you, and you love me. And yes, I do want a special relationship, but it's not the right time.'

'It will never be the right time for us,' Ashley replied. 'If you resonate with Jasmine, like you said you did, then it would be a mistake to let her go.'

'But if she wanted to stay, she would. Why's she going then?'

I threw my hands up. 'Because you didn't ask her to stay, you idiot! She loves you, and it's painful to stay around someone you love who doesn't reciprocate. She needs to hear you say it.'

'Particularly after last night,' Ashley said. 'If you didn't express how you feel, no wonder she's taking off.'

'That's game playing. I don't play games.'

'Telling someone how you feel is not playing games,' I said. 'You're too detached for your own good. Maybe it's best she leaves.'

Ashley nodded. 'I agree. She'd be better off without you. She needs to get on that bus and go. There's nothing for her here. It'd just be a pain in the arse for you.'

We heard a sound and turned to see Jasmine go past the bedroom door. Footsteps moved quickly down the passageway. The front door slammed shut.

'She overheard us!' I leapt out of bed and went into the kitchen.

A note lay on the kitchen table. I picked it up; it had

186

tearstains on it.

Ashley came up behind me. 'What's it say?'

'It says, "Dear Maggie, Ashley and Drom. I hate goodbyes and I especially hate saying goodbye to all of you. I can never thank you enough for what you've done for me. For saving me and avenging my sisters. You are so courageous and kind. As soon as I'm on my feet I will repay the money I owe you. I promise. Thank you all for everything. Thank you, Drom. I understand. Stay safe. All my love. Jasmine." And then there's hugs and kisses.'

'Ah, jeez,' Ashley said, 'I would've liked to have given her a goodbye hug.'

'Me too. I'll miss her. She had such a peaceful presence.'

Drom sat at the kitchen table and rested his head in his hands.

I started making coffee. 'We need to make a move once we've had this.'

'I'll pack and clean up,' Ashley said.

Drom stood. 'I'll have a shower first then.'

I nodded at his tattoos. 'If you don't get soap on them or rub them, they should stay put for a couple of days.'

He went into the bathroom and closed the door.

Ashley looked at me. 'I'd thought he'd go after her.'

'That's our Drom. Other worldly.'

'More like stupid.'

When we were ready to depart, Ashley checked his watch. 'Ten twenty-five. Jasmine will be on her way in five minutes.'

Drom had returned to the kitchen table where he sat gazing into space. As I watched him, something tapped away at my brain, trying to break through. I sat in front of him and let out the words that were hammering for freedom. 'To fear love is to fear life, and those who fear life are already three parts dead.'

Drom started and his eyes latched onto mine. 'Why did you say that?'

'It wasn't me. It was someone else.'

He leapt up from the table, sending his chair flying. He pushed past Ashley and raced out the front door. It slammed behind him.

'Jesus, Maggie. What was all that about?'

'He's given himself permission to love on an earthly plane.'

Ashley looked frustrated. 'Why does everyone speak in riddles around here?'

'There's no doubt Drom can love. He loves on an ethereal level. His love is all encompassing. He doesn't do well loving on a personal level, with all the nitty gritty that goes with it. He's had a change of heart. I reckon he's gone after her.'

Ashley checked his watch. 'Crikey, he's left his run a bit late. Let's get the truck and go to the bus stop.'

We raced down the stairs and clambered into the truck. Ashley took off before I'd even had time to shut the door properly. The bus stop was five minutes away. In the distance, we saw Drom running flat out. He leapt over and around anything that got in his way. The bus pulled out just as Drom hit the back panel with his fist. There was nothing to hold onto. He was too late.

Drom stood in the road, his fists clenched, staring after the bus.

We pulled up next to him. Ashley nodded his head. 'Get in, mate, you're blocking the road.'

He climbed into the truck. 'I was too late.'

'It's never too late, mate.' We were pushed back in our seats as Ashley accelerated, the engine roared as he chased the bus. Once he was behind it, he blasted the horn and flashed his lights. He had one arm out the window indicating for the bus to pull over.

The bus kept going. So did Ashley. A face appeared at the back window. Jasmine. Then she disappeared. After a minute, the bus slowed and pulled over. We drove in behind it.

Drom leapt out and ran to the front of the bus. When the doors opened, Jasmine launched herself into his arms. The force nearly knocked him off his feet. He spun her around. They kissed, deeply and passionately.

The bus driver jumped out and opened the luggage compartment. He grinned as he placed Jasmine's bag next to them. The driver gave us the thumbs up before getting back in the bus. We could hear cheering as the bus pulled away. People were at the windows, clapping and smiling.

Drom and Jasmine walked back to the truck. They were both beaming. I ran to Jasmine and hugged her. 'I'm so glad we have you back.'

'Thank you, Maggie, it was you, it had to be.'

'Actually, I'm not sure who it was.'

Drom helped Jasmine into the truck. 'Thanks, Ash.' He looked at me. 'That quote. It was my mother. It's by Bertrand Russell. Mum said it was a quote I should take heed of. I'd forgotten all about it until the words came out of your mouth.'

'Your mum's passed on?'

'Yes, died early from breast cancer,' he said softly.

'Well, she's still watching out for you.'

'Thanks, Mum.' Drom leant over and kissed Jasmine.

Ashley checked the rearview mirror. 'Oh, jeez. It's gonna be like having two lovesick teenagers on our hands.'

'Lucky them,' I whispered.

'Too right.'

---

[24] *Maggie's Playlist: Scared of Love — Nate Dog*

A sense of foreboding dogged me as we drove along the highway: destination, Hanging Rock. It seemed to be my general "go to" state these days. My gut instinct screamed. *Turn around! Don't go! Run!*

But what could I do? We had to go there.

Maybe it would be okay. Maybe I was wrong. I was stressed, after all. How bad could it be?

My phone beeped. A text from Dad. 'Dad said we need to let Fox know when we get to the city. He'll follow us to Hanging Rock. By the way, the photo of our surfer friends fooled everyone 'cept Fox.'

'That figures,' Drom said. 'He's a detective after all. I would've been disappointed if he didn't pick it. It's amazing the others didn't twig.'

I adjusted my wig, tucking up a piece of stray hair. 'Yeah, the disguises are awesome. Can't wait to get a couple more costumes.'

Ashley raised his eyebrows. 'A French maid costume would be nice.'

'Oh, I asked for that, didn't I? Mister one-track mind.'

Something caught my eye on the console — a small, smooth

rock. It gleamed with opal highlights as I picked it up and held it to the light. 'Hey, what's this rock?'

'It fell out of your jeans pocket when I was folding them,' Ashley said.

'Fair dinkum.' I ran the smooth rock between my fingers and jumped as my brain buzzed with a deep, low rattle that shook the bones in my cranium. I dropped the rock in fright. 'Jesus!'

'*What?*' Ashley said. 'What is it?'

'The rock. It must be from the Nargun. Its voice was in my head.'

'A communication device?' Drom asked.

'Must be.' I picked up the rock and slipped it in my pocket.

Ashley grinned. 'Maggie's got a magic rock.'

'Well, Nargun did say all rocks are our friend. I hope he changed his mind about the bit where if we fail, all rocks will be our enemy.'

Drom sharply inhaled his breath. 'He said *that?*'

'Yes, but I told him he was being a bit harsh. I think he came around.'

'I hope so,' Drom said. 'We have enough problems without rock enemies.'

'Ain't that the truth,' Ashley said.

'Still no word or sign of Jason?' Jasmine asked.

I shook my head. 'No, nothing. Fox has pulled out all stops, but it's as if he's vanished.'

Ashley glanced at me. 'It's the same as when the Prof went missing.'

'Hopefully, like the Prof, Jason will return to us unharmed,' Drom said.

'It's the worst thing in the world when someone you love goes missing,' I said. 'They vanish and you don't know if they're dead or alive. You can't move on with your life. You can't grieve because you don't want to give up hope. At what point do you decide to grieve? To draw a line in the sand and say, they're dead.

It's the most horrible experience.'

'About 35,000 people are reported missing in Australia each year. One every fifteen minutes,' Drom said. 'About ninety five percent are found, but there are a significant number who remain long term missing.'

'That's so many people!' Jasmine said. 'And now my brothers and cousins will be on that list. I feel sad for my parents, even though they caused so much pain. My parents will never know what happened. I have to carry that knowledge. I wish I didn't. It's another pain to bear.'

'It weighs heavy on us all, Jasmine. All the people taken by roaches, gone in black holes, no evidence, nothing. I feel sorry for Fox most of all, in the role he has to play. It sucks,' I said.

The conversation sent us off into our own thoughts and made me feel depressed. The scenery as we approached Melbourne made me feel even more depressed. The suburban sprawl with its voracious appetite was silently and efficiently devouring the countryside. Farms, orchards and green spaces now grew McMansions, huge homes that took up entire blocks. A sea of rooftops replaced a sea of green. I wanted to run away.

The city was no better. Huge towers of ugliness poked skywards, block after block of tiny apartments with tiny balconies, displaying sad pot plants and limp washing.

In the midst of the modern ugliness, occasional old buildings remained. A delight to the eye, like rare flowers, they illuminated the grey concrete surrounds with warm red bricks and pleasing designs. They were diamonds in the dross.

The sound of a motorbike disturbed my musings. A Ducati Diavel motorbike cruised along next to us.

'It's Fox!' I said excitedly, and felt my spirits rise. He lifted his visor and grinned. I waved. 'It's so good to see him!'

Jasmine laughed. 'Check out the dog!'

'That's Schmoo. Boo will be very happy.'

Fox had attached his custom-made Royal Enfield sidecar to

the bike. Schmoo sported a pair of goggles and sat up proud in the bullet shaped pod. Boo poked her head out of the tarpaulin as soon as she heard Schmoo's name. Her eyes were bright and her pink tongue was out, ears flapping in the breeze.

I would like to ride with Schmoo, Maggie. Do you think Fox would let me?

'I'm sure he would, Boo. Maybe on the way back?'

As we left the city, we passed DFO, The Direct Factory Outlet. Rows of huge billboards loomed above us, advertising all the brands we needed to feel like we'd made it. Streams of cars sat bumper to bumper, queuing to get in, desperate to donate their hard-earned money at the shrine of consumerism.

Ashley shook his head. 'Have a look at it. It's insane.'

'I'm on the wrong planet,' Drom said.

The scenery became more pleasing to the eye as we approached the Macedon Ranges. An unusual abundance of rain had transformed the normally brown landscape into rolling hills of lush green.

'Not far to go now,' Ashley said. 'I haven't been to Hanging Rock for years. The place does get to you. It reeks of mystery. It's straightforward going up, but boy, did I get lost trying to come down.'

'The Aboriginal people wouldn't climb the rock due to the harmful spirits that live in the crevices,' Drom said. 'Many indigenous people feel uncomfortable on the rock and don't hang around long. They say the rock has a presence they don't like. They did use the forested flats around the rock for thousands of years though. Oh, and don't souvenier any bits of rock. Apparently, it's similar to Uluru. People have sent back their rock samples because of the bad luck it brought them.'

'Oh great, that's just what we need, harmful spirits,' I said. 'I hope there's none in the crevices I'll be looking in.'

There weren't many cars left by the time we drove into the car park. It appeared most of the tourists had headed off. Fox pulled in next to us and dismounted. He took off his helmet and held out his arms. I rushed over and flung myself into them.

'It's good to see you, Maggie.'

'Ditto, Fox. I've missed you and Schmoo. I know Boo has too.'

Boo floated out of the truck and sat in the sidecar next to Schmoo. They were in a face licking frenzy.

Ashley grinned. 'Jeepers. Check out the dogs. Ain't love grand.'

'Dogs aren't allowed up on the rock,' I said. 'They can hide in the back of the truck. That way if I need Boo, she can get out.'

'Okay, let's get going,' Ashley said.

I shivered. 'Christ, it's *freezing*. I'm going to need my jacket.'

Ashley grimaced into the icy wind. 'Spanner weather.'

Spanner weather? I hadn't heard of it.

'Tightens your nuts,' Ashley said, in response to my questioning look.

'Oh, ha ha.'

'You'll warm up if we go to the top. It's a steep climb,' Ashley said. 'Are you picking up any signals?'

'Not yet.'

'Well, put your head in gear and lead on before I freeze to death,' Fox said.

We walked along the path and I stared up at the rock looming above me. The group followed behind as I dissolved into myself and opened my mind to the crystal vibration.

'Don't let Maggie out of your sight,' I heard Ashley say softly to Drom. 'She can go a bit loopy under the influence of crystal.'

'No worries.'

I had no thought. My body moved under the pulse of a vibration that now hummed in my mind. At the foot of the rock, huge moss-covered shards and pinnacles thrust upwards. We were in shadow. It was icy cold, and my heart beat in time with the sound of dripping water.

194

I followed a path to the foot of some stairs and began to ascend. We passed under the hanging rock, a huge boulder suspended between two rocks, and then to an escarpment from which we could see the land stretched out beneath us. The racetrack below was a ring of white around a field of green.

I clambered through rock crevices near the edge of the rock, keeping my eyes firmly on the ground under my feet. The humming increased, driving me onwards. I couldn't have stopped if I'd wanted to. Through narrow hallways of rock, I leapt over angled holes that opened out to the ground. I wondered vaguely how I was going to leap back over those jagged spaces.

'Christ, Maggie, slow down a bit,' Ashley yelled. 'We can't keep up. It's dangerous.'

'I can't. You'll have to let me go.'

'I'm right up your hammer,' Drom said. 'I'll go with you. The others can slow to a safer pace. I'm loving this.'

Up and around, down and around, in and over, over and under, my feet flew across the rock. I clambered up boulders as sure footed as a goat, and then stepped forward into nothing. Drom grabbed my jacket and hauled me backwards. I fell on top of him.

'Jesus *Christ!* You would've gone straight down.' He helped me up and slapped me gently on the cheeks. 'Maggie? *Maggie, wake up.'*

I awoke as though from a dream and found myself staring into Drom's blue eyes as they worriedly gazed back at me. I started as I registered the sheer drop below. 'Crikey, that was close. I was in a trance.'

'Tell me about it.'

'Well, that's where I have to go. Down there. Through that hole.'

'You're kidding.'

'Nope.'

'Surely there's another way? I mean exactly where do you have to go?'

I stared down at the jagged rocks surrounding the void. 'I'll find out once I go.'

The sound of footsteps and heavy breathing reached our ears as Fox, Ashley and Jasmine caught up. They were so puffed they couldn't speak. When Ashley finally managed to utter a word, it was what we all expected. 'Fuck me. I thought I was fit. You're not fit, Maggie. How the hell?'

'I don't know how the hell, Ashley. It's the crystal energy pulling me. Drom saved me, again.' I pointed to the hole in the rock. 'If it wasn't for him...'

Ashley craned his neck over the edge. 'Holy snapping vertebrae.'

I screwed up my nose and whispered, 'I have to go down *there*.'

Ashley lay down on his stomach and stuck his head into the hole. 'Can you hold my ankles, Drom? I feel like the rock's pulling me in.'

After a moment Ashley said, 'If you can let yourself down through the hole, there's a ledge. Once you're there, it's almost like stepping-stones, boulders sticking out all over the place. In fact, it's a bit of an optical illusion. If you had gone through, Maggie, you may well have fallen on the side of the ledge.'

'Well that's comforting to know,' I said.

'Can we use your climbing ropes to lower me down?'

'Yep, cos there's no way you're gonna be free climbing on my watch. I'm not thrilled about this.'

'Me neither.' A peculiar clenching sensation struck my nether regions as I registered the drop below.

'Do we *all* have to go?' Jasmine asked.

'No, luv,' Ashley said. 'We'll get Drom down first, then Maggie. See where Maggie reckons it is.'

'I need to go first,' I said.

Ashley eyed me. 'Have you rock climbed before?'

'No.'

He turned to Drom. 'You?'

'Yes. Lots.'

'And so have I,' Ashley said. 'So, Maggie, it would behoove you to have two people who know what the hell they're doing on each end of the rope, comprendo?'

'And it would behoove you to not get so snarky with me, Mister Big Shot Rock Hopper. I didn't see you keeping up with me. I'm going first and that's it.'

Ashley snorted.

'Okay, let's get you harnessed up,' Drom said.

They lowered me down through the hole, and I immediately saw what Ashley was saying. It *was* an optical illusion. There was a ledge within easy reach of my feet. I dropped onto it and looked around. I felt like an eagle on a perch. The sun broke through the clouds and illuminated the escarpment. The warmth on my face was a welcome relief. I turned and looked behind me. There was a cave going back into the rock wall behind me.

I stared into the gloom where sunshine disappeared into blackness. One thing came to mind — one thing only. Cave crickets. I couldn't face another encounter with those creepy bugs. I hated them worse than the roaches, and that was saying something.

'You right there?' Fox shouted.

'I'm on the ledge, and there's a cave going back into the rock. It's where I have to go.' My head vibrated intensely.

'I'm coming down,' Drom said.

Drom lowered himself through the hole. He had no ropes and swung onto the ledge with consummate ease. He grinned. 'Hi, Maggie.' He was enjoying himself. 'I have a torch.' He shone it into the cave and slid forward on his belly to explore further. 'It goes back about fifteen feet and then there's a hole going straight down. A long, narrow chamber.' He slid back. 'I can't see the bottom.'

'Crap. Next you'll be telling me it's only wide enough for me to fit.'

'Yep. Sorry 'bout that.'

'Double crap.' I repressed a dreadfully strong urge to let off a chain of expletives about crystals and life in general. I yelled them loudly in my head instead.

I can hear you from down here, Maggie. That's appalling.

'Shut up, Boo. Now's not the time.'

Can I help you get the crystal? I don't mind tiny, narrow, dark, claustrophobic spaces that have all manner of flora and creepy fauna in them.

'I wish you could, Boo, but no. Thanks for the descriptive offer anyway. Made me feel a whole lot better. *Not.*

Drom grinned. 'Cheeky dog! Here's the torch. Sit here and chillax. I'll fill in Ash with the situation.' He stood on the ledge outside the cave and I heard his muffled speech. Sitting in the rock cave was quiet and peaceful. The dark jagged cave entrance framed the sky and clouds. It reminded me of being in the Nargun's Den. I was a bat in a hidey-hole. It was almost cozy.

The crystals had never led me astray, never let me get hurt, well, not that much, anyway. However, I couldn't be totally sure; it was early days. Perhaps crystals were totally dispassionate. I could simply be disposable—collateral damage in the fight for light. Fingers crossed that wouldn't be the case.

The humming buzzed in my bones, and despite the doubts running through my mind, I had an overwhelming urge to slither down into that hole.

I crawled on all fours and leaned into it. It was wider than my shoulders. Just. I swung myself around and sat on the edge. My legs dangled inwards. I kicked my heels against the side of the tunnel. A waft of moss and decay filled my nostrils. My atoms throbbed with the crystal hum.

Tucking the torch in my bra, I crossed my arms over my

chest. Gravity took me as I pushed off into the blackness.

I crawled into the dank blackness at the back of the cave. 'Maggie, are you there? Maggie!'

Nothing.

'Ashley's coming down. We're going to lower you into the hole. Maggie?'

From outside I heard Ashley yell, 'Drom, what's going on?'

I crawled out onto the ledge, my gut twisted with fear. 'Get down here! Bring a torch!'

He landed on the ledge with a thud, carabiners and metal anchors clinking on the ropes round his neck. He switched on the torch and shone it towards the back of the cave. 'What's happened to the other torch? Where's Maggie?'

'She's gone. Quick! Give me the torch.'

'What do you mean, she's *gone*?'

'Exactly that. She's vanished.' I shone the torch into the hole. 'She's in a harness, and the end of the rope's still here.'

Ashley grabbed the rope and pulled. 'There's nothing attached! This is a fifty metre rope, about forty's been used.' He pulled until finally the end appeared with an empty harness attached. His voice was a low growl. 'What the hell did I say to you, Drom? Don't take your eyes off her!' He leant over the hole and shone his torch into the darkness. There was a note of panic in his voice. *'Maggie! Maaaaggggggiiieeee, make a noise!'*

Nothing.

Two kookaburras shrieked outside. Their hysterical laughter bounced around the walls of the cave and created layered echoes of mocking cackles that assaulted our ears.

Ashley shone his torch all around the cave walls and ceiling.

'Maybe there's another way out.' He felt across the rock, looking in every nook and cranny. 'Nup. There's nothing. She's in there. She couldn't have gone over the edge because you were standing there. So, she must've fallen in the hole.' Ashley dragged his hands through his hair. His jaw was clenched and his eyes blazed. He looked at me, shook his head and turned away in disgust.

'So now what, Drom? Any ideas?'

In the background, someone was yelling over the kookaburra's maniacal laughter.

'Ashley, someone's calling. Outside.'

We moved to the ledge and looked up. Fox's face appeared through the hole.

'We've got trouble, guys. Get your arses up here.'

I jumped off the ledge and swung myself up through the hole. I was glad to get away from Ashley. His anger towards me was palpable, and in that enclosed space it was overwhelming.

Ashley followed behind me. 'We've got trouble too. Maggie's missing. Vanished. Drom took his eye off her and she's gone. No sign of her, and I just pulled an empty harness out of the tunnel.'

'*What?*'

'Yep. She's not responding to our calls,' I said.

Fox walked over to the edge. 'Have a look down there. We may have to deal with this first.'

A fleet of motorbikes rumbled up the road next to the rock. I counted twelve. Each bike was towing a small trailer. It was hard to see clearly, but they looked similar to greyhound trailers.

'Bringing their dogs to race at the track?' Ashley suggested.

Fox pointed. 'See the symbol on the large trailer?'

'A Catherine wheel, three interlocking sixes, *shit!*' Ashley said. 'We have roach people.'

The bikers dismounted, and each of them went to the back of their trailer and opened the doors. Large black animals leapt out and gathered around one man. The creatures stood silently, waiting.

'Christ, they're some weird dogs. They're *massive*,' Ashley said.

The biker gave a command and the animals turned as one and raced in a pack up the path. Their gait was swift but erratic.

An involuntary shiver ran down my spine. 'They look like a pack of gigantic huntsman spiders.'

'They're coming up the rock,' Fox said. 'I've got one gun, fully loaded, and one magazine.'

'We've got a gun and a spare mag each,' Ashley said.

'Ninety bullets, around seven bullets per animal,' Fox said. 'It's gonna take a few to bring those things down if you don't get a head shot first off.'

'We're going to kill them?' I asked.

Ashley gave me a look. 'What else do you suggest? Give 'em a pat on the head and a couple of bickies?'

'I've got nine throwing knives. I can get head strikes no worries.'

'You'll need something more like an axe to get through those skulls. Those things are mammoth,' Fox said.

'What if we go down on the ledge, in the cave. They'll never get us there,' Jasmine suggested.

'Yes, but we'd be trapped. There's no way out. They'll be waiting for us,' I said. I held out the harness. 'You go into the cave, Jas. You'd be safe there. Come on.'

Fox helped me lower her onto the ledge, while Ashley checked the bullets in his magazine. 'Now, whatever you do, guys, if you see a dog, don't run. Don't stare it down either, or turn your back. Get up against a rock so they can't flank you. For an instant kill you'll need to shoot them through the top of the skull. A level shot at the base of the ear may do it. With our 9mm pistols we'll have to get close. If not, be prepared to empty your gun.'

'And you know this how?' Fox asked Ash.

'I was attacked by a pack of wild dogs in Iraq,' he said grimly. 'And they were half the size of these suckers.'

Fox looked horrified. 'I'm out of my depth here.'

'Me too,' I said. 'The thought of having to kill a dog makes me sick.'

Ashley whacked the magazine back into his gun. 'Well, if you don't, you'll certainly be feeling sick when it rips out your throat and tears you limb from limb. If you can't hack it, I suggest you go hide in the cave with Jasmine.'

I didn't answer. His sarcasm was fuelled by anger.

'What we need in this situation is a nice big shot gun.' Fox imitated the action. 'Chk. Chk. Boom! I've called the troops. Hopefully they'll be here soon.'

The baying of the dogs echoed around the rock and mingled with the harsh laughter of the kookaburras. The wind sprang up and whistled eerily through the rock crevices. Dark clouds gathered overhead. The air held the scent of rain. Eucalyptus trees around the rock swayed in the wind, and the rustling of their leaves whispered sinister warnings.

'Both find yourselves a strategic position,' Ashley instructed. 'Preferably where they can't get behind or above you.'

We spaced ourselves around an area away from the cave. Surrounded by rocks, it gave the impression of an arena. Each of us crouched on top of a rock to give us the best angle. It was hard to find the perfect spot, but we figured we could cover each other if things went pear shaped.

Fox looked around anxiously. 'It's a friggin' gladiator ring.

Do we yell to attract them?'

Ashley pointed with his gun as the first creature poked its head around a rock. 'Don't need to. Holy abomination. What the *hell*?'

'Another Tapakah mutant creation by the looks of it,' I said.

What came into the arena wasn't any dog. It was twice the size of a panther and as black as the night sky. Large ebony eyes glittered in a dog like face. The skull was exceedingly large and square, with small ears that lay flat back against the side of its head. Rows of glistening white teeth were set in a wide, cavernous mouth. A black tongue flicked out as saliva dripped and pooled at its clawed feet.

That's where the similarity to a canine ended. It hissed rather than snarled. The torso was covered in plates of chitinous panels, which served as body armour. Six muscled legs gave it movement peculiar to an insect.

The head was held low as it swayed slightly from side to side. The eyes were hypnotic, drawing me in. It held me in its cold, dispassionate stare. Its nose quivered as it read the air, and then it scuttled sideways up a rock and stopped. Its claws adhered to the lichen-covered surface, holding it horizontally on the steep rock.

'Jasmine, will be trapped!' I whispered, feeling the panic in my chest. 'It can go *anywhere*.'

'Go get her out. I'll distract it.' Fox clapped his hands together.

The effect was instantaneous. The creature scuttled, half flew, over the rocks at speed. It made a beeline straight towards Fox, its mouth a hissing, drooling cavity of white teeth.

I made a dash for the hole and leaned through it as a shot echoed around the arena. Jasmine sat on the edge looking terrified.

I held out my hand. 'You have to move! They're not dogs, they're *things*. They can crawl anywhere.'

Her voice shook. 'Yes. I saw them coming up.'

She grabbed my hand and I hauled her out. This was my worst nightmare. I had to protect her; she had no weapons. I was no longer a free agent. How the hell would I keep her safe? I hated having to feel like that.

Three more shots echoed out, and we turned to see the creature collapse on its side, legs twitching. Black fluid flowed from its head and pooled on the ground. The body lay right at Fox's feet. Its jaws twitched around his ankle. He kicked it away in disgust and wiped his sleeve over his face. He was covered in a dark, tar-like substance. The stink of gangrenous flesh filled my nostrils and made my stomach turn. Fox made odd noises as he dry retched.

The sky grew dark, and the wind howled around us, whipping up dust and ripping leaves from trees. Thunder cracked overhead.

The heads of more beasts appeared over the top of the rocks behind Fox and Ashley. They were sneaking up the outside of the rock.

'Ash, Fox, behind you! Get into the middle. Now!' I grabbed Jasmine by the hand and pulled her with me to the centre of the arena. Fox and Ashley scrambled off the rocks to join me.

'Stand back to back!' Ashley ordered

We stood with our backs together, and Jasmine in the middle, as the creatures crawled down over the rocks towards us. We were surrounded.

A loud noise filled my mind. *What on earth?*

The soundtrack of *Apocalypse Now* blasted into my brain as a black shape rose up over the rocks. Resembling a mini Blackhawk helicopter, it was Boo, channelling *Ride of the Valkyries*. Metal glinted in the light; Ashley's samurai sword was clenched between her teeth, and his Desert Eagle pistol was secured in her paws, clutched like a favourite bone.

Da da dah daaa da, da da dah daaaa da ... Boo to the rescue! I have weapons, Ash!

Ashley reached up to get his weapons. He grinned at Boo. 'You bloody little ripper! Now hang around, but don't you dare try and tackle these bastards, okay? That's an order.'

HU-AH! Over and out.

Boo flashed us a crazy grin and hovered away like a floating submarine, tail spinning in circles. We laughed despite the situation.

The creatures were distracted. One of them reared up and snapped at Boo as she flew past. Boo barked and snarled at it as Fox took aim and fired. The creature slumped to the ground. A direct head shot.

I spun around to see one in midair, target Jasmine. Its claws were outstretched, jaws aimed straight at her neck. She fired and hit it in the shoulder. The creature didn't flinch. Ashley turned and fired the Desert Eagle into its ear, just as its teeth were about to rip into her throat. Its skull exploded into a cloud of black blood and brains. A shower of stinking filth splattered us from head to foot. Jasmine screamed.

Fox stood, legs spread, in a double-handed gun hold, emptying his magazine into two creatures. These things didn't die easily. They fell at his feet, jaws snapping in uncontrolled spasms. Three came for Jasmine and me.

Jasmine was on her knees, finger jammed on the trigger. She squeezed off seven rounds. Her gun was in its mouth before the thing died.

I chose to save ammo and flicked off four knives. Direct hits right through both eyeballs. Blinded, the creatures staggered around before keeling over.

Fox shouted, 'I'm all out!'

'Get in the middle and give Fox your gun,' I yelled to Jasmine. She saluted me and handed over her weapon. Her face

---

[26] *Maggie's Playlist: Apocalypse Now (Main Theme) — The Intermezzo Orchestra*

was covered in black slime. The whites of her eyes blazed as she flashed me a beautiful, brave smile. She raised her hand to her mouth and blew me a kiss. A surge of love for her erupted in my heart. Its energy ran like fuel through my body.

Three more creatures slithered over the rocks and in a split second launched at us. Thunder exploded so loudly my eardrums and bones shook. A blast of lightening rent the air and smashed into a nearby tree.

Ashley clutched the Desert Eagle pistol in his left hand and the samurai sword in his right. He let rip with the pistol, and one more head disintegrated into a cloud of black jello.

'Faaaaaaahhhrrrkkk!' His terrifying battle cry reverberated around the arena as he ran the sword through the creature, cleanly separating its head from its shoulders. The head flew through the air and landed neck down on the top of a rock. The rest of the creature's body slammed into Ashley and knocked us all down like dominos. We flailed around and slipped in the black ooze as we tried to find our feet.

It took eight rounds for me to bring the last one to its knees. It crawled towards the edge to escape, hissing and snarling, its claws dragging through the slime.

It's not a dog; it's not a dog; it's not a dog, was the mantra playing in my mind as I plunged my knife into its skull.

'I think we got 'em all!' Fox shouted. He helped Jasmine up and counted the corpses piled around him.

I bent to retrieve my knife from the creature's skull just as Jasmine shrieked, 'Watch out, Drom!' Something whacked into me from behind, sending me flying into a nearby rock. Winded and gasping, I stood to see Jasmine in the jaws of a creature. It had her by the hair. Her red raincoat flapped in the wind as it dragged her towards the precipice.

'No!' I took a flying leap and grabbed the end of her jacket. The creature locked its eyes on me and gave a violent yank. It pulled her over the edge like a rag doll, and her coat was torn from my grip. I stared over the edge, a piece of red material clutched in my hand.

Below me, Jasmine hung in midair, clutching onto a woody shrub with one hand. The creature had lost its grip on her hair and had her raincoat in its mouth. It dangled below her, legs clawing wildly in the air as it tried to find a foothold.

Another crack of thunder and the rain came. It fell in fist size droplets that pounded into the ground. Cascades of dirt and water erupted around me. I could barely see through the water running down my face.

'Hang on! I'm coming!'

An electric flash. The ground in front of me exploded. Shock waves rattled through my body. A king hit to the head. I staggered and fell to the ground, my brain spinning. One thought rattled through my brain. *Save Jasmine. Save Jasmine. Save Jasmine.*

I dragged myself to the cliff edge. Ashley and Fox were already there, leaning into the abyss. Looking over the edge, a black and red shape spiraled down through the rain towards the ground.

Time slowed. An eternity passed before the shape stopped falling.

At the bottom of the cliff, a skeletal hand of lichen-covered rock stretched its bony fingers skyward. The bone-crunching thud echoed in my head as Jasmine and the creature smashed into its unforgiving grasp. The hand displayed its treasure. A slash of red cradled in its palm blazed out through the muted grey atmosphere and somewhere, a kookaburra laughed.

'Drom … Drom … Dromeus … *Drom!*'

A familiar voice broke into my consciousness. It was Ashley. He was shaking me.

A peculiar sensation of unreality overcame me. 'She's dead. It was Jasmine, wasn't it? She saved me?'

Ashley clutched my shoulders. 'Yes, Drom. She did. She pushed you clear of the creature.' His brown eyes stared into mine. I'd never noticed he had a scar on his forehead. His hair was plastered against his face. The rain ran in rivulets down the side of his neck. His biceps flexed as he helped me to my feet.

'Did we get them all?' I croaked.

He nodded. 'Yes, we got them all.'

We stood knee high in piles of black sludge, and I threw up violently as the stench finally reached my consciousness.

Lightening flashed and thunder roared around us. The trees below whipped backwards and forwards in the wind, dancing a crazy, evil dance.

A huge black cloud swirled above us, spinning like a Catherine wheel. The air held a malevolent intent that was palpable. Lightening flashed and hideous ghostly faces appeared in the rock crevices and then disappeared.

I screamed over the thunder and wind, 'We have to find Maggie!'

Fox gripped my arm. 'It's too late.'

---

27 *Maggie's Playlist: The Worst Day Since Yesterday — Flogging Molly*

Chapter 27: FUBAR

Fox's face was a picture of frustration. 'Ash, please talk sense into Drom. He's not being rational.'

'No worries, mate.'

Drom hung down through the hole in the rock trying to see any sign of Maggie, an impossible task in this weather. I yelled over the wind and driving rain. 'We have to leave the rock! It's nearly dark, and it's dangerous. You were hit by lightning, mate. For Christ's sake, you're lucky to be alive.'

Drom heaved himself out of the hole and stood shielding his eyes to keep out the rain. 'No! We *have* to find her.'

'Drom, listen! We can't do anything in these cons, other than get ourselves killed.' I grabbed his arm. He yanked free and pushed me away.

'Drom, please, listen to me. We have to go now. Trust me just this once. I know what's best.'

'Jasmine … Maggie … gone.' Drom shook his head and mouthed the words over and over. I put my arm around him and guided him towards the descent.

The rain didn't let up. It was slippery and treacherous all the way down. As our feet finally reached the main path, we saw flashlights waving up through the dark towards us.

Drom moved for his pistol.

'Police,' I shouted to him.

Police or not, we were still on high alert as they took us to the information centre. Our clothes were soaking wet, and even the pounding rain hadn't made much of a dent in the black stinking sludge that coated us. I wondered how Fox was going to explain it.

The foul-smelling black ooze proved to be a godsend. The stench was so abominable no one wanted to come near us.

Fox came over. 'We can use the facilities here to clean ourselves up. There are hot showers and we can stay on site tonight. The café owners have opened up for the troops, so you can stay too. The search and rescue team will be here at first light to search for them.'

'What happened to the biker gang?' I asked.

'All rounded up for questioning.'

Drom looked as white as a ghost. 'Lead the way to the showers, Fox. I can't stand this stink any longer.'

It took a whole lot of soap, hot water and scrubbing to get that shit off us. We binned what was left of our clothes and got fresh duds from the truck. Boo and Schmoo were ecstatic to see us. I gave Boo a massive tummy rub as a small reward for her military support. 'I'll get you something nice to eat from the café, Boo.'

Ashley, I want to fly out and search for Jasmine and Maggie.

'No one is going out in this weather, and that includes you, Boo. We'll go at first light. Hopefully the weather will have improved by then. I don't like the thought of Jasmine's body being out there overnight, but there's nothing we can do. As for Maggie, let's hope she's in a cave somewhere and can last 'til morning. It's totally FUBAR, Boo. Absolutely total.'

What's a FUBAR, Ashley?

'Fucked Up Beyond All Recognition.'

I knew I shouldn't have asked.

By the time we reached the café, Drom and Fox were getting stuck into the beer, and they had a cold and frothy one waiting for me. Their faces were a portrait of exhaustion and distress. Fox downed his pot in one go. 'I hope that black shit doesn't have any toxic after effects. I can still smell it in my nose.'

Drom skulled his beer and stood up. 'I'll get us another round.' He staggered off to the bar.

Fox watched him go. 'He's had six already.'

'On the road to annihilation,' I said. 'The whole thing sucks. I don't think he's going to handle this well. He took a chance, opened himself up, went against his own code, and look what happened. What a total shit of a day. And I'm sick with worry about Maggie.'

Drom came back with the beers. His face was pale. I chugged back my beer and took the next one. 'Let's drown our sorrows.'

Drom downed his in three seconds flat.

'Take it easy, mate. I need you with your wits about you tomorrow.'

'I'm fine, Ash. I'll be fine,' he said quietly.

'If you want to talk, I'm here for you.'

'Me too,' Fox said.

'I'm fine, really. Shit happens. All you can do is accept it.'

'Well, just saying … if you want. There's nothing you could have done. It's not your fault.'

He looked and me and laughed. 'It's *all* my fault. If I hadn't gone after her, Jasmine would be safe in Sydney by now.'

'You can't look at it that way. It was her choice. She wanted to stay. It was what she wanted most in the world, after everything that had happened. She loved you, Drom, and she gave her life for you. No thought, no hesitation. She wouldn't have wanted it any other way,' I said. 'Even with this outcome.'

The café was too quiet, despite the wind and rain howling outside. Someone cranked up the juke box. The sound of bongo drums filled the room as Santana's *Soul Sacrifice* pumped out. It had a frantic belly dance beat, and as I stared out through the rain streaked windows, Jasmine was dancing in the rain, her blue scarf flying as her hips flicked from side to side.

What the fuck?

I jumped up and pressed my hands on the cold glass, staring out at ... nothing.

Christ, I was seriously starting to lose it.

Fox put his arm around Drom. 'Jasmine gave you the ultimate gift.'

Drom's face twisted with bitterness. 'More like the ultimate curse.'

He slumped over the table and rested his head in his arms. His body shook with emotion as he let sorrow take him.

---

[28] *Maggie's Playlist: My Curse and Cure — Hercules & Love Affair*

I was going to hit rock bottom.

Shattered spine. Smashed ankles. Paraplegia.

Bending my knees slightly, I attempted to relax my body as I plummeted.

A fifty-metre drop would take about three seconds, I figured, but I kept on falling. I started to do my thing, and counted … one cat and dog, two cat and dog, three cat and dog, four cat and dog. I fished out the torch from my bra and switched it on. The tunnel was too narrow to see anything below me. I shone the light upwards. The rock walls blurred as I fell. All I could see was a halo of light above my head. Nine cat and dog, ten cat and dog, eleven cat and dog…

I turned off the torch to save battery power. How fast was I falling? Was I falling faster *now*? There wasn't much air resistance. I tried to recall an applicable Newton's law. I couldn't.

The experiment an astronaut carried out on the moon came to mind. He'd dropped a hammer and a feather simultaneously, and they'd reached the ground at exactly the same time. I wasn't sure how this was relevant.

My body tensed with each passing second as I anticipated that the next second would be the one I smashed into the ground. I needed that online splat calculator. I wondered what my speed on impact would be. Twenty cat and dog, twenty-one cat and dog...

It didn't feel as if I was falling anymore. More like floating. Suspended in darkness. Maybe I'd run out of air before I hit the bottom. I couldn't work out if I was horizontal or vertical. It was as though I was in outer space but with no stars. I needed to relax. There was no point trying to be ready. I needed to surrender. What would be would be. I felt each muscle fibre ping as it let go. Fifty-three cat and dog, fifty-four cat and dog...

It was dark. It was warm. I was weightless. I lost count...

When I opened my eyes, I was lying on a path in a eucalypt forest. The sky through the trees above me was grey, but sunshine shone down upon my face. Its rays illuminated the forest with a soft golden light. I sat up and wiggled my toes. My body seemed to be in working order. I stood and looked around. Everything was lush and green. Gentle bird song filled the air. Swathes of white flowers, similar to snowdrops, covered the ground through the forest. A creek, full and flowing, followed the pathway. It was beautiful.

I walked forward a few steps and my feet crunched on gravel. The air smelt of sweet blossom and eucalyptus. I turned around to look behind me, and I stared into blackness. It was as though I'd closed my eyes and the world disappeared. I stretched my eyes wide to ensure they were open — yes, they were. I turned and the world appeared as before.

Weird. Obviously, I needed to keep moving forward.

My mind started to come back online. Questions ticked over in my brain. How long had I been gone? One minute? One hour? One hundred years? I had no idea. Where was I? How would I get home? Where was the crystal? I had no idea about any of these questions either.

A knot of anxiety formed in my gut. I took a deep breath and continued along the path. What else could I do?

I rounded a bend and saw a girl sitting on a bench. She had a bunch of white flowers next to her. Long blonde tresses cascaded over her shoulders as she leant over and sorted through the blossoms.

She looked ready to attend a tea party, in a beautiful white lace dress with a drawstring waist and pin tuck pleating.

'Hello,' I said. 'My name's Maggie. Can you tell me where this path leads?'

'It leads to wherever you want it to lead,' she said brightly.

'Where are you from?'

'From here.'

'I'm lost. Where *is* here?'

She smiled up at me. 'It's hard to say. I'm lost too. But it's beautiful. You'll love it here.'

'What's your name?' I asked.

'People call me Miranda. So, it must be — *Miranda,'* she said, as though saying it for the first time.

'What? Like in the story Picnic from Hanging Rock?'

'Yes! *Yes ... that's it!'* she said excitedly. 'Hanging Rock. That's where we are! I keep forgetting. I know my name's Miranda because I hear people calling it out all the time.'

'You can't be *that* Miranda,' I said, more to myself than her. 'It's a made-up story.'

'I *am* Miranda.'

'How do you stay alive here?'

'*People* keep me alive.' She stood and held out her hand. 'Come, I'll show you around. You can help me stay alive too.'

I moved to take her hand and felt a strange sensation. Her hand had a magnetic quality that I could feel myself being forcefully pulled towards. I jerked back my hand.

'Don't be afraid. It's beautiful here. We can help each other stay alive.'

I stepped away from her. 'Thank you, Miranda, but I should

be getting on.'

It was as if I was moving through mud. My legs felt like lead. It was similar to a dream where you're trying to run but your legs won't work. My mind felt sleepy, sluggish, drugged.

It was beautiful here. This was real; this was what I was looking for. I should stay. She was right. We needed each other. I'd be safe.

No, Maggie. Run!

I suddenly realised what this was! I shook my head vigorously until my cheeks flapped, and with every ounce of will I had, I moved myself along the path away from her. When I looked back, everything was black, and my legs moved normally and my head felt clear. Thank God I'd twigged before it was too late. Miranda was a thought form.

Fifty years of people's energy, thoughts and attention had created it. An energy entity that believed it was real. And it was. Its immense power had nearly drawn me in. I was lucky. Once in the embrace of a powerful thought form you really were lost. Billions of people spent their lives caught up in them. They lost their awareness, trapped in an illusion. It was usually at death's door people woke up to the fact they'd been living a lie and had spent their life caught in a dream. Or a nightmare.

I continued along the path and crossed a small wooden bridge. A Tawny Frogmouth sat on the railing and regarded me with its golden eyes. It had feathers the colour of paperbark, and its presence was so *still*. So still it resembled a granite statue.

'Do you know where I might find ... the ... the crystal?' I asked it. Crikey, it was getting hard to remember why I was here.

The vibration I usually felt when looking for a crystal was totally absent.

'It will find *you*,' the bird said.

'So what do I do?'

The bird fluffed up its feathers, doubling in size. '*That's* the wrong question.'

'Look, can you help or not?'

'I be, not do.' The bird turned its head and looked the other way. I glanced that way too and everything was black. Staring into the blackness, I recognised a familiar shape. For an instant, I thought I saw Jasmine.

I turned to look along the path and the world appeared. I left the bird and continued until I came to a seat-shaped rock that backed onto a huge boulder. I moved past it and stepped into darkness, so I backed up and turned around. The world reappeared. I experimented. One step forward and one step back took me into darkness. If I stood still, in this slice of light, the world remained. Right here.

I sat on the rock, closed my eyes, and leant back against the boulder. The warmth from the sun-drenched rock penetrated my bones. A slight breeze kissed my cheek. Birds chirped. Leaves rustled. Water bubbled and trickled. Insects droned and buzzed. The myriad of sounds were stitched together by a continuous deep, low call: *oom-oom-oom-oom-oom-oom*.

It was the Tawny Frogmouth teaching me to be, not do.

I was the call of the Tawny Frogmouth. There was nothing else.

Nothing and Everything.

I heard the sound of voices in the background. Oddly familiar, but I couldn't place them.

'What's that woop woop sound?' voice one asked.

'It's a Tawny Frogmouth,' voice two answered.

'It's close by. It's loud,' voice one said.

'They don't usually call during the day,' voice two replied. 'Holy hell! The rock moved!'

'It's *looking* at us.'

'Oh my *God!*'

Drip. Drip. Drip. Water splashed on top of my head.

It was awfully loud. The drips echoed through my brain as they hit my skull.

Drip. *Crash*. Drip. *Smash*. Drip. *Crash*.

I opened my eyes.

A pair of eyes looked back into mine.

Suddenly *I* remembered. Who *I* was. *I* ... was. *I* ... am.

I ... is.

I stood and shook myself. Droplets of water, feathers, rock and lichen flew into the air. In a slow-motion dance, the feather, water and rock particles radiated out in expanding concentric circles. Reality buckled and rippled, bending the world into soft prisms. I stepped out and into the arms of Ashley.

I whispered, trying to find my voice. 'I didn't find the crystal.'

'Yes, you did, luv. You're holding it.'

I stared down in surprise at the glowing crystal in my hand. 'I feel discombobulated.'

'No wonder, Maggie. You just stepped out of a rock.'

---

[29] *Maggie's Playlist: Miranda — Fleetwood Mac*

I found myself in the middle of one of the biggest bear hugs I'd ever had. Ashley, Drom and Fox surrounded me, and it appeared they weren't going to let me go anytime soon.

Drom's voice broke. 'I can't tell you how glad I am to see you.'

His psychic tidal wave of emotion hit me and I knew immediately. I ducked under and out of the arms that enfolded me. 'What happened to Jasmine?'

Ashley explained everything on the way back to the café. Drom walked next to me in silence. I took his hand and held it tightly.

'Search and rescue are trying to retrieve her body as we speak,' Fox said.

I shifted into a state of unreality, unable to believe she was dead.

Fox pulled twigs and grass from my jumper. 'You look remarkably well for a night spent out in the bush.'

'I don't think I was actually in the bush. I tried to mind meld with you guys, but all my circuits were dead. I couldn't get anything coming in or out. It was a kind of limbo, another dimension.' I filled them in with the details as best as I could recall.

'It's amazing that you encountered Miranda,' Ashley said. 'What about the other girl?'

'No. Only Miranda. But strangely, I thought I saw Jasmine. When I turned back and looked into the black, I had a fleeting glimpse of her, like charcoal on black, and then nothing.'

'What does that mean?' Drom asked. 'She's alive?'

'I'm sorry, I don't know.' A physical pain wrenched my heart seeing the grief etched on his face.

Fox put an arm around my shoulder and gave it a squeeze. 'I'm glad you're safe, but I'm sorry you came back to this awful news.'

'It's the pits. And I'm obviously going to have to lie about what happened to me.'

'Yep. That's the standard MO now.' He rolled his eyes. 'Say you can't remember anything.'

Back at the café, members of the search and rescue team came out to greet us.

Fox gave them the thumbs up. 'We found Maggie!'

'Thank Christ for that, mate. Where was she?'

'Up the path, where it turns right towards the steps going to the hanging rock. There's a hollow where the water drips down from the rocks above it. Right there, mate, sitting in a puddle. She can't remember a thing.'

The thud of boots approached. Eight members of search and rescue stomped down the path. One held a red raincoat in his hand. Drom inhaled sharply as he saw it.

'We can't find her body, mate. There's no sign of it anywhere. Only this.' He held out the raincoat to Drom. 'The coat was in the rocks, on top of a pile of disgusting black sludge. Right where you said she landed. But no body, mate. We'll keep looking.'

Drom clutched the raincoat, his knuckles white. He looked at me desperately. 'Maggie, do you get *any* sense of Jasmine?'

'Nothing. It's like when my dad went missing. Radio silence.'

'So, there's a chance she's trapped in the rock? You said you thought you saw her … in there.'

'Yes, I did get a sense of her in there, but it was fleeting. And I don't know the time. Maybe she was still alive when I saw her. She may turn up. Look what happened with the Prof. It's a bloody bastard, the not knowing. It kills you, slowly.'

'I saw her body hit the ground. She must be dead.'

Fox put his hand on Drom's shoulder. 'I'm sorry to say this, because it's horrible, but is there any chance one of the creatures finished her off during the night?'

'I thought we took 'em all out,' Ashley said.

Fox shook his head. 'The police who went up to our arena said it's full of stinking black sludge. They can't make out specific creatures or features. Just piles of gunge, so we can't be one hundred percent sure.'

A search and rescue guy ran over. 'The media are here, Fox. News leaked out. Another mystery at Hanging Rock. The press will be all over it.'

Fox pulled a face. 'Just what we need. I'll talk to them. I'm the master of vague when I have to be.' He muttered and walked off.

Ashley and Drom took me into the café. I felt strange, out of it; a sense of unreality pervaded everything. It was as if I wasn't back in my body. I was a cardboard cutout.

Ashley put a mug of hot chocolate and a toasted sandwich in front of me. 'You okay?'

'No. I feel weird. I'm not even hungry.'

He put his hand on my forehead and looked worried. 'Crikey, that's a bad sign.'

'It is, isn't it?' I was worried myself. The food in front of me looked synthetic. It had no odour. I held up the plate to my nose and sniffed. I couldn't smell a thing.

Christ, what had happened to me in there? It was as if I

222

wasn't fully alive. There was no scent to anything. I couldn't even smell the eucalypts outside. And my emotions … they were missing. Shouldn't I have been feeling more upset, more happy, more … anything? I was in a sensory deprivation tank. It was as if I'd had numbness ramped up to alien intensity.

I pinched my leg hard. Even that sensation didn't register properly. It felt as though my etheric body hadn't fully integrated into this dimension. What if I never fully returned?

Ashley rubbed his beard and stared at me worriedly. 'Have a sip of hot chocolate and see how you go. God, it's good to see you. I feel like I've aged ten years in the last fifteen hours.'

'You both look exhausted.'

'Didn't sleep a wink,' Drom and Ashley said simultaneously.

'I'll get us another coffee.' Ashley went to the counter.

Drom fiddled with a serviette, twisting it into knots. 'I have to ask you. Why the hell didn't you tell me you were going to jump into that hole?'

'It was as if nothing else existed. Nothing else mattered other than going down there. I was under a spell. I still feel like it now. I'm NQR. There's no way I would have done what I did in my right mind. I'm sorry for what I put you through.'

'Ashley gave me so much grief over it. He said it was my fault we lost you. I was irresponsible, couldn't be trusted. I've never seen him so angry. I don't think he'll ever forgive me.'

'Did he punch you or put his fist through any walls?'

'No.'

'Then he wasn't really angry.'

Drom looked miserable. 'Well, he must've been holding it in, 'cause I sure felt it psychically.'

Ashley plonked a cup of coffee in front of Drom. 'Felt what psychically?'

'Your anger. About Maggie.'

Ashley made a fist. 'Yeah, you're lucky I didn't punch your head in, mate. I sure wanted to.'

'It wasn't Drom's fault. I was hypnotised. I had no thought of consequences.'

'Yes, and we know that's how you go when you hunt crystals, which is exactly why I told him not take his eyes off you.'

Drom stared blankly at the other side of the room. 'I'm sorry, Ashley … for letting you down,' he whispered.

Ashley took one look at Drom's grief-stricken face and pulled him out of his chair by his lapels. He enveloped Drom in his arms and held him in for an Ashley special. This was a bear hug that lasted for a significantly long time. It went longer than the point when you tried to break free, and he didn't let you go until you'd completely surrendered. He reserved them for the most special of circumstances.

Drom and Ashley had developed a strong bond. I knew Ashley loved Drom like a kid brother, and Drom loved and admired Ashley. Ashley's anger generally dissipated as quickly as it erupted, and he rarely held a grudge. I could see Ashley was dismayed at how much he'd upset Drom.

Ashley rubbed Drom's head with one hand. 'Bloody hell. I'm sorry, mate. No one could have stopped what happened. That's how shit rolls with this stuff. I was so worried about Maggie that I took it out on you. I shouldn't have. It was wrong. I trust you more than anyone. With my life … with Maggie's. I love you like a brother, and you've way more sense than me. I'm an arsehole sometimes. Can you forgive me?' Ashley pushed Drom back to see his face.

'I felt I'd let everyone down, including myself. I deserved your anger. But I thought I'd lost your respect.'

'I respect you more than anyone, Dromski, and *I'm* sorry.' Ashley pulled Drom in for stage two of the Ashley special.

Drom was smiling when Ashley finally released him. The tight sadness stamped on Drom's face had gone, and his normal calm expression had returned.

I sipped my drink, and the aroma of chocolate, vanilla and

spice suddenly sang in my senses. The scent of golden, crispy cheese toast followed, and I went in for a bite.

I jerked as a billion atomic doors slammed shut throughout my body. The feeling ricocheted from my head down to my toes and out through my feet into the earth.

I shuddered as one final thud hit my body. The world felt real. I felt real.

Ashley gave me a look. 'Are you okay?'

I smiled at him and hoed into my sandwich. 'I'm back!'

'You are indeed, and I'm bloody glad of it.'

* * * * *

The rain had set in and it was going to stay that way all day, apparently. We sat in the café staring out through the rain-distorted glass, the landscape outside resembling a Monet painting.

Fox traced a pattern on the glass with his finger. 'We may as well head off. Search and rescue will come back tomorrow. The conditions are too dangerous to continue today.'

'We're not far from Beechworth. There's a crystal there we could try for,' I suggested.

'I suppose we could do a bit of a recky,' Ashley said. 'If it's not an easy find, we'll come back when the weather's better.'

'Why don't we swing by the Vic Hotel in Woodend for lunch?' Fox said. 'I've got to check in with someone there, and they do a great counter meal.'

Ashley looked at Drom. 'Are you okay with the idea of leaving?'

'I guess so. None of us are getting any sense of Jasmine, so what's the point?'

I hoped a lunch at the Vic would lift our spirits. We could move on from there.

* * * * *

I was imagining a parma and chips with a glass of local wine when we arrived at Woodend. Since full re-entry, my body was screaming out for sustenance to keep me grounded. A couple of steaks were on list for Boo and Schmoo too.

Ashley ordered drinks and we sat around the fire staring into the flames, waiting for the bistro to open. Despite the soft light of the fire, my musketeer's faces were dog-tired, sad and grey.

'You know what? I'm making a call. Forget Beechworth. We need to take time out. I want to go home,' I said. 'I want to see the Prof, Bella, the Maestro, Christos and Luca. I have to see Fraser and talk to him about Jason and the business.'

Ashley looked at me gratefully. 'I was hoping you'd say that.'

Drom nodded. 'Me too.'

'Ditto,' Fox said. 'It's a wise move.'

I felt my face quiver. 'More than anything, I want to curl up in my own bed and cry my eyes out. For Jasmine, Jason. I can't…'

I stopped talking before I started crying. Once the floodgate of emotions opened, that was always it for me, so I bit my lip and stared at the ceiling, focusing all my attention on a diamond wire cage light fitting. I counted the wires, the number of intersecting diamond shapes — eleven around the bottom, four large, six small, twelve wires holding it up, creating another two sets of hexagons.

Ashley watched me, and I knew he knew what I was doing. He leaned forward. '*Maggie?*'

I shook my head. 'Just leave me to count stuff.'

I always counted things when I was upset; it helped me keep control.

Ashley focused his gaze on the racks of wine behind the bar. 'I need to join you.'

Drom pointed at the wall. 'There's a lot of exposed bricks in here. I've counted one thousand and sixty-three so far.'

Fox laughed. 'Seventeen stairs going up, that I can see, and six rails on each side. By the time we leave here, nothing will be left uncounted.'

Fox's laugh was so infectious it set us off on a laughter bender that left us gasping and wiping tears from our eyes.

Drom downed his beer. 'Oh, God, I so needed that. My shout. Same again folks?' He headed off to the bar.

I was reluctant to leave the warmth of the fire. 'I have to go to the ladies. Can you mind my chair, Ashley?'

'No worries, luv.' He grabbed my hand and gave it a squeeze. 'Remind me to tell you about my samurai sword. There are *developments*,' he said mysteriously.

In the ladies, I washed my hands and wondered what on earth he'd meant by "sword developments".

As I splashed my face with water, a clear image of Jason flashed into my mind. I jolted involuntarily. Jason was never out of my mind for long. I wondered where he was, how he was. I wished with all my heart I could see him.

I looked up at the mirror and gasped with shock. I clenched the basin and stared, as the image of my pale, shocked face registered Jason's reflection staring back at me.

His laser beam blue eyes were fixed on mine. He smiled softly. 'Hello, Maggie.'

I drank in his face and that gorgeous smile. 'Jason! You're alive!' Warmth erupted from my heart and flooded my body.

He held out his arms. 'I've missed you.'

I turned and ran to him. 'I can't tell you how much I've missed you, how worried I've been!' I threw my arms around him.

He looked at me sadly. 'I'm sorry for everything, so sorry.'

I caught sight of his reflection in the mirror. His eyes were black as he plunged a syringe into my neck. It stung like fire. The room turned as black as his eyes. Ice ran through my veins and my heart pounded as I collapsed to the floor.

Ashley

'Another beer, Ash?' Fox asked.

'I'll pass, thanks. Maggie's been gone for a while.'

Drom looked at his watch. 'Thirteen minutes, twenty seconds. I was just going to check on her.' He headed toward the toilets. Three minutes later, he came back, looking white. Fox and I leapt off our chairs.

He held out a blood-stained paper towel. 'She's gone. They've got her.' Nestled in the blood-soaked paper was a tiny cylinder the size of a grain of rice.

'Fuck. *Fuck!* It's Maggie's microchip!' My gut knotted.

'I found it on the sink in the ladies. This was this on the floor.' He held up a syringe.

'Jesus. They've cut it out of her!' My stomach heaved. 'No chip. We're screwed.'

Fox hightailed it to the bar. 'They've gotta have CCTV. You guys, go outside, keep looking!'

I ran into the beer garden and out the front gate to the street. There was no sign of her.

A bloke was eating fish and chips in front of the shop next door. The smell made me salivate. I was so hungry I could eat the arse out of a low flying duck. 'Hey, mate, have you seen a girl, long black hair, pale skin, slim, good looking?'

'About five minutes ago. Carried out that gate by a bloke. I asked is the sheila okay. He mumbled something about her being pissed and he was takin' her home. He shot out from that laneway, down the side there, nearly knocked me over. Black Audi A7, the wanker.'

'What did he look like?'

'You a cop, mate?'

'She's my friend. Kidnapped.'

'He was tall, probably six foot, blond sandy hair, bit of a looker, serious face … reminded me of Bowie a bit, I reckon.'

'Bowie?'

'Yeah, mate, you know, *David*. Well, sort of.' He pointed upwards. 'The shop's got a security camera. I know the bloke. Come with me.'

We ran into the shop. The owner was helpful, and I came away with what I'd hoped for. I was coming out of the shop as Drom and Fox were heading in.

'No CCTV from the pub,' Fox said.

'No sign of her,' Drom said.

I pulled out my phone. 'Check this out. I filmed the shop's CCTV.'

I ran the clip. You didn't even need to sharpen or enlarge it. You could see as clear as day it was Jason, with Maggie slumped in his arms, a dark patch staining the arm of her jumper. Blood, where the bastard had dug out the microchip. The car sped from the laneway, a black Audi. The number plate was illegible.

Fox was on the phone before the clip even finished running. 'All available resources are on to it as we speak. They're gonna try and get the chopper.'

I started to run. 'Get to the truck! Jason went down that road. We need to get him!'

Drom was right behind me. As we ran, our footsteps pounded on the asphalt, and my heart matched them beat for beat.

---

[30] *Maggie's Playlist: Lost & Not Found — Chase & Status, Louis Mattrs, Lost & Found — Shane Harte, Alex Zaichkowski*

I opened my eyes to pitch blackness.

Silence.

Deafening silence.

Not a skerrick of light.

I held my hand in front of my eyes. No hand to be seen, just a slight warmth radiating against my face.

I was in bed. Naked. The room was warm. Comfortable. The sheets were flannelette. Soft and cosy. Snug. I felt like a bug in a rug.

Where was I? At home? My brain ached. I rubbed my head. A sickening sensation of fear ran through my body. Where the hell was my hair?

I touched my head again. Nothing. I had no hair. The bald skull was alien under my fingers. I felt all over my body. Completely smooth, hairless. Everywhere. I was totally bald.

I froze. My heart pounded in my ears. I took long, slow deep breaths trying to bring my heart rate down and control the fear coursing in my veins.

Eyes open, eyes closed. No difference. Just black.

I felt around the bed. It was huge. At least a king. I had a pillow. Top sheet, bottom sheet, doona. Quality linen.

I slid over to one side and extended a hand. No side table. I tried the other. Nothing. I leant over the bed and touched the floor. Carpet.

I moved back to the middle of the bed and lay still. Maybe I was in hospital. But hospitals didn't have carpet. I wasn't at home.

Then where the hell was I?

A memory of Jason kicked open a door in my brain. I shot upright and cried out loud in shock. I stiffened as a voice in the room spoke. 'Hello, Maggie, it's nice to see you again.'

The blackness in the room dissipated. I pulled the bed covers around me, clutched them tight. My hands shook uncontrollably.

'There's no need for modesty. I've already seen everything.'

The darkness was replaced by a murky red light.

The space revealed itself. A plain, windowless room with a hospital trolley pushed up against one of the walls. Aside from the bed, the only other piece of furniture was a wingback armchair in a corner of the room.

The figure sitting in the chair looked older, mature. He was bald with no facial hair, and his physique was muscular, but there was no doubt who it was. It was unmistakably Tapakah.

I gasped.

He laughed. 'Don't say you're surprised to see me? It was only a matter of time. I told you that.' He came over to the bed.

I leapt out and pulled the sheet with me. 'Get away! Don't you dare touch me!'

'Relax. I already have,' he said quietly.

My knees gave out from under me and I collapsed to the floor and sobbed. What had he done to me? How long had I been here? Where *was* here? Think. I had to think!

He wrapped the sheet around me and lifted me up. His hand stroked my bald head as he pulled me in close to him. 'Hush, Maggie. *Hush.*' He rubbed my back. 'It's okay.'

Bile rose in my throat.

'I'm not going to hurt you. You're precious. Get back to bed and I'll bring you something to eat. You've been through a lot. You need to rest. I need you strong.'

He held up the doona and I slid underneath, trembling from head to foot. All strength had deserted me.

'What have you done to me? *What?*' I croaked.

'You're tired. Rest. I'll be back soon.'

He went to the door and held his hand over a keypad. The door slid open silently, and I caught a glimpse of the corridor outside before it slid shut. It was as dimly lit as the room.

I opened my mind and screamed for Ashley.

He answered immediately. 'I'm here! I've been here all along, but you didn't respond. Where are you? Is Jason there? Are you hurt?'

'It's Tapakah. Jason must've taken me to him. Tapakah's holding me prisoner in a room with no windows. It has electronic security. He's left to get me food. I'm extremely weak.'

'You've been gone for four days.'

'Four days! I've just woken.'

'Let me see through your eyes. Give me sight.'

'I can't.'

'Can't or won't?'

'I can't.'

I could give him sight, but he didn't need to see this. It wouldn't help. It would distract and upset him.

'Any idea where you are?'

'Nope. The room must be soundproofed. There's a bed, a chair, carpet and a hospital gurney.'

'A gurney? Go! Check it out. Does it have any ID on it? Check the sheets, the bed, the door, anything.'

I slid out of bed and wobbled over to the gurney, holding onto the wall for support. 'It has a label on it, half peeled off. It says Gendron, USA.'

Now the chair. I'd have to tip it over. I didn't have the

strength. I couldn't see anything else because the light was so dim. Tottering over to the security pad, I peered at it, squinting to gain focus. 'It says BJS Biometrics on the keypad. Sorry, I have to lie down. Bye.'

I collapsed on the bed and crawled under the sheet. Sleep took me immediately.

The aroma of Thai green curry broke into my consciousness. I opened my eyes to see Tapakah sitting on the bed next to me. My heart sank.

Damn it. I'd thought I was home. I hated him. I hated him. I hated him.

At the end of the bed was a small, round, ornate table and two antique chairs. The table was set with cutlery, crystal wine glasses, flowers and a candle. The hospital gurney had gone.

'We have your favourite, Thai green curry. Jason made it especially for you. I thought we could share a meal together.' He stood and handed me a black silk robe.

'I'm not hungry.'

'You're starving. You must eat.'

'I won't.'

'Jason will be disappointed. He said you would definitely eat this. He must be lying. There will be consequences for him.'

'I'll eat.' I took the robe and put it on under the covers. The material was soft on my skin. Creepy soft. I slipped out of bed and Tapakah grabbed my arm as I swayed on my feet.

'What have you done to me?'

'Nothing, you've been unconscious. You've just woken.'

'I've been unconscious for *four* days!'

'How do you know that?'

'I … I just know things.'

'Yes, indeed you do.'

'I have something for you.' He pulled out a length of shiny black plastic. It caught the candlelight and sparkled with a strange opalescence. 'Hold out your right wrist.'

'What is it?'

'Something to keep you safe.'

'I don't want it.'

'At this point you have no choice.'

My mind raced. The cutlery on the table. The crystal glasses. I could smash a glass and jam it in his face. Or stab him in the heart with the knife, then cut off his hand to use it to get me out of here. That might work.

I made a move for the knife, but my head began to spin and blackness encroached on the edges of my vision. I grabbed the side of the table to steady myself as the room whirled around me. Tapakah leapt from his chair and stopped me from falling. He held me by the shoulders until my head cleared.

'Are you okay now?'

I nodded mutely.

'Your wrist?'

With no energy left to fight, I stretched out my arm. Something had sucked the life out of me.

Tapakah tapped the black strip against my wrist and it sprang to life. I jumped. My skin felt icy cold as it coiled itself tightly around my wrist. The pressure of it increased until I thought my hand would explode, but abruptly the black strip vanished, leaving my skin with a black, snake-like tattoo. It glowed briefly, and I felt a subtle pressure around my temples. It was as if I was wearing a hat, one that was way too tight. So tight, all psychic connection was impossible.

I tried to reach Ashley and winced in pain. 'What have you done to me?'

'It's a psychic dampener. It won't cause any long-term damage, at least I don't think so. I wouldn't want that, but it will stop you dialling out, so to speak. Or people dialling in. I don't want any unwelcome visitors. Once you get to know me, you won't want to leave, and then I'll get rid of it.'

I held my head as I tried to break through to someone. The

pain of trying made me sob.

'If you don't try, it won't hurt.' He spoke softly and poured me red wine. 'It's your favourite.'

'Yeah, yeah. Don't tell me. Jason picked it up special like. You've sucked him dry haven't you, you stinking, slimy piece of scum sucking shit.'

Tapakah stared at me, his expression shocked. 'Before you say something that might offend me…' His mouth twitched and his hand flinched. I pulled back expecting a slap, but instead he sat back and laughed. Then he laughed some more.

I stared daggers at him. '*What?* What's so funny?'

His mirth surprised me. It was a genuine laugh, not the usual *Buahaahaha* evil kind. It made him appear strangely attractive, in a roguish kind of way.

'You are. That's why I would never "roach" you, as you call it. I love your feistiness. It's refreshing. Much more so than the quivering terror people usually offer me.'

'Oh, I can do feisty, mate. No worries there.' I threw the wine in his face. 'If you want to impress me, pick your own wine, arsehole.'

His eyes blazed as he raised his hand. His mouth quivered in an odd kind of way. 'Enjoy your meal.' He wiped the wine from his shirt with a serviette and threw it on the table. Flashing me a death stare, he walked to the door and left.

That was the thing about fancy sliding electronic doors. You couldn't slam 'em. An angry exit loses something with just a piss weak hiss of the door. At least he hadn't hit me. I was pushing my luck. I should watch my mouth.

I took the lid off the casserole dish, and the scent of coriander filled the room.

'You beauty. Alone at last.'

It made sense to eat, build up my strength and get the hell out of this shit hole.

I picked up a serving spoon, but paused when I heard a

mechanical whirr. A television lowered from the ceiling. A Catherine wheel logo flashed on the screen, followed by Tapakah's face. He looked directly at me. The camera panned back. Jason was behind him, chained to a wall, stripped naked, arms above his head, feet splayed and chained.

Tapakah had a thin, nasty looking crop in his hand. 'Count, Maggie. I can hear you. *Count!*'

'No, please. Don't hurt him. I'm sorry. I apologise. Don't do this. Please.'

'Count! It will be worse for him if you don't.'

'No, I'm sorry. I was angry and upset. I don't feel well. I shouldn't have—'

Tapakah's eyes narrowed. His face was a quintessential portrait of menace. He snarled at me. 'Start. Counting.'

'Wh … wh … one.'

Tapakah took the whip to Jason's back with a vengeance. The crop left a bleeding, red slash. Jason twitched but remained silent.

'Count.'

'Tuh … two.'

Slash. Welt. Blood.

I winced at the fury of it. *What had I done? Oh, my love. Jason. I was so sorry.*

Tapakah smiled at me.

I screamed, 'Please, please stop! Hit *me*. Not Jason. I'm *sorry*.'

Tapakah shook his head. 'Three!' He struck Jason's back with all his might. 'I will not tolerate disrespect. Repeat! What did I say?'

'You will not tolerate disrespect. So much for feisty,' I mumbled under my breath.

'I beg your pardon?'

'Nothing.'

The television went black. I retched, over and over again, but there was nothing to come out. The TV fizzed and turned on

236

again. Jason's face stared out at me with blue eyes, not black. 'Use it, Maggie. To escape. There's no other way.' Then his eyes rolled up and turned black, as did the TV, retracting back into the ceiling.

That was Jason. *My* Jason. He was still in there, somewhere.

Tapakah was going to pay for what he'd done. I picked up the knife and stood next to the door. I could barely stand, but I was going to kill that cocksucker, or die trying.

A voice boomed from above. 'I can see you.'

The low growl with the tinge of ice was unmistakably Tapakah's voice.

Damn it! There were no apparent surveillance devices. Should've known.

Replacing the knife on the table, I sat back down and waited. Smoothing out the tablecloth, I felt a bump. Surreptitiously, I felt under the cloth and found — a razor blade. I managed to flip it just under the bed as the door opened. It landed close to the edge. If I could see it, then so could Tapakah. Maybe it was on CCTV.

Mister Roach strode across to the table and stood hands on hips. 'What did I say?'

'You will not tolerate disrespect.'

'Excellent. You learn quickly.'

'What I don't get is how that fits in with feisty. The way I see it, you can't have both. I get feisty, you say it's disrespectful and beat the crap out of Jason. Work with me here, Tapakah. It doesn't make sense.'

'It will. I have a new wine, one I picked myself. I hope you enjoy it.' He poured me a glass. 'You had better eat something first though.' He served me a small portion of curry and rice.

Well, wasn't this cozy?

The food was delicious. I knew Jason had made it. No one made a Thai green curry like Jason. The thought that he'd made this with his own hands gave me strength and hope.

Tapakah kept serving and I kept eating. He watched in amazement.

'What?'

'You have an exceptionally healthy appetite.'

'Yes, that's what everyone says. But according to you I haven't eaten for days, so?'

'You will sleep now. Tomorrow I will show you my work.'

'Can I shower and brush my teeth?'

'No. Tomorrow. I'll give you one of these now.' He pulled out a wallet full of syringes.

'No! *Please*. No syringes.' I gasped, as the room turned into a tunnel. My heart started to pound as hard as a butcher hammering out a piece of cheap steak.

'It's only a multi-vitamin shot.'

'Please, no needles. I'll take all the friggin' pills you want, but please, no needles.'

'You have a bad reaction to them?'

'No shit, Sherlock. Yes, thanks to you and your minion Dylan, I have PTSD.'

'Okay, no more needles.' He stood and left the room.

Thank God, for small mercies. Thank God. Breathe. Breathe.

I took a swig of wine to steady my nerves, even though I knew it probably wouldn't help.

That was actually a nice drop. I'd have another sip. Oh, shit. It was probably drugged. What the hell.

I skulled the wine and collapsed on the bed as my chest tightened. I imagined drinking a mug of Ashley's hot chocolate and biting into a soft vanilla cookie. I thought of dolphins and cuddling Jason. My heart quieted and my breathing eased. Blessed sleep took me so quickly I didn't even make it under the sheets.

---

[31] *Maggie's Playlist: Puppet Master — Chris Major. Puppet Master — Walter Trout*

When I awoke, I was under the covers — naked. Someone had removed my gown and put me to bed. I had no doubt who that someone was. My skin crawled, and an anxious knot tightened in my stomach as I contemplated what might have occurred over those four days.

The door slid open. Tapakah.

'Good morning, Maggie. How did you sleep?'

'Like I was drugged. What's with the hair thing? Why have you shaved my hair?'

'I lost my hair after you torched my etheric body. It hasn't grown back. So smooth and hairless it is for everyone.'

'I wondered how you fared after that. I thought you might die. How disappointing.'

'I very nearly did, but I recovered. Everything except for my hair.'

'So now you're so bitter and twisted, you won't let anyone else have hair. Is that it?'

'Maybe at first, yes, but then I realised smooth is erotic. It turns me on. Did you know cockroaches *eat* hair, Maggie? We love the keratin. I keep the shaved hair for feed.'

'Way too much information, thanks.'

'You look lovely with no hair. You have a beautifully shaped cranium.'

'Why is it so dark in here? Could I have a brighter light please?'

'It's my preference. I like dark. I like warm.'

'Could I have my clothes back?'

'You don't need clothes in here. I prefer not to wear them.'

'But you're wearing them.'

'Simply to make you feel more comfortable.'

'That's kind of you. It would make me feel much more comfortable if I could have at least jeans and a T-shirt. *Please.*'

'I'll see.'

'So now what?'

'Lilith is coming to bathe you, and then you can have breakfast. After that I will show you my work.' He walked to the wall and pressed it with his hand. A panel moved sideways to reveal a large bathroom. It looked way bigger than the bedroom and was well appointed, similar to a hotel ensuite. There was a huge shower next to a large raised area made of timber boards. A sunken bath was set into the timber area.

'Impressive. Why so huge?

'Cleanliness is next to Godliness. Lilith will be here shortly to look after you.'

'I can look after myself, thanks, I've being doing so for quite some time.'

'You can't do everything yourself, and I have particular standards.' He turned and left the room.

I didn't like the goddamn sound of that. Okay, I only had minutes. I had to move it.

The first thing I did was pick up the razor blade and hide it in the mattress. Then I went into the bathroom, wanting to get a good look around before Lilith arrived.

The glassed shower area was so large it also held a toilet and bidet. The fixed showerhead was gigantic, with a detachable showerhead and an exceedingly long stainless-steel hose.

Opposite the shower was wall to wall glass, behind which was a sauna. Between the sauna and the shower area was a washbasin and mirror.

I opened all the drawers and cupboards looking for anything I could use as a weapon. Nothing. I'd have to pull a fixture or fitting off the wall in the shower, or maybe unscrew the tap. A voice behind me made me jump.

'I'm Lilith. Take off your robe.'

I turned around. 'And nice to meet you too, Lilith.'

A tall, slim woman dressed in a white lab coat stood with a utility basket full of brushes, loofahs and bottles of various concoctions.

She must have been in her late sixties and would've been a real looker in her day. Her blonde hair sat at shoulder level. Almond shaped brown eyes sat above high cheeks bones and a wide jaw. Her mouth was pursed as she put her basket on the wooden platform and began setting out her equipment. I didn't like the look of some of it.

She ran the bath and tested the water temperature with the inside of her wrist. I noticed a black Catherine wheel tattoo there. She pointed in the direction of the huge glass enclosure. 'Robe off. Get in shower.'

'I need to go to the toilet first.'

'Well, go.'

'I need privacy. It's a glass box.'

She rolled her eyes and turned her back. I quickly looked at all the stuff she'd laid out, but couldn't see anything I could use.

Going into the glass box, I did what I had to do whilst looking at Lilith's back. I'd never used a bidet before, so always up for a first, I gave it a go. Lilith turned around and looked even more peeved. She tapped her foot.

Not wanting to get on her wrong side, given my vulnerable position, I took off my creepy black robe and hung it on a hook.

Lilith entered the glass room and pointed. 'Get in shower.'

I did as I was told, and she picked up the detachable showerhead. She didn't have to tell me what was going to happen next.

The blast of warm water nearly knocked me off my feet. At least it was warm. I reckon the showerhead must've been a Commando 450. Lilith operated the hose like a fire fighter, blasting me with water to within an inch of my life. I needn't have bothered with the bidet. I supported myself against the tiles to keep myself from slipping over.

Lilith flicked a lever on the nozzle and finished me off with an icy cold jet spray. I gasped for air as the icy torrent pummeled my body.

Some warning would have been nice, thanks. Bitch.

Lilith obviously took pleasure in her work, so I wasn't looking forward to what was coming. I tried to make conversation and find out information.

'How long have you been in Tapakah's employ?'

'Get into the bathtub.'

'Hokay.' This broad was hard work.

I slid into the huge tub. Lilith had filled it with hot water and scented oils. It smelt divine. My aching muscles gave thanks to the uncommunicative one standing there watching me.

After ten glorious minutes, she ordered me out.

'Lie on your stomach there.' She pointed to a large towel she'd laid on the floorboards next to the tub.

I lay down and the scent of cedar wood enveloped me. Lilith took out a spatula and dipped it into one of her no name plastic jars. She put dollops of stuff on my back and legs and then began massaging and rubbing. It felt abrasive, and I wondered if I'd have any skin left.

'Turn over.'

I turned over. No modesty towel here. I wouldn't be recommending this place on TripAdvisor. She set to work with a vengeance, leaving no part of me untouched. And I mean, no part. She massaged between my legs, buttocks, between my toes and even behind my ears. You couldn't say she wasn't thorough. She was creepily thorough.

'Get back in shower.'

Wobbly on my legs, I staggered back to the glass box for the inevitable hose down. I was beginning to feel water logged. Lilith finished, hung up the nozzle and slapped me on the bum. 'Get in sauna.'

I gave her the stink eye, but settled myself on a cedar bench in the sauna. I loved the smell, but hated saunas. I speculated as to how long Nurse Ratched would leave me in here.

After around fifteen minutes, just as I was about ready to expire, Lilith opened the door. 'Get in shower.'

Oh, for fuck's sake. Not again. This was getting monotonous.

I gave her a look. 'You could say the word please occasionally. Haven't you heard the quote, "Friends and good manners will carry you where money won't go?"'

In response, she gave me a 'humpf' combined with a severe dose of stink eye and one raised eyebrow. Lilith did the evil eyebrow raise well. Combined with the pursed lips, it was a scary combo.

Another viciously cold jet spray left me gasping for air. Following that, Lilith toweled me down and slathered me with a fragrant lotion. She held out a fluffy white bathrobe. 'Use things on basin. Toothbrush, makeup … everything there. Fifteen minutes be ready. Take these clothes.' She held out a denim skirt and a tank top.

'Any underwear?'

She shook her head. 'Not required. Soon you need shaving and waxing. I'll be back.'

'Well, that sounds tickety-boo. Let me tell you, it was an absolute pleasure to meet you, Lilith. Enjoy your day.'

Lilith bitch face walked away, stopping before the door to turn around. Her eyes were black. She spoke in a flat voice that had a rhythm totally different from her own. 'Don't bother checking. There's nothing in here you can use as a weapon.'

A shiver ran down my spine. The black-eyed thing freaked me out, and even worse, I had the feeling it was Tapakah staring back at me.

* * * * *

I stood at the basin and looked in the mirror, feeling my bald head. A few years ago, I'd shaved my hair off to raise money for charity, so it wasn't such a huge shock to see myself bald. But my beautiful long hair was gone, taken against my will.

I'd been violated. So fucking violated. This was punishment and prison. He wanted to demean me. What the motherfucker didn't get was that this was war, and I would win.

Having no hair made my eyes, nose and mouth stand out. Deciding to make the best of things, I put on eye makeup and lipstick. I pulled on the black tank top and denim skirt and went into the bedroom. I sat in the chair and waited for El Roacho.

It wasn't long before the door slid open, but it wasn't the person I expected.

A young boy around eight years of age stood in the doorway holding a tray. He didn't have any hair either and wore a simple black shift.

'I have your breakfast, Miss.' He placed the tray on the table in front of me. Scrambled eggs, grilled tomato, bacon, sourdough toast, and a flat white coffee, sat beautifully presented on the tray.

'Did you make this?'

'No, Jason did.'

'What's your name?' I almost sobbed out loud.

'Billy. I hope you enjoy your breakfast, Miss.' He walked

towards the door.

'Wait, Billy. Do you know where this place is?'

'No, Miss.'

'How long have you been here?'

He furrowed his brow as though trying to remember. 'I'm not sure, Miss.'

'Are you happy here? Do they treat you well?'

'I guess so. I've got to go now, Miss. I'm not supposed to talk to you.'

'Thank you, Billy, you're very kind. I hope I see you again.'

'Thanks, Miss.' The door closed behind him.

I burst into tears. Those few words of conversation meant the world to me. He was such a lovely boy and I wondered about his story and how he came to be here.

Taking a breath, I pulled myself together and focused on breakfast. No wonder Jason had been given kitchen duty; he was such a great cook. Whether it was true or not, it made me glad to think Jason had prepared my food. I ate with a sense of reverence and love, savouring every mouthful.

I checked the tray for hidden things, but there was nothing. The crockery and cutlery were real, but I couldn't take them; it would be too obvious.

I was finishing my coffee when the door slid open, and this time, it was Tapakah. And Jason. My heart skipped a beat at the sight of him.

'You're looking lovely, Maggie. How was your breakfast?' Tapakah asked.

'Delicious, thank you.'

'Jason made it for you.'

I feigned ignorance, not wanting to get Billy in trouble. 'Oh, really? No wonder it was so delicious.'

'Jason's looking well, is he, Maggie?'

'Aside from having dead eyes, being brainwashed and having angry welts all over his back, he looks fine. Is it permanent, what you've done to him?'

'He's a strong man, physically and mentally. It took five roaches to finally have him submit to me.'

I couldn't take it anymore. I couldn't take him anymore. I wanted to annihilate him from existence, and I didn't care if I died doing it.

The knife glittered on the table begging me to pick it up. I moved my hand slowly towards it keeping my eye on Tapakah. Jason's brow creased slightly. I took it as a warning and arranged the knife and fork neatly on the plate instead.

'How can he live with five roaches in his brain?'

'The roaches atomise into the host's neural circuitry. After the initial pain of insertion, you don't realise they're there. That is, unless you try to override them, then it's immensely painful.'

'Can you deactivate them?'

'Yes.'

'Would you consider doing a deal?'

'What sort of deal?'

'I stay here with you, willingly, for as long as you want, if you deactivate the roaches and set Jason free, unharmed.'

'But I thought you'd enjoy having him around. That's why I acquired him for you.'

'What use is he to me here? It's a distraction. You won't let me near him. I can't talk to him. He's not Jason. He's an automaton. What's the point?'

'I'll consider it. But I want you to see my work first.'

'Can you really deactivate the roaches? I don't believe you.'

Tapakah smiled. 'I know your games. But I'll give you what you want. You have three minutes with your precious Jason.' I saw Tapakah's eyes turn black before he closed them and placed his fingers on Jason's temples.

Jason reacted immediately, his eyes strobing from blue to black, and his head shaking from side to side. His face contorted with pain. He screamed.

246

Tapakah pushed Jason towards me. 'I forgot to mention, deactivation hurts like hell too. You have three minutes.' He closed the door.

Jason staggered to one side, moaning in pain. I guided him towards the bed and helped him sit. He leant forward, groaning and holding his head.

The seconds were ticking away.

'Jason? *Jason?*'

He looked into my face and his eyes came alive. He whispered, as though waking from a dream. 'Maggie! Oh, my God, *Maggie.*'

He pulled me into his arms and kissed me like there was no tomorrow. In the joy of that kiss, I had the sickening feeling there was no tomorrow.

We held each other's faces, drinking in the sight of each other.

'We have three minutes, Jason. I love you. You said you didn't love me anymore ... is ... is that true?'

'That was Tapakah speaking. You know I love you more than life itself. I *love you*, Maggie. Always believe that, no matter what happens. Don't do the deal. You don't realise what you're in for, what goes on here. There is no escape. No way out. Believe me, I've tried.'

'But the blade,' I whispered. 'You said to use it to escape ... that, *was* you?'

He put his mouth to my ear and whispered, 'Death is the only escape. That's what it's for. It's your only way out.'

Jason sat back and stared into my eyes. 'Goodbye, Maggie. I love you.' His blue eyes changed to black, and he slid onto the floor, writhing in pain as the puppet master took control.

---

[32] *Maggie's Playlist: Puppet Master — Jenefer Siân*

Jason groaned and quivered at my feet, while I sat stunned, trying to process what he'd said to me. The door slid open and Tapakah stepped in.

'Ah, lying prone at your feet. That's how I like it too.' He nudged Jason with his foot. 'Get up. Get out.'

I helped Jason stand. He didn't appear to fathom who or where he was.

'What have you done?'

'He'll come good.' Tapakah grabbed Jason by the arm and shoved him out the door. 'Happy now?'

I didn't answer. My stomach was heaving. If I opened my mouth I'd lose my breakfast, and there was no way I was going to let that happen.

Tapakah held out his hand. 'Let me take you on a tour.'

I cringed inside as I took his hand, but I wanted more than anything to get out of the room and see where I was, and hopefully, find a way out.

It felt like freedom stepping out of that room. In the corridor, shiny floors stretched into the distance. The place reminded me of a hospital or institution, but it was windowless, the only light that infernal dim murky red, similar to a photographic dark room.

I noticed a row of hooks outside my door. Various ropes and implements hung from them. Tapakah selected a black collar and placed it around my neck. It made a mechanical clunking noise as it snapped shut. I jumped in fright.

'This is to keep you close. I wouldn't want you to get hurt … or lost.' He attached a lead to the front of the collar and the other end to his belt.

'Come, the new world awaits.' He tugged on my collar and pulled me forward. I can't describe how I felt at that moment, but the thought of the razor blade gave me comfort.

It was an old building. Probably a hospital. Large black and white tiles paved the floor of a corridor that appeared to stretch to infinity. The width of the corridor was twelve tiles across. The walls of the corridor were painted brick. Three small pipes ran along the top of the wall where it joined the ceiling. The ceiling itself was made of panels, four across. The panels adjoining the walls were angled down so the ceiling resembled part of a hexagon. Solid doors, all shut, were set back into the walls. The place seemed deserted.

Tapakah stopped halfway down the corridor and pulled a piece of material from his pocket. 'Blindfold. Just for a short while.'

He tied it over my eyes and pulled it tight. 'Walk. I won't let you fall.'

We walked on for a while, paused, and then he guided me into what I assumed was a lift. There was a slight movement under my feet, then a tug on the collar to indicate I should move.

'We're here.' He removed my blindfold.

The space was huge. It reminded me of an exhibition centre, divided into different areas by partitions. The light was slightly brighter here.

A row of narrow stables, or pens with wire doors lined one wall. We looked inside one and saw a young woman confined there. Naked. Bald. Pregnant. She looked at me in surprise. She was tethered to the wall with a collar around her neck similar to mine, and one on each ankle. There was a small, elevated bench in her pen, with a mattress to sleep on. The flooring was white and red tiles. There were one hundred, two-inch holes in each tile. Ten down, by ten across. My urge to count was strong.

At the back of the pen, a gap of about three feet ran between the floor and the ceiling. A tube with a teat on the end hung from the wall. The woman took the tube and sucked at the teat.

'Water,' Tapakah said, by way of explanation. 'These are the maternity pens. They're clean, warm and comfortable, as you can see. The opening at the back of the pen is designed to give technicians easy access to the females. The females are examined regularly, given medication and also milked for secretions. The bed doubles as an examination platform. Their health is of paramount importance for the growing fetus.'

I ran my eye along the row of pens and lost count at around one hundred.

I wanted to throw up. 'T ... tuh ... toilet?'

'None. They go on the floor in the corner. The pens are hosed out regularly, as are the females. Cleanliness is paramount. These are the females who give birth to my creatures. I believe you met one of my earlier creations, Leon. He was a stage one prototype. My most successful at the time, but we have progressed a great deal since then.'

I lost my breakfast all over Tapakah's feet. As I heaved, a couple of men in white lab coats ran out and coupled up a hose. They hosed away the offending material from the floor, and with Tapakah's nod, the vomit from his gumboots.

I wiped my mouth. 'Sorry 'bout that. I did ask for a toilet.'

He looked concerned. 'What's wrong? You're feeling ill?'

'Something isn't agreeing with me,' I muttered.

'Do you need to lie down?'

'No. Let's push on.'

'As you wish. I'll show you the technician's access area.' He led me around the corner and down some steps. A sense of unreality washed over me, as if I wasn't really there. I wished I wasn't.

The floor in the technician's area was covered with the same red and white perforated tiles. Above and below the access gaps to the woman, were stainless steel panels. Blue plastic tubes with stainless steel suction devices hung on chains outside each pen. A gauge was attached to each hose. Above the gap was a number identifying each pen, and a computer control panel inset into the stainless steel. Three stainless steel pipes ran along the floor at the bottom of the pens. The blue plastic tubes connected into these pipes.

An electric bell sounded, and five technicians wearing black plastic overalls, latex gloves and gumboots instantly arrived. Machinery clunked and whirred in the women's pens.

'It's a fully automated system. The tethers retract, and the females are pulled into the examination apparatus. Only five technicians are required to service one hundred females.'

One of the technicians stood at a control panel. He pressed various buttons and the examination benches slid forward presenting the technicians with a row of women's genitalia. The sound of clanking steel cascaded from one end of the room to the other as steel ankle restraints snapped into place.

Tapakah guided me back a couple of steps. 'You might want to stand back for this.'

The technicians picked up hoses and systematically hosed down and washed the women's genitalia.

'We have technicians on the other side hosing out the enclosures and washing the females' bodies. After washing, each female is given a digital pelvic examination, injected with medication and finally the electronic stimulation and collection devices are inserted to generate, and milk, their secretions.'

The sound of Tapakah's voice droned on, and I found myself

disassociating. I counted the buttons on the computer panels over each pen. There were two panels; one had seven buttons, the other had twelve.

'…the process lasts for thirty minutes and is conducted three times daily. The vaginal fluids that make up the females' sexual secretions are a valuable source of amino acids, proteins, carbohydrates, prostatic acid phosphatase, glucose, fructose, and other acids produced by the normal lactobacillus bacteria, along with antimicrobial compounds including elements such as zinc…'

I watched from outside myself as the technicians moved methodically from one woman to the other inserting gloved fingers into their vaginas. The technicians made notes on computer tablets.

'…females with an enhanced ability to ejaculate their glandular secretions are more valuable to our production targets along with having an evolutionary advantage for successful reproduction. Unproductive females are weeded out and used in other areas. The secretions are used as part of a feed formula for our roaches. They thrive on it.'

I noticed there were black rubber knobs and black squares running along the panels. I started to count them.

'Come, let me show you the gestation area.' He guided me back up the steps. I turned around to finish my count and saw one of the technicians with his face buried in a woman's genitalia. Tapakah registered my shocked expression.

He smiled. 'One of the perks of the job. Some of the females enjoy it. As long as production and hygiene standards are maintained, the technicians are free to do whatever they want to the females.'

We walked a short distance and entered the Gestation area. Racks of women lay restrained, face down on steel shelves. The shelves were stacked up like bunk beds, eight high. Their breasts protruded from holes cut out for the purpose. Baby creatures lay on steel trays below and suckled from the available breasts.

'This system allows newborns to suckle safely from the breeding females. The separation has reduced the high rate of infanticide we had in the past. This process has to be used for ninety percent of human females. It won't be necessary long term as we'll progressively replace these females with hybrids.'

I walked towards the shelves. 'Why do they want to kill their babies?' I took one look at the monstrous suckling creatures and knew why.

Tapakah's leash pulled me ever onwards, through laboratories populated with people in white lab coats, facemasks and glasses. They sat around hexagonal workstations and peered into microscopes, decanted coloured fluids with pipettes and dissected bits of black flesh and God knew what else.

Pipes and tubes, too numerous for me to count, ran down from the ceiling. Glass cabinets and rooms were plastered with biohazard and radiation signs. It was a sea of stainless steel, laminex, computer screens and fluorescent lights.

'The money ... for ... for all this—'

'Countries have paid me handsomely for my work with DNA and genetic engineering. I have developed a new protein that can alter the DNA in living cells. It is highly precise as opposed to the methods currently in use.'

'Are all the people working here roached?'

'Most of them. However, a handful of leading scientists work here by choice. I have infiltrated the highest levels of government, in Australia and globally. This state-of-the-art facility wouldn't be possible without having that sort of influence.'

'You're kidding me. The government knows about this?'

'Only the people who matter.'

'But why would politician's support something like this?'

Tapakah raised an eyebrow at me. '*Really*, Maggie?'

'Yeah. Sorry, dumb question.'

'They're interested for military and health applications, but primarily, they want a ticket to play in the new world.'

We walked on and turned a corner. Tapakah put his thumb on an electronic scanner and a door slid open.

I gasped at the sight in front of me. Hundreds of glass jars lined hundreds of shelves. They were backlit and filled with the most hideous creatures.

Decapitated hybrid heads with nightmarish features, wrinkled fetuses crammed into bottles, strange insectile limbs combined with human features, experiments gone wrong. Or maybe — right.

Some jars were exactly the same as my mum's preserving jars, the ones she used for apricots. These jars, however, contained the stuff of nightmares — tiny hybrid babies.

Jar one. The dainty creature looked so peaceful. Eyes closed, its arms and tiny hands clasped around itself as though for comfort. The feet and toes were bundled together at the bottom of the jar. The mouth had a gentle smile. The innocence of it made me want to pick up the jar and rock it in my arms.

Jar two. Two cloven-hoofed fetuses embraced, limbs entwined. Their shared cranium had the appearance of the devil incarnate. The tiny creature was the essence of evil. I had to turn away.

Jar three. A baby with a skull so huge it filled the whole container.

Jar four. A perfect baby, except for its head. It floated in a sea of formaldehyde with the umbilical cord still attached. Its bulging eyes stared out from under multiple antennae; the insectile jaws were open in a twisted smile.

Jar five. Tiny twins attached at the belly floated open mouthed in their liquid home, holding each other as though waltzing, their long thin strands of red hair rippled around them.

As we walked the jars became larger until we reached a section that was filled with life-size jars containing — *things*.

254

Creations more hideous than anything I'd ever seen. I started to count them.

'This is the GMO lab. Here we modify an organism's genetic composition by artificial means. Genes and specific traits are transferred from one organism into an animal of an entirely different species. In this lab, it's primarily cockroach to human. The resulting organism is called a GMO, a genetically modified organism or transgenic. Leon was transgenic.'

'So, it's like cross breeding?'

'No, cross breeding is when genes are exchanged between closely related species. This is genetic engineering, genes from completely different species are inserted into another. For example, in your world, Chinese scientists have inserted jellyfish genes into pigs to make them glow in the dark. I have been able to accomplish much more, as you can see from the newborns in the gestation section. I have even built in a self-destruct mechanism that reduces the organism to sludge once it's been compromised.'

'The creatures at Hanging Rock.'

'Yes. That was an interesting experiment.'

'Yeah. Fascinating. So how did you come about?'

'I crawled into the mouth of a pregnant female and merged with her fetus. So technically, I modified myself.'

Oh, Jesus. I was seriously going to throw up again. Breathe. Breathe. Stay focused. Stay interested. Lead him on. Look for ways to escape.

'So why do you have to use genetic engineering to reproduce. Why can't you reproduce naturally yourself?'

'Well in a sense I do. I provide the genetic material and we work with that. Natural reproduction is not quick enough for the new species I want to create, in the time frame I've set.

'So, you haven't reproduced in the good old-fashioned way then?'

'No, I haven't. Surely you understand? That's why *you're*

here.'

I felt the blood drain from my face. The gift Jason gave me, the razor blade, was suddenly even more precious.

We moved onwards, past huge glass walled rooms that housed Tapakah's offspring prior to him becoming a hybrid. These were the roaches that had the ability to infest humans and generate black holes. There were millions of them. Wall after wall, row after row. The scuttling creatures froze as Tapakah passed, turning towards him as one, their antennae twitching.

'They recognise you.'

'They should. Technically they are me.'

Tapakah led on, past the barracks housing adult hybrid males, adult hybrid females and mixed barracks for selected couples. There were two barracks for hybrid children.

He steered me up a flight of stars. 'The newborns are with their birth mothers for eight weeks before they're removed and raised independently.'

He pointed to an area with rows of barred cells. 'This is the "Stock In" section. These are captured humans awaiting processing.'

Blank and frightened faces stared out from behind the bars. Voices yelled and screamed for help. Tapakah pressed a control and the door slid shut. All noise disappeared. 'The place is especially well sound proofed,' he said proudly.

'How can you get away having a place like this in Victoria, without anyone finding out about it?'

'What makes you think it's in Victoria?'

'Well, I ... I...'

'You assumed. It could be anywhere. You could be anywhere.'

Oh, my God. Four days. I'd lost four days. I could be anywhere. The missing women were from Victoria. It *had* to be Victoria, hadn't it? Maybe not. They could've shipped them anywhere. I might not even be in Australia.

My knees buckled as the realisation hit me, and my brain spun like an out of control merry-go-round. Tapakah caught me and guided me to a seat near a water cooler. He handed me a cup of water. An alarm sounded.

He touched his ear to activate a communication device. His face clouded with anger as he listened. 'Get things under control. I'll be right there!'

He clipped the end of my leash onto a metal wall fixing. 'There's something urgent I must to attend to. Wait here. I'll be back.' He raced off down the corridor.

I examined the lock on my lead. It was similar to a handcuff. If I had a hair clip or thin piece of metal, I could break out. I scanned the vicinity but there was nothing to use. I yanked hard on the lead and collar, but no go, I was securely tethered. Now I understood how dogs felt.

Anxiety churned in my gut. I took a sip of water. The plastic cup!

I tore at it with my teeth trying to detach the surround at the top. It sliced my lip as the plastic ripped apart. Using that initial tear, I managed to peel off a narrow strip. Taking the sliver of plastic, I inserted it under the latching mechanism of the cuff. My hands shook and blood dripped from my lip onto the floor.

Voices echoed up the corridor. I sat back down on the chair, secreting the piece of plastic into my skirt pocket.

Two men in black plastic overalls approached.

'What the hell's that female doing here? Must've been left behind from the last stock transfer. We'll get our arses kicked if we don't get her processed.'

A tall man ran up to me and unlocked the leash. He yanked my collar. 'Come along, pretty one.'

I pulled back. 'I'm with Tapakah.'

The second shorter man guffawed. 'Yeah, right. That's a good one.'

'No seriously. I am. I'm Maggie.'

'Yeah, right. Good try, sweet cheeks.' He pushed me forward as the other one pulled. Tall man put his hand up my skirt and groped me. He sniggered. 'Nice. I might take care of you myself.'

'Get your hands off me!' I spun around and delivered a flick kick to his crotch. It worked just like Drom had taught me it would. Blunt force trauma. The man crumpled to the ground, moaning in pain.

Behind me was a loud snap, followed by a rapid, monotonous clicking sound. Each click felt like a punch from a heavy weight boxer. I was being tasered!

My legs collapsed. I couldn't move. I couldn't think. I screamed and twitched. Stabbing. Cramping. Burning. My muscles were tearing themselves apart. And then, it stopped.

Short man hauled me to my feet. 'Get up, bitch!' I could barely stand. The muscles in my legs burned, and my body was so much jelly.

The tall man I'd kicked grabbed my other arm and together they dragged me along the corridor. My feet trailed behind me and squeaked on the polished floor. They stopped in front of a door and short guy looked through a peephole. 'Exam room's free.'

They unlocked the door and dragged me inside. I felt a slap on my arse. 'She's all yours. Enjoy!'

I was shoved into an examination chair. The plastic was cold on my skin. Restraints were snapped into place around my wrists and ankles. I screamed. Duct tape was wrapped around my mouth. The man kept going until the bottom half of my face was covered, then he stood back and admired his efforts.

Not satisfied, he wound more tape crisscross over my nose, around the back of my head, and finished off partly over one eye.

Stainless steel instruments were lined up in neat rows on a nearby bench. I began to count them, as tall man picked up a pair of stainless steel shears.

My brain flashed back to the morgue, and Adam.

No. Not again.

Not thinking, I screamed psychically for help, and then screamed from the pain generated by the psychic dampener.

I couldn't even leave my body anymore. I couldn't escape.

Tall man moved towards me, cutting the air with the shears. His expression was menacing. The scissors spoke to me with each open and close of the blade. '*Weaker, weaker, weaker, weaker, weaker, weaker, weaker.*'

Déjà vu slapped me in the face. It was Tapakah wielding the shears as tall man cut off my top and skirt and yanked the material out from under me. My heart pounded in my ears. My brain wouldn't work. Sounds were soft or ear shatteringly loud. Echoes of a deep, slow-motion voice, a vague perception of tall man's mouth moving.

'There are a series of examinations we need to perform to ascertain if you are optimal breed stock. What's your name again?' He tapped the screen on his tablet. 'Oh, sorry, of course, you can't speak.' He snickered. 'It was Maggie … Maggie *something*. No record of any Maggies here.' He scratched his head. 'Well then, looks like it's my lucky day. No records mean you don't exist in this world, sweet cheeks.'

He ran his hand up my leg. 'We have a state-of-the-art garbage disposal system here. All waste is reprocessed into feed. That's where a piece of trash like you is going to end up, after I've finished with you. Roach food, that's what you'll be.'

I moaned and twitched as my mind slipped into madness.

'Time for your digital exam.' He looked around the room. 'Hmmm. No gloves. Looks like it's au naturel for you.'

He squirted lubricating jelly between my legs. 'You're going to pay for what you did to me, my pretty.' He thrust his hand between my legs. 'Oh baby, time for you to find out what it's all about.' He stepped back and pulled down his trousers. 'I'm looking forward to this!' He grabbed my thighs and pulled me

259

towards him.

I screamed through the duct tape, and his head disintegrated into a cascade of blood, brains and bone.

Jesus Christ! Had I done that?

My mind processed the vision in slow motion. A spectacular red peony firework sprayed across the room, sending sparkling globules of blood into the air. It hung in suspension against the background of shiny white tiles. Time stopped. Silence.

An ear shattering bang and it crashed in a wave to the floor.

A sliver of cranium impaled itself in my arm.

The not so tall anymore, tall man, toppled backwards and hit the floor with a thud. A fountain of blood pulsed from his neck, spraying out against the tiles. The resulting spatter decorated the wall better than a Pro Hart painting.

Saved by the gun. Again. But why, oh why, such a large calibre bullet? So. Much. Mess.

I started to hyperventilate as blood trickled down my body and a piece of brain slipped down my thigh. Somewhere in my mind I prayed the shooter was Jason.

It wasn't.

It was Tapakah. He held a severed head in the palm of his hand. It belonged to the short man. Now even shorter.

I laughed hysterically on the inside and convulsed on the outside.

[33] *Maggie's Playlist: Click Go the Shears — Snake Gully*

 **Chapter 33: Paradigm Shift**

"Go to the ant, O sluggard; consider her ways, and be wise. Without having any chief, officer, or ruler, she prepares her bread in summer and gathers her food in harvest." — *Proverbs 6:6-8*

I crossed my fingers and prayed that when I opened my eyes, I would be in bed at home, and everything that had happened would be an extremely bad dream.

Okay. Eyelids open. Nope. Still there. Damn it.

Tapakah sat on a chair next to my bed. Billy sat on a chair nearby. Jason stood in the corner, staring straight ahead.

Tapakah noticed I was awake and moved to sit on the edge of the bed. He went to touch my hand and thought better of it.

'I'm sorry, Maggie. I sincerely apologise for what happened. It was totally unacceptable what they did to you, and I made them pay the ultimate price. I saw it on the CCTV, but I couldn't get to you fast enough.'

'It was fast enough by about one second,' I said flatly. 'How long have I been sleeping?'

'Twenty-four hours. You were in a bad way. We had to sedate you. I'm furious about what happened. What you had to go through. I don't think I've ever felt so much rage.'

I picked at a thread on the sheets. 'You need to use smaller calibre bullets. Get a .22, effective and far less messy.'

Tapakah looked at me oddly.

'What's this all about, Tapakah? I've had the tour. What's

261

your mission statement?'

'To create a new species. In their current state, Homo sapiens are a scourge on the planet. A disease. They are removed from the natural cycle of life, exterminating insects, flora, fauna and polluting the planet with pesticides and chemicals. There are currently over seven billion of them on the planet. I plan to eliminate five billion to allow the planet, and all that depends on it, to recover.'

'And how do you plan to exterminate five billion people?'

'Disease. The new species, Blattodea Humanus, will be immune. Homo sapiens will die. Did you know that Homo sapien is a Latin phrase meaning "wise man"?' It's a joke, don't you think?'

'I don't find too much of anything funny these days. What's Blattodea?'

It's the scientific name for cockroach, from the Latin "Blatta", an insect that shuns the light.'

I couldn't help laughing. 'That's hilarious. An insect that shuns the light, and I'm a keeper of light. We're exact opposites.'

'Yin and Yang, light and dark. We're meant to be together.'

'Until the disease gets me.'

'You will be immunised, along with those of your choosing.'

'Okay, I'd better start my list then. Got a pen?'

'You're being sarcastic.'

'You're so astute.'

Tapakah stood. 'Billy is going to stay with you and make sure you're okay. Jason will make dinner for us. I'll be back later.'

'*Whatever.*'

'Come, Jason,' Tapakah said, and they both left the room.

'How are you feeling, Miss?' Billy asked.

'Physically okay. Mentally, not so good.'

'I can make you a nice cup of tea. That always makes me feel better.'

'You drink tea?'

262

'Yes, strong with milk.'

'That's how I like it too, Billy.'

'Shall I make us both a cup? Tapakah let me bring up a tray with everything I need. It's in the bathroom.'

'That would be lovely.'

Billy trotted off, and five minutes later he was back bearing two mugs of tea and some biscuits. He picked up an Arnott's fruit biscuit. 'I call these fly biscuits.'

'Jason calls them that too. They're his favourite. How did you come to be in this place?'

'Tapakah found me on the streets. I was living under a bridge. I ran away from home. Mum and Dad were doing drugs. Home was horrible, so I left.'

'Weren't you scared out there on your own?'

'It felt safer on the streets than at home.'

'Did Tapakah make you go with him?'

'No. He offered me a home. I can leave anytime I want.'

'*Really?*'

'That's what he said. But I don't wanna go.'

'He trusts you to keep all this secret?'

'S'pose so. There's nothing out there for me anyway. Mister Tapakah's not so bad once you get to know him. He's nice.'

'Yeah, real nice.'

'He's nice to me. Once he trusts you, I guess. He's super strict, but. You can't cross him.'

'I thought you weren't allowed to talk to me?'

'After what happened he said I was allowed to talk to you. He thought it might help.'

'Did he now? Well, it's lovely to talk to you, Billy. I like you.'

'I like you too, Miss.' He smiled and dunked a fly biscuit into his tea.

'I'd love to have a bath. Is that allowed?'

'I'd better check.' Billy headed towards the door. 'I'll be back in two secs.'

A deadly, unforgiving blackness descended upon me. I was cut off from everything, but most of all, cut off from myself. I traced my finger over the black snake around my wrist and tried to reach out to someone. A piercing pain ran through my temples, and I cried out in agony.

I pinched myself on the arm. I couldn't register pain. I didn't feel real anymore. I was so alone. Empty, a cardboard cutout of myself. The sense of unreality was growing stronger every day. Everything appeared foreign to me … strange. I was no longer part of the world. My sense of interconnectedness with all things had gone. The words of a Simon & Garfunkel song ran through my mind: *I am a rock. I am an island.*

I stared at the cup in my hand, and the hand holding it. It didn't seem to be mine.

I am a rock. I am an island. And a rock feels no pain. And an island never cries.

Billy raced into the room. 'He said you can have a bath after dinner, Miss. Jason's bringing it, any minute.'

Billy busied himself laying the table for dinner. I fixated on the cutlery gleaming on the table, and imagined how I would lean across the table and plunge the knife into Tapakah's eye. I'd have to be fast. And accurate.

Tapakah was extremely fit, and his reflexes were razor sharp. I pictured myself doing it, over and over. I'd done it twice before, stabbed someone through the eye, while fighting for my life. But the adrenaline had been pumping. I'd done what I had to do. Stabbing someone in the eye over a nice dinner for two would be a different matter.

The door slid open and Tapakah entered. Jason followed carrying a tray. Billy took the contents of the tray and placed them on the table.

Tapakah waved them away. 'You two can go now.'

---

[34] *Maggie's Playlist: I Am a Rock — Simon & Garfunkel*

Billy and Jason turned to leave. I gazed at Jason's back, the broadness of his shoulders, the way his jeans hung on his hips, the way his bum moved with his long, relaxed gait, his strong arms and hands. I drank in every detail that I could in those few seconds and wondered if I would ever lie in his arms again.

The door closed. I returned my attention to Tapakah. He stared at me.

'What?'

'I have clothes for you.' He handed me a drawstring bag. 'You can get changed in the bathroom. Here's a new robe. Try it.' He held the robe up in front of his face, so I could slip out of bed and into it without him seeing me naked.

What was the point? What was his game? He'd already seen everything there was to see of me. Arsehole.

I took the bag of clothes and went into the bathroom and closed the door. I pulled open the bag and removed its contents, laying out the items on the wooden platform near the bath.

There was a pair of black leggings, a long sleeve black top, a cute blue hoodie jacket and a pair of red sneakers, similar to the ones I used to have. There was also underwear, a bra and knickers.

I put on my new clothes, enjoying the process of dressing. It was wonderful to be properly clothed. It gave me a sense of security.

Tapakah was up to something. Why was he doing this now? Being all charming and considerate.

When I returned to the bedroom, he was sitting at the table having a glass of wine. 'You look lovely. Are the clothes okay?'

I felt genuinely grateful. 'Yes. Thank you.'

'We have something simple and light to eat. Vegetarian lasagna and salad.'

I sat at the table. 'Thank you.'

This was too weird. It felt like an awkward first date, except on this date my beau was going to end up with a knife through his eye.

I sipped my red wine while Tapakah served my food.

'Wine okay? I picked it myself.'

'Delicious. Thank you.'

I took a mouthful of lasagna. It was Jason's all right. I closed my eyes and savoured the flavours.

This could be my last meal if things don't go to plan.

When I opened my eyes Tapakah was staring again.

'*What?*'

'You're beautiful.'

He was weirding me out. I had to change the subject. 'Why haven't you roached Billy?'

'Because he has a pure heart.'

'What do you mean?'

'He's similar to an animal. Innocent and pure. Without guile. I trust him. I protect him.'

'How can you be so unspeakably cruel to all those women, men and children out there?'

Tapakah did the one eyebrow raise. It reminded me of Jason.

'Define cruel.'

'Well, where do I start?' I tapped my fork on the table. 'You're capturing women against their will, holding them in pens, and using them as breed stock. You restrain them when they feed their babies. You take their babies away from them after eight weeks. You perform experiments on them and milk them for their bodily fluids. They've been removed from their family and friends; they see no natural light. You put collars on them. And leashes. They have no freedom. No choice. No options. That's cruelty in my book.'

Tapakah regarded me for a while before he spoke. 'Humans are animals. Tell me, how does the way I farm humans differ from the way humans use and farm animals?'

I ran over what I knew about the factory farming of chickens, cows, pigs, sheep, turkeys, ducks, laboratory animals,

266

and all the other myriad of ways humans used animals. I thought about puppy farms and pets. About Boo and Schmoo. Dogs were collared and leashed. They only had the freedom we allowed them. It was for their protection. It was for the best. Greyhounds, horse racing, whales, fish, elephants, ivory, animal testing, experiments … *shit*, the list went on and on and on.

'Well? You've been silent for a long while.'

'I guess your practices don't differ from how humans farm animals, except in the case of free-range farming. But that doesn't make what you're doing right.'

'I do this by necessity. It's a short-term plan to achieve my goal.'

'The things you did to me, tried to do to me, and are doing to me. They're cruel.'

'The things I did … I thought that's what you wanted. How you liked to be treated. I found it all in your head.'

'It's not *my* stuff, for God's sake. It's other people's stuff. I see their fantasies, their hidden thoughts and desires, their sick obsessions. I put those images away. Lock them in compartments in my brain so I can function normally. Well, as normally as possible for me.'

'Then I'm truly sorry. I'm mature physically, but I'm still so young. I'm learning, growing and changing every second. I barely sleep. I have a lot to learn. I make mistakes. I'm sorry.'

Huh. It was probably an act, but he seemed genuinely remorseful. All I could do was play along and find out as much as I could.

'How long will you live?'

'I don't know what my life span is. I'm unique. Perhaps I could die tomorrow. Maybe I could live for a hundred years, or more. I have no idea how long I've got.'

'I guess that's the same for all of us.'

'I'm not evil. I'm half insect. Insects are not evil.'

'But you're half human, and humans can be hideously evil.

And what about the dark force? You're aligned to it. It uses you.'

Tapakah lowered his voice. 'The dark force feeds on the negative energy created by humans. Once there are only my species, and humans of pure heart, the dark force will have nothing to feed on. It will starve or go elsewhere. You won't need your crystals anymore. The fight will be over. You won't ever have to go through this suffering again.'

'That's all well and good, but right here, right now, I'm *dying*. I'm losing my soul. *Please*, let me go. Let Jason go. Please. I'm *begging* you.'

'I can't do that. You can't leave. Not now.'

His answer was the catalyst. Moving my elbow, I knocked over the wine glass and dropped my knife on the floor. My heart pounded as I bent to retrieve it. Tapakah leant over to pick up my glass. This was it!

I lunged and thrust the knife at his face.

In that split second, his hand grabbed my wrist and held it fast. Staring into my eyes, he squeezed my hand until I dropped the knife to the floor. 'I thought we were making progress.' He released my wrist with a dismissive flick.

'So did I. Can I have a bath now? I've lost my appetite.' I rubbed my wrist and he tapped his comms device. 'I'll get Billy to clear up here and run a bath for you.'

I couldn't think straight. Nothing made sense. My head ached all the time. Tapakah's words rattled around in my brain.

You can't leave. Can't leave. Can't leave. Can't leave.

Oh, yes! I could.

I laughed.

'What's so funny?'

'I remembered something a friend once said.'

'What's that?'

'You always have a choice. It's just that sometimes, the choices suck.'

'What choices do you have?'

'You tell me.'

'You can stay and let me make you happy, or you can stay and be sad.'

'Only two choices?'

'I prefer to keep things dead simple.'

'It is that simple, isn't it? Dead simple.'

Billy stuck his head around the door. 'Your bath will be ready soon, Miss.'

'Can I have privacy, or do you need to watch your human bathe? Silly me, you probably have surveillance in there anyway. Enjoy then.'

Tapakah opened the door. 'You have complete privacy in the bathroom now. I'll be back to check on you in a couple of hours.'

I smiled. 'Missing you already.'

My smile felt as soulless as his.

---

[35] *Maggie's Playlist: Paradigm Shift — Alphaville*

I undressed and placed my clothes on the bed. As I pretended to straighten them, I surreptitiously retrieved the razor blade from its hiding place in the mattress and went to the bathroom and closed the door.

The bath water was bearably hot. Exactly how I wanted it. Billy had added lavender essential oil. The aroma smelled heavenly. I slid down into the water and felt the heat instantly relax my body.

I turned the razor blade over and over. It was brand new. Never used. I had two hours to die. Two hours to bleed out. It probably wouldn't take that long, but I'd better get cracking. The thought of escape, of freedom, excited me. It seemed to be the only emotion I could feel.

Cut the right arm first, my strong arm. If I started with the left, I might not have the strength to finish, and I intended to finish.

I examined the pale skin on my forearm, and traced my finger along a blue vein. The vein was defined at my wrist but faded out soon after. Holding my arm below the elbow, I squeezed tight, whilst clenching and unclenching my hand. A blue line appeared, running down the centre of my arm.

I'd cut down the middle, starting from halfway along my forearm and finishing at my wrist. Not too deep. I didn't want to sever any tendons and not be able to finish the job. But deep enough to bleed. Bleed a lot. Fast.

My flesh opened up as I drew the blade along my arm. A line of blood followed the blade, soon turning into a river of red.

I swopped hands and cut a similar red line down my left forearm. It was harder; the blade was slippery with blood. I placed the blade on the side of the bath and watched as my blood trickled down the sides into the water. It reminded me of red paint.

I dipped a finger into it and wrote the words *"Freedom. Maggie's choice."* on the white tiles near the bath. I doodled a flower next to the writing then put my arms under the water. The pain was excruciating.

Gradually, the water changed colour. I focused my mind on that, rather than the pain. So many different shades. Rosé. Fairy floss. Flamingo. Turkish Delight. Strawberry. Cherry. Ruby. Shiraz.

Tiredness weighed upon me. My eyes were heavy … I couldn't keep them open … any longer. The pain and fire in my arms faded.

I closed my eyes and embraced freedom.

---

[36] *Maggie's Playlist: Breaking Free — Skillet, Lacey Sturm*

"Darkness cannot drive out darkness; only light can do that. Hate cannot drive out hate; only love can do that." — *Martin Luther King, Jr.*

I sat in the control room and checked the monitor, replaying the recording of Maggie's room.

Why had she undressed in the bedroom? She knew she was under surveillance there. Was she being deliberately provocative? Or had she simply forgotten?

I replayed it again.

Christ, she was beautiful. The ridge of her collarbone, the rise of her breast, long slender arms, a perfect bottom. But what was she doing?

I zoomed in and tried to avoid looking where I shouldn't. I would give her privacy. Soon. She was fiddling with the bedclothes. I rewound and zoomed in again. There was something in her hand.

Rewind. Zoom. Rewind. Zoom.

I wanted to take her to the opera. Salome. In public. On my arm.

Rewind. Zoom. Zoom. Focus. Focus. A sliver of metal. *Shit!*

I checked my watch. It'd been thirty minutes. I ran down the corridor and called the medical officer on the way. 'Room 206, second floor, medical emergency. Get there, *now!*'

Fuck! *Fuck!* I was yelling.

'Billy, Jason, get to Maggie's room, *now!* I'll meet you there.'

I raced up the stairs, along the corridors. The bloody corridors. So frigging long. My breath burned in my lungs.

Please. Please, don't let it be. Don't let it be. Not a blade. Not Maggie.

No one was there yet. I opened the door and steeled myself for the worst.

Her clothes were on the bed where she'd left them. I opened the bathroom door.

The bath must've been internally lit with one of my red safelights. It had to be.

A rim of dark red ran around the inside of the bath. Maggie's tangle of long limbs rested under the water — arms, legs, crossed over each other, the colour of rosé. She was asleep, her face as white as the ceramic tiles. Snow White. She appeared to be bathing in Shiraz. Her favourite.

Footsteps. Billy and Jason. Billy shrieked. Jason fell to his knees.

Frank, the medic, pushed me out of the way. 'Jesus, holy mother of God. Don't just stand there, Tapakah.'

Frank felt for a pulse on Maggie's neck. His hand changed to the colour of Cabernet Sauvignon.

'There's a faint pulse. Help me get her onto the gurney and apply pressure to the wounds. *Move!*'

Maggie's body was limp and slippery. Everything was covered in blood. Frank handed me a large dressing to press on the wound. Jason was up and attending to her other arm. Billy was crying. So was Jason.

The medical team arrived and took over. Blood dripped from the gurney onto the floor as they rushed her away.

There was writing on the tiles, and a flower.

'Freedom. Maggie's Choice.'

The letters had spidery red trails.

I dropped to my knees. I had blood on my hands. Maggie's

blood. I was covered in it.

Déjà vu. I was back in Maggie's ballroom covering myself with her blood.

This was *wrong*.

This wasn't supposed to happen.

I stared at the water in the tub. A bloodbath.

The chilling howl of a wolf echoed off the blood-stained tiles. Startled, I looked around and realised … it was me.

* * * * *

'It's lucky you had the foresight to get so much autologous blood when you captured her, Tapakah. Expecting something like this, were you?' Frank asked. He adjusted the tube feeding Maggie's own blood back into her veins.

'Not *this*.'

'It'll make her chance of survival much better. Her arms are pretty wrecked, but we've done a good job repairing the damage.'

'Make sure it's more than good, Frank.'

'Don't worry; she'll be as good as new. In a while. The transfusions are going to take hours. We're going as fast as we can, but we can't give more than her heart can handle. I'll keep her sedated and comfortable, with vital signs constantly monitored. I'll let you know when you can talk to her.'

'Thanks, Frank.'

'Now bugger off and leave me to my work.'

I returned to the surveillance room and watched Maggie from there. I dialled up Frank on the comms.

How's Billy doing?'

'Sedated. I'll keep him that way for a while, until Maggie comes around. He's traumatised, poor bugger.'

'Aren't we all. Thanks, Frank.'

I missed having Billy around. And what to do with Jason? Maggie must've obtained the blade from him. Billy wouldn't have done it. I had no evidence. I'd scoured hours of footage. Maybe she found the blade when those two bastards got to her. But I doubted it.

Why would Jason want Maggie to die? He must've done it to get back at me. For revenge. He poisoned her mind. What a monster. Jason needed to go. Maggie deserved better. He was a distraction. Maggie had said so herself. She wouldn't move on with him around. With him out of the way, she'd recover more quickly. She could rely on Billy and me. It was for the best. A monster like that didn't deserve to live.

I called security, made the necessary arrangements, and took the lift down to the basement.

I'd have to find another cook. Pity. Jason was great in the kitchen. Who to get? Maybe that restaurant in New South Wales. Where was it? Mollymook. That was right. Bannisters — Rick Stein. He seemed to have a pure heart and was used to travelling. I'd see if I could get him. I could be extraordinarily convincing, after all.

I walked into the holding room. The security team had Jason in cuffs. He wasn't putting up a fight. He couldn't, with me in his brain. I wanted my roaches out of there before he died. Lucky for him that he'd have full control of his mind when he heard what I had to say.

'Three things, Jason. One. I'm giving you your brain back. Two. I have news you need to hear. But first, let's get my babies back. Oh, and this is going to hurt.'

I touched his temples and initiated the removal process. All my creatures are linked to me, part of me, yet separate. I locked onto their energy and began to materialise them out of Jason's neural circuitry. That was the part that hurt.

The tendons on Jason's neck stood out like rope. His mouth stretched into a scream. He squeezed his eyes so tightly shut it was as if they'd been stitched together. Creases fanned out across his nose and eyes. The ebb and flow of his scream was exquisite.

The sides of his nose expanded as a cockroach emerged from each nostril. He bent over and retched, and my final three babies crawled out of his mouth and onto my waiting hand. They scurried up my arms and rested quietly on my shoulders.

Jason hunched over, sobbing and gasping. He couldn't hold his head, as his hands were cuffed.

Finally, he straightened and looked me in the eye. He was staring me down. The fury in his face, the set jaw, the icy blue eyes, the muscular physique. I could see why Maggie found him attractive.

'Now that's out of the way, there's something you need to know.'

He attempted to speak, but had trouble controlling his vocal chords. His circuitry would still be a bit fried. Maybe it would stay that way.

I stared straight back at him. 'Maggie is *dead*.'

Those words delivered more impact than any weapon I could ever use against him.

His head snapped up. 'No! You're lying,' he croaked.

'Unfortunately, not. *You* saw her. In a bath of her own blood. We did everything we could to save her. But it was too late. Congratulations. Your plan was successful. I hope you're happy. It was you who gave her the blade?'

Jason sank to his knees. His head hung down, and his shoulders shook as he sobbed soundlessly.

'What I can't understand is how you could do that to someone you supposedly love? Was it an act of revenge? To take her away from me?'

Jason looked up at me. His eyes blazed. They bore into mine like laser beams.

'It was a *gift*, Tapakah. A gift. I gave Maggie the gift of *choice*. She didn't have to use it. It was *her* choice. *Maggie's* choice. She wrote that in her own blood. Are you so bloody stupid? She chose *death* over you. She hates you so much she chose death.'

'So not revenge?'

'It's called *love,* Tapakah. Something your insect brain has no concept of. Haven't you heard the saying, "If you love something, set it free. If it comes back, it's yours. If it doesn't come back, it was never meant to be."'

Jason's voice broke. He could barely speak. 'I loved … Maggie … so much I gave her … choice, even though there was the chance … I would lose the person I loved most in this world. You think you love her? You were killing her … slowly, bit by bit. She's dead because of *you* … not me.'

'I disagree. You put the weapon in her hand. You planted the seed. It's on your head, not mine.'

Tears streamed down Jason's face. 'What's the third thing?'

'You're going to die.'

'I figured as much,' he croaked.

'Perhaps you and Maggie will finally be together. Take him away.'

They led Jason out of the room. Even though he had his own mind, he didn't struggle. He was broken. He went willingly because he wanted to be with Maggie.

I laughed at the thought.

* * * * *

Finally, the call came through from Frank. It had been hours. I couldn't concentrate on the things I had to do. Maggie was constantly on my mind.

The words Jason said turned over and over in my brain. *She hates you so much she chose death. She chose death over you.* I couldn't believe it. Wouldn't accept it. I wasn't that bad. She simply needed more time to get to know me. I did love her. I was sure it was love. But I couldn't set her free. Not yet. She'd learn to love me. I was learning. I'd made mistakes. She'd come around. I knew it. She had to.

I opened the door to her room. She was in bed, propped up by pillows, talking to Billy. Billy sat on the bed next to her holding her hand. He jumped up when I came in.

I put my arm around him. 'Relax. How are you both doing?'

'Much better now Miss Maggie is okay.'

'How are you feeling, Maggie?'

'Disappointed,' she said flatly.

'Why?' I asked, already knowing the answer.

'Because I'm still here.'

I knelt down beside the bed and took her hand. Her arms were swathed in bandages. Her beautiful eyes filled with tears. Her bottom lip quivered. I wanted to kiss her.

'I will give you your freedom. Do you understand me? But not yet. You need to talk to me more. Tell me how you're feeling. It was a mistake what you did. It was unnecessary suffering for you, for everyone. And Maggie, I'm sorry, but your choice, your action, had consequences. Terrible consequences.'

She gazed at me intently. 'What do you *mean*?'

'Jason is dead.'

Billy gasped.

'No! No. *No!* You're *lying!*' The small amount of colour in her face drained away.

'Unfortunately, not. When Jason saw you in the bath he thought you were dead. He took his own life shortly afterwards. I'm sorry. We've disposed of his body. Exceedingly messy. He should've used a smaller calibre. I guess he wanted to be sure. I'm so sorry, Maggie.'

I waited for her to throw her arms around me. To sob and cry so I could comfort her. I would hold her in my arms and kiss her. Make the pain go away. But nothing happened. She sat there and stared straight ahead with a blank expression.

'Maggie? Talk to me. Say *something.*'

Her eyes were dead. Unblinking, she stared into space. I reached out and touched her arms. They were rigid. I grabbed

278

her by the shoulders and shook her gently. Her whole body was stiff and unresponsive.

I took her arm and shifted it upwards. It behaved mechanically. I let her arm go and it stayed put, frozen in the air. I twisted her hand around; it remained exactly where I positioned it.

It was the same with her other arm. I moved her head to the side; it stayed there. She was a human mannequin.

I waved my hand in front of her face. No blink response. Nothing.

'Maggie. *Maggie.* Come back to me,' I whispered. 'Say something … *anything.'*

Billy was crying. 'What's happened to her, Mister Tapakah? Is she dead?'

'I don't know what's happened. Please, run and get Frank, straight away.'

He left the room sobbing. Poor Billy.

I pulled the blankets back. Maggie's naked body lay rigid. Holding a slender ankle, I moved her leg up and let go. It remained suspended in space. I pulled the pillows out from under her head. Maggie's head and shoulders remained fixed, as though resting on invisible cushions.

I touched her breasts; they felt full and soft. 'Can you see me, Maggie? Your eyes are unseeing, but can you *see* me? Can you *hear* me?'

I bent forward and kissed her gently on the lips. They felt warm.

I bent her other leg at the knee and moved it upwards.

She was a mannequin. An exquisite doll. I could take her like this. I could, if I wanted to. And I *so* wanted to.

I gently pulled her legs and arms straight and placed the pillow back under her head. Covering her with the duvet, I sat and held her hand, waiting for Frank.

* * * * *

Frank covered Maggie up. 'She has retarded catatonia. All the symptoms are there — staring, posturing — the inhibited movement, rigidity, mutism.'

'What's caused it?'

'Sometimes it's a symptom of schizophrenia. It can be brought on by depression, post-traumatic stress disorder, bipolar conditions. I recommend immediate treatment with benzodiazepines or ECT. This must be treated promptly. Malignant catatonia can be fatal.'

'ECT, really?'

'Electroconvulsive therapy, absolutely. Tapakah, she was fine when I brought her back. What happened?'

'I told her Jason was dead. He committed suicide.'

'He did?'

'Yes.'

Frank shook his head. 'Well, there you have it. That's what tipped her over the edge. Good one.'

'Can she hear us?'

'She may be able to hear us, but whether her brain comprehends what we're saying, I'm not sure. I would surmise it probably isn't registering.'

'So, she's like the living dead.'

'Well, she's not dead. But she will be if we don't treat her. If she's not eating, she'll require parenteral nutrition and fluids. It's an IV, the nutrients are absorbed directly into the blood.'

'I've fucked up.'

'Yes, to the level of FUBAR.'

I appreciated Frank felt safe enough to say what he really thought. I needed people like that around me, and I realised I *had* fucked up beyond all recognition.

I'd had a good man killed and destroyed the love of my life.

I was no better than a human.

---

[37] *Maggie's Playlist: Déjà vu — King Henry Maejor*

Chapter 36: Back at HQ

Bella plonked a cup of coffee in front of me. 'What's up, Ash? You're staring into space.'

I squeezed her hand. 'Thinking. Or rather, trying not to think.'

The place wasn't the same without Maggie and Jason.

The Maestro and Christos had returned to the Maestro's apartment, the Prof home to try and sort out his life and career. Fox was consumed with work and trying to find our missing Musketeers. He'd taken Schmoo with him, so Boo was extra miserable without her buddy around. Luca had thrown himself into his medical studies, and Drom always disappeared during the day. He didn't say anything, but I knew he was going back to Hanging Rock. That left Bella and me keeping the house running and looking after Boo.

I spent time cruising on my Harley looking for Maggie and Jason. My heart would leap at a familiar appearance in the crowd, a man's stance on a footpath, the curve of a woman's face. I started seeing them everywhere.

Bella briefly considered returning to New Zealand, but she and the Prof needed each other, and I needed Bella. Sometimes having her around made it harder. Things she said and did reminded me of Maggie. I missed Maggie so much I ached. Now, I knew how Maggie felt about Jason.

The police hadn't been able to come up with anything. It's as though Maggie and Jason had vanished from the planet.

The Maestro tried to lock onto their life forces with her bracelet, but there was nothing. I worried it meant they were dead. The Maestro disagreed. She thought they were being held in a shielded environment. That gave me a sliver of hope.

Bella rubbed my arm in sympathy. 'Why not focus on what to cook for dinner tonight. Everyone will be here and we can catch up and plan what to do next. It'll be great to have us, well, most of us back together again.'

* * * * *

I looked at the faces around the table. It made me so damn happy to see them. 'Glad you could make it.'

'It's great to be here,' Fox said.

I raised my glass. 'I want to propose a toast to Maggie and Jason. May they soon be safe and sound with us. And to Jasmine, much missed, always in our hearts.'

Everyone raised their glasses, clinked, and downed the contents.

'Thanks for dinner, guys,' Drom said. 'It was delicious.'

'Bella and I thought Thai Green Curry, in honor of Maggie and Jason, would hit the spot. We've got lemon tart for desert, Jasmine's favourite.'

'I really miss her,' Drom said.

Bella sighed and twisted a serviette into knots. She was on her fifth serviette already. 'I wish I'd met her. She sounded lovely. I miss Maggie and Jason so much.'

Everyone nodded sadly in agreement.

'Do you have anything new to report?' Luca asked Fox hopefully.

'Yes, and it's not good. The Feds will be taking over all the missing persons cases, including Maggie and Jason's. I'm being frozen out. It's becoming political. All my lines of enquiry are being shut down.'

'All the information on the web relating to Maggie and Jason has disappeared,' Drom said.

Fox looked surprised and flicked through his phone. 'No it hasn't.'

'It has. Check again. Type in their names; nothing shows up.'

'Jesus. You're right. When did you notice that?'

'This morning. Their footprint has been eradicated.'

Fox checked his phone again. 'None of the other missing persons have been removed. But there's definitely nothing for Jason and Maggie.'

Bella grabbed her iPad. 'They're gone from the missing persons sites we put them on too.' Her eyes filled with tears. The Prof handed her a tissue and put his arm around her.

'Tapakah must have done this. He's obliterated all reference to them,' I said.

Bella's expression became defiant. 'Well, we'll keep reinstating everything.'

The Prof shook his head. 'Tapakah will just keep shutting everything down. We can certainly keep trying, but perhaps we should focus on print media, the newspapers. He can't stop us advertising. We could tell the media about how they've vanished and now all reference to them is being wiped. We don't have to mention the whole unbelievable story.'

'That's a great idea, Prof,' Drom said. 'I have friends who are journos. I'll talk to them.'

'I do have one lead,' Fox said. 'Ash, remember in your last mind meld with Maggie, she described a hospital gurney with the brand name Gendron USA?'

'Sure do.

'Well, they're not readily available in Australia. We managed

284

to track down a shipment that came in from the USA a few months ago. It's a convoluted trail, but we've narrowed it down to a delivery address in Canberra. There doesn't seem to be any of these gurney's anywhere else, so I'm thinking Maggie could be there.'

'In *Canberra?*' Bella said.

'Yes. I'm working on this in my own time, and I've a couple of good cops helping me. Not sure how long we can keep going before I'm shut down. But, here's the other thing. By chance I was speaking with a friend who works in security at Parliament House. He saw hospital gurneys on the premises a few weeks ago. Nick didn't know what type they were, but thought it was strange they were on site. He counted twenty gurneys in a basement storage room. Thinking it was odd, he made enquiries as to who, or what, they were for. No one knew anything about them. When he went back for a closer inspection, they'd gone.'

The Prof shook his head. 'Parliament House, Canberra. You're kidding. This puts a whole new light on things. If they're Tapakah's gurneys, that means we're operating in a very different and much more dangerous space than we thought, if that's even possible.'

Bella looked anxious. 'What are you saying, Dad?'

'I'm saying that whatever Tapakah is up to, it's possibly being sanctioned by the government.'

'*What?*'

'That's what I was wondering,' Fox said. 'ASIO must be involved in this as well.'

I thumped my fist on the table. The cutlery and crockery rattled with the force of it. Everyone jumped, including Boo and Schmoo. 'Fair dinkum. Everything keeps getting better and better, doesn't it?'

The Maestro squeezed my arm. 'Settle, Ashley. I realise you're upset. We all are. But that doesn't help.'

'Well, what the fuck are we going to do?' My frustration was growing by the second. A low growl emanated from underneath the table — Boo, voicing her displeasure at my language.

'I've set my MAESTRO device to track Maggie and Jason's life force twenty-four seven. If they're removed from a shielded environment, even for a split second, this device will latch on and get the coordinates. If I give you, Fox and Drom a device ring, we can immediately jump to the location. The problem is that operating the 24/7 tracker uses up a lot of energy. I may have to top up from a crystal again.'

'We have to do it,' I said. 'It's the one slim chance we have.'

The Maestro handed out the rings. 'Put them on and don't take them off.'

'What about Christos?' Bella asked.

'I need him to stay behind as back up. In case something goes wrong.'

Christo's deep voice rumbled forth. 'Bella needs me here. I will look after her.' He smiled at her, and she blushed.

Looked like they still had the hots for each other. I was glad Bella would have something good to take her mind off things. I wished I had something to take my mind off Maggie. I skulled my beer and went for another. Drom gave me a look.

'What, little brother?' Want another?'

'You're drinking a lot, Ash.'

'Yep. What another?'

'Yep.'

'So what does this jumping business feel like?' Fox asked.

'You get used to it,' Christos said. 'Our first jump was interesting. It made us vomit and hurt like hell. I felt as if my atoms had been torn apart in a blender and then smashed back together by nuclear fusion.'

Drom wrinkled his brows. 'The word *interesting* is an understatement then?'

Christos grinned. 'Absolutely.'

'It's not that bad,' the Maestro said. 'You men, for heaven's sake. He's exaggerating. You'll feel slightly dizzy, is all.'

'What's the plan exactly?' Drom asked.

'As soon as I get the alert, your rings will vibrate and glow red. You'll need to get yourself somewhere private to jump. You'll have three minutes. The ring will flash green for ten seconds and beep before it changes to yellow. When it turns yellow you will jump in the next second. Don't hold your breath. Relax. You'll have to be ready, dressed and armed. I have programmed the jump location to be three-hundred metres from the life-force coordinates.'

'Why three-hundred metres?' Luca asked.

'Because the jumpers will need time to recover from the jump, and we need to keep this technology secret. At the moment, it appears to be our only advantage. We can't blast down right in the middle of things.'

'You're right,' I said. 'We appreciate you helping us, Maestro.'

She moved and sat next to me. 'Oh, Ashley. You look so distraught.' She encircled me with her long arms and kissed the side of my face. Her breasts pressed against me. 'Christos and I are going to stay until this is resolved, one way or another. You have our complete support, so whatever we can do to help, we will do,' she said softly.

Her hand massaged the back of my neck and the tension released. She stood and massaged my shoulders with firm, deep strokes. Every touch from her was charged with sexual energy. She didn't mean it; that's how she was. How they both were. My body responded to her touch. I started to tingle from head to toe. Her touch made me feel drunk. In another second, I would be hers, and there'd be nothing I could do to resist.

'Stop, now! Please.' She ceased immediately. 'Ah … thank you, Maestro.' I shook my head. '*Phew.*'

Everyone laughed. The Prof looked at her with adoration. No wonder he loved her. Or maybe he was just an addict. Addicted to her kind of love. I definitely didn't want to add a

Maestro addiction to my substance abuse list.

Drom slapped me on the back. 'That took your mind off things. Can you get me another beer?'

'Get it yourself, little brother.'

He grinned. 'Yes, I guess you won't be able to stand up for a while.'

The Maestro smiled at me. 'You should let yourself go, Ashley. You don't know what you're missing.'

'I'm saving myself.'

'For who? And why, for heaven's sake? You Earthlings are so uptight with your sexuality.'

'It's ... it's something I've promised myself.'

'You've made a pact with God, haven't you?' Luca said.

'Not God, Luca. *Definitely* not God.'

The Maestro whispered throatily into my ear. 'I don't understand you, but I admire your resolve.'

I wished it was Maggie doing the whispering.

The Maestro whispered again. 'I know who you're holding out for.' She kissed the top of my head and sat down.

'You don't have to be a rocket scientist to work that out.'

'I guess not,' she said sadly.

---

[38] *Maggie's Playlist: Officially Missing You — Jayesslee*

'Maggie. Feel. Can. Hear. What. You. How. Change. Christ.'

Words babbled and jabbered outside … somewhere.

I curled up inside my tiny container. It was safe there. No one could reach me. No one could get me. I liked it and thought Maggie may stay forever.

I was vaguely aware of things going on outside, but I ignored them. Outside was bad. Inside was good. I made myself even smaller and my container shrank with me. I felt as tiny as a pea. If they tried to get in I would make myself so small I'd disappear. Forever.

Something tapped on the outside of my container. I pulled open the slide on my tiny glass window and peeked out. A pair of black eyes stared in at me. My own reflection was mirrored in them — except, it didn't look like the me I used to see when I looked in the mirror. Maybe it wasn't me. I couldn't be sure who me was. Who were you, me? What *was* me?

The voices babbled on. I couldn't understand them; it was noise with odd words.

'Sorry. Love. Back. Need. You. Please. Something. Say. Sorry.'

The black eyes vanished. A hand waved back and forth

across my window. A pair of arms stretched out from behind me. Or was that me? Who was me? Strange hands moved the arms. Moved the hands. The hands appeared to be made of wax.

'Response. Nil. Shock. Nothing. Help. Drugs. Hope. Shut.'

I didn't like what I saw. I didn't like the words. I closed my peephole and went back to sleep.

* * * * *

Tapakah

I stared into Maggie's blank eyes. 'It's been five days, Frank, and there's no change. Maggie, can you hear me? Can you see me? Christ, Maggie, I'm sorry. Please come back to me.'

Frank waved his hand in front of Maggie's face. 'She can't hear you, and she can't see you.' He lifted her arms and manipulated her hands.

'Still no response after all those drugs. You have to help her get over the shock, Frank. I can't take much more of this.'

'Neither can Maggie, Tapakah. If you want her back you have to do what I say. You have to remove the psychic dampener. She's an intuitive, and you've effectively shut down the part of her brain she needs to operate effectively in the world. You've removed her coping mechanism, how she processes the world, her connections to all the energies she accesses for support. You've essentially crippled her, and as a psychic, it'd feel like she'd had her heart cut out.'

'If I take it off, they'll find her.'

'If you don't, she'll be safe, but dead. You also need to get her out of this place. She'll never recover in here, even with that device removed. She needs the outside world. Sunshine, trees, the sky, things of beauty. She'll respond to that. It will draw her out better than any drug I have here.'

'Do you guarantee it?'

'I'd stake my life on it.'

'You are,' I said.

Frank rolled his eyes. He thought I was joking.

'Okay, I'll do it,' I said. 'I have a property in Western Australia. It's two hundred kilometers from the nearest made road. It'll be damn hard for anyone to get to her in that place. It's beautiful out there, and the wild flowers will be out. You and Billy will come with me. I'll also need security. Get what you need. I want to leave in an hour.'

'Who's going to run the show while we're gone?'

'Cafard, my eldest. He's up to speed and seems healthy. The challenge will be good for him. How long do you think we'll need?'

'Maybe ten days, depends on how quickly you remove that thing.'

'I'll do it now.'

'I'll take off the bandages.'

Frank peeled off the bandages and gently placed Maggie's arm back down on the bed cover. The sight of it made me gasp. Her limb was parchment white with a thick, raised red scar running down the centre. It was vandalism. I felt sick.

I touched my finger to the black coil around her wrist and it began to pulse with light. Drawing my finger up along her arm, I lead the device away from her damaged veins and up to the top of her arm. It obediently followed my finger until I stopped. Maggie's skin rose slightly as it removed and re-atomised itself into my hand.

Frank seemed fascinated. 'That's it?'

'All done.'

Frank peered into Maggie's face. 'No reaction yet.'

'It's too soon. It'll take time for her brain to adjust and realise it's no longer restricted.'

'Okie dokie.' Frank scribbled out a list of requirements. 'Shall I organise a pilot?'

'Yes. Get Mark. I like him best.'

'Frank adjusted his collar and grinned at me. 'Will do. A change of scenery will be welcome, especially since my life's on the line.'

I smiled back. 'Indeed.'

He still thought I was kidding.

* * * * *

Billy played with the blind on the aircraft window, opening and closing it. He gently kicked his legs back and forth against the chair. 'How long will it take to get to Western Australia, Mister Tapakah?'

'It's about six hours to where we're heading, Billy. It's in the middle of nowhere, an old cattle station covering over a quarter of a million acres.'

'That's pretty big, isn't it?'

'Incredibly big. When you're out in the bush, standing on one of the hills, you can't see anything that's human made.'

Billy was excited. He'd never been anywhere, let alone in a private jet.

Maggie sat opposite me. I'd positioned her head so she could look out the window. She would stay in whatever position we put her in, for hours, if we let her. Her food was still intravenous.

When Jason had kidnapped Maggie, she'd been wearing a blonde wig. I'd decided to let Maggie grow her hair back, and in the meantime, she could wear the wig.

To my surprise, my own hair had started to regrow vigorously. In two days, I sported a shock of thick black hair, plus an extended goatee. I decided to leave it. I thought hair would make me more appealing to Maggie.

Lilith had done Maggie's hair and makeup. She looked beautiful with blonde hair, as well as black. Perhaps if she caught a glimpse of herself looking like she used to, it would help her recover.

Soon a red ochre landscape appeared below us, dotted with green and grey scrubby bush. The plane circled around to land. 'There's the cattle station, Billy.'

Assorted sheds, trucks, cars, and corrals littered the area around the station. The homestead was a sprawling colonial farmhouse, built in the late eighteen hundreds. It was surrounded by trees and stood out as a lush green patch in a sea of red dust.

Hugh and Elizabeth, the station managers, were waiting for us at the side of the airstrip. They had two four-wheel drives ready to transfer us to the homestead.

Frank placed Maggie in her wheelchair. Even though I found it difficult, I'd decided not to touch her anymore, to keep my distance. If, like Jason said, she hated me so much, any physical contact would hinder her recovery.

The jet had a built-in hydraulic wheel chair hoist, which made it easy to get Maggie in and out of the plane. Billy and I waited outside as the hoist gently deposited Maggie and the wheelchair onto the ground.

'Can you push her?' I asked Billy.

He grabbed the handles. 'Sure thing!' He propelled the wheelchair forward towards Hugh and Elizabeth, and the wheels sent up spirals of red dust. He kicked up the soil with his shoes. 'This is *amazing!* I've never seen dirt this colour!'

Hugh grinned at the boy's enthusiasm. 'You haven't seen anything yet.'

We arrived at the homestead, and the two station dogs, Dundee and Nulla, were there to greet us. They yapped excitedly around the car as we rolled into the driveway.

Billy seemed anxious. 'Do they bite?'

'They guard the place, and they only bite bad people,' Elizabeth said.

Billy thought for a while and said hesitantly, 'What if they think we're bad people?'

Hugh smiled. 'Don't you worry, young Billy. You stick with me. I'm the boss dog. Null and Dee are looking forward to meeting you. What you have to do, is step out of the car all confident like, and ignore them. Don't talk to them, don't look at them, and don't touch them. That way, they'll think you're a boss dog too. After a while, when they're quiet and settled, you can get to know them.'

Billy grinned. 'Okay, I'm a boss dog!'

We unpacked the cars and Frank and I settled Maggie into one of the large guestrooms. The homestead was a faded beauty, with tall ceilings, verandas and a spacious covered courtyard in the middle. Maggie's room was peaceful and cool with a view onto the gardens.

We put Maggie in bed to rest, and supported her with pillows so she could see outside. There was a comfortable chair and footstool by the side of the bed so someone could be with her at all times.

Frank and I sat on the veranda outside her room and had a beer. Billy, who was now a firm friend of Dundee and Nulla, played with them on the grass.

'It must take a fair bit of water to keep it so green around the homestead,' Frank said. 'I thought it'd be nothing but red dirt.'

'It's not just for looks. It's a necessity, a buffer zone. Back in the day when there was nothing around the homestead but soil and scrub, windstorms would fill the house with dust. It would get in through every tiny crack and the whole interior would be coated with red dust. The women would spend hours cleaning it, before the next windstorm blew it all back in again. The trees, shrubs and lawns keep the house cool and stop the dust.'

Frank sculled the rest of his beer. 'Jeez. Must've been hard going back then. Get you another?'

'Please.'

While he was gone, I looked through Maggie's window. She

sat motionless on the white cast iron bed, her body surrounded by decorative pillows. A feeding tube line ran into her chest. A bedside lamp lit the walls with a soft pink glow. She didn't see any of it, just stared unblinkingly out of the window. Frank went into the room, tilted her head back and squeezed drops into each eye, and then tilted her head down again.

'Still no change,' he said grimly, when he came back out.

'It's early days.'

'We need to get her outside. I've talked to Hugh. He can drive us to the wildflowers.'

'Okay, let's. The weather's not too hot.'

'I'll disconnect her feed tube and get her ready,' Frank said.

Hugh drove us around to the other side of a ridge. The track was bumpy in spots, and it was a rough ride. Hugh and I were in the front; Frank and Billy sat in the back next to Maggie to make sure she was okay.

Rounding an enormous expanse of red boulders at the end of a ridge, the landscape opened up. We gasped. A sea of white flowers spread out before us. It was as though a storm had dusted the red soil with drifts of white snow that stretched out for miles in each direction.

'That's the most beautiful phenomenon I've ever seen,' Frank said. Hugh pulled over and we all jumped out. Billy was speechless.

Frank carried Maggie to a spot right in the middle of the field of flowers. Billy spread out a blanket and helped her to sit cross-legged on the rug. They returned, leaving her sitting alone in a field of white.

'Should she be on her own?' I asked.

'I think so. Only for a short while,' Frank replied. 'We should remove ourselves from her line of sight. It might help if she can't see us … you.' He pointed to a nearby boulder. 'You have your telephoto lenses and surveillance gear. You can watch her from over there.'

I set up my camera and recording equipment by the boulder. The monitor captured Maggie perfectly. We made ourselves comfortable and settled down to watch.

* * * * *

Maggie

Perfume of earth and rock. Warmth penetrated my bones. Fragrance of flowers. Sounds of nature. Thousands of whispers tickled my ears. Something touched my skin, caressing it with a gentle breath.

Whisper. Rustle. Whisper. Rustle. Whisper. Rustle.

What was that sound? It didn't stop. It was calling me. Go away.

Whisper. Rustle. Whisper. Rustle. Whisper. Rustle.

I hated to look out there. I didn't want to. But something was calling me.

Sliding open the cover of my peephole, I peeked out.

White flowers. Nothing but white flowers. Hundreds. Thousands. *Millions* of white flowers. Star like in appearance, their heads nodded in the breeze, moving as one. A creature made of flowers. I thought it surrounded me, but I could only see straight ahead. Beyond the flowers was a wall of bright blue. Bluebell blue. The bluest of blue.

I stared and stared and stared and didn't want to close my window. The whiteness and the blueness made me feel bigger. Softer. Something tickled my ankle.

Whisper. Rustle. Whisper. Rustle. Whisper. Rustle.

The flowers. The flowers were calling. They wanted me.

I felt safe. I didn't know who or where I was, but I felt safe.

I closed my window and it was dark. I opened my window and the flower creature and the blue were still there.

Open. Close. Open. Close. Open. Close.

Back in the dark, a room appeared. It had doors. There were doors all around me. The floor was wooden. The doors were rusted shut. Many were bolted and padlocked. One door was open. I walked towards it and stepped through.

The room had thousands of shelves, with thousands of books stacked to the ceiling. Many of the shelves had collapsed or tipped over. Books littered the aisles. Row after row of broken shelves stretched into the distance. Books lay higgledy-piggledy everywhere.

I touched a book and it lit up, sparkling iridescently. It triggered other books in other sections. Cascades of colour rocketed around the room. I dropped the book in fright.

I touched another one, and it lit up in different colours. I opened the cover. A man with sandy hair and bright blue eyes looked out at me. The image made me feel like crying. I slammed the cover shut and put the book down.

There were books bound with wire. Books locked in chests covered in cobwebs. Ancient books covered in black leather with "Do Not Open. Ever." scrawled in red across the front. New books were mixed with old books, and the whole place was one overwhelming, frightening mess.

This was my library. I was the librarian. It appeared to be the biggest library in the world, and it was in ruins. It had been trashed. I'd have to clean it up. Make sense of it. Repair it. Sort it. Fix the shelves. Catalogue it. Index. File. Register. Log. Record.

I backed out in terror, overwhelmed at the task in front of me.

There was a shiny new book sitting near the entrance. I picked it up and flipped open the front cover to see white flowers and blue sky. I liked the book. It was beautiful. This book was the only book I needed. Whatever the rest of those books contained, I didn't want to know.

I stepped out of the library and shut the door.

The door disappeared into the wall. The library was gone. The room with the doors dissolved into the dark. A sense of happiness descended upon me as I looked out of my peephole.

I could start a whole new collection, beginning with just this one book.

* * * * *

Tapakah

The camera lens was filled with Maggie's pale and frozen beauty. I stared, spellbound. Her dark lashes fluttered slightly.

'She blinked. Frank, she blinked, I swear it!'

I zoomed in on her face. Her eyelids fluttered. She glanced slowly from left to right and then straight ahead. Her eyes were alive. She was seeing! Her arm jerked towards a flower near her ankle. Her hand twitched as she caught the stem and the flower head broke.

Her limb functioned robotically as she raised the flower to her face. Her fingers played stiffly against the paper-like petals.

I realised I was holding my breath in excitement and anticipation as the edges of Maggie's lips twitched and a smile lit up her face. Her expression was one of beaming radiance and joy. Her eyes shone with green luminescence as she directed her gaze straight down the lens of the camera into mine. A dart of energy pierced my heart. I jumped back with the shock and intensity of it. Clutching my chest, I looked back down the lens at Maggie. She mouthed the words, *'Thank you.'*

My body pulsed with strange sensations. *Emotions?* I'd never felt this way before. It was as though I'd been transformed as she was transformed.

A small hand grasped mine. 'Why are you crying?' Billy asked. 'You should be happy.'

'I don't know why. I've never cried before. Ever.'

---

[39] *Maggie's Playlist: I'll Fly Away — Alison Krauss & Gillian Welch*

298

Frank looked at me with raised eyebrows as I wiped the fluid from my face and tasted it. Hmmm. Salty. 'But I am … *happy*. I think.'

Frank smiled. 'Guess I get to live another day then?'

I pulled him into my arms and hugged him. 'Many, many days!'

'Jesus. I'm not used to *this*,' Frank said, as Billy joined in the hug.

I looked back at the monitor. Maggie had vanished.

'She's *gone*!' I broke into a run. Frank and Billy were right behind me.

My heart was pounding as I reached the blanket.

She lay on her back, obscured by the flowers. Her arms were spread out to the side, and she stared at the sky, smiling. An angel in a flowing gown of white.

'*Maggie?*'

She raised her head and smiled. 'Hello, there. Who are you?'

Billy knelt down and took her hands. 'Maggie, it's me, *Billy*.'

She gazed at him blankly. 'Do I know you?'

'Maggie, this is Frank. He saved your life,' I said. 'And you should certainly remember me, Tapakah.'

'I'm sorry, but I don't know you.' She indicated the surrounds with jerky movements of her arms. 'All I remember is the blue and the white.'

I shot Frank a look. 'Excuse us for a minute, Maggie. We'll be right back. Billy, can you stay here with Maggie?'

Frank walked me out of ear shot. 'She has amnesia. That device of yours has screwed up her brain. I'll have to do further investigation to discover what sort of amnesia she has.'

'Can it be treated?' I asked.

'There's no actual cure for it. Sometimes it resolves itself. I can treat any underlying medical conditions, give her therapy, but if she has hippocampal damage, she may never get her memory back. What are you going to tell her?'

'As little as possible. Follow my lead.'

We returned to where Maggie and Billy were waiting. This must have been divine intervention. If her mind was wiped, I'd have a clean slate to work with. I could start again. Make things right. This was my lucky day.

'Can you remember me now?' I asked her.

'Sorry, no.'

'What can you remember?'

Maggie furrowed her brow and thought for a while. 'Nothing. Just the blue and the white. It's strange, I don't know how I came to be here,' she said calmly.

'You're not frightened?'

'No. Should I be?'

'Definitely not,' I said. 'Maggie, you've been ill and we've been looking after you, helping you recover. Your ability to remember things has been affected. We're your friends, and we're doing everything we can to help you. We need to get you back to the homestead now.'

'Okay.' She tried to stand, but her legs didn't have the strength to support her. She slowly collapsed back on the blanket.

'I'll carry you,' Frank said.

I bent down to help her up. 'No, I'll take her. Maggie, can you put your arm around my shoulder?'

'Yes.' Slowly, she lifted her arm and placed it around my neck. I scooped her up and walked back to the car. She must have lost weight as her body felt so light. She leaned her head on my shoulder and was instantly asleep. As I walked, the paper daisies crunched under my feet. Her body felt warm against mine. Holding her this way, carrying her, filled me with joy. At least, I thought that was what the sensation was.

On the return car journey, I sat in the back with Maggie and Billy. I didn't have to keep my distance anymore. She couldn't remember me. It was a blessing.

I cradled her in my arms as she slept. She was stretched out across the back seat, her legs resting on top of Billy's. He made sure she was secure as we travelled over the bumpy tracks.

'This is nice,' Billy said.

'What is?'

He shrugged his shoulders and smiled. 'Everything.'

Maggie was still fast asleep when we arrived at the homestead. I carried her back to her room and put her to bed.

'Is she okay?' I asked Frank.

'I think so. She's tired. I mean, she's been catatonic for days, so this has been a marathon for her. I'll reconnect her feed tube in the meantime, but I want to try her on light food, soup, jelly, that sort of thing. I'll have something ready for when she wakes.'

'I'll sit here with her.'

I sat in the armchair and watched Maggie sleep; her face was peaceful and relaxed. I struggled with the intense sensations that coursed through my mind and body. What was happening to me? I was different. She felt real to me now. Not an object. I had an intense sense of connection to her.

I held her hand in mine. Her arms were still bandaged. Powerful feelings flooded through me as I thought about the damage to her beautiful body. Damn Jason.

'You look sad, Tapakah.'

She was awake, watching me intently.

'Is that what I'm feeling? Then I'm sad about what happened to you, to your arms.'

'What did happen to me?'

'We're not sure. I found you on the streets and brought you in. You couldn't remember anything. It appears you tried to take your own life.'

Maggie gave a little gasp. 'I must've been desperately unhappy to do that.'

'It appears so.'

'How long have you been looking after me? What is our

relationship?'

'We've looked after you for a few weeks now, but it seems you've lost those memories too. We hoped that by bringing you here, it would help heal your mind. With regard to us, it's complicated. Since you've lost those memories, I guess it's like starting over for you. But from my point of view, I ... I love you, Maggie.'

Her cheeks flushed pink. 'Oh. *Really?* Do ... do I love you?'

'You'll have to discover that for yourself.'

'Did I love you?'

'No. I'm fairly certain you didn't. And don't.'

'But why? You seem so ... so kind.'

'You had a lot to deal with. I don't think love was on your agenda.'

'So why are you telling me now how you feel?'

'Because ... because I wanted you to know. It just came out. I'm sorry, I shouldn't have said anything. I'm not myself. I don't want to make you feel uncomfortable. If the feeling isn't mutual, I can deal with that.'

She bit her lip. 'I'm sorry. I feel awkward around you now.'

Frank returned and placed a small bowl of jelly on the bedside table. 'Don't worry. Everyone feels that way around Tapakah. Oh, and mail's in. This is for you.' He handed me a brown envelope.

I ripped open the packet and pulled out a thin gold bracelet. 'Ah, what I've been waiting for.'

'What's that?' Frank asked.

'It's a tracker for Maggie. If she loses her memory again, or gets lost, we'll be able to find her. Can I put it on your wrist, Maggie?'

She held out her arm. 'Sure.'

I snapped it shut. 'It's light and waterproof, so it shouldn't bother you.'

'Hopefully, I won't need it.'

I handed Maggie a buzzer. 'We'll leave you to rest now. If you need anything, press this.'

She snuggled under the covers and looked up at me gratefully. 'Thank you for everything.' Closing her eyes, she was instantly asleep.

* * * * *

'Okay, Tapakah, what is that bracelet, *really?*' Frank asked.

'Like I said. It's a tracking device.'

'And?'

'And a life force shield. Her people will be looking for her. They have advanced technology. If you imagine life force broadcasting similar to Wi-Fi waves, the bracelet shields the wearer's energy and essentially makes them invisible.'

'I knew it! It's not going to mess with her mind, is it?'

'No. Definitely not. Do you think her memory will come back?'

'I'll give you my opinion when I've had time to investigate further. So, you're not going to tell her what actually happened?'

'No.'

'And if her memory returns?'

'I'll deal with it. What are you looking at, Frank?'

'Your hair. It's amazing how fast it's grown back. If we could synthesize whatever's at work there you could make a fortune.'

I smiled. 'You'd better get onto it then.'

'I'll add it to the list.' He ran a hand through his own thinning hair and grinned. 'Might have to make it a priority.'

---

[40] *Maggie's Playlist: Amnesia — Guy Sebastian*

Maggie

Chapter 38: Absence Makes the Heart Grow Fonder

Once Frank removed all my tubes and I was eating normally again, I felt much stronger. The weeks had flown by, and my body was my own again. It was wonderful not to feel tired all the time.

I was in the kitchen eating breakfast with Frank, Billy, and Hugh. Hugh had cooked up a big breakfast especially for me: free range bacon, eggs, grilled tomatoes, hash browns and toast. My favourite.

Tapakah had been away for over a week on business, and the place felt strange without him. He was due back tomorrow. We were all looking forward to seeing him.

After he'd declared his feelings for me, it had felt a bit awkward, but he kept things light and friendly. I began to relax and enjoy what was. Everyone was so lovely. Whatever my past was, it must have been unhappy for me to attempt suicide. Tapakah had saved me and given me a new life. I couldn't remember my old life. By the sounds of it that was no great loss. I was grateful for everything he'd done for me.

I decided to give up my struggle to remember. I was scared that if I did remember, it would ruin what I had now.

Footsteps echoed down the hallway. The kitchen door

opened and Elizabeth and Tapakah walked in. My heart gave an unexpected leap as I laid eyes on him. He was dressed in black jeans and a dark charcoal T-shirt with four buttons down the front. A black leather jacket with zips in the sleeves and black lace up hiking boots completed the picture.

He'd had his hair cut and styled. It was swept back off his face and highlighted his brown, almost black eyes. His dark eyebrows, Roman nose and extended goatee made him appear like a brooding Spaniard.

Everyone stopped eating and stared.

'What?' he said.

Frank chuckled. 'You've had a makeover. I think I'm in love. We were expecting you tomorrow. Everything all right?'

'Yes, Cafard's doing a great job.'

'Wow, you look like a movie star.' Billy ran over to Tapakah and threw his arms around him. Tapakah picked him up and swung him around.

'I've missed you, little Billy,' Tapakah said, putting him down.

Tapakah locked onto me with his dark eyes. 'Hi, Maggie.'

'Hello.' I looked down, suddenly feeling shy and silly. I wished I'd made more of an effort with my appearance.

'You're just in time for breakfast,' Hugh said. 'There's plenty left.' He stood and put a couple of plates in the oven.

Tapakah pulled out a chair for Elizabeth. 'Fantastic. I love a good Hugh breakfast. I was hoping we'd make it in time.'

Tapakah sat opposite me and Hugh put a cup of coffee in front of him. He sipped his coffee and stared at me. I felt self-conscious as I tried to finish my breakfast without shoveling it down.

Tapakah nodded approvingly. 'You have your appetite back.'

I smiled at Hugh. 'The food's so fabulous here, it would be hard not to.'

'Any memories?'

'No. Nothing.' Looking up from my plate I thought a look of

relief flashed across his face.

'I'm sorry you find yourself in this situation.'

'Don't be. I don't care.'

He cocked his head in surprise but didn't comment. 'Oh, I have something for you. Billy, in my bag at the front door, there's a present for you, and one for Maggie.'

Billy leapt off his chair and ran down the hall, returning with two brown paper packages.

He took one and slid it across the table to me.

I loved surprises. I ripped off the paper and opened the box. Inside was a shoulder length black wig.

'It's identical to your own hair. I thought you might prefer it to the blonde, or as a change,' he said softly. 'You don't have to wear a wig at all, but I thought it would be nice for you to have options while your hair grows back.'

'Thank you. It's lovely. I can't remember how I looked with my own hair. Was it exactly the same as this?'

'Yes. *Exactly*. There's something else.' He pulled another small package from inside the box and handed it to me.

'How exciting! What could this be?' I tore off the paper and gasped. 'An iPod touch and AirPods!'

'You said you loved music. It's been loaded with all the tunes you mentioned you loved, and more. I hope you like it.'

'Like it? I *love* it!'

Oh, my God. Music! All those songs that played constantly in my brain. I'd be able to search for them. Hear them for real. What a beautiful gift. He was very thoughtful.

'Thank you so much, Tapakah. I don't know what to say, how to repay you.'

'You don't have to. Seeing you happy is its own reward.'

'Billy, what did you get?' I asked.

'A knife, Miss. It's awesome.' He handed me a dagger with an exquisite handle.

'It's beautiful!' I removed it from the scabbard and held it to the light. 'It seems ancient. I *love* it.'

Tapakah smiled. 'Maybe I should've bought you a knife rather than a wig. It is ancient, made of Damascus steel.'

I was thrilled. 'I know about Damascus steel! It's supposed to have magical properties. It can split a feather in midair, yet cut through armor and rifle barrels. The pattern of the steel looks organic, similar to rippling water.'

How did I know about Damascus steel? Why did the blade look familiar?

Tapakah looked concerned. 'Maggie, is there a problem?'

'It's okay. I appear to be acquainted with Damascus steel. I've seen it before, but I can't remember where, or why. Never mind.' I turned my attention back to the remaining piece of crispy hash brown on my plate.

When I looked up, Tapakah was still staring at me. He was so intense. Even though he made me feel uncomfortable, there was something exciting about it. I found him intriguing. My shoulders shuddered as a chill ran down my spine. A peculiar sensation clenched in my base chakra. I knew it was the feeling that came upon me when looking down from a great height, as if I was going to fall. Why I felt that, sitting safely at the breakfast table, I didn't know.

'I'll clean up,' I said. 'You guys go and do whatever you need to do.'

'Won't argue with that,' Hugh said.

Everyone left, and I was glad to be alone. I didn't mind cleaning and enjoyed washing dishes. I was looking forward to listening to my iPod, but in the meantime, I hummed a song that had been ear worming around in my head all morning. I couldn't remember where or when I'd heard it, it simply popped into my brain.

'If it makes you happy, it can't be that bad. If it makes you happy, why the hell are you so sad?'

Standing in front of the sink, I swayed to the melody in my

mind. Someone gripped my waist from behind and I just about jumped out of my skin.

'I missed you, Maggie.'

It was Tapakah.

'You scared the hell out of me!'

'Sorry, I didn't mean to.'

I turned around and my rubber gloves dripped soap suds all over his new jacket. 'Oh, shit. I'm sorry.' I tried to rub off the soap and made things worse. Flustered, I pulled off the gloves. 'I'll get a cloth.'

He laughed and wouldn't move out of the way.

'Relax. I really missed you.' He held my shoulders and stared into my soul with those dark eyes.

'I … I … actually missed you too.' I felt hot and bothered and wished he wasn't standing so close. The scent of leather from his jacket, the warmth of his body. He radiated heat. I could hear his heart beating along with mine. A strange mix of fear, excitement and adrenaline coursed through my body. I couldn't work out if I was scared or aroused.

His gaze was hypnotic in its intensity. I couldn't look away. He held my face and kissed me, pressing his body hard against mine. The stainless steel of the sink dug into my back. My knees buckled as terror and passion intermingled in my brain. I wilted away from his kiss.

He held me up. 'What's wrong?'

'Um, it appears I have a knee problem.'

He looked at me worriedly. 'I'll get Frank to check you out.'

'Frank's not going to be able to fix them.'

'Why not?'

I put my arms around his neck. 'Because you are the cause and the cure.' I stretched up on my tippy toes and kissed him back.

A cocktail of emotions exploded in my head as we kissed — fear, passion, disgust, danger, lust, excitement — they were all melded together in my brain. I couldn't tell the difference anymore.

I didn't care. He had set me on fire.

After the kiss, Tapakah held me tight. His heart pounded in his chest. I could sense emotions flooding his body, feel them pulsing under his skin. I didn't know what to do, so I did nothing.

Finally, he spoke. 'That was a surprise. I was expecting a slap across the face.'

I buried my face in his chest. 'I'm sorry, I don't understand what came over me.'

'Don't be sorry. I'm certainly not.'

He leaned back and lifted my chin to see my face. I looked away as I felt myself flush. It was hard to sustain his intense gaze.

'What's wrong?' he asked.

'I hardly know you, yet I feel as if I know you. All my emotions are mixed up … crazy, good, bad … terrifying. I can't explain it. It *scares* me.'

'I scare you?'

'Maybe.'

'I'm sorry. I shouldn't have kissed you. It was wrong. I was carried away. I won't do it again.' Tapakah put his arms around me and sighed. 'I'm afraid you're my obsession.' He kissed me on the forehead, then turned and left the room. I stood and watched him go, wishing he would stay. I was relieved he was gone, but I wanted him back.

What the hell? What was my problem? No wonder I'd tried to commit suicide. I was a fruitcake. I needed to go for a walk and clear my mind.

I went outside to look for Hugh and Elizabeth. Hugh was chopping wood, and Elizabeth was feeding the chooks.

'Can I take the farm bike and go up to the ridge? I need to

---

[41] *Maggie's Playlist: If It Makes You Happy — Sheryl Crow*

clear my head.'

Hugh nodded. 'It's okay with me. Better ask Frank.'

Frank came out of the shed. 'Someone mention my name?'

'Can I take the farm bike and ride to the ridge? I need space.'

'You can ride a motorbike?'

'Yes.'

'How do you know?'

'I just know.'

He tossed me the keys. 'Well, show me.'

After four fast laps around a tricky circuit, I slid to a stop right next to him, spraying his feet with red dust.

'Oops, sorry 'bout that, Frank.'

He grinned. 'Yeah, I get it. You can ride a bike. Be back well before the sun goes down.'

I dropped a wheelie and blasted down the dirt road. Something caught my eye in the doorway of a shed. A man stood tall, with the posture of a gun slinger, mouth tight, shoulders squared, legs apart. He looked ready for a gunfight, hands open at his sides, ready to draw. He was dressed in black and wore aviator sunglasses.

It was Tapakah.

I pretended not to see him.

The red dust, the white flowers and blue skies were calling me. I loved trail bike riding, and had my eye fixed on the ridge with colossal red boulders. The landscape replicated Mars. I couldn't wait to climb to the top.

* * * * *

Tapakah

'Frank, what the *hell?* Where's Maggie going? I said, striding across the yard.

'Taking a ride up to the ridge. She wanted to clear her head.

310

What's the problem?'

'She could disappear, fall off, get hurt, try and escape, any number of things, you idiot.'

'She's a fine rider, you saw her. She has a tracking device on her wrist. There's no problem. You want her to recover fully from catatonia? This is part of the process.'

'Can you guarantee her memory won't return?'

'I can't guarantee it, you know that. But from the investigation I've conducted, it's highly unlikely. Nothing I've tried triggers any memories. Her mind's a closed shop. Everything starts from here.'

'Just way I want it.'

'So, you're not going to give her any information about her past?'

'Nope. I have no choice. Well, I do, but I'd lose her. I'm not prepared to do that.'

'You're not going to bring her back to the lab?'

'I'm not sure yet. I'll have to wait and see.'

---

[42] *Maggie's Playlist: The Nearness of You — Norah Jones*

Red soil and grey saltbush stretched out before me. I blasted along the road, which was worn into two sections by the tyres of four-wheel drives. The saltbush covered the landscape with soft pastel tones of grey. Red, flat-topped mounds of anthills punctuated the grey, appearing like stepping stones leading to the ridge.

I slowed to a stop near a tangle of burnt out brush and fallen trees. I didn't want to get lost out here, so getting my bearings was important.

A flash of gold caught my eye, and there was a rustle in the brush. As I kicked down the stand on my bike, a huge goanna flew out of the bush towards me. I pulled my feet up and kept still. It froze, and then, rose up on its hind legs and regarded me with dark eyes.

I held my breath. It was a whopper, at least two meters long, speckled with light and dark brown spots that glowed amber in the sun. My breath caught with the beauty of it, an Aboriginal painting come to life.

A black band of pigment ran around its head and through its eyes, reminding me of the mask of Zorro. Each powerful leg was kitted out with five formidable claws.

Hugh had been educating me about the local flora and fauna. I remembered he said goannas could give you a nasty bite. The bite wouldn't kill you, but apparently goannas have venom glands in their mouth and the wound can flare up for years. He also said that goannas generally run away when confronted. Sometimes, they've been known to mistake human bystanders for trees and have tried to run up them. Looking at the size of those claws, it wouldn't be much fun for the innocent bystander.

Given that was the extent of my knowledge about goannas, I decided to get off my bike and move slowly away. I didn't want to make like a tree.

I dismounted and the goanna rose even higher on its back legs. A black forked tongue flicked in and out. It hissed, and the skin around its neck inflated. I backed off a couple of steps. It hissed again, loudly, and something about that hiss made my blood run cold.

The goanna's eyes locked onto mine. Its stare was intense, reminding me of Tapakah. I swore it was trying to tell me something. Then with a flick of its powerful tail, it spun around and vanished into the brush. Small billows of red dust floated up in its wake.

Vague notions about animal totems stirred in my mind. I was sure I knew about them, but the memories flickered out of reach.

I climbed back on the bike and headed along a track leading to the left of the ridge. The trail was rough, so I took it easy and cruised along at around forty clicks. A glint of water shone in the distance, so I travelled towards it. The day was warm with a light breeze, a bright blue sky, and a few token puffs of white clouds.

Something moved in my peripheral vision. I looked over my shoulder. A massive red kangaroo bounded along beside me. Its hind legs pounded out a rhythm in the red dust, its tail moved up and down propelling it forward with grace and ease. It seemed to be enjoying running next to me, which was incredible. After a while it stopped and watched me go. I turned the bike around and slowly motored towards it, stopping about ten feet away.

From its size, it was obviously a male, and the biggest red kangaroo I'd ever laid eyes on. Its body was a deep rusty colour; a tinge of red ran up the nose and over the top of its eyes. The muzzle and ears matched the grey of the saltbush. Its charcoal colour nose twitched as it caught my scent, and its dark liquid eyes looked at me with a soft gaze.

It lowered itself slightly and leapt. In one bound it was up against my bike. It stood on its hind legs and towered above me. It must've been over six feet tall. Whack a white singlet on him and he would've doubled for Arnold Schwarzenegger in his heyday. Probably bigger. Definitely on 'roids. His chest rippled with muscles. Bulging biceps popped with veins, and strong forelimbs were finished with black-gloved paws and five lethal looking talons. Scars old and new crisscrossed his flesh. I hoped I wasn't in for a dose of 'roid rage.

He did have a kindly camel-like face, but as it loomed above me, it didn't feel especially kindly. I knew it could rip my guts out in two seconds flat. Unlike my encounter with the goanna, this time I decided to make like a statue.

A soft whiskered muzzle bent down and snuffled my ear. It tickled and I screwed up my face as it moved around exploring my head and neck. The scent of grass and scrub filled my nostrils. Two clawed paws placed themselves firmly on my shoulders. I was totally at its mercy.

My mind was spinning. I could floor the bike to get out of its clutches, but half of me may be left behind. The bike couldn't get up enough initial speed to outrun it. That plan may only serve to make it angry, and there was no way I wanted to make this fella angry.

Maybe I could tickle his tummy. What animal didn't enjoy a tummy tickle?

Slowly, slowly I moved my hand and gently rubbed its belly, just under the chest. The fur was woolly and soft. The roo quivered slightly and stretched up even higher on its back legs. Its eyes were closed, and its ears moved backwards and forwards.

Encouraged, I scratched and tickled with more enthusiasm. The roo made soft grunting noises, and I cogitated on how long I should continue. After a couple of minutes, I stopped, and the pressure of its claws increased against my flesh. I took this as an indication that it would behoove me to continue. This time I leant forward and used both hands to give it a thorough going over.

After about ten minutes my hands were ready to drop off, and I had a severe crick in my neck and back. My fingers felt waxy and dirty.

'I can't do anymore, Big Red,' I said softly. 'Please let me go. I'll come back tomorrow and give you another tummy tickle.'

A loud grunt-cough rumbled from its chest, and the roo released my shoulders from its grip. A paw plonked down on top of my head, the claws pressing hard against my scalp. I was going to lose what little hair I had. But no, it patted me on the head, a few light whacks, and then nuzzled my ear.

The muscles on its body rippled as it moved away. The roo thumped the ground with its back legs raising a cloud of red dust. It turned, met my eyes, and then launched itself into the air. Five explosive bounds later and it had disappeared from sight.

Hooley Dooley. That was one intimidating animal encounter. My hands were trembling as I hit the throttle and headed off towards the glint of water.

As I rounded the winding track, a large expanse of water appeared before me. Short, snow-white eucalypts grew in twisted sculptures around the lake, and the red earth was carpeted in shades of yellow, orange, rust and luminescent greens. Streaks of orange floated on the surface, making it look as though the lake had merged with the land.

I turned off the motor and sat in awe. Mother nature was the artist, and she had created a painting, a divine watercolour of exquisite hue, shade and texture. It stretched as far as the eye could see. The scene was accompanied by music, my ears resounded with it. The insistent chirruping of a billion insects, mingled with the bell like calls of birds, created an all-encompassing symphony of sound. I was transported to another realm as my soul absorbed this heaven on earth.

In the distance, a black shape floated above the water. It headed straight for me at speed. In flight, it cast a shadow on the earth as black as night. That blackness, the shadow, a recognition — something — caused a jolt of fear to course through my body.

It grew closer, gliding like a B52 bomber. I recognised the shape, the curve of the wing — a wedge-tailed eagle. The shadow underneath it seemed to have a life of its own. As black as Vantablack, it slid threateningly across the earth and I was paralysed by its deadly approach.

The rush of air from its wings buffeted me as the massive raptor slowed and extended its claws towards my face. I covered my head and braced for impact.

A eucalypt branch above me bowed and shook. I looked up through my arms and into the piercing gaze of the eagle. Black talons curled around the branch. It flapped its magnificent wings. The nine-foot wingspan was a waterfall of chocolate, rust, silver grey and amber feathers. The wings stretched, shook and then retracted to nestle neatly against its body. The head extended towards me, a powerful hooked beak and hooded amber eyes conveyed an expression of dominance and disapproval.

Slowly, I took my arms away from my face and gripped the handlebars of the bike.

The shadow had left me with a strong feeling of foreboding, which made my body twitch with the urge to run. When I moved my foot to kick-start the bike, the eagle jumped off the branch and landed on my arm. One taloned foot clenched the throttle and my hand, the other curled around my forearm. My shoulder sagged with the weight of its body.

The beak, with a hook like a claw hammer, was mere inches from my face. Its nostrils quivered and the ridge of pink flesh on the side of its mouth, pursed upwards as it considered which of my eyeballs to prise out first.

The raptor had four black talons around my arm, one at the back and three at the front. As it held me in its gaze the vice like grip increased. Three talons were pressing into my skin causing it to pucker. The eagle gave a quick and powerful squeeze and the three front talons pierced my skin. I cried out in pain and my hand flew away from the throttle as the raptor pushed off and launched into the air.

A lone feather floated down and landed in my lap. I picked up the feather and tucked it into my pannier. I knew eagle feathers were important, but I couldn't fathom why.

Blood trickled from the puncture wounds on my arm. They formed a triangle of three dots spaced two inches apart. A red line emerged from one of the wounds and flowed in a spiral creating a circle in the middle of the triangle. A line of dark blood flowed from the other wounds and connected to the circle. The lines of blood defied gravity and moved with purpose and intelligence. The finished work was a three-pronged Catherine wheel of blood.

I tried to rub the blood away, but my arm stung like fury. I pulled out an old hankie from the pannier and tied it around my arm. I suddenly felt bone weary. The intensity of the experiences had taken their toll on my limited reserves. I kick started the bike and decided to return to the homestead.

As I passed the ridge a renewed surge of energy hit me. My head and bones hummed with a strange vibration. The red rocks of the ridge called to me, their song ringing in every cell of my body. I had to follow the call.

I reckoned I could ride up to the top of the ridge. I'd done rougher trails before, I was sure of it. The rocks were flat and pathways wound between them. As I slowed to a stop and took in the view above me, I changed my mind and decided to go on foot. The whole place had a sense of the sacred. Taking a motorbike up there didn't feel right.

The humming in my brain grew stronger until I could barely think. What the hell was it?

The red rock was flat and steep, and as I looked back, the landscape opened up below me, a vast expanse of green and grey. Huge red boulders were scattered around resembling gigantic marbles and dinosaur eggs. Great slabs of red rock had sheared away from massive boulders. It was as if a giant had cut off slices with her mammoth breadknife and left them laying on top of one another like so many pieces of red rock toast.

She had sculpted out caverns, caves and flowing waves from the red boulders. Dragons heads, lizards and strange creatures leapt out from the surface of the rock.

The sun had started to retreat back down the hill, and as it left, the rocks below burst into flame, shining like pools of molten orange lava.

I was nearing the top and paused to look out over the land below. The sea of land that stretched out around me was unblemished by any sign of civilisation. The majesty of it was breathtaking.

The clatter of hooves sounded nearby and I started. Horned heads emerged from above the rocks as a group of feral goats leapt up onto a precipice. They appeared strong and proud, a cluster of horned devils silhouetted in the falling light.

A noise came from overhead and I stepped back from the overhanging rock to see what was above me. I froze. A strange creature perched on the edge of the rock.

It was largely in shadow. I had to squint to try and make sense of what I was seeing. A large, powerful torso. Wings. A twitching tail. A horned head. The shadow outline of it rippled with movement, and the edges of it flowed with ceaseless motion as though it had no fixed form.

Sensing I couldn't outrun it, I held my breath and waited for it to pounce. Minutes ticked by. There was no movement other than the shimmer and flux of the creature's outline. Slowly and quietly, I moved away. The buzzing in my mind reduced somewhat. Whatever the buzzing was, the vibration had left me feeling strong and energised. I decided to work my way around behind the creature so I could discover exactly what it was. I couldn't wait to tell Hugh.

I picked my way through the rocks heading to where I thought I would emerge behind it. As I rounded a boulder, I came out right beside it. The sun's rays chased away the shadows and illuminated the creature in a blast of light.

Seated on the edge of the rock, creatures of every description surrounded the beast. A kangaroo, a billy goat, goannas, lizards, snakes, pythons, skinks, geckos, rock dragons. The wedge tailed eagle perched proudly on its head. Tawny Frogmouths, hawks, kestrels, falcons, honeyeaters, magpies, owls and numerous other birds I couldn't identify. Thousands of spiders, moths, beetles, wasps, crickets, cockroaches and other bugs swarmed over its body creating the undulating outline.

The creature slowly turned towards me and the other creatures followed suit. A thousand eyes fixed their gaze on me. The gaze was identical to the creature sitting in the middle of it all. Tapakah.

'Hello, Maggie. I've been waiting for you.'

As he stood, a tidal wave of creatures swept away from him. Birds and insects took flight and a wash of lizards, bugs and spiders raced past my feet. He smiled and walked over to me, gently pushing my open mouth closed. 'Are you okay?' he asked, examining the hankie around my arm.

I nodded mutely, finally managing to stutter. 'W... wh ... *what?*'

Tapakah laughed. 'I have an affinity with creatures.'

I felt seriously spooked. *Who the hell was this man?*

I finally found words in my brain. 'You don't say. That was the most amazing thing I've ever seen, well, at least in my limited recollection. Does Hugh know about this?'

'No, he doesn't.'

'It's good to see you, Tapakah. I've had an adventurous day.'

'I know.'

I smiled up at him. 'I thought I was going to finish the day off by having to battle a multi headed bush critter. How come you're out here?'

'Just making sure you're safe.'

'Well, your mate, the eagle was a bit rough.' I pulled off the hankie. 'Look what he did to me.' I displayed the Catherine wheel scar.

Tapakah took my arm and scrutinised it, examining the scar that ran up my forearm. 'The eagle was a she, by the way, and I'm glad she didn't open your wounds.'

'Thank you for looking after me, Tapakah. I appreciate everything you've done. You're certainly one strange and amazing bloke. I still can't believe what just happened.'

I couldn't get my mind around it. Perhaps he was an alien. He had to be. Creatures generally didn't trust humans, and with very good reason. If all those creatures felt safe with him, trusted him, then so should I.

He took my hands and said the words I was hoping he'd say. 'Can I kiss you?'

'Yes.'

He embraced me and his mouth found mine. As I began to dissolve into the kiss, he suddenly pulled away and pushed me roughly to the ground. 'Get down!' The crack of multiple rifle shots echoed across the land.

There was a dull *thunk*. Tapakah fell backwards, collapsing against a rock. He held his side. Blood leaked through his fingers. It was black. Bullets ricocheted around the rocks as I moved

320

toward him.

'No, Maggie! Get down!'

I ignored him, hooked under his arms and dragged him behind a rock. A bullet whizzed past my ear. My hands shook as I undid the buttons on his shirt. Blood was everywhere. Pulling off my T-shirt, I formed it into a pad and pressed it over the wound. 'Hold this and press down. Can you lean forward? I need to get your shirt off.'

He complied and I took off his shirt, tying it tight around his torso to hold the pad in place. 'Keep up the pressure on that pad. How did you get here?'

'Truck. Parked on the other side of the ridge. Forty-minute walk away.'

'Shit. That's too far. I'm going to get the bike. Sit still and keep the pressure on that wound. I'll be back in ten minutes.'

Tapakah grabbed my arm. 'It's too dangerous. We'll stay here 'til light. Hugh will come.'

'It'll be too late. You'll bleed out and die. Trust me. I'll be fine.' I pulled free of his grip and ran back down the path.

I swear I was channelling a billy goat as I leapt from rock to rock. I certainly felt as sure-footed and confident as one. Energy surged through my body as the buzzing in my brain returned. There was a strong pull to change direction, but I ignored it.

My mission was to get to the bike. To save Tapakah. After all he'd done for me, I had to. The humming in my head was starting to hurt, to take me over, but I pushed on.

The bike was where I'd left it. I leapt on and kick started the motor. It fired into life with one go. Sorry, sacred space. I revved the bike and shot up along the rocks. I had to get to the top and back down before dark. Maybe Hugh was already out looking for me. I hoped so.

Going as far as I could with the bike, I walked the rest of the way on foot. It was only a couple of minutes until I reached Tapakah. He was still conscious.

I helped him up and for the first time noticed the tattoos running down his arm. The strange designs started at the shoulder and writhed in the dimming light. There were odd symbols, insects and Catherine wheels. *Huh. The Catherine wheel is the same as mine.*

He put his arm around my neck, and I assisted him to the bike. 'I hope you have the strength to hold on.'

'I have,' he said quietly.

'Then try and hold onto me with one arm and keep the pressure on your wound with the other.'

I kick started the bike and hoped it would take us safely home.

'It's going to be a rough ride. Hang on.'

He gripped me around the waist as I took off. It was harder with someone on the back; I wasn't used to it. It took me longer than anticipated. When I reached the bottom, it was nearly dark. How the hell was I going to find my way back?

I gasped as a huge red roo appeared in the headlight. Its eyes glistened black.

'Follow it,' Tapakah whispered.

The roo took off with me right up its hammer. I followed the graceful ebb and flow of its enormous tail back to the homestead. Tapakah's head started to nod and his grip loosened. People were out the front waiting for us. Frank ran towards the bike as I skidded to a stop. The roo hightailed it into the bush.

'He's been shot!' I yelled.

Frank and Hugh helped Tapakah off the bike. Billy appeared with a wheel chair. Tapakah slumped down into it, and Billy wheeled him into the house at a million miles an hour. His little legs pounded away like pistons in the red dust. Frank followed behind.

My legs had turned to jelly and my arms were shaking. Hugh supported me as I swayed on my feet. 'Are you all right, luv?' he asked, helping me into the house.

The tone and words of that sentence rang bells in my mind. It was as if a dear, dear friend was speaking to me from the past. An image of brown eyes set in a kind and rugged face flashed into my mind and then was gone before I could keep it, treasure it, recognise it. I shook my head and the voice was Hugh's again.

I stared at the Catherine wheel on my arm, and the black blood gleaming in pools on the kitchen floor. My mind stirred, quivered. Something was knocking on a door deep in the recesses of my brain.

---

[43] *Maggie's Playlist: Up on The Ridge — Dierks Bentley*

Frank came into the kitchen looking tired. It was three hours since I'd brought Tapakah home.

'How is he?' I asked.

'Your first aid and getting him back here so quickly saved his life.'

'So, he's okay?'

'Well, a normal hu … ah, person, would recover quickly, but Tapakah has … um … unique medical issues, a syndrome that makes his body react strangely. We may have complications.'

Billy's eyes were wet, and his face was scrunched as he anxiously twisted his T-shirt into knots. 'Then we need to get him to a big hospital. Get the plane. We shouldn't wait.'

'It's not that simple,' Frank said. 'The doctors wouldn't know how to treat him. They'd do more harm than good. I understand more about his physiology than anyone, and I have all the specialised equipment. Moving him wouldn't be helpful.'

Billy's eyes glistened with tears as he asked the question I was too afraid to voice. 'Is he going to die?'

Frank plonked himself into a chair. 'Not if I can help it.'

'He saved my life,' I said. 'Pushed me out of the way and took the bullet himself. Who was shooting at us? How did he know?'

'He said he saw a reflection, a glint in the bushes. He knew there was nothing human made in the bush that would shine that way, like a scope. His reflexes are superfast. Lucky for you. We think it was someone shooting feral goats.'

Hugh caught Frank's eye, and in that glance, something exchanged between them.

'But we're two hundred kilometers from the nearest road. Who the hell would be out here shooting goats?'

'We've got station hands checking things out,' Hugh said.

'Why do you say human made, rather than man made?'

'It's a Tapakah thing. I've picked it up from him. Another one of his idiosyncrasies.'

'Can I see him?'

'Five minutes.' Frank motioned for me to go.

I walked down the long corridor to the room Frank had set up as a surgery. The door was slightly ajar, so I pushed it open and went in. Nulla and Dee were lying under the hospital gurney looking worried.

Tapakah was asleep; his eyes moved slightly under his closed lids, and his long dark lashes fluttered slightly. His arms were outside the covers. I noticed the tattoos on his right arm had faded. I checked my own scar. It had faded too. Weird.

Tapakah's face was pale against his black hair. He had muscular arms and strong hands. I picked up a hand and held it gently. Somehow, I knew I'd seen terminally ill people before, and Tapakah had that look about him. His breath rattled slightly as he exhaled. His skin was icy to the touch, his forehead cold and clammy. A rush of emotions overwhelmed me and tears streamed down my cheeks. I ripped a handful of tissues from the box and blew my nose.

When I looked up, Tapakah's dark eyes were open, staring at me. I jumped. The intensity of his gaze always had that effect.

He smiled weakly and whispered, 'How am I supposed to

recover with all that racket?'

'Sorry ... so sorry ... I ... I...'

'I'm joking. It's good to see you.'

'You saved my life and now you're ill. You should've let me take the bullet. Frank said you have medical issues that cause complications. I would've taken a bullet for you, after all you've done for me—'

Tapakah cut me off. 'I don't want you taking a bullet for anyone. You've been through enough.' He caressed my face. 'I'm sorry we didn't get to finish our kiss.'

'Me too.'

He closed his eyes and seemed to be asleep again. His chest was uncovered. Faint lines resembling scars, crisscrossed his torso. There were three on each side of his chest spaced about five inches apart. They appeared identical and slightly raised. I reached out to touch one. Tapakah moved as fast as lightening and grabbed my wrist. I cried out in surprise.

'What are you doing?' he whispered.

'Sorry, I didn't mean to wake you. I wanted to touch you ... the scars...'

'Don't.' He brought my hand to his lips and kissed my fingers. His lips were ice on my skin.

The floor creaked and Frank's face appeared round the door. 'Times up. And bring the dogs out with you.'

Tapakah released my hand and seemed to be asleep again. Outside, I spoke to Frank. 'How does he do that? He grabbed my hand with his eyes closed.'

'He has amazing reflexes.'

'Yes, I appreciate that, but with his eyes closed? It freaked me out.'

'He's sensitive to air currents.'

'Right.' I walked off down the hall, feeling the need for a stiff drink. In the kitchen, Elizabeth took one look at me and said, 'How about a brandy and dry? You look like you could use a

326

pick me up.'

I grinned. 'You're an angel. You need to give me jobs. I'm no good hanging around with nothing to do.'

'No problems there. You can help me feed the baby 'roos tomorrow.'

'Really?'

'Really. But first a drink.' She poured a heavy-handed slug of brandy into a glass, followed by a splash of dry. She made one for Hugh and Frank, and a small snifter for Billy. She raised her glass. 'For medicinal purposes only.'

We clinked and after a couple of sips, I was warm and relaxed.

Hugh pulled up a chair at the table. 'The colour's come back to your cheeks. Oh, I see, Lizzie's medicinal brew.' He picked up his glass and sculled it.

I needed more information, and fast. Hugh and Elizabeth were lovely, they'd fill me in. 'Can you tell me about Tapakah?' I asked.

Hugh looked uncomfortable. 'Best to mind your own business, is my advice. Not meaning to be rude, you understand?'

'Yes, fine. I understand.'

I couldn't get information out of anyone. Even Billy was a closed shop, and he was my best buddy. He'd say; I've no idea, Miss. I couldn't say, Miss. I know as much as you about Mister Tapakah, Miss. Everyone was extremely awkward with any questions about Tapakah. If I didn't know better, I'd say they were frightened of him. I guess they were paid to be discreet, but Billy? It was really starting to bug me.

Billy came back into the room from a quick visit with Tapakah. His eyes were red from crying. I held out my arms and he flung himself into them. His tears ran down the side of my neck.

'He looks so sick, Miss Maggie. He's going to die, isn't he?'

'He's not going to die.' I untangled his arms from around my neck. A glob of snot hung down from his nose, Elizabeth shoved a bunch of tissues into my hand.

'Here, blow.' He made a noise similar to a trumpet. 'You sound exactly like me.'

He giggled. 'Yes, I've learnt from the best.'

'Oh, ha ha.'

'Mister Tapakah said you woke him up with your trumpeting. He said between the two of us we should be in a band, 'cept we're out of tune.'

'He said that, did he? Well, I wonder how he sounds when he blows his nose? Like a whale, I'll bet.'

Billy giggled. 'I've only seen Mister Tapakah cry once, when you came around. Oh, and I thought he was going to one time when he found you in the ba—'

'Billy!' Hugh cut in sharply. 'Here's a snifter Elizabeth made for you.' He slid it across the table giving Billy a look.

'What were you going to say?' I asked,

'Ah, nothing, Miss, I don't know.'

I decided not to push it. I didn't want to get Billy in trouble. When Tapakah had found me where? I had a jigsaw puzzle with pieces that didn't fit.

'It's getting late, you should rest up,' Elizabeth said, looking at me. 'And you too, Billy.'

'I won't be able to sleep. I feel wired.'

Billy nodded. 'Me too.'

Frank came into the kitchen looking drawn and tired. 'Tapakah wants to see you again, Maggie. Go in.'

I tried not to run back down the corridor. I stuck my head around the door and Tapakah looked the same, pale and half dead. I sat down by the side of the gurney. 'You wanted to see me?'

'Yes.' He lifted his hand and I held it. His voice sounded a little stronger than before.

'Um … what?' I asked.

'Nothing. I simply want to look at you.'

I felt my face flush. 'Oh.'

He smiled.

'Thanks for saving my life.'

'Well, we're even. You saved mine.'

'Maggie, if I don't make it, I want you to know I've provided for you. You will have everything you need. I don't want you to worry.'

'Don't say that. You're going to make it.'

'I wanted you to hear it from me.' He gave a sudden gasp and grimaced with pain. He squeezed my hand. 'Whatever happens, don't leave. You have to wait. *Wait.*' His whole body jerked violently. The pressure of his grip on mine tightened. He was having a fit. The scars on his chest opened. Flesh glistened underneath. Air rushed out through the vents, hissing loudly as though his lungs were collapsing. I couldn't get my hand free, he was crushing it. His eyes rolled back showing the whites. The colour of his skin had changed to bronze. 'Frank! *Frank, come quickly!*' I screamed.

Tapakah's eyes rolled forward. They were completely black — iris, whites, the lot. I screamed some more.

Frank burst into the room and pushed me roughly aside. 'Get out!'

'*Hello?* I can't!' I showed him Tapakah's hand clenched around mine. He rolled his eyes, prized open Tapakah's fingers and pushed me out the door.

Billy stood there looking as white as a sheet. I leaned my forehead against the wall, and breathed, and breathed, trying to control my emotions. I would not break down in front of Billy. He needed me to be strong.

His tiny voice held a million questions. 'Maggie?'

'It's fine, Billy. Let's go back to the kitchen.' I put my arm around his shoulders and guided him there. Hugh and Elizabeth were waiting at the end of the corridor, two anxious faces posing their own questions.

'He had a bit of a turn and I over reacted,' I said.

The look on Hugh's face told me he knew I was lying. Same for Elizabeth. Billy bought it.

'Oh, you scared me,' he said.

'Sorry, Billy. We're all a bit on edge I guess.'

He grabbed my hand and gave it a squeeze.

'Let's sit in the courtyard,' Elizabeth suggested. 'It's cooler there, and I've made drinks and nibbles.'

Hugh turned on the fountain in the centre of the cobblestone courtyard. We sat back in the comfy chairs and listened to the sound of water bouncing off the walls. We sat and waited. And waited. And waited.

Billy and I wandered up and down the corridor next to the courtyard looking at old relics — an ancient typewriter, a boomerang, spearheads, old photographs with serious sepia faces from the past.

Eventually, Frank's voice echoed up the corridor. 'Maggie, Billy.' He beckoned for us to come. Billy ran. I walked. I could sense what he was going to say. His grief-stricken expression told me everything. He didn't have to say the words, but he said them anyway.

'I'm sorry, Maggie. He's gone. I tried everything. He won't come back. Tapakah's dead.'

---

[44] *Maggie's Playlist: Dead and Gone — The Black Keys*

Maggie Chapter 41: The Last Stand

He's dead. He's dead. He's dead. Dead. Dead. Dead.

Frank's words rang in my head. How could it be?

'Can I see him?'

'Perhaps remember him the way he was. It's for the best. I need to make arrangements now. Please, excuse me.' He rushed off along the hall.

I heard Hugh and Elizabeth attempting to console Billy somewhere. I followed the sound of Frank's voice. He was in the room opposite the surgery, talking on his phone. His tone was urgent, almost angry, as he barked out orders. I tried the door to the surgery. It was locked. I stepped up to the door and listened to Frank.

I heard fragments of conversation. 'Get the plane here *now*. Yes, he's gone. We need to get him on ice, ASAP. I can't do that here. DNA preservation is crucial. Yes, yes, of course we'll dissect. Keep me posted.'

I heard the beep of another number being dialled. '… tell the minister … yes, he knows who I am … yes, he'll understand what I mean. For fuck's sake, just do it!'

I didn't know how I knew, but I knew. In fact, there were a lot of things that I knew, without knowing how I knew.

Two things I did know, right at that moment, was one, Frank had a gun down the back of his pants, and two, I knew what I was going to do.

I hid behind a grandfather clock as he crossed the hall and put a key in the lock to the surgery. Sneaking up behind him, I flicked up his jacket and snaffled the gun, a 9mm Glock 17 semi-automatic pistol. Nice.

He spun around. 'What the hell?'

I released the magazine, checked it was loaded, and clicked it back in. 'Back away from the door, Frank. Tapakah isn't going anywhere. Drop the keys and kick them over to me. Not too hard, not too soft.'

'What are you *doing*? Are you crazy? Come on, you're upset, we all are. There's nothing else we can do. Be a good girl and put the gun down. Come on, Maggie, give me the gun.' He took a step towards me.

I released the slide with a click and pointed the gun directly at his chest. 'Don't call me a good girl, Frank. I really hate that. This gun is locked, loaded and ready to fire. I won't tell you again. I will use it.'

'You're not kidding, are you? Who *are* you?'

'I wish I knew. You probably understand that better than me. The *keys*…'

He kicked them across as requested.

'Back away and then walk to the second door on the right.'

He did as he was told.

'You can't comprehend what you're doing, Maggie.'

'Maybe so.' I stepped into the surgery and locked the door.

I grabbed a towel, wet it in the sink, wrung it out and then laid it across the crack under the door.

There was plenty of adhesive tape around. I used it to cover the keyhole and any other evident cracks around the window and door. I jammed a large stainless-steel tray over the window opening, slamming it in tight with my fists.

A heavy cabinet was nearby. I could use that. I sat on the ground and put my back against it. Using my legs against the wall as leverage, I pushed that sucker right across the door. I dragged another set of shelves across the window to be sure. Things were as secure as I could make them. For the moment. Frank was banging and shouting to be let in.

I turned my attention to the body on the gurney. It was in a body bag. I had an intense feeling of déjà vu as I unzipped it. It fell open and revealed a body covered in what appeared to be cling wrap rather than skin. It resembled an anatomy model, with everything visible. Every muscle, tendon, the white of ligaments, the creeping spread of veins ... and the unmistakable musculature of Tapakah's face. It was a body that appeared to have been skinned alive.

I threw up in the sink.

As I wiped my mouth I noticed three sealed plastic bags against the wall. They were filled with strips of translucent plastic. The label said: "epidermis".

He said to wait. He said to wait. He said to wait.

So I'd wait.

Instead of zipping up the bag, I draped a towel across the corpse. I couldn't bear to look at it. I sat on a chair next to the gurney and started counting the stars in the pressed metal ceiling.

Frank was still banging on the door. 'Open the door, Maggie. This is your final warning. We'll kick it down.'

'You will not take his body, Frank. The only way you're taking it is over *my* dead body.'

'There's no problem there. I can tell you that right now. You don't know what you're doing. We have to preserve his body or everything will be lost. Do you understand?'

'I have to wait, Frank. I'm sorry. He said to *wait.*'

The banging on the door was furious, but then it stopped. Peace. Quiet. I was up to one thousand three hundred and two. Then it started again. They were using something more substantial, a battering ram of some sort.

I waited for a lull in the noise. 'If you make it in, I will kill every one of you,'

Urgent whispers, running footsteps, noises outside the window. The sound of breaking glass. Someone had smashed the window. More voices.

I yelled, 'I have a fully loaded gun. I *will* use it. I will kill anyone who makes it in here!'

'Maggie, if you won't let me in, I need you to do something for me. Are you listening?'

'Yes.'

'You need to keep Tapakah's body cold. This is not going to hurt him. There are thermal cooling blankets on the table nearby. They're already hooked up to the machine near the gurney. You need to put them over his body and secure them with the Velcro straps. There are various sizes, for torso, head, arms and legs. Put them on and then I'll tell you how to turn on the machine. We need to keep him as cold as possible.'

'Why didn't you do that before?'

'Because he was being flown out of here. There's equipment in the plane.'

Doubt crept into my mind. *Was I doing the right thing? Was I? No, I had to trust my gut.*

I pulled off the towel and tried to get Tapakah's body out of the bag. He was heavy, and I didn't want to handle him. I picked up a shiny pair of stainless-steel shears from the instrument trolley, and a wave of nausea hit me. I thought I was going to throw up again. I cut the body bag to pieces, and after putting on blue plastic gloves, I gently maneuvered the pieces of bag out from under his body.

The whole while I was on high alert for any activity outside the room. There didn't seem to be any.

Working methodically, I picked up the sections of thermal blankets and attached them to wherever they seemed to fit.

'All done, Frank. He's covered in the blankets.'

'Okay. Now listen carefully. The machine is already programmed. It's not hard. This is what you have to do.'

I followed his instructions to the letter. The machine whirred into action, and the thermal blankets filled with water.

'Done. Now what?'

'Well, ideally you let me in so I can take Tapakah to the waiting plane.'

'I'm not going to do that. I heard you. You're going to cut him into tiny pieces. I'm not going to let that happen.'

There was a howl like a feral cat. It was Billy.

More voices. '... gas ... could work ... might affect the tissue ... tissue will be useless anyway...'

'...smoke her out ... blow the door...'

'...it's all going to compromise the tissues...'

'...water ... through the roof ... starve her out ... can't be that hard ... for Christ's sake.'

I checked the ceiling. There was no obvious way to get in, so I settled myself on a chair in the corner of the room. It was a mushroom coloured, vinyl monolith of a thing — cold but comfortable. I covered myself in a blanket and discovered the chair was electric and turned into a bed. Well, I wasn't going to use that. Sleep was not an option.

I propped my arms on my bent knees and pointed the gun at the door. I had seventeen bullets, and I was ready to use every one of them.

Another flash of déjà vu hit me. Why was I so comfortable with a gun? Who the hell *was* I?

The oversize plastic clock on the wall ticked away the seconds, minutes and hours. It was quiet outside. Everyone had given up and gone to bed. Or maybe that's what they wanted me to think. Six hours had passed, and I'd nearly dozed off numerous times. Holding the gun the way I did helped me to stay awake. It felt comfortable and familiar in my hand.

Needing to do something, I crossed the room to get a drink of water. I did fifty push-ups off the wall. I did twenty squats. I looked in the mirror and pulled off my wig. My hair was growing back, about half a centimeter all over. I could've easily snagged a role in Mad Max.

I was so bored. An electric razor sat on the side of the sink. I turned it on and ran the side of the blade in a line across my head. It left a neat thin strip of bare skin. I did another one underneath it. And another.

The buzzing of the razor in my hand brought me back to reality, and I gasped at the image in the mirror. I seriously didn't recall doing *that* to myself.

I checked the time. Twenty minutes had passed without me realising it. My skull was a complex road map of geometric designs. Now I really resembled something out of *Mad Max*.

The room was untidy, so I put everything in order and wiped the benches. I polished the mirror and the stainless-steel implements. For some reason, handling them made me feel sick, so I stopped and went back to the mammoth chair and resumed my position.

I was extremely hungry and tired. I stared up at the ceiling and wondered if I should resume counting. As I ran my eye along the wall trying to locate where I'd left off counting, I noticed a small hole about seven feet up from the floor.

I picked up a cotton ball and tape, and pulled a chair over to the wall.

Standing on the chair, I examined the hole. It wasn't a hole. It was a shiny camera lens. I stuffed the cotton ball over the top of it and taped it in place. Friggin' peeping toms. I cast my mind back over my actions and hoped I hadn't picked my nose or something.

Jeepers, what else had I missed? I sat back down.

The ticking of the clock was getting louder. My head felt dizzy. A new sound, a slight hissing. Gas!

I dashed across the room, wet a cloth, and held it over my mouth and nose. The nozzle of a tube poked in through the corner of the broken window. Squeezing my arm behind the cabinet, I bent the tube around so it was pointing back out. It wouldn't be immediately apparent, if at all. I pondered how long it would take them to discover I wasn't gassed.

Another hour passed and then I heard voices at the door. 'She'll be well and truly out to it by now,' Frank declared.

A chain saw screamed into life. I ran across the room and banged on the wall. The chain saw died.

'I'm still awake and I still have a gun. Just giving you the heads up is all!' I yelled.

I'd been in the room for nearly eight hours. It was doing my head in. The novelty was wearing thin. I was bored. And tired. And annoyed.

Tapakah's body was completely covered in thermal blankets, except for the main part of his face. After having handled his body, I was more at ease with the gruesome sight. I took a closer look at him.

The muscle fibers around his eyes, mouth, jaw and chin flowed in neatly ordered strands, reminding me of pink rhubarb. Veins wound themselves in, over and around the muscles — a network of tributaries wending their way with purpose and design. Amazing.

He looked fairly peaceful, given the circumstances. Well, he was dead after all.

Why the hell was I doing this? Because he said wait? He probably meant wait, stay here a bit longer. Wait, I want to tell you I love you. Wait, I'm thirsty. Wait, it's been nice knowing you. Why wait? I was an idiot. I'd put all these wonderful people through hell.

Everything was quiet again. I was starving. My stomach was growling.

A scratching noise came from the door. I bent down to see

what was going on. A stick poked the wet towel aside. They must be going to try the gas again.

A long thin piece of cardboard made its way into the room. Resting on top of it in a long, neat row, were twelve single Salada crackers. Each cracker had a small slice of cheese on the top, neatly cut to fit. A note, secured with an extra piece of cheese, read: *For you, with love, Billy xxx*

Oh great, they were using Billy to get at me. The cheese was probably drugged. Could that be done?

Lying on the floor, I peered underneath the cabinet. An eyeball looked at me. Tiny fingers wiggled under the gap. It was Billy.

I collected the crackers from the cardboard, and he whisked it away. I laughed out loud. God bless Billy!

I sat crossed legged on the humungous, ugly chair and devoured my cheese and crackers. It was the best meal I'd ever had. Ten minutes later, the cardboard appeared again, with another six crackers, and a piece of toast with butter and Vegemite. The toast had been flattened so it would fit under the door. I picked off a dust bunny and scoffed it. *Delicious!*

I was feeling a bit better. I didn't do well on an empty stomach, and Billy knew that. All I needed now was a nice cup of tea.

I was wide awake after the food, so I sat on the chair bouncing my legs up and down. Boring. Boring. Boring!

Another noise at the door. Something else was being poked underneath the crack. I reached out and grabbed it — a sealed sandwich bag filled with brown fluid. It was hot. I opened the bag and decanted the fluid into a glass. Billy had made me a cup of tea. I teared up as I drank it. That kid was fair dinkum unbelievable. So smart. I wanted to adopt him.

It was coming up for ten hours, and it appeared everyone had given up. Gone to bed. I wished I could.

I walked across to the gurney and touched Tapakah's face. It was icy. This was ridiculous. It wasn't right.

I turned off the machine and began to remove the thermal cooling pads. I averted my eyes from his body. It was too hard to take. Medical issues or not, he needed to die in peace and not like a piece of frozen meat. I didn't understand why I was doing what I was doing. I was working on instinct.

Warm and dark. Warm and dark. Warm and dark.

Frank really would kill me now. But I didn't care. It seemed like the right thing to do.

Warm and dark. Warm and dark.

I finished removing the pads, covered him with a sheet, and turned off all the lights except for a small one over the sink.

Now what? I sat back down and kept on waiting, gun in hand. The clock ticked by another hour. Without the whirring of the machine the room was deathly quiet.

I must have dozed off. A loud noise made me jump off the chair in fright. A dreadful, tortured screeching came from the gurney. The cloth over Tapakah's face was sucked in tight against his mouth. His torso arched back violently as his body tried to suck in air. I ripped off the sheet and cried out in surprise. The clear tissue over his body had turned opaque and appeared almost like normal flesh. Fluids bubbled and flowed beneath his skin. His body twitched and jerked twice before he collapsed back down and was still.

As I continued to watch, his skin solidified and he was Tapakah again. I clutched the steel rail of the gurney and held my breath.

The clock ticked by. Nothing happened. He lay there looking dead.

I put my ear against his face to check for breathing. Nothing.

I touched his neck to feel for a pulse. Nothing.

I tried to find a pulse in his wrist. Nothing.

Five more minutes passed. Still nothing.

Thirty minutes.

Nothing.

I kissed him gently on the lips. They were cold.

Sitting back down in the vinyl chair, I gave way to emotion. Shuddering sobs wracked my body as I let go of my grief. All was lost. The man who'd saved me, cared for me, loved me, the only true friend I had was gone.

I'd done the wrong thing. I shouldn't have interfered. What the hell had I been thinking. What was going to happen to me now? How could I live without him?

Exhaustion swaddled my brain. I lay back and let sleep take me.

I didn't give a rat's anymore. I gave up. I was done. They could drag me off and kill me for what I did. Who cared? I didn't. I probably deserved it.

A crash of steel wrenched me from my slumber.

They must have broken in! I was screwed.

I leapt up, legs braced, arms straight, gun drawn. My eyes were blurry; I couldn't see. The light was dim. I blinked rapidly to better see the shapes around me.

One? Two? How many? Why weren't they moving? Shit!

My heart pounded in my ears. The room narrowed.

Racking the slide, I squinted trying make out who the hell was in the room. 'Don't move. I'll shoot!'

A dark shape came to life and took a step towards me.

I started in fright and the gun jerked in my hand. '*Stop!* Don't come any closer. I'm warning you. I *will* shoot.'

The room became clearer. The gurney was empty. *Shit.* They'd taken the body. Now they're going to make me pay. Frank. It had to be.

Frank took another tentative step forward.

'Stop! One more step and you die, motherfucker.'

The tiny backlight from over the sink left Frank's features in shadow.

'That's ... no way to ... greet me, Maggie.'

The voice was gravelly and rough, but I recognised it. It couldn't be.

'Tapakah?'

The figure moved, and I backed up and hit the chair. My knees shook uncontrollably, but my hands were steady.

Zombie. He was a zombie. He'd turned into a bloody zombie! Jesus Christ. What the hell? This was the start of it. The Zombie Apocalypse.

My mind raced over the movies I'd seen. You had to smash their heads to smithereens. At this close range, a gun would do it. No handy baseball bats.

It took a jerky step forward and I stepped up onto the chair.

'You've got 'til three to move away or I'll put seventeen bullets in your brain. Capeesh? One ... two...'

The thing took a defiant step forward.

'Three!' I squeezed the trigger. The gun fired. My ears rang. The gun was ripped from my hand.

In that split second, the creature moved so fast I didn't register it. The bullet hit the mirror, exploding it into a crystalline shower of glass.

What the hell? Now what?

I climbed onto the back of the chair and balanced with my back pressed up against the wall. I was cornered. Screwed. The creature held the gun and regarded me quietly for a couple of seconds before turning away and moving towards the glass that was tinkling to the floor.

Oh, thank God. Maybe it was fascinated by sound? Oh, duh! Of course, zombies were attracted to noise. Stupid me. There was no way I could get out. It was too bloody fast. Better stay still and quiet. Someone would rescue me soon, wouldn't they?

The creature stretched out an arm and hit a switch on the wall. As the fluorescent tubes flickered into life, it turned around and stared at me.

Don't move, Maggie. Make like a statue. Damn my knees.

I held my breath and froze as the lights flickered and strobed to full intensity. The flickering stopped and finally I saw clearly what stood before me.

Holy, holy hell.

The creature was buck naked except for a torn piece of thermal blanket around its waist. Slowly, it stretched its arms towards me. The head tilted, and the face broke into a crazy, crooked grin. Its expression told me everything I needed to know. Adrenaline surged through my limbs as I prepared to move.

It wasn't a zombie that stood before me. It was Tapakah.

I shrieked and launched myself at him. He laughed as he caught me, and I made like a koala. He swayed slightly on his feet.

'I don't believe it. You're *alive*!'

'I am,' he croaked into my ear. 'And you're my gorgeous koala. An exceptionally dangerous, gutsy, stubborn one at that.'

I jumped out of his arms and stepped back to appraise him. 'Are you okay, really okay?'

'Other than feeling a bit stiff, I've never felt better. Thanks to you.' He yanked me back into his arms and hugged me. 'Still, you nearly blew my head off. What's with *that*?'

'I mistook you for a zombie,' I said sheepishly. 'I thought you were gonna suck my brains out.'

His body shook with laughter and he hugged me tighter.

'It's not funny. I was scared.'

He hugged me even tighter and chuckled. 'I didn't mean to scare you.'

'I … I can't *breathe*,' I gasped, and he released his hold.

'Sorry, I'm feeling really strong. Let's get out of here.' He grinned. 'I can't wait to see Frank's face.'

I attempted to help him shift the heavy cabinet, but he pushed it away one handed, like so much balsa wood.

'Crikey!'

Tapakah opened the door and was nearly bowled over by Billy hurling himself into his arms. Billy blubbered with joy. Tapakah held him gently, another little koala.

Hugh and Elizabeth were crying, and Frank, well, he was making a first-rate impression of a stunned mullet. He reluctantly met Tapakah's stare, and his impersonation morphed into one of an exceedingly frightened mouse.

Tapakah's voice held a deadly undertone. 'Whatever calls you made, Frank, unmake them now.' He turned to Elizabeth. 'We need to eat.'

She nodded and dashed off to the kitchen dragging Hugh with her.

Tapakah untangled Billy's arms from around his neck and placed him gently on the floor. 'Go help Elizabeth. I'll see you in a minute.'

Billy's face was beaming, and his cheeks were wet with tears. 'Sure thing, Mister Tapakah.'

'Well, you're certainly barking out orders. Those people love you. They've been through hell too, you know. You shouldn't speak to them that way.'

I made a move to follow Billy, but Tapakah grabbed my wrist and pulled me into an adjoining room. He pressed me up against the wall by my shoulders. Energy coursed through his body. His eyes blazed with it.

Crikey. I was in trouble here. I'd pissed him off.

His jaw was clenched, his mouth was tight and his breath fast.

At this rate, he was going to hyperventilate. I needed a brown paper bag. Well, any colour would do, wouldn't it? In the movies, it always seemed to be brown. Christ. Too intense. Too intense.

'Tapakah, you're scaring me. It feels like you're going to hit me, or eat me.' I winced, expecting a blow at any second.

'Oh, I want to eat you all right. Eat you and a whole lot more.' He took a deep, shuddering breath. His arms shook and his body quivered. He seemed to have one hell of an internal battle going on.

'Tapakah, you're struggling. You should rest. I mean, you're just back from the dead, for Christ's sake.'

He pushed up hard against me. 'I'm struggling, all right. Struggling with everything I have … not to rip your clothes off … and fuck you to kingdom come.'

'Tapakah!'

His fists were clenched; his breath was ragged and fast. 'I need to run. Run off the energy.'

My skull cracked against the wall as he let me go with a push. Rubbing the sore spot on my head, I peeked around the corner and watched him run.

The sun shone through the fly screen door at the end of the hallway giving the linoleum a soft sheen. The walls of the narrow hall appeared to buckle as he bounded along it, his powerful silhouette filling the space.

It must have been a trick of the light.

'You're half *naked!'* I yelled after him.

The screen door slammed shut and a cloud of red dust rose up in his wake.

Bloody hell. I rubbed my head and massaged the sore spots on my shoulders where he'd gripped me.

He'd come back to life full of vim and vigour. That was certainly some God awful, weird medical syndrome he had. Frank should write a paper on it.

I made excuses for Tapakah's inappropriate behaviour. I figured coming back from the brink of death would make a man want to procreate as quickly as possible. For me, I didn't get it. After a flirtation with death, a nice cup of tea and a cheese toastie would float my boat.

On reflection, I wouldn't have minded taking him up on his

crudely put offer. However, in the state he was in, I would've come out worse for wear. Much better he ran off that energy.

Even though I hadn't come back from the dead, I was absolutely stuffed. I collapsed on the bed and was asleep before my head hit the pillow.

---

[45] *Maggie's Playlist: The Zombie Song — Stephanie Mabey*

Something touched my hair, jolting me to consciousness. I scrabbled for my gun.

'Hey, take it easy! It's only me.'

I was disoriented. Where was I?

Tapakah sat on the edge of the bed holding a tray of toast and coffee. 'What are you doing?'

'Looking for my gun. I was dreaming about ... zombies.'

He smiled. 'Frank has the gun. You've been asleep for fifteen hours. I thought it was time you had something to eat.'

'Thanks, but I'll get up. How are you feeling?'

'Fine. Better than fine. I wanted to apologise for my crude behaviour. It was unacceptable. I'm sorry. I was out of control with the energy, the sensations ... emotions, I was feeling.'

'I'm sure everyone would behave erratically after coming back from the dead. By the way, I would've taken you up on your offer.'

'You're kidding me?'

'Not kidding.'

'Why the *hell* didn't you say something?'

I could tell he was kicking himself and I laughed. 'I was too tired and with all that energy you had ... I don't think I would've survived.'

'I can't believe I missed the opportunity.' He mock punched the bed.

'How far did you run?'

'To the ridge and back.'

'That's over eighty kilometers!'

'Indeed. In bare feet and a loin cloth.'

'Crikey. Is that a one off or can you do it again?'

'I could do it again, probably not as fast though.'

'Pity you couldn't channel that energy somewhere and tuck it away for "ron".'

'Tapakah looked puzzled. 'Who's Ron?'

'It's slang for later on. *Ron.*'

He smiled. 'Energy has to flow. You told me that.'

'I'm getting up. I'll have my breakfast in the kitchen.'

'Sure thing.' He leant over and kissed me on the forehead. 'I'll see you there.'

I had a quick shower, made myself look presentable, and headed off to the kitchen. I was starving and hoped Hugh had cooked up a storm. It was late though, so breakfast was probably off.

I walked into the kitchen and Tapakah, Hugh and Billy were sitting around a laptop laughing at something. There didn't seem to be any sign of a big breakfast. Disappointing.

'Hello, all. What's going on?'

Tapakah chuckled. 'We're watching the CCTV footage from the surgery yesterday.'

'You're extremely resourceful and determined,' Frank said.

'I'm glad it all turned out for the best. Here was me thinking I'd disabled that camera.'

'You missed one, right above the gurney. It wasn't easy to spot,' Tapakah said.

'I'm curious as to why you stopped the thermal cooling,' Frank asked.

I thought for a while before answering. 'I'm not sure. I was operating on instinct. The words warm and dark kept coming to mind, so I went with it. I can't fathom why. Sorry.'

'Well, you saved his life. Thank you for doing what you did. It took a lot of guts.'

'I like the part here where you clean up the surgery and put everything in order,' Tapakah said.

Billy looked at me. 'Maybe you were in the police force? You knew exactly what to do, how to use a gun and everything.'

'I have no idea, Billy. As I've said before, I know many things, but I don't know how I know them.'

Frank snorted with laughter. 'I love the bit where you nearly blew Tapakah's head off. All that good work could've been for naught.'

'Don't remind me, Frank.'

Billy giggled. 'And what about the bit when Maggie was getting bored and shaved all those patterns in her hair. That was so funny and awesome. I want to do that to my hair.'

I smiled. 'I'm glad everyone is having fun at my expense.' It warmed my heart to see everyone so jubilant.

'Tapakah told me you thought he was a zombie,' Billy said, giggling. He leapt out of his chair and staggered around the kitchen doing a zombie impersonation.

I laughed at his antics. 'Well, you're ingenious and resourceful, Billy. Thank you for feeding me in the clever way you did. If you hadn't, I don't think I would've had the stamina to continue.'

'My two brave heroes,' Tapakah said. 'I owe both of you a great debt.'

'You do?' Billy's eyes were wide with delight. 'What are you going to do?'

'First off, right now, I'm going to take you both on a picnic. I have somewhere special in mind. Elizabeth has made us a picnic basket. The truck is packed and ready to go when you are.'

348

Tapakah smiled at me. 'That's why there's no big breakfast. I could see you were disappointed, but I hope the picnic will make up for it. Have your toast and coffee to tide you over, and then we'll go.'

I was excited. 'Sounds great! I love picnics.'

'Me too,' Billy said.

After toast and coffee, we headed off in the four-wheel drive. Nulla and Dee barked around the wheels and chased us until we reached the end of the road.

'Where are we going?' Billy asked.

'Somewhere you haven't been before. One of the station hands told me about it and said that we need to go now.

'Did they find any evidence of the shooter?' I asked.

'No, but everyone's on high alert. I have pistols and rifles in the car. Don't worry. We'll be fine.'

'I hope so.' The thought of snipers lurking in the bush made me anxious.

After thirty minutes of bumping along rough bush tracks we rounded an outcrop of boulders and pulled to a halt.

'Wow!' Billy's eyes were as big as saucers as he stared at the scene before us.

The ground rose upwards in a gentle slope, and someone had spread out a red blanket for us. The blanket covered the entire slope and extended to the horizon. It was made of flowers.

We leapt out of the car and I stood speechless. I'd never seen anything so beautiful. An army of tiny alien forms — millions of strange, bright red flowers, with shiny black bellies — marched across the land.

'What are they?'

Tapakah saw the expression on my face and smiled. 'Sturt's Desert Pea.'

'They're incredible. It's as though we're on another planet.'

'They're beautiful, aren't they? I haven't seen them before

either. Apparently, this is the most spectacular display in years. Just for us.'

Billy bent down to take a closer look. 'Wow! That black bit in the middle, all shiny and swollen, looks like a spider's belly.' He reached out a finger to tentatively touch it. 'You know, like a Redback that's gonna have babies.'

'I hadn't thought of it that way, but yes, it does,' Tapakah agreed.

I marvelled at the beauty surrounding us. 'Where are we going to have our picnic without damaging the flowers? The ground is thick with them.'

'Over there by that stand of trees and boulders. It will give us shade too.' Tapakah pulled a picnic basket and two large Eskys from the car.

'Looks as if we're in for one hell of a banquet,' I said.

'We are. Come on, Billy, you can take the basket and I'll take the Eskys.'

'I'll take one,' I said.

'You grab the picnic rugs in the back.'

Tapakah picked up the Eskys as though they were empty. His strength obviously hadn't diminished. Anyone trying to tackle him would definitely come off second best. The thought made me feel comfortable and uncomfortable all at the same time.

It was a perfect day. No wind, quite warm and a cloudless blue sky. I spread out the rugs while Tapakah unpacked the picnic basket.

'Champagne, Maggie?'

'Yes, please.'

'Champagne, Billy?'

'*Really*? Can I?'

'Yes, you can. This is a special occasion, but only a small glass, okay?'

'Okay!' Billy beamed from ear to ear. 'We're very lucky aren't we, Maggie?'

'Yes, Billy, we are.'

Tapakah handed us our drinks. 'I want to propose a toast. To Maggie and Billy. Without your heroic efforts, I wouldn't be alive today. My heartfelt thanks to you both.' We clinked our glasses and sipped the delicious wine.

'To all of us,' I said, as I polished off the lot.

Billy crinkled his face and giggled. 'The bubbles tickle my nose.'

Tapakah looked at my empty glass and raised his eyebrows. 'You must be thirsty.'

'I seem to enjoy champagne. A lot.'

'Well, there's plenty more where that came from,' he said, topping up my glass. His hand brushed mine as he steadied the glass, and a rush of energy ran up my arm. I started and spilled wine on the rug.

'Did you feel that?' I asked.

He grinned. 'Yes, there's definitely a spark between us.'

'Weird to have static outside though.'

'I'm still full of energy, Maggie.'

'So it seems.'

'Now, Elizabeth gets most of the credit for this fantastic spread, but there's one thing I made for you myself.' He gingerly removed a golden-crusted pie from the basket. 'Egg and bacon pie. Especially for you. Made with free range eggs and bacon, of course.'

'You made this yourself? It's perfect!'

'Well, you haven't tasted it yet, but I'm sure it will be splendid. Elizabeth told me what to do, but I made it,' he said, proudly.

I handed him a knife. 'We'd better get stuck in then.'

Tapakah cut us all a generous slice and served it with Elizabeth's homemade relish. He looked at me expectantly as I took a bite.

'Mmmm. Crisp, golden, buttery pastry, tasty bacon with

exactly the right amount of crispness, eggs cooked to perfection, not too hard, not too soft, a hint of parsley, a tang of Dijon mustard. Perfect, Tapakah!'

He beamed at me and wiped a crumb from the side of my mouth. 'You love your food don't you? And you describe it well. Unlike those cooking shows where they taste the food and say, "Mmmm. This tastes great", and you've absolutely no idea what they're experiencing.'

'Do you enjoy cooking then?'

'I think I do. It made me happy to make this for you, and to see you relish eating it.'

'I'm not sure if I can cook. I can't remember.'

'I'm sure Elizabeth wouldn't mind if you helped out in the kitchen.'

'That would be great. I need to be busy, to have things to do.'

'What else have we got to eat?' Billy asked.

'Why don't you have a look, and bring out the rest,' Tapakah said.

There were dainty club sandwiches, potato salad, carrot salad, bean salad, tiny sausage rolls, delicate savoury tarts, scotch eggs, fresh bread rolls, creamy butter, a lemon meringue pie for desert, plus fluffy scones with homemade jam and cream.

'Oh, my goodness, we'll never be able to eat all this,' I said. 'What a feast.'

'It won't go to waste. Billy has the appetite of a horse, and whatever's left, the station hands will polish off.'

We sat on the picnic rug surrounded by flowers, gazing out at the beauty that encircled us. The food was delicious and we ate, drank and laughed, feeling the warmth of the sun on our backs as it filtered through the trees.

Billy tucked into his second piece of lemon meringue pie. 'This is the best day ever!'

'Food always seems to taste better when you eat outside,' I

said. 'Thank you, Tapakah, this is wonderful. I feel so happy.'

'I'm glad.'

Tapakah was right. Billy had hollow legs, and soon most of the food had gone. Once Billy was full as a goog, he lay down and dozed on the rug as I packed away the leftovers. Tapakah squatted down nearby examining the flowers.

Once I'd finished cleaning up, I lay next to Billy and stared through the branches of the stunted eucalypts to the bright blue sky above. The air smelt fragrant. A slight breeze rustled the leaves, and they shook and sparkled in the sunlight. I was full to pussy's bow, blissful and sleepy. Closing my eyes, the sounds of the bush enfolded me. The insects and birds created a complex symphony of sound that ebbed and flowed with the wind. The effect was so mesmerising and calming, I drifted away.

Tapakah sat down beside me and stroked my head, tracing the patterns I'd cut into my hair.

I'd taken off the wig because it was too hot. I didn't care. I reckoned I looked all right bald, and in the outback, I didn't have to make a fashion statement. I thought Tapakah bought me the wig because he didn't like bald, but he didn't care, he liked me any old how.

I muttered to no one in particular, 'I think I'm in heaven.'

Tapakah lay down beside me, looking up at the sky. He stretched out an arm. 'Cuddle?'

I moved next to him and cuddled up, my head on his shoulder, my arm across his body.

He closed his eyes and whispered, 'I'm in heaven.'

We dozed blissfully until Billy spoke. 'I'm not tired anymore. Can I go explore?'

'Sure, but stay within earshot,' Tapakah said drowsily.

'What's that mean?' Billy asked.

'Don't go further than calling distance. Promise?'

'Promise.'

Billy scampered off, and I drifted back to my delightful

dozing. Sounds faded away, the breeze caressed my face, the scent of the earth and the warmth of the sun enfolded me, along with the arms that held me close. My body was smiling. An unusual sense of freedom encompassed me. It was as though a bubble around me had burst and let the universe in.

Tapakah's lips brushed mine as his body pressed close against me. I opened my eyes and gazed into the darkness of his.

'Can I kiss you?'

'You just did.'

'A proper kiss.'

'I'm not sure I know what a "proper kiss" is. You'd better show me.'

So, he did, and it was deep, passionate and divine.

'Oh, my God, I can play you like a musical instrument. You're so responsive,' he said.

My body undulated to an internal rhythm to which he moved in sync.

'If that's a proper kiss, what's an improper kiss?'

He laughed and then looked serious. 'Do you remember having ... other men?'

'No. I can't remember anything. Who knows, I might never have had a boyfriend.'

'I wouldn't imagine that would be the case. They'd be lining up at your door.'

'Well, I'm flattered, but I can't remember being with a man. You are my first kiss.' I felt suddenly shy and awkward.

'Essentially, you're a virgin then.'

I laughed. 'Essentially, yes. A pretty old virgin.'

'Hell, I have a huge responsibility.'

'I wouldn't worry. I've nothing to compare you to, and, so far so good. Don't be so sure of yourself, anyway. What makes you think you're going to get lucky?'

Tapakah straddled me and pressed his body against mine. He held my face and kissed me again. My body began to dissolve as passion overtook me. He pulled my arms above my head and then jerked sharply away from our kiss. He gasped.

I opened my eyes. 'What's wrong?'

Tapakah was staring at my wrist. 'Where the fuck is your bracelet?'

My wrist was bare, except for the ugly scar along the centre of my forearm. I hated the sight of it and turned my arm over.

'I don't know. It was there this morning.'

He looked around anxiously. 'Bloody hell. Are you sure?'

'Yes, I'm sure. Does it matter? I'm not going to get lost.'

'Yes, it does matter. Very much,' he snapped. 'How do you know it was there this morning and you didn't lose it before that?'

I started to feel annoyed at the interrogation. 'It was there because Frank checked it.'

'Frank checked it?'

'Yes. Is there an echo around here? Frank was checking it.'

Bloody hell. You've spoilt everything with all your hoo-ha about the friggin' bracelet.

'Why would Frank be checking it?' Tapakah said, more to himself than me. 'It has nothing to do with him.'

Tapakah was still straddling me and it made me hot and bothered. He pressed down on my wrists and locked on to me with those eyes.

'I'm sorry, but we have to go. Right now. It's not safe. I'll make it up to you, I promise.' As he bent down to kiss me, he froze, his body tense.

Behind him was the sound of four pistols being cocked.

---

[46] *Maggie's Playlist: Too Good To Be True — Rhys*

'Get your filthy hands off her, you motherfucker!' The man's voice was a deep, low growl. 'Now! Get off her ... slow ... hands in the air and kneel down on the rug.'

Tapakah did as he was told, and as he moved away I could see who stood before us.

Three men and a woman, all pointing guns. Big guns. Their aim was directed at Tapakah.

The man with the deep voice stared at me. 'Maggie, oh, my God. What the hell has he done to you?' He leant forward and stretched out his hand to me.

I recoiled. He was tall, over six foot, with a huge, muscular build. His biceps bulged under a dirty white T-shirt, his jeans needed a wash, and his black biker boots looked as if they'd kicked in a few heads. His hair was wild, his beard unkempt. He reminded me of an outlaw.

'Maggie, *come on*. Let's go,' he urged.

I inched further back on the rug. There was no way I was going anywhere with him.

He looked at me exasperated. 'Come on, luv. Let's get you out of here.' He gave me a smile. His teeth were nice. White and even.

I was wise to his game. A smile wouldn't win me over.

'No way. I don't know who you are. Please leave us alone.'

'*Maggie?* Maggie, it's me ... *Ashley.*'

'I don't recognise you. Should I?'

'Yes, you bloody well should, luv. You recognise Drom?' He pointed to a young man with knives sticking out of his sleeve pocket. Drom was wiry and strong. His blue eyes looked directly into mine. Something tickled inside my brain. He had an air of sadness about him.

'No. I don't know him either.'

'What about Fox?' He indicated a man with a broad jaw, strong chin and hair that flopped across his forehead. There was a scar on his top lip. He wore a black T-shirt, jeans and desert boots.

'No. Never seen him before in my life.'

The man called Fox, muttered, 'Bloody hell.'

'Well, you *must* remember the Maestro.' He pointed to a tall, stunning looking woman in the tightest jeans and top I'd ever seen. She wore black, over the knee stiletto boots and a couple of choice pieces of exotic jewellery. Her glossy black hair caught the breeze and flowed behind her.

Not the best fashion choice for the outback, but she could get away with anything. She was mesmerisingly stunning.

The Maestro stepped forward and placed her boot on Tapakah's leg, digging the heel into his flesh. She ran her eyes over every inch of his body. 'Well, look at you, Mister Tapakah. You look quite handsome, for an evil son of a bitch!' She gave him a kick.

Tapakah didn't flinch, and stared her down in the way only Tapakah could.

The Maestro bent down and looked into my eyes. 'Maggie, darling.' She spoke softly, took my hands and turned them over. I let her. She seemed charming, albeit scary.

She gasped at the sight of my scars. The others looked

shocked. 'What happened to you, sweetheart?'

'I can't remember much. But I do remember that this man, Tapakah, saved me. Rescued me. I tried to kill myself. He saved my life, brought me back from death's door. If it wasn't for him, I'd be dead. I was awfully sick and he made me better. I owe him everything. Please, please don't hurt him.'

The four of them exchanged looks and seemed at a loss as to what to do next.

Tapakah spoke. 'It's true what she—'

The man called Ashley cut him off. 'Shut up, arsehole.' He glared at Tapakah with such hatred it gave me goose bumps.

The Maestro nodded at Tapakah to go ahead. 'Let him speak, Ash.'

'It's true what Maggie said. She's just recovered. There's no way she can handle another shock. She simply can't. It would send her back. We may never be able to reach her again.'

'Back to what?' the man called Drom asked.

'She was catatonic. She nearly died. We had to feed her by a tube to keep her alive.'

The man called Ashley bent down on one knee and spoke softly to me. 'Can I see your arms, luv?'

I turned them over and felt my face flush.

'Crikey.' His face twisted with emotion and his eyes brimmed with tears. 'Maggie, we're your friends, your family, we love you. Tapakah did this to you. He's the one responsible. He's wiped your mind. He killed your friend Jasmine and probably Jason too. Jason's missing, Maggie.'

'Who's Jason?'

'Jason is the love of your life, your partner, your lover. The person you love most in the world.'

What the fuck was he on about? What was going on? I didn't know him; I didn't know Jason. Why was he here? I wanted him to go away.

'I don't know any Jason.'

'That's because Tapakah's wiped your memory. He's holding you captive. You don't understand what he is. He's a monster.'

'He's not holding me captive!' A rising sense of hysteria brewed in my gut. 'He said I can go anytime I want. I'm here because I want to be, and I do understand what he is, and he's not a monster. He's kind and caring and … and … *I love him.*'

'You *what?*' the four of them said simultaneously.

'You heard me. Please … leave us alone. I don't know who you are. *Please.*' I started to sob.

These strangers were going to take me. Take me away from the one thing I knew and trusted, the people I loved. It couldn't be. I wouldn't go. I wouldn't let them take me. After everything, I was happy. They couldn't. I wouldn't!

My body started to shake and my head hurt. I clutched at it.

'*Please,* Tapakah pleaded. 'Please stop! Can't you see what you're doing to her? I'm begging you,' he said, his voice breaking.

Ashley patted my hand and spoke softly to me. 'It's okay, luv. We're not here to hurt you. Relax. Take a deep breath and think of dolphins.'

The tone, the sound of his voice made the shaking stop.

He stood, brushed the hair back off his face and glared at Tapakah. 'Jesus H. Christ. This is a friggin' turn up. You fair dinkum piece of low life scum. Take that smirk off your face, before I take it off for you.' Ashley clenched a fist and took a step towards him. The woman stepped in front of him.

'Back off, Ashley.'

'We can't leave her here,' the man called Fox said.

Ashley growled, his eyes burning with hatred. 'Let me kill him. Right here. Right now.'

I froze as the sound of footsteps crunching on gravel came from behind me. Silence, then the *Chk Chk* of a shot gun being cocked. A voice, trying to sound deeper than it was, rang out. 'Everyone, drop your weapons or you're dead where you stand.'

It was Billy. 'Put your guns on the ground. Slowly. Back off. You're not taking Maggie anywhere. You're not hurting my friends.'

Broad grins spread across the faces of the four as they sighted their opponent.

'Well, well, well, look what we have here,' Fox said.

'I may look small … and young … but I can still blow your head off.'

'Please, don't hurt him. He's just a kid,' I said.

'We're not in the habit of killing children, Maggie. You should know. Tapakah is the one who does *that*,' Ashley said, with venom in his voice. 'What's your name, kid?'

'Billy.'

'Billy the kid 'eh? Have you shot a gun before?' Ashley asked.

'Yeah. All the time, mate.'

Ashley chuckled. 'You're outnumbered four to one, Billy. You're brave, but you don't want to be a silly Billy.'

Billy was defiant. 'I won't let you take Maggie. She was very ill, and if you take her she'll get sick again. She could die. I don't want her to die.'

'I want a word with you all, in private,' Tapakah said.

Ashley was defiant. 'Say what you have to say right here.'

'Fine. Here's the deal. I'll go with you. Willingly. Take me. Do whatever you need to do with me. But leave Maggie here, with Billy. If you take her, you will destroy her. Take me. Leave her.'

Ashley rubbed his beard and nodded. 'Good plan, Tapakah. We could do that.'

'*No!*' I shouted. 'Who are you people? You can't do this; you can't take him. I won't let you!' I jumped to my feet. My head was raging, hurting. The man called Drom kept staring at me hard. I grabbed the rifle from Billy and pointed it at Ashley.

'Back off. Go away. You're not taking me and you're not taking him.'

'It's the same odds, Maggie. Four to one. We're your friends, for Christ's sake. Put the gun down and let us take you home. You want to go home don't you?'

'I don't know home. I don't know you. All I know is here, and I'm not giving up the only thing I know. *This* is my home.'

'But you will remember. It will come back to you. Please, give me the gun. You could never hurt me.' He took a step forward.

'Stop! I *will* shoot.'

'No, you won't.' He took another step.

'I will. I'm warning you. One more step and I *will* shoot.'

The Ashley man was supremely confident. I couldn't let him get any closer. One more step and he was dead. Please. Don't. Make. Me. Do. It.

Ashley took the step.

I pulled the trigger.

The butt of the rifle slammed into my shoulder. My ears vibrated with the blast.

The man called Ashley collapsed to his knees. Tapakah leapt to his feet. The others pointed their guns at him and motioned for him to sit. He did.

Where was the blood? The guts?

Ashley stared up at me, his face white with shock. He staggered to his feet and dusted himself off.

How could it be? There was no blood. I'd missed. Impossible. It was point blank range.

Ashley stepped forward and spoke softly. 'Want to try again, luv?'

He couldn't beat me. He couldn't. The bastard. I wouldn't let that happen. Somehow, they were in control. But they weren't in control of me. I was in control of me.

'Yes, I'll try again; with a slight modification.'

I cocked the rifle and held it under my chin. The Catherine wheel tattoo on my wrist appeared to spin as I placed my finger on the trigger.

My voice was quiet, but firm. 'I will do it. I've done it before. I have nothing and everything to lose, so don't push me. I'm *deadly* serious.'

'Maggie, put the gun down,' Tapakah said. 'Listen to me. Don't do this. I love you. Don't. I'll go with them.'

Billy sobbed. 'I love you too.'

'I don't *want* you to go with them. Don't make decisions for me. Don't tell me what to do. I would rather die than be without you. *I'm* not going. *You're* not going. I refuse to have everything I love taken from me. It's not going to happen.'

The man called Ashley had tears running down his face.

But why? What the hell was going on? I was confused. My head was hurting. Had everyone taken leave of their senses? Had I?

Tapakah watched the tears run down Ashley's face, and his mouth twitched with the shadow of a smile.

'You *will* pay for this, Tapakah.' Ashley pulled out another gun from the back of his jeans and pointed both at Tapakah.

I tightened my finger on the trigger. 'If Tapakah is going to die, then I will too.'

Tapakah looked at me with a desperation I'd never seen before. 'Don't, Maggie. Do not do this. Please.'

I took a deep breath and closed my eyes.

'No, Maggie. *Stop!* Stop. Please. I won't shoot. I promise. Open your eyes.'

I did, and Ashley lowered his weapons. 'Take your finger off the trigger, Maggie.'

The woman spoke. 'It's okay. We're leaving. Listen to me. Listen to this. We love you. We would never hurt you. We're leaving because we love you. Remember our names; we're your family. Ashley, Drom, Fox and me, the Maestro. Your dog Boo misses you, and your father — The Prof, Christos, Luca and your sister, Bella. *Remember us.*

'We love you and miss you and want you to come home. But

because we love you, we are letting you go, letting you be. Au revoir, sweet Maggie.' She motioned for them to back off.

The men called Drom and Fox pulled Ashley away. He didn't want to go. His shoulders heaved; his face contorted with emotion. Fists clenched, he swore and struggled as they dragged him towards the boulders.

'I love you, Maggie. *Remember.* You *have* to remember!' He yelled and raised a fist in the air. His little finger pointed skywards.

Had he meant to use his middle finger? What did a raised pinky finger signify? I had no idea.

Tapakah smiled as he watched them retreat.

The Maestro walked backwards, her eyes and gun fixed on him the whole time. She covered her friends' backs until they disappeared behind the rocks.

Tapakah leapt up, grabbed the rifle and took off. His form appeared as a blur against the landscape, and he reached the boulders in two seconds flat. Spiderlike, he scaled the rocks and vanished over the top.

My knees buckled, and I slowly collapsed into the red dust. Billy rushed to my side and threw his arms around me. He was shaking from head to foot.

'I'm okay, Billy. Everything's fine now. You're exceptionally brave. You saved the day.'

Billy sobbed into my shoulder and hugged me tighter.

I picked up a handful of red dirt and let it run through my fingers. It reminded me of my past — just so much dust.

In the distance, the shape of a man appeared from around the boulders. We started with fright and then relaxed, recognising the familiar shape speeding towards us. Tapakah ran like a demon, his arms and legs pounding the earth. Red dust swirled around his imposing silhouette. His eyes were fixed on me. The image captivated me, and gave rise to a feeling of simultaneous terror and safety.

By the time he reached us, he hadn't even raised a sweat.

'They've vanished. There's no sign of transport. They've disappeared into thin air.' He shook his head. 'They have serious technology at their disposal. And your gunshot … It's as if they had a force field. You couldn't have missed at that range. I can't even believe you pulled the trigger. It's incredible.' He held out his hand to me. 'Come on, let me help you up.'

Tapakah hoisted me upright, took me in his arms and kissed me.

Billy sobbed and put his arms around the both of us. I stroked his hair. 'Relax, Billy, they're gone. You were so brave.'

Billy wiped his nose against my T-shirt. 'I'd do anything for you, Miss.'

'That was a crazy stunt you pulled back there, Maggie. Please, don't do anything like that again.' Tapakah's expression was serious and concerned. 'Are you okay?'

'Yes. But I'm confused. My brain hurts. Those people. Who are they? The things they said. They said they're my family … that they love me. Could it be true? What's going on?'

'They're after me not you. They're lying. They'd do anything to hurt me. Say anything. They're using you to get to me. Don't believe them.'

'But they left … and the things she said. It was kind. Why would they do that? Why would she say those things?'

'That, Maggie, is something I'm just starting to learn. To be honest, I'm as shocked as you are that they left. Don't worry about it. They've given us a lucky break. I'll make sure they never find you again. Or me. Never threaten you again. I promise.'

I knew Tapakah to be a man of his word. I believed him. I felt safe.

He ran to the car and made a call on the satellite phone.

'I've called for the chopper to come and get us. It'll be here shortly. We need to move. One of the station hands will drive the truck back. I don't want you out here any longer than

364

necessary. They won't give up that easily. They'll be back.' He tucked a gun down the back of his pants, checked the magazine of another pistol, and handed it to me. 'You obviously know how to use one.'

I took the pistol from him. 'So it seems.'

'Bring the rifle, Billy,' Tapakah said.

Billy picked up the rifle and rested it on his shoulder. 'Can we walk through the flowers while we wait?'

Tapakah smiled at him. 'Sure, let's go.'

The three of us set off, our arms around each other.

The sun setting over the ridge transformed the boulders into the colours of molten lava. The Sturt's Desert Peas stretched out to the horizon and beyond, their heads nodding as one in the gentle breeze. We stopped and stared at the glowing, undulating wash of red flowers that encircled us.

In the falling light it was as though we were standing ankle deep in a vast lake of blood.

A shiver ran down my spine as a door slammed shut in my head.

The clunk of a key turned in a lock.

I knew it. My past had gone forever.

This was the first day of the rest of my life. This was my life, now.

My new life.

The Beginning ...

---

[47] *Maggie's Playlist: For New Beginnings — Eliel Arrey*

Appendix — Maggie's Playlist

1. White Flag — Bishop Briggs
2. Wild Hearts Can't Be Broken — Pink
3. Never Get Over You — Paul McDonald
4. Hitchhiker — Demi Lovato
5. Knife Thrower — Charming Disaster
6. In the Outback — Dreamtime
7. Gunpowder & Lead — Miranda Lambert
8. Always Looking Out for You — The Beez
9. Psychic Attack — Ruts DC
10. Ghost City — Thomas Azier
11. Can't Fight This Love — Austin Mahone
12. Shot-Gun Boogie — Tennessee Ernie Ford
13. Transformation — Nona Hendryx
14. Prototype — Viktoria Modesta
15. When You're Evil — Aurelio Voltaire
16. My Demons — Starset
17. Autumn Leaves — Ed Sheeran
18. Pigs Can Fly — James Bourne
19. Under the Water — Dirty Heads
20. Gone Missing — Tod Moses, Fujita 5
21. Because I Love You — The Master's Apprentices
22. The Burning Pain of Love — W.E.T.
23. Disguise — Dirty Heads
24. Marco Polo — Loreena McKennitt
25. Scared of Love — Nate Dog
26. Darkness into Light — The Meltdown
27. Apocalypse Now (Main Theme) — The Intermezzo Orchestra
28. The Worst Day Since Yesterday — Flogging Molly
29. My Curse and Cure — Hercules & Love Affair
30. Miranda — Fleetwood Mac
31. Lost & Not Found — Chase & Status, Louis Mattrs, Lost & Found — Shane Harte, Alex Zaichkowski
32. Puppet Master — Chris Major. Puppet Master — Walter Trout
33. Puppet Master — Jenefer Siân

Book Four: Search for Truth

The Crystal Sphere Series by Ingrid Fry

Accidental contact with a mysterious crystal sphere changes the nature of a group of humans and a dog, forcing them on a terrifying quest to save the world.

Maggie has lost everything. Friends, family, her mind, even the clothes on her back. Fate has conspired to give her arch enemy exactly what he wants.

The action moves from Melbourne to Daylesford as Maggie experiences a devastating betrayal. Paranoia takes hold as she struggles with knowing whom to trust.

A new man on the scene seems set to win Maggie's heart, and the sexual chemistry is too hot to handle.
Circumstances force them together as they battle to ward off increasing deadly attacks.

The action escalates to new heights as passion and emotion run high on all sides.

Is Maggie doomed to be with her nemesis, forever unaware of the past?
Are the Musketeers powerless to help? Will they be able to track her down?
Who will Maggie choose? Who can she trust?

The lines between good and evil blur, as opposing forces face an unexpected new enemy and Maggie makes a heart-breaking decision.

The fate that awaits one of the brave Musketeers will shock and surprise.